THE
NIGHT CALLS

MURDER ROOMS:
THE DARK BEGINNINGS OF
SHERLOCK HOLMES

DAVID PIRIE

arrow books

Published in the United Kingdom in 2004 by
Arrow Books

1 3 5 7 9 10 8 6 4 2

Copyright © David Pirie 2002

The right of David Pirie to be identified as the author of this work has
been asserted by him in accordance with the Copyright, Designs and
Patents Act, 1988

First published in the United Kingdom in 2002 by Century

Arrow Books
The Random House Group Limited
20 Vauxhall Bridge Road, London, SW1V 2SA

Random House Australia (Pty) Limited
20 Alfred Street, Milsons Point, Sydney
New South Wales 2061, Australia

Random House New Zealand Limited
18 Poland Road, Glenfield
Auckland 10, New Zealand

Random House (Pty) Limited
Endulini, 5a Jubilee Road
Parktown 2193, South Africa

The Random House Group Limited Reg. No. 954009

www.randomhouse.co.uk
www.murder-rooms.com

A CIP catalogue record for this book is available from the British Library

Papers used by Random House are natural, recyclable products made
from wood grown in sustainable forests. The manufacturing processes
conform to the environmental regulations of the country of origin

ISBN 0 09 941659 X

Typeset by SX Composing DTP, Rayleigh, Essex
Printed and bound in Great Britain by Bookmarque, Croydon, Surrey

THE NIGHT CALLS

David Pirie was a journalist and film critic before he became a screenwriter. His numerous credits include the BAFTA-nominated adaptation for the BBC of *The Woman in White* and he also collaborated with Lars Von Trier on the script of the Oscar-nominated film *Breaking the Waves*. David Pirie lives in Somerset. *The Night Calls* is his second novel.

PRAISE FOR DAVID PIRIE'S *MURDER ROOMS* SERIES

'A convincing Victorian world of eerie moors and fearless detectives, impenetrable ciphers and strange hooded assassins. A pacey, enjoyable yarn, with a surprising twist that ranks with the best of the Doyle canon' *Times Literary Supplement*

'This evocative, superbly crafted mystery thriller paints a striking picture of Victorian *mores* and the tight and imaginative plot is excitingly developed in a strong narrative that demands (and deserves) to be devoured at a single sitting' *Publishing News*

'A satisfying Borgesian mix of library riddle, fact and conjecture' *Guardian*

'Pirie presents an evocative picture of Victorian life, blending fact and fiction in a gripping narrative which never lapses into anachronistically modern language or attitudes. This is a breath of fresh air in the crime genre – a fascinating read' *The Good Book Guide*

'It is the combination of style and scholarship . . . that gives this atmospheric yarn the heightened thrill of intellectual challenge' *New York Times*

For TW

AUTHOR'S NOTE

This is the second in the 'Dark Beginnings of Sherlock Holmes' cycle of novels. As in the first novel, *The Patient's Eyes*, some parts of the story overlap with the very first film, in which Doyle met Joseph Bell, but most of it is original, chronicling their earliest dealings with the figure Doyle generally preferred to call 'him'.

PROLOGUE

10.07 a.m., 14 October 1898

I woke up early this morning and it was almost as if he stood there in the room. The feeling of fear and dread in me was so palpable.

A few feeble rays of early sunlight gleamed on the mantelpiece of the dressing room where I have slept since my wife became ill. My window was ajar and, as the curtains shifted slightly in a breeze, I kept telling myself there was nothing unusual. Yet I felt his presence so keenly that I almost expected him to be crouched on the sill behind them. It is strange to think that the reader of these words has no idea of who he is or what he has done. Of how many women have died in what vile circumstances. And of how I will be dead – yes, perhaps, if I am fortunate, long dead – before this is ever read. All I can tell you is that if Satan himself were behind those curtains, I do not believe I would have been more frightened.

Some weeks ago I received a parcel containing a picture from one of my stories. There was writing disguised in the picture and, though he had contrived a puzzle for me, it was effectively an announcement of his return. Last night another parcel came. This time the handwriting with its wild vowels and fanciful elongated consonants, was unmistakable. I can be absolutely sure now he is coming back. The man who destroyed so much of my young happiness and hope, and who stands for everything in the future that the Doctor fears and despises, has returned.

Of course in my heart I suppose I had known as soon as I deciphered the first puzzle, but I shrank from the knowledge. I thought he was dead; there could be no reason to think otherwise, but now I can be absolutely sure it was a deception. And his timing as always is lethal. There is a reason – to do with my personal life – why he might have chosen this time. Knowing the author of those parcels, I would be surprised by nothing, but I cannot allow myself to entertain such fears. They will only paralyse me.

As soon as I was certain of his return, my mind naturally turned to the Doctor. But the loss of his son affected him so badly that I have decided for the moment to deal with this on my own. The postmark on the second parcel was Dumfries in Scotland and, given my tormentor's propensity for games, I believe I may have a little time before he makes a firm move. And so I must leave word of my encounter with him. It is a strange unnerving story, set in many different places, which encompasses horrors I have always fervently wished to forget, horrors enough for several tales. Nothing about it was constant; lulls would be followed by a sudden descent into the blackest hell. Inevitably there were connections to my working life and I suppose it was no coincidence that I wrote the death of my own fictional detective just a few months after a black flag outside Newgate appeared to bring our ordeal to an end. Of course, I am aware that to describe all that took place is to break the Doctor's trust, for I swore confidentiality. But I do so now because I cannot be sure what will happen to me.

Therefore I got up, assured myself that my wife was untroubled – indeed she was still asleep – and came down to my study where I stared at the parcel before me. Then, like a diver not wishing to think before he plunges into an icy pool, I tore it open. Unlike the one before, there was fine tissue paper inside and I felt something within the paper.

At once I dreaded what I might find, for more than once he has sent human remains. But it was not like that. In many ways it was far worse.

Inside the parcel was a pale blue silk scarf.

I did not flinch or cry out. I suppose a week or so earlier I would have, but not now. Partly because I was prepared for anything, but I also had to pause to take in the enormity of it. I could recall the garment below me so clearly. Once again I was back on a beach long ago. And I heard a song.

> And one could whistle
> And one could sing
> And one could play on the violin
> Such joy there was at my wedding
> On Christmas day in the morning

But that was enough. I thrust the garment aside, telling myself that only my own application of the Doctor's principles could have any hope of defeating the man. I am not someone who resents progress. In many ways the fabric of our lives has seen improvement in my time. But the idea of a murder for no reason – the idea of a man killing a series of women for nothing more than a minor thrill – was, when the Doctor and I first came together, as incomprehensible as it seemed impossible. There had been barbarism and bloodlust in the mid-century, of course, and plenty of it, just as there was in the last. But murder as a casual and sophisticated game had not yet been invented or even foreseen. *He* was one of the first to give us that, perhaps he was the first, which is why his shadow seems cast over the start of the next century.

And so it is that I put the parcel to one side and take up the box I have long dreaded to open. The first item I see is a map, though of a bizarre kind. Handdrawn, it marks in a curious way the streets and byways and medical buildings of Edinburgh. Some of the streets are tinged with scarlet, others with black, some of the names are odd, others conventional. It is in fact a diagram marking the dark night-world of the city and the scene of several of his crimes, starting in 1878.

Beside it there is a sketch of what seems to be a labyrinth – which indeed it was, though I reflected often enough that I would far rather face a monster in there than what I found. This drawing in fact follows the corridors and cupboards and staircases and roofspaces – yes and the bedrooms – of a notorious Edinburgh establishment, a building long since shut down, called Madame Rose's.

It is unnerving to see these things again, for I know

where they lead. I have placed them beside the scarf, which lies there mocking me as I go back to that time when I was just a young and somewhat disillusioned student in my second year of medical school. How aimlessly I walked the streets that winter. Until there came a night I shall never forget, when I heard that lilting, other-worldly music from a beggar's violin, and I am sure even then I sensed him somewhere. Waiting . . .

PART ONE: HIS COMING

The Tune from Another World

I always think of the beggar as the beginning. His name was Samuel and, with his ancient red shirt and sky-blue eyes, he stood there like some vision from heaven on the corner of one of the most colourful and depraved streets in the whole of Edinburgh. I never once heard him play a real tune, only a series of wild and rambling flights of musical fancy which sounded eerie enough in themselves but all the more so in that spot, only yards away from the town's more notorious brothels and drinking dens.

The night I first heard him, I stood there for a long time, drinking in his music. To me it sounded a hundred times more spiritual than all the empty catechisms of the Jesuit boarding school I had just left. And the playing healed some of my anguish, for it so happened that evening had been particularly miserable at home.

My mother was away delivering some mending. And for some reason I never fathomed, my small brother Innes, then still a very young child, climbed the stairs and ran along the red corridor which led to my father's study. For some years our house had been blighted by my father's condition. Now he was barely able even to speak, his mind utterly fogged by drink and near-insanity. Yet, unusually for him, he happened on this occasion to hear the infant playing and opened his door.

Both of them undoubtedly had a shock as they faced each other. By this time my father, with his lank beard, unshaven pallor and stale clothes, was rarely sane or sober enough to venture downstairs. No doubt my mother was relieved that her four younger children, Innes and his three sisters (for the two older girls were seldom at home), saw him so rarely. I am sure at times he would hardly have recognised them.

Even so, beyond a little fright for both of them, the incident might well have come to nothing. Except that someone else now appeared. Our so-called lodger Dr Waller, who was then in his mid-twenties and not so much older than myself, had come out of his room and witnessed this unlikely meeting. I say 'so-called' lodger for really it was more as if we were *his* lodgers. For some time, Waller had paid the entire rent for the house as a favour to my mother and, though he was careful to be civilised and even fawning with her, I knew quite well in my heart he felt an unspoken power over all of us. Nor was he by any description a kind man. I will acknowledge that he was cultured, and when I was away I had on occasions corresponded with him about literature. But by this time I knew that his mask of sensibility concealed much that was arrogant and inhumane, including a deep distaste for children, which ensured that they generally kept out of his way.

I can still see the little tableau in my mind's eye, framed in the dim light of the flickering corridor lamp. Innes was still, puzzled by these figures. My father was about to retire, the shadows playing over his whiskered head. But Waller stood upright beside them, a look of great irritation on his face. And then, quite suddenly, without the slightest provocation, he slapped Innes hard around the face and sent him, howling, away. After that, he gave my father a brutal shove that sent him back into his room and closed the door.

I am quite sure to this day Waller did not know he was observed, and the sight confirmed all my suspicions. I had always strongly suspected that my father's illness and our poverty suited the man admirably. It had allowed him to rule a roost of his own without all the tiresome effort of building one for himself. As he slammed my father's door, he had never looked to me so much like a sadistic jailer.

And then he saw me and we faced each other with poor Innes's sobs still ringing in my ears from below.

Given Waller's arrogance, and his position of authority, you would think perhaps that I, then an eighteen-year-old student, would often have come into conflict with him. This was the opposite of the truth. My mother had enormous faith in the man, and never tired of reminding me of the unpleasant fact that he had kept us from the workhouse. So for her sake he and I both generally kept an uneasy peace. The night I describe was one of the few occasions our hostility erupted into the open.

I walked towards him in fury at what I had observed and told him he had absolutely no right to strike Innes. 'You are not even his father any more than you are—'

I could not go on for I knew at once that I had given him his opening. Waller was aware I had been about to challenge his position in our house, and he stared at me, his brown eyes gleaming. 'Any more than what? Would you like to consult your mother? I think you will find she enjoys my company here in this house.'

I wanted to strike him. He was, as I have said, only a few years my senior, yet he was not a physical man, and always dressed with the meticulous care of someone much older. Tonight, as ever, he was immaculately groomed and coiffured, not a whisker of his thick dark hair was out of place. I clenched my fists, longing to let fly with a punch that would have ruffled that fine appearance. But, as ever, the thought of my mother restrained me and I offered no answer.

'And where would you be? Where would that child be?' he continued. 'Where would your father and mother be if I were not here?'

Still I would not reply.

'I will tell you, you would be in the workhouse. I wonder if you realise, Arthur, I am not exacting even a farthing for what I have done for you personally. I could, if I wished, insist it came out of any future earnings you make as a doctor – that is, if you make any at all.' And with that he turned and walked away.

I am sure the exchange had only occurred because my mother was out of the house. Even Waller would never have dared to express his own sense of power and supremacy so crudely in her presence. Of course, I could have tried to tell her, but I knew from countless arguments on the subject she would not have listened. And the bitter truth was that, even if I could have persuaded her to see the dreadful hypocrisy of our arrangement, I would only have hurt her more deeply. What, after all, was the alternative?

So, as often before, I took to the streets. And it was this very night, with my emotions already stirred, that I first heard Samuel's music and stood there on the pavement, quite overwhelmed by it.

After a little while, I offered the player a coin I could ill afford, but he only wished me to buy him a cup of something warm. Naturally I thought he meant strong drink but it turned out he was an abstainer, or near enough, and we went to a little stall, not far away, where he had a mug of some hot cordial, made from blackberries. As I handed him his cup, I told him his music sounded like it came from another world.

The large genial stallholder laughed at this. 'That's what I say, sir. Why can he not play an air like everyone else?'

He moved away as Samuel looked over the steaming mug at me with a twinkle in his faraway eyes. It was impossible to tell his age, twenty-three or sixty-three. 'Another world? D'you believe in one, sir?'

The question was as unexpected as its speaker. I did believe in something, I knew that, but the discipline and eagerness for hell that I had seen at Stonyhurst, my Catholic boarding school, had clouded my vision.

'I do not know,' I said simply. 'Do you?'

He smiled. 'Well, as for my music I was taught by a man who sailed wi' me. And aye, I believe in something. Something else. But I hope to bide hereabouts in this world a wee while longer. For I like to watch all that goes on. Some strange things there are too, sir, but the police willna hear o' them from me.'

With that he downed the drink and was soon back to his post where he raised his violin and took up an even sadder and more poignant form of that strange music. I walked on, trying to avoid the eyes of the women in the doorways as I reflected on his last remark. There was no doubt that any beggar on that street would see some odd sights, but his mention of the police inevitably brought my mind around to a subject I had been avoiding and to a person I had not seen for many weeks.

Dr Joseph Bell was the extraordinary teacher at the university, who had first asked me to be his medical clerk, and then in great confidence initiated me into his pioneering study of criminal investigation, or what he called his 'method'. I was of course intrigued and flattered, all the more so after he allowed me to accompany the police on a highly confidential case. But, although I was impressed, I had never from the beginning quite been able to accept the vast claims Bell made for his system of deduction. And so it was that one afternoon in February, shortly after he took me into his confidence, I had been bold enough to try and test the man's deductive powers.

Among the many claims Bell made for his precious method, one of the most outlandish was that a close study of any object could lay bare the character of its owner. I was highly dubious of this and had therefore offered him my father's watch as a trial. It had been recently cleaned so I felt absolutely confident that he could get nowhere with it. However, Dr Bell proceeded to use every mark and feature of that watch – certain indentations, some pawnbroker's notches, the tiny scratches around the key – to expose in unbearable detail its owner's mental condition. It was utterly horrifying to me to hear the secret my family had struggled to conceal being analysed and reviewed in so casual a fashion. To his credit, the Doctor saw my anguish and tried his best to make me aware he had been indulging in pure deduction. But even so, for some time after that day, I did my best to avoid him and pleaded my studies as an excuse.

Now, with the fiddler's melancholy notes still in my ears, I thought of that incident with the watch once again. And I found that I missed my jousts with Bell even if, despite my painful lesson, I still had doubts about the man's 'method'. Perhaps he had won that particular contest, but was there not, even here, some plain old-fashioned luck? After all, in his attempt to divine human character from an inanimate object, I had fed his ego by handing over a damaged artefact. But supposing that cursed watch had belonged to some fussy old solicitor rather than an artist whose mind was giving way? If the thing had been in utterly pristine condition, what could Dr Bell have had to say then beyond some vague and useless observation? Much of my old spirit returned as I remembered how disconcerted the Doctor had looked at first when he realised it had been cleaned.

Supposing it had not only been cleaned, but bore no marks whatsoever? Bell's expression might well have remained just as unhappy for the whole test.

As the music faded behind me I smiled to think of that, and before the walk was over I had made up my mind that I was ready to see him again. Not that I would abandon my scepticism. Perhaps now a part of me wanted to challenge his method because it had inflicted such pain. But surely such challenges were good for him and for me, just as long as I took more care?

And so the next morning I made my way along the dark stone corridors to Bell's strange vault-like room in the university. As you entered it, you passed through a kind of tunnel between huge shelves of various compounds and chemicals until you arrived at an enormous tank which ran halfway to the ceiling. Today that tank was dry, rather to my surprise, for I was used to seeing strange things in its watery depths. Beyond it a huge bookcase towered to my left and I came past it to find his empty desk.

'Well,' said a familiar and sharp voice from somewhere below me.

I whirled round. At first I could see nothing at all in the shadows, but eventually I made out a shape lying down very flat between two low bookshelves. The space was so confined you could hardly see Bell's wiry body. But slowly I made out his features and saw he was staring at me. He was indeed quite horizontal, lying between two shelves that were so close together only the smallest volumes could possibly have fitted them, and yet Bell had somehow clambered in and managed to lie flat. He had a watch in one hand.

'Doctor?' I said in amazement.

He ignored me and looked at the watch. Then his legs moved and he wriggled out from under that tiny crevice and drew himself up to his full height, which was more than six foot. His expression was fierce. 'Your business?' he said.

'But what are you doing?'

'I am establishing whether a man called André Valère was truly able to lie in a chimney space much smaller than a grave in order to conceal himself from the constabulary of Rouen in 1780.'

'1780?'

'Nothing has been presented to me in months, but I do not wish to remain entirely inactive in the field. If I cannot obtain fresh material, I can at least occasionally exercise my powers with older cases, especially those unsolved. Perhaps you are not aware of the Rouen matter? Valère was a suspected strangler, but they could not place him near the scene. I think he was in a chimney crevice no bigger than this when the third murder was discovered. He seemed to vanish into thin air and, though there was speculation, they thought the space was too small. This bookcase is a few inches smaller and I could have stayed longer; he only needed twenty-three minutes. So I am convinced.' He had taken up a brush and was removing some dust from his jacket lapels as his tone became more clipped, but his eyes never left me. 'Now, your business, please, I have a lecture to give.'

And he continued to stare at me with a somewhat pugnacious expression.

As I think back to this small reunion I sense again

how energised and indefatigable the Doctor was in those days. Recalling his eager yet assertive gaze, I can see now that there was still almost an innocence in him for he had not as yet been fully tested. His most recent case at that time, involving a man called Canning, had proved a typical triumph, even if it had irritated the local constabulary. The Doctor was yet, in fact, to be seriously bloodied in any quest he had undertaken. That would come, and a good deal sooner than either of us might have wished.

'I merely came to tell you I could make myself available again for my duties.'

He looked at me with a certain amusement. 'Your letter said you were obliged to undertake intensive studies for another course. So in that at least you must now be accomplished?'

After the business with the watch I had written him a polite but vague letter, explaining that I had to take a leave of absence as his clerk to further my studies and his written reply did not press me though he must have guessed the real reason.

'I feel enough time has been devoted to them.'

'Do you really, now? Well, you may assist me in my operating theatre today.'

Of course it was the lowliest task he could have offered, and an hour later I was running around like a madman, fetching instruments and dressings as he desperately tried to speed the progress of a woman patient having an emergency amputation. In those days patients survived in a fairly direct ratio to the speed with which their doctors worked, and I truly sensed the Doctor's frustration for I had to mop his brow over thirty times as he cut and cleaned. I had rarely seen him so determined, but he managed to get the woman off the table alive.

Later, as I performed the mundane chore of sorting through his surgery papers, he sat in his workroom making a few notes and offering very little in the way of conversation. Then he got up, without even glancing in my direction, and disappeared through the locked door leading to the extraordinary room where he kept relics and other more private records of criminal cases. Clearly I was not to be admitted to this inner sanctum again for the moment.

It took me some time to finish my work and at last I walked home, deliberately extending my journey until I reached the street where the beggar Samuel played his violin. The night was cold yet clear, and the stars above made a perfect setting for the player, who seemed in a kind of trance and did not notice me. But I paused some minutes to listen and am glad that I did, for it was a sound I was destined never to hear again in this world.

The Strange Student

Next day I resumed my studies and found myself sitting mournfully alongside my friends in Macfarlane's pharmacology lecture hall. I say 'mournfully' because among the many dreary teachers in Edinburgh at that time, Macfarlane was without contest the dreariest of all. In fact he was probably the dullest lecturer I have ever known in my life.

The man's idea of teaching was to walk up and down reciting endless lists and formulae that several centuries ago he had learned by heart. A small, nervous, bespectacled figure with a trim white beard, he rarely looked at his audience, and sometimes the words themselves became entirely incomprehensible, little more than a mumble.

'I have in my time,' he was saying on this occasion, 'counted nineteen compounds which may be of use to help a patient suffering from the condition. And we list them for you in order of strength . . .'

On one side of me was Colin Stark, a cheerful student from Dundee. On the other was Neill, from the colonies, at that time my closest companion. He was a little older than me and his features generally bore an expression of amusement, but today he looked pained by Macfarlane's ramblings and leaned over to whisper in my ear, 'This is purgatory.'

'Far worse,' I said quite loudly, for I knew Macfarlane would never be distracted by noise from the floor. 'We have to pay for our torment.' Stark agreed with this equally loudly and started to outline his hopes for the forthcoming medical society ball.

All of us were perfectly confident nothing would stop Macfarlane's flow, but on this day we were wrong. As he doddered up and down, murmuring his compounds, there was a sudden cry of excitement from behind us, followed by a screaming noise. I turned quickly and at first all I could see was the main door of the hall being flung open. Anything seemed a great relief from the tedium of the lecture hall and heads craned round.

Suddenly, to our general amazement, a dozen panic-stricken sheep raced into the room, frightened and bleating. The hall was flat rather than raked, with movable desks, so within a few seconds there was complete and utter chaos. People were jumping to their feet, scaring the animals further, desks and test tubes went flying. The sheep darted about the place like white billowy waves in the sea of dark jackets. Now I saw the students who herded them, a gang of young bloods I had observed often enough before, led by a wild, somewhat rebellious, scion of Scots nobility called Crawford.

To one side of me a chair went over and glass

sprayed up from a broken beaker. Some people ran for the door, others tried with difficulty to hold their ground and discover the purpose of this latest madness. The whole place was in uproar, though as yet none of us could understand the purpose. Crawford dashed past me, his eyes dark and fiery, his jet-black hair falling over his forehead, screaming incoherent abuse. His eyes were fixed on the front of the hall. And now at last I saw why. His mob were heading straight for the women.

In that year the controversy about admitting women to medicine was reaching its height. Passions had been roused to a frenzy, and any women who braved our classes endured the grossest behaviour. During the worst disturbances, they had been spat upon and called prostitutes and Jezebels. There had also been cases of assault.

Partly as a result, many staff refused to teach them though, to his credit, Macfarlane was not one of these and nor was Bell. Among the students, Crawford had a reputation as one of the women's fiercest opponents and often led the mob against them. Indeed he seemed to have all the prejudice and bile of a religious zealot.

'See, we have more students here for you.' He was shouting at the women now. 'If you insist on attending, we may as well make doctors out of mutton.'

His followers roared approval as they poured in behind him, no doubt seeing the whole thing as a splendid opportunity to indulge in insults and other abuse of a kind they would normally have kept to themselves. Fortunately several students, including my friends, took the opposite view, for we believed there was no serious reason to keep the women out. I was strongly of this belief and would love to ascribe this to my enlightened nature but, if I am being honest, I ought to admit there was another factor too. Our 'lodger' Dr Waller regularly expressed fierce opposition to the women in medical school, and this may well have spurred me to their defence as strongly as anything else.

But on the occasion I am describing, it is hard to see how any civilised person could possibly have sided with Crawford. The women before us looked terrified as he herded the sheep right at them, screaming incoherent biblical abuse.

In her hurry to get out, one girl tripped and Stark ran to help her up before a sheep trampled on her. 'Mothers of whores, the abomination of the earth,' Crawford screamed down at her as she backed away in terror. Another of his group, a pale Englishman with a little blonde moustache, had a more comprehensible cry. 'Go away and find yourselves husbands!' This was taken up by other men in Crawford's gang as the women were pinned against a side wall, for the men were close and the sheep made it difficult to get away from them.

'They have every right to be here,' I cried above the din and one of the more forthright of the women with a bob of ginger hair, whose name I think was Sophia, took it up. 'Yes we have every right to be in this building. There is an act of parliament now.'

I turned to appeal to Macfarlane, but need not have bothered. Crawford's followers were quite aware of his timidity and had raced two of the sheep down close to the front so that even now he was moving quickly off through the wings of the hall without daring to turn around.

Stark, in his decent Dundonian way, had been arguing directly with Crawford, repeating the women's rights, but Crawford just bellowed back at him. 'Do you not read your Bible? They *have* no rights here. I did not come to a hallowed medical school to supervise a brothel.'

'Since you seem to confuse women with sheep,' said Neill, my friend from overseas, laughing, 'I am glad of that. And you have no idea how to herd animals.'

An idea struck him, and he turned to me. 'But why do we not show you? Doyle, drive them back from the left. Stark, come round the back, we'll clear the beasts out of here directly and give these poor women some room to breathe.'

His idea was inspired for, once they saw what he was about, the rabble turned back from the women to rescue the sheep they had no doubt borrowed from a farmer. Meanwhile Neill, who had done some herding in Canada, grabbed a ruler from a bench and slapped a couple of the animals smartly on their flanks, turning them back towards the door.

I had little experience of sheep myself but I managed to get between the flock and the women and coerce them into following Neill, who turned back to help me. Soon, fired by his manic energy, we had got most of the animals out into the quadrangle where some sunlight was piercing the clouds. I was even starting to feel a little cheerful, for Crawford and his gang had been forced to follow us out and were soon desperately trying to reassemble the scattered sheep before they disappeared into the streets of Edinburgh.

My friends and I stood there in the late winter sunshine, chuckling to observe their efforts. 'The most lively lecture we've had yet,' concluded Stark as he and Neill walked off, for they had another class which, thanks to my lack of funds, I had not yet paid to enter.

The women were now mostly dispersed, and I entered one of the corridors leading to the main entrance for I wanted to see if the university had yet selected a medical team to play rugby against the vets. Ahead of me, I was amused to observe a stray sheep trotting happily along, and then my attention was caught by a good-looking young man walking beside me. He wore a loose coat and a high collar and I recalled now that I had noticed him earlier in the lecture hall, observing the mêlée with furtive anxiety. For some reason I felt a sympathy for him. Evidently he disliked Crawford's activities as much as I did, so I spoke to him, nodding at the sheep.

'Well, this one seems to know where it is going. The sheep show greater intelligence than the shepherds.'

I expected some friendly reply, but my companion only nodded silently and distantly, turning his face away.

I was slightly surprised by this rudeness, and even more surprised when he moved away from me into a nearby doorway. Was this why I acted as I did? Mere curiosity?

I stopped. And then on an impulse I turned back and moved towards the entrance he had taken.

The door was ajar and I passed through it into an

unused demonstration room. As soon as I entered, there was a sudden movement by the window. A figure whirled to face me.

Now that I could see him properly with the collar down, attempting to pin up the disobedient hair, I wondered how I could ever have been taken in by the disguise. For this was no man. Before me was a very beautiful, strong-boned woman, quite tall in height with long reddish fair hair and high cheekbones. Her eyes were particularly striking, brown-green eyes that were both soft and also defiant. They were certainly defiant now. 'Yes,' she said to me, 'my preference is to attend without being assaulted. You know Latimer has excluded us completely.'

She was referring to the most virulent opponent of the women in the whole university. But I hardly took her words in. I was so startled by the sudden revelation of her sex that all I could manage was some foolish remark about my surprise.

She abandoned her attempts with her hair and stood there, her eyes flashing. 'We merely wish to be taught. You think it is too much to expect?'

'No,' I replied quickly, 'and it may sometimes occur, but it is not something I personally have experienced yet.'

The joke was feeble enough even if it were almost true, but its effect on her was striking, for her face was momentarily transformed by a luminescent smile. I started to introduce myself, learning that her name was Miss Elsbeth Scott, and perhaps we would even have walked out of the university together but it was not to be. For suddenly there was a great cry of outrage behind me.

I turned, and Crawford was there. He must have come after the stray sheep and heard our voices. But the sight of this woman in a jacket, with her hair down, acted as a terrible goad to his anger. 'My God!' he said. 'So this one parades herself as a man to snare us. She is among the foulest.'

I think he would have attacked her, but I stepped in his way. 'Leave her,' I said.

He brought his face unpleasantly close to mine. His breath smelled of stale brandy and tobacco as he stared at me.

'The knight errant. But she is no lady. Do you not see their aim, Doyle? Now they are among us, they seek to destroy this place.'

With this he made to walk past me, but I was so angry that I seized him by the collar and pushed him to the doorway. Rather to my surprise he did not offer any great resistance.

'Much you have to learn, Doyle,' he said with a smile. 'We will deal with her in time.' And then he was gone.

I was relieved to be rid of him and turned back to her. But there was no one in the room. Another door led to the quadrangle, and it was ajar. I moved over there and stared out but there was no sign of her or anyone else.

So I retraced my steps, moving back to the stone corridor, as I tried to come to terms with what had happened. The idea that Miss Scott felt so persecuted that she resorted to disguise had naturally made a profound impression on me. As did the woman herself. I could not forget her radiant smile, a smile as much of surprise, that a man could be human enough to make a joke, as of amusement. But the incident had also concentrated my mind on Crawford and his associates. How could it be right they should be allowed to continue this reign of terror?

There was only one man who might offer some help, and so I made my way to the Doctor's room.

As I came through the tunnel of shelves, he was standing by the tank in his greatcoat, pulling on his gloves.

'Doctor Bell, I wish to . . .' I began.

He put out a hand for silence, securing the last glove and bending to pick up the silver-topped cane he always took with him. Then he turned. 'If you come with me, there will be time to discuss whatever you wish to say on the journey.'

I knew his mood well enough: at last he had a case and at these times he hated to be interrupted. A hansom had been called by the porter and the Doctor was still preoccupied as we entered it, nodding to the driver, who had evidently been given his destination. We moved north through the blackened streets leading to the docks. The sun had retreated and it was becoming colder as late afternoon turned to evening and the rain began to descend in a thick drizzling mist. I stared out at the grimy pavements and shops, selling spirit and cheap provisions, until at last the Doctor broke his silence, asking me what I wished to say.

After that I spoke to him in no very coherent fashion about my concern for the women and the disturbance that had interrupted Macfarlane's lecture. He looked at me for a moment as if shifting his mental focus. 'Yes, I heard something of it,' he said at

last. 'My belief is it is the first time Macfarlane has
been successfully interrupted since 1863. On that
occasion there was a fire.'

I was annoyed by this flippancy and did not
hesitate to show it, pointing out that the women were
being seriously harassed. But he stopped me with a
raised hand and a piercing look. 'No, I am not jesting.
On the contrary it is a measure of the seriousness of
what occurred that Macfarlane was interrupted.
Whatever his style as a teacher, he is nothing if not
indefatigable. The situation is becoming deeply
distasteful to all of us. But, as you are aware, there are
many differences of opinion in the university. I will
take note of what you say. I only wish, Doyle, that
they would try some of their antics in my lecture hall.'

'But they never would,' I protested. 'They pick
their victims with care. Not least the women themselves.'

The cab had come to a stop outside a narrow,
nondescript, three-storey building. Bell had agreed
with me, yet I felt a deep dissatisfaction that he
would not promise more action. At the time I was
indignant that he was not doing more to back up his
beliefs.

The cab waited as we entered the building which
was at the end of a row of similar houses on a road
close to the docks. There was nobody about, and at
first I could not understand what we were doing in
what appeared to be an ordinary domestic house. I
suppose I could have asked the Doctor, but I had
already distracted him enough, so I waited.

Closing the door, we turned into a room which was
quite large, with two new sofas, an armchair and a

large cabinet. In an attempt to make it more cheerful, someone had applied a coat of red paint to the walls, but the effect was overdone. The Doctor glanced at all this without much interest.

Rather to my surprise, the only other rooms on that floor were a small scullery with a basin and an even smaller bedroom. We moved up the stairs, which were clean if not well lit, until we came to a carpeted corridor and three more rooms. Again, all of them contained rather basic beds and most were decorated with dull etchings, showing country scenes, of a kind that can be purchased by the dozen in any cheap saleroom. Though free of dust and dirt, the bedrooms were dauntingly similar: all of them had side tables with basins and jugs, all had fireplaces, all were rather overpainted. The largest had a tatty sofa as well as a bed, but that was the only difference.

Apart from these sticks of furniture there was absolutely no sign that I could see of any personal possessions in the whole place. I reflected on this oddity as the Doctor went back to the larger room near the top of the stairs. Outside it was starting to get dark, so he lit some candles, before bending down to examine a stain he had found on the rug beside the bed. It was not large, but from the colour I assumed it was blood. And then we heard the noise.

It was like a kind of humming, though it was hard to make out a tune. The notes were strange, high-pitched. Bell was out on the landing in an instant. I had assumed we were on the last occupied floor but now I saw there was a ladder to a skylight and the noise came from a small door one side of it.

The Doctor went first, climbing quickly ahead of

me till he reached the opening. Then, holding his candle high, he flung the hatch-like door open.

It was a boxroom. I could see some empty cases, but there was also a makeshift bed, this time with sheets and blankets. And there, sitting in it, sucking a stick of sugar, was a small boy.

The creature had bright eyes and dark curls and looked up at us with mild curiosity but without the slightest flicker of fear. He was reading something by the light of his own small candle and took another lick of his long stick of barley sugar. Although small, I decided he must have been almost twelve years old, and he certainly had a marvellous confidence for his years. Bell stared at him, and his features softened, but it was the boy who spoke first.

'And who might you be?' he said, putting down his book which was one of the most lurid of the old Penny Dreadfuls called *Varney the Vampire*.

Bell moved forward, smiling. 'Oh, I am a doctor who is looking around, perhaps with a view to buying this place for my practice. And this is my helper, Doyle. How is it you are here?'

'My mam left me here last night,' said the boy, and though he spoke well in the English manner I began to wonder if he did not have a slight foreign accent. French perhaps. 'She said my grandmam would come.'

'You must have hidden, then,' said the Doctor. And both the boy and he eyed the trunks where he had evidently concealed himself. A small bag was packed beside it.

'You will not say I am here, then?' The boy looked at us.

This evidently presented Bell with a problem. 'We will warn you if we do,' he said. 'But of course you would not want to stay here for ever.'

This seemed to satisfy the boy as, to my amazement, he took another lick and went back to his reading.

A few minutes later Bell and I were conversing in the room below. 'Well?' he said with a slight twinkle in his eyes revealing not the slightest surprise at this development. 'Are you apprised of all the details of the case?'

I considered a moment. He was playing with me, of course, but I was determined to show my powers of observation as well as I could. 'From the arrangement of rooms it is obvious,' I said, 'that this is a boarding house, one that by its very emptiness has fallen on evil times. Since the whole place has been cleared, I can only conclude a very serious crime has been committed. I believe you were examining a bloodstain by the bed in the larger room and I assume that is where the body was found. A stabbing I take it.'

'Very good,' he said thoughtfully. 'And the boy?'

'His mother is evidently foreign, but to be living here must have entered a period of poverty which has, I presume, led to problems of an even more serious nature. She has told him to hide and hoped to summon his grandmother. Therefore I conclude the mother is either dead or accused of the crime.'

There was a cry from below us, someone calling for 'Davey' and footsteps on the stairs. 'Excellent, Doyle,' said Bell. 'And if I am not mistaken that is the grandmother now.'

Sure enough a woman entered the room, but she

was not as I had expected. The boy had about him an air of foreign manners. There was nothing foreign or refined about this good woman who wore a filthy apron and looked terribly worried. 'Oh, gentlemen,' she said. 'I am so feart. Have you seen him? Have you seen my wee Davey?' The stench of fish from her apron suggested she must work in one of the fish shops by the docks.

'You need have no concern, madame,' said Bell, smiling at her. 'All is well, he is here.'

At this the woman gave a great cry of thanks, coming forward to shake his hand, evidently so relieved that she could not stop talking. 'Oh, that is a kindness, sir. Her mother said I would find him here but she didna tell me till she got out this afternoon and she is worried to come back here. She loves Davey and the boy is all I have of my son, but still it is terrible what she seems to think the poor lad can endure.'

'Well,' said Bell, 'he seems to have endured no harm. He was left with a supply of barley sugar and enough reading to last him a week. You will find him in the room above.'

At this her face brightened even more – she fairly leapt up the ladder and we heard her cry of joy as she found the boy. Soon they were both coming down with Davey still clutching his sweetmeats and the little bag so neatly packed. His mother was evidently not as negligent as had first appeared, or as his grandmother thought.

The woman offered profuse thanks, and the boy seemed pleased enough to see her, before the two of them disappeared down the stairs and into the darkness.

By now, I was starting to feel rather pleased with myself, for the grandmother had appeared as living proof of my deductions and no doubt Bell saw my satisfaction. 'Well done, Doyle!' he said, putting down his candle. 'I am grateful for your analysis, and the grandmother arrived to prove you right.'

'So my deductions were not too wide of the mark?'

'Well, I would myself hesitate to call the grandmother a deduction when the boy had already told us in plain English he was waiting for her,' he replied.

'And the rest?' I asked.

'Oh, it was a fine piece of work,' he said, looking out of the window. 'Even though every single observation you made was wrong, and every conclusion you drew false.'

Not for the first time with the Doctor it was as if I felt the ground giving way under me. But at least Bell never gloated, and already he had returned to his inspection of the bloodstain and the bed beside it.

'The boy's mother, who I am glad to say seems to love her son, is neither victim nor accused.' He bent down reflectively. 'She is merely a witness, but not of anything the police are taking seriously, for no serious crime has been committed. If it had been, do you really believe even Inspector Beecher would have left the place unattended only hours after the deed?'

Beecher was a senior detective of the city's constabulary, a pompous man who the Doctor had crossed more than once. 'And I can assure you,' Bell continued, 'that if someone had been stabbed to death you would expect to see far more blood than this; why, it might have come from a bleeding nose.'

He stopped looking at it and straightened up. 'As

to this building, it is, you must agree, Doyle, on any
showing a very odd boarding house. Where is the
dining room in which the landlady can offer food to
her guests, and the kitchen in which she cooks it?
How on earth can it be cleared so quickly and
efficiently of any personal things, including even
those of the landlady herself? You put this down to a
crime but it is hardly common for the police to clear
a house after a crime. An infection might have been a
better theory though it is not the answer. And you
hazard the place has fallen on hard times but, if so,
why is it kept so clean?'

I knew there was logic in what he said. And I began
to see where he was leading.

Bell looked at me. 'Yes,' he said. 'It was used as a
place of assignation. There are far more elegant
establishments in the old town, you may have heard
of Madame Rose's. This one is more basic. It was run
efficiently but nobody ever lived here.'

'So why is it empty?'

'In fact it is empty for much of the day. But it is
true something curious happened here last night.'

'And the women ran off?'

'It was not so dramatic as that. After much deliberation, the women called the police but Beecher, as
is his way, refused to give them any credence as
witnesses and took them all down to the cells for a
night. The mother of the boy is a wise woman and
made him hide before they came. In doing so, she
spared him a good deal.'

'But why did Beecher summon you?'

'Oh, he did not,' said Bell. 'As you know, he has not
consulted me for months and he will not do so again

unless he is desperate. No, I was told about the matter by a police constable to whom I once offered some medical assistance. He was here last night and heard their story and felt I might be interested. I have come here today to follow up what he told me. And not only am I interested, I will tell you I am extremely concerned.'

'Were they attacked?'

'There have been attacks. Mainly in the street. On this occasion they were not exactly attacked, but a client who they will only describe as being a good-looking gentleman demanded certain things. He made it out to be a game of will. For example, he made one of them eat some grapes.'

'Not so onerous unless they were poisoned?'

'And they were not. But he stood before the mother of that boy and held them out and insisted she ate them. That was the beginning. There were three women here. At first they took it as a game, though they were frightened. He asked another to drink some brandy which she did not want. Another was cut. You saw the stain.'

'Good God!'

'Only a tiny cut. She bled a little, but it was little more than a scratch. The man tired of the game and left, apparently without doing anything more, not even claiming any sexual favours though he had paid amply for them.'

'Yet they told the police.'

The Doctor turned to me, looking very animated. 'Perhaps I have been unfair with you, Doyle. There is no reason why you should have been able to deduce what in itself may be regarded as an odd trifle. All the more since I can hardly claim to have used my own method when I was told most of the details by my Constable. But I am delighted to see that now you have put your mind to it and reached the heart of the matter.'

I was pleased, if surprised. But the Doctor was quite serious. 'Oh, yes! The heart of it! *They told the police*. Consider, Doyle, the implication of that for one instant. Women of this kind will do anything to avoid them. They will run through streets when they see them coming. Hide in ditches if necessary. They can expect nothing but trouble. Yet they called them to this house. They were taking a great risk and were treated to a night in custody as a result. But there must have been a reason, and there was. Namely that they were absolutely terrified. Not, of course, at the beginning. They were all a little drunk. They assumed at first that he was being playful. And then, suddenly, when he used the knife, they became convinced they were all going to die. I believe that they nearly did.'

'And what happened?'

'It seemed to be all he required. He put the knife away. Told the woman there was nothing to fear from such a tiny incision, which was quite true. And then he left.'

'Perhaps he was drunk?'

'Perhaps. I can prove nothing. But their fear greatly concerns me. Especially when I am sure, from their description, it is the same man who has committed attacks elsewhere. But we will learn nothing more here. And Beecher has decided the place will not reopen, so our man has no cause to return.'

We made our way out of that house. By now the thought of this pointless exercise in cruelty had begun to haunt me, and I was very glad to be away from it.

At the door, Bell stopped and looked back.

'Well at least nobody was badly hurt,' I said.

'That is part of what occupies me,' said Bell, and I could sense the feeling in him. 'In one way it was almost childish. Like a child testing his own power. I hope it is not his idea of a rehearsal.'

Hair and Knife

I lay in bed that night, thinking of the house we had seen. That word the Doctor had used, 'rehearsal', appeared curiously apt, for there was something about that shell of a building which almost seemed like a theatre without the performers. It was the first time I had ever ventured into such a place, and I was both repelled and intrigued.

I thought too of the student, Miss Scott, who I had met under such strange circumstances. Of all the strange things that had happened to me that day, our meeting had made the strongest impression. I could still visualise the sudden flash of her impish smile before Crawford interrupted us. I tried to recall exactly what had passed between us, all that she had said. And now, for the first time, I remembered that she had mentioned Latimer.

Professor Neil Latimer was a fierce-faced anatomy teacher who had made it a pledge of honour never to admit a single woman to his class. Indeed the lack of anatomy tuition was becoming one of the women's greatest handicaps. The man would argue his case constantly in front of us, and I recalled one occasion in particular when he was brutally dissecting a frog. 'Besides, gentlemen,' he said, looking up at us from his dissection with an expression on his face that was positively obscene, 'there are traps even you may not have thought of. What after all is to stop a Magdalene from the streets coming here to study?'

He smacked his lips as he said the word Magdalene, and we all knew what he meant, indeed some of the men guffawed at the thought of a prostitute in our midst. 'Oh yes,' he said, 'there is a place for everything.'

It was, I suppose as I look back now, among the stupider observations I heard from any teacher in the whole of my career at university. Not only was it utterly fatuous to imagine a woman of the streets without any education entering the university to study medicine. But supposing even that impossibility happened, what exactly could she do to corrupt us? Beyond the open soliciting that we endured every day on the streets, the answer was nothing at all except in Latimer's own fevered imagination. His words were nothing more than a lustful fantasy masquerading as an argument. My blood boiled to think of that now, and to recall that Crawford had been one of those who guffawed the loudest. And what did it say about our sex that on the one hand we could try to hound women out of learning the practice of healing and on the other use their services in houses like the one I had just seen?

That night such thoughts went round and round in my head but it would be entirely dishonest to pretend that, during this confused time, I always occupied the moral high ground. On the contrary, I was as torn as any eighteen-year-old about my true emotions with regard to these subjects, and no doubt my encounter with Miss Scott added to my confusion. For the honest truth was that, outside of my immediate family, I barely knew what I should expect of a woman when the examples around me were all so manifestly different.

On the one hand there was the Edinburgh landlady, who in this era was a notorious breed, grasping and viciously prudish almost to a point of madness. On the other, in the streets, we students were constantly being importuned by girls who seemed tender-hearted and were no older than ourselves. There was one woman in particular I had encountered regularly, on the corner where Samuel played his violin, who had a merry twinkle in her eye and a kindly mischievous manner.

I never really dared to talk to her, yet once this woman had come upon me unawares, and offered a sweet kiss, and the memory of that kiss lingered uneasily with me. I knew well enough it was only an attempt to part me from my money, but in her way she still seemed far less hard and grasping than the landladies I had encountered at my friends' lodgings. Indeed, when Latimer had first spoken, I certainly felt a guilty fascination at the thought of a 'Magdalene' appearing in our class to tempt us to unspeakable acts of lust.

But, by the night I describe, I know I was at last becoming aware of a vague sense of right. Whatever my reservations about Bell (and these reservations had by no means disappeared), I could see quite well that he had a good deal more rationality than Latimer or Crawford, and also I needed little persuading to honour Miss Scott as a shining example of sense and fortitude.

As a result I longed to meet with her again, and looked for her the next day and the day after. But, after Crawford's cruel prank, the women were much less in evidence at the university and there was no sign of her. Eventually, since there were already rumours on the subject, I told my friends of Miss Scott's disguise and they were both amazed and impressed. Neill's response was that, as gentlemen, we should now insist on offering the women a safe escort into the university, but his scheme gained little support and I felt a bitter disappointment when Macfarlane's next pharmacology lecture came and went without any women attending at all.

I walked home after it, wondering gloomily if I would ever see her again. The weather seemed to fit my mood, for the city had suddenly thrown up one of those late frosts that make its streets a treacherous misery, even in early spring. It was, I reflected, inauspicious weather for that night's medical society ball, an annual event I usually managed to avoid. But on this occasion Waller happened to have been given a ticket, though he never attended, and my mother insisted I make use of it. So a few hours later I found myself in the ballroom of the Waverley Hotel, which once stood at the end of Chambers Street, doing my best to dance an eightsome reel.

It might be thought that a medical society ball in Edinburgh at that time would be a smart formal event. In fact it was nothing of the kind. The hotel was a dingy place, lit by an inadequate series of gas lamps, which made for an eerie spectacle, sending flickering shadows of the dancers on to the floor beneath our feet. As an economy measure there was little in the way of food, but a plentiful supply of brandy punch had been provided in steaming bowls set to one side.

Partly because of the absence of food, and partly because of the cold, it was soon obvious as we staggered through our dances that too much punch had already been consumed, though more by the men than the women. My partner in the reel was the daughter of the hotel owner, and by the end her father came over with a grim countenance, looked me up and down (though I was perfectly sober, having had only one glass) and pulled her away, obviously concerned about the propriety of such partners and the reputation of his establishment.

I was rather irritated to be treated in this way and sauntered over to where Stark and Neill were pouring themselves liberal glasses of punch and laughing, for they had witnessed it.

Neill put a comforting arm round me. 'You are not respectable enough in his eyes,' he said. 'Like the heroes of our favourite Poe stories, you are "plunged in excess".'

'And I may as well be,' I said bitterly. 'He judges without evidence.'

'Well, I hope he has no cat for you to attack.' He was referring to Poe's strange tale, 'The Black Cat', one of the many stories by that author Neill and I constantly devoured.

'I have not seen one,' I rejoined. 'But if it appears I may well be tempted.'

All of a sudden we were interrupted by a commotion on the stairs to one side of the room. I could hear women's voices raised, and the sound of running feet. Several men, including Stark, Neill and myself, ran up there, and women pointed along the corridor. Loud screams and sobs were coming from a room at the end.

Stark was first there and Neill and I ran behind him as he flung open the door. We were in a ladies' powder room, which was brightly lit with a red carpet. Directly ahead of us a woman was on her knees. She was as white as a sheet and quivering with terror. Another woman was trying to hold her, but she was hysterical. A man, who turned out to be her brother, pushed past us and put his arm round her, trying to console her.

'Kathy,' he said. 'It is all right, you are unharmed, but what has happened?'

She calmed down a little, but it was a while before we heard the full story, and it came out only haltingly after some brandy. The woman, whose name was Miss Katherine Morrison, had entered alone and there had been a man behind the door. The instant she closed it, he pulled her towards the window and covered her mouth. She was terrified enough, and then he produced a blade and said he might cut her throat.

What happened next she would not say, but her friend knew and she told Stark, Neill and me the story downstairs as Miss Morrison's brother stayed with his sister to comfort her and await the police. At first this friend had been reluctant to go into details, but I told her we were medical students and she need not spare our feelings. And so, after drinking a glass of punch, she told us the facts. Evidently the man had said he would cut some of her hair now, and one day might return to cut more of her. That was horrible enough, but he also made it clear that the hair he wanted was not on her head. Miss Morrison had had to keep still as his knife went within an inch of her belly. Hearing this, we naturally assumed the worst but it turned out the man had not lied. Using the knife, he had snipped a bit of pubic hair and done nothing else. It was odd but even so, as we all knew, it amounted to an indecent assault of the most disgusting kind.

Already, as word spread of what had happened, much of it grossly exaggerated, the place was in an uproar. All thoughts of dancing had been abandoned and a search of the upper rooms had begun, though it was obviously useless, not merely because the man had almost certainly fled but because most of the searchers were demonstrably the worse for drink.

I was trying to get a description of the man, but she had not seen him properly. All that could be ascertained was that he was lean and dressed in black. At a formal ball this amounted to nothing at all and soon, to my disgust, such frenzied portraits were circulating among the pursuers that I could see he would shortly be accorded fangs, gigantic stature and a forked tail. In any case so much noise was being made, so much bellowing and bravado, that we might as well have hunted him with a herd of elephants in front of us.

45

Neill and I gave up in disgust and decided to look downstairs rather than up. The ballroom was empty now, and we moved into the kitchen area, which contained a multitude of corridors, sculleries and storage rooms.

The first space was filled with pots and pans and a basin. I entered it and glanced around, but it seemed to be empty and I moved back into the corridor as Neill turned to the next door along. I was just behind him as he opened it.

The figure on the other side was huge and covered in blood and gave a great cry as he came out at us like a bull. The sheer impact almost knocked Neill to the ground and forced me to grab out at my friend as the assailant darted off down the corridor.

I made sure Neill was only winded and then raced after the man. He was already pushing his way into a kitchen, knocking a great pile of plates down as he went. I reached the door, managing to dodge the broken crockery. It was obvious the figure was aiming for the open kitchen window. Once out in the street, there would be little hope of catching him so I tried to dive for his legs.

It was a feeble attempt, for he only kicked out at my head, sending me flying backwards into the hard wood of a cupboard door.

I was dazed and took a little while to get to my feet, feeling very foolish, for by now he was through the window, and would have easily escaped into the darkness.

I reached the sill, which was covered in ice, and saw that it gave on to a narrow dark wynd. There seemed little point in pursuit now but I started to clamber out. And then I stopped in astonishment. For sprawled on the paving stones below me was a large black shape, streaked in red. I stared, but there could be no doubt. It was my assailant.

Naturally I waited, fearing some kind of trick. But he seemed to be still, so I eased myself out and jumped, every muscle poised for his attack.

None came. He was lying there, just as I had seen, in the bitter cold, and he was quite unconscious.

Neill was soon beside me, and after a few minutes the police were on the scene too. Our fugitive was dead to the world, and the stench of brandy convinced me I had been a witness to the wildest stage of drunkenness, inevitably followed as it was now by oblivion. Quickly we ascertained that the man was a waiter in the hotel and that the blood on him was not his own. A chambermaid had been stabbed, though fortunately her wound was minor. Being the hero of the hour, I took the opportunity to ask one of the policemen if he would summon Dr Bell and, although the man was a little reluctant, he agreed.

About an hour later I was waiting expectantly when the Doctor strode into the ballroom, dressed so scrupulously in his immaculate topcoat with silver-cane and bag, that you would never have thought he had been dragged rudely out of his bed. But if I expected any kind of thanks from him, I had quite forgotten his ways. He merely nodded in my direction and then went upstairs to talk to the victim of the first assault.

This surprised me a little, for she was after all the least afflicted, but I knew better by now than to question his style. In any case there were more pressing matters, for the police had proved utterly incapable of finding the knife that had been used in both attacks. The first victim described this weapon in some detail: a long-handled, double-edged blade of a kind that sounded almost surgical. The second merely saw it glint in the darkness and felt its sharpness cold as it entered her shoulder. But her attacker was so drunk that she was able to force it from his hand and even heard it drop while he fled. It therefore seemed certain that the blade must be in the room where she was stabbed, but the police had combed the place and found absolutely no sign of it.

I was still pondering this problem when Bell returned from talking to the first victim. Together we watched the waiter being carried out to the police cab as a large man with whiskers and an official manner entered the premises. This was Inspector Beecher, who seemed in excellent spirits for he nodded to me, even though I knew quite well that my presence on the earlier case had irritated him.

'Well, Bell,' he smiled. 'Judging by the business upstairs this seems to involve your mysterious assailant.'

'I agree,' said Bell guardedly.

'Then you must also agree your anxieties about the man appear to have singularly little foundation. He is only a drunken waiter, so drunk in fact that he made a very ineffectual attacker.'

Bell looked at Beecher without expression. 'I do not believe that Miss Morrison upstairs thinks he was ineffectual. Nor was his weapon.'

'Ah, the weapon,' said Beecher with irritation. 'You will always seize on any awkward little points. It is true we have not found it yet. But you cannot deny the man's drunkenness. No doubt he had more brandy after his encounter with Miss Morrison, which would explain why his second attack was less calculated.'

'On the contrary,' said Bell, 'I have already looked at the statements and, according to several witnesses, the waiter you have locked up was deeply intoxicated for hours. It was why the chambermaid was trying to avoid him. He had courted her for months and had been rejected in favour of a local shopkeeper. Now, if you have no objection, Doyle and I would like to examine the room where she was stabbed. I would ask only that you leave Miss Morrison for a short while. She has been subjected to a good deal of questioning, and I promised her as a doctor that we would give her a little time to recover.'

'Very well.' Beecher nodded ungraciously. 'But I cannot wait too long.' And I could see that already the man was beginning to lose his good humour.

A few minutes later, Bell and I approached the room where Neill and I first saw the figure. Bell stopped before we entered and went to an open window, staring out.

'I can assure you,' I told him, 'he could not have disposed of the weapon there. He never went near it.'

The Doctor turned back and, rather to my surprise, he had a great look of satisfaction on his face. 'Very good, I accept what you say. Now let us see the room.'

We entered what turned out to be a bare, dark storage room, lit by a single tiny gas lamp. I stared around me. There were signs of the chambermaid's bleeding on the floor, where they found her, but almost nothing else. The windows were closed and shuttered, and there was absolutely no place of concealment.

Bell examined the walls, then the lamp and the windows. I had noticed the room was warm and, near the bloodstains, a hot-water pipe ran through it at skirting level, but we could both see there was nothing beneath this. Bell studied the pipe and the wall for a moment and then he turned to me.

'So, Doyle. The weapon. Where is it?'

I looked around me. 'It was not on his person or in the wynd, I am sure.'

'Indeed. The victim insists the weapon was dropped here,' he replied.

'Then,' I said, 'either she is mistaken or—'

'There is no mistake. She has a cut on her hand where she grasped its blade.'

'So it is here. It is hidden or it has fallen.' I went to the windows but the shutters were sealed tighter than a drum.

'No,' said Bell, watching me. 'That is not the answer. They have not been open for years.'

I was baffled. 'Well, it cannot have disappeared. Doctor, you must . . .'

'No,' interrupted Bell, rejecting my appeal for help. 'This is your case. You were first to see him. Think.'

I turned from the walls back to the floor and then back to the walls again. There was absolutely nothing in this room. I thought that perhaps there was some trick to the blade, that its knife collapsed into the hilt. I had heard of such things before, but what good was that to me when I could see not even the tiniest object?

'Use your sense,' said Bell. 'When you have eliminated what is utterly impossible, then where do you turn?'

I stared around me. 'Well, I can ascertain exactly where she fell.'

'Good,' said Bell. 'Do so.'

I could see the bloodstains and pictured the scene easily enough. The door had opened. She faced him. Yet still I had nothing. The Doctor sensed my helplessness and now he came at me as the man had, holding a feigned weapon in his hand. 'Relive what happened. You are as she was.'

I retaliated just as she had. 'She said she heard it fall,' I said to him. 'I would guess this meant it hit the pipe.' Slowly I followed what I imagined was her fall to the floor. 'The knife would surely now be somewhere a few inches from my hand.' And I stretched out with little hope for I could see there was nothing there.

To my astonishment I did feel something cold. And I sat up at once to look. 'There is water,' I said in surprise. 'Is the pipe leaking? Perhaps a hole . . .' But I touched the pipe, which was very hot and quite solid. The Doctor was watching expectantly. 'No. It seems intact and hot. But this leak is . . . cold . . . almost ice-cold.' I knew by his face I was close. 'Sharp and cold, the maid said.' And suddenly I felt the bolt of illumination. 'My God! It was ice. It was not a dagger at all. He had an icicle.'

Bell stood there, a broad smile on his face. Then he turned and led me out through the door to the open window he had inspected earlier. There had been water dripping off a low roof here and several icicles had formed. He broke one off and held it up. It was about the size of a dagger.

'The girl was very unlucky indeed,' said Bell. 'This man merely seized what was to hand and hit upon a deadly weapon, but at least he was in no position to use it very effectively. I am very glad, Doyle, you have learned something trivial, though I fear in a rather more important matter you have proved a grave disappointment.'

'I do not understand,' I said, as ever brought down to earth after what I had thought was my deductive triumph.

'You should have called me as soon as the first incident occurred. Not only had the trail gone quite cold by the time I arrived, but, if you had, I could have told you at once there was absolutely no connection whatsoever between the drunken jealous brawl you interrupted here and the vicious, pre-meditated and indecent assault on Miss Morrison. As it is, this business, which is utterly predictable, has completely obscured what is far more serious. Now let us go and tell Inspector Beecher what he has no wish to hear.'

Beecher was standing in the ballroom grinning from ear to ear, having evidently recovered his good humour, as Bell approached. 'Well,' he said, 'are you satisfied we have got your man?'

'No,' said Bell. 'Because you have not.'

'Oh, come,' said Beecher with impatience.

'Oh, Miss Morrison has already confirmed it,' the Doctor said lightly. 'She saw the waiter with me and will swear on oath that he is not the man who assaulted her.'

Beecher's smile disappeared so rapidly I thought he was going to choke. 'You had no business to see her before I did. And how do you explain the fact that they used the same weapon?'

'Because they did not. The man upstairs used a blade which was seen in full light. Your drunken waiter merely seized the first common article to hand.'

'And was lucky enough to find a dagger?'

'No, only this.' And so saying the Doctor thrust an icicle into the astonished Beecher's hand. 'There are plenty of them about tonight and you will find the traces of his one lying under the pipe, inches from where the maid knocked it from him, mixed with her own blood. Your pathologist Summers will confirm it for you, I have no doubt.'

Beecher was speechless as Bell moved off and I followed. 'Our mystery man is still very much at large,' the Doctor called back to him. 'His activities are a matter of enormous concern. And now another opportunity has been squandered.'

THE COINS IN THE GUTTER

Perhaps the Doctor felt he had been a little hard on me, for he was very friendly on the journey back. Indeed, though it was late, he proposed some refreshment. I was delighted to be readmitted to his inner sanctum, the large room which lay up a flight of stairs behind the locked door in his official work place. Here he had gathered an extraordinary collection of criminal artefacts and would even refer to it as his own black museum, for there was at that time some interest in the newly opened Black Museum in Scotland Yard.

I never quite understood who, besides Bell, looked after this chamber, but it was well tended and soon we were glad enough to be seated in two comfortable old armchairs before its fireplace on that bitter night. Behind us those towering shelves, containing so much history of infamy, were illuminated by the flickering firelight. The Doctor offered me some brandy, which I declined. He was an abstemious man himself, for his family were members of the Scottish dissenting Free Church, so I was quite surprised when he poured out a small amount and added water from a carafe. Then he took a sip of it and stared into the fire.

'I do not like it,' he said at last. 'Nor do I feel any nearer to understanding it.'

I knew he was referring to the attack on Miss Morrison. 'But surely,' I said, 'it is only a form of sexual attack. Odd, I agree, but that crime has always existed. And we are fortunate he did not take it further.'

Bell turned to me and the firelight, flickering in his face, made his sharp features look almost sinister. 'If I were convinced that the attack merely had a sexual motive, I would be a good deal more confident about our friend. Clearly passion is there in part. He is drawn to attack women, but even so his crimes are among the odder I have known. Edinburgh has a long history of vice, but I have never in my life heard of anything quite like this. Today's attack was foul, but it was also daring. If his timing had been wrong by even a few seconds he would have been seen and perhaps caught. It is as if . . . as if he is telling us something.'

'But what?' For I truly thought the Doctor was guilty of romancing a little in his description.

'I have an idea and I hope it is wrong. That is all I will say.' He was staring at the fire as he spoke, but now he turned back to me. 'I believe my own anxiety caused me to be a little churlish with you earlier, Doyle. Of course I would like to have been there sooner, but if somehow your drunken waiter had got away, no doubt Beecher would have been all the more insistent that he had perpetrated both crimes. So in that sense you performed a very useful purpose and were ill thanked for it. Now it is time to lock up and go to bed, for tomorrow I have to make a journey.'

I was pleased he had said as much, and slept well, but next morning, when I returned to the university, I reflected that I was still no nearer to finding Miss Scott. There was quite a crowd of students around the square and I heard laughter and cheers. Then I recalled with a sinking heart that this was the day one of the School of Medicine's most important patrons, Sir Henry Carlisle, was being given a 'royal' tour.

I had seen Carlisle often enough and had no high opinion of him. A large, bewhiskered, self-important man with raffish good looks and a swagger, he had made a packet in the colonies and now seemed to like nothing better than to parade himself before the students. I had no doubt his money did some good, nor did I care if he wished to flaunt it, but what always irritated me about Carlisle was the way he sought to ingratiate himself. He would endlessly wink and joke and snigger for our amusement, and had consequently built up a sizable band of followers, some of whom I knew from the rugby field. Indeed there was a story that on one hot day he had declared after his usual tour of the university that the 'men' looked a little parched and he would buy them all some beer. At which there was a great cheer and he was carried shoulder-high to Bennett's Bar, where no doubt they laughed at his jokes for as long as he wished.

As I drew closer, I saw that on this occasion Carlisle was being escorted by one of the most pompous and unctuous medical teachers in the university, a physiologist called Gillespie. 'If you come this way, Sir Henry,' he was saying, 'I would like to show you how our newest operating theatre is progressing, thanks to your generous help.'

Sir Henry grinned at the crowd, and I noticed for the first time that there were women among it. 'Delighted,' he said, looking round him. 'Though I have to admit I am almost expecting to find lace tablecloths draped over the instruments of surgery. After all, much as we may abhor it, it seems you have the tender sensibilities of women to consider now.'

Here was the kind of humour he favoured, even though today, unusually, his wife Lady Sarah Carlisle was beside him. She was small and fair and looked rather ill at ease.

'Yes,' Gillespie answered with a smile. 'It has been left to each teacher to decide whether to admit women.'

'Quite so,' Carlisle replied, climbing the steps to the theatre, and winking at one of his acolytes, a sly man who played fullback in the university team. 'And I hear Latimer for one stands out agin it.' Here he raised his voice for the benefit of the men by the door. 'He says the only women in his anatomy class will continue to enter feet first!'

There was a great guffaw of approval and a whoop of delight from Crawford's gang, who were standing not far away. Moreover, as soon as he was in the theatre and the door had closed, a great jeer went up against the women standing by the entrance. I walked away to my class, but my blood was boiling and Latimer's dissection did nothing to improve my mood. How could Carlisle abuse his position in this way to stir up feeling against the women? He was not a doctor or a teacher. He had no jurisdiction over any of us. He was merely meant to be involved in charity and good works. And now he was using his money to further his own prejudices. By the end of the class, after an hour of watching the red-faced Latimer pulling amphibians apart, I had made up my mind to do something. It would be no use to approach Carlisle directly, but the unctuous Gillespie would surely hear my complaint. I knew quite well that the man hated trouble of any kind, and I fully intended to cause as much of it as I could.

Not wishing to be distracted, I crossed the square and walked straight down the corridor to Gillespie's office. The door was half open, and I could hear voices. A woman's voice sounded angry. I made out the phrase 'compromise yourself'. Perhaps some of the women were already making their feelings known to Gillespie. I knocked on the door and entered.

To my astonishment, Miss Scott stood there, a little flushed in the face, staring at me. I was equally startled. It was the first time I had seen her since the incident with Crawford and I was struck, as before, by her physical beauty. The reddish fair hair was combed out and fell round her face. The eyes were less defiant now, sadder, though surprised enough at the sight of me.

I tried to compose myself. 'I am sorry,' I said. 'I was looking for Dr Gillespie.'

I turned, expecting to see him, but the other person in the room was the small, somewhat fragile yet elegant figure of Carlisle's wife. Miss Scott saw my confusion.

'He is not here, Mr Doyle,' she said. 'May I introduce my older sister? Lady Sarah Carlisle.'

Of course I went forward and shook her hand, marvelling at this. Now that I thought about it, there was a faint resemblance between the two sisters, though Lady Carlisle was some years older.

'Mr Doyle,' she said. 'Dr Gillespie has been approving the new wing with my husband. I am sure you can interrupt them.'

I was emboldened now to say what I had come for, and I wanted Miss Scott to hear it. 'Well, to be honest, ma'am, I only wished to point out to him it is hard enough here for your sister and her colleagues without our own patron airing his feelings against them.'

If I had expected Miss Scott to look pleased with me, I was disappointed. Her eyes were fixed on Lady Carlisle. The latter did not seem put out, but her reply had dignity. 'Mr Doyle, if certain of my husband's views incline to the traditional, it is his affair and not particularly unusual.' And then she smiled over at her sister. 'But Elsbeth here will make a very good doctor. I am proud of her.'

It was a touching moment, and Miss Scott was about to answer when suddenly the door swung wide open and Gillespie and Carlisle swept in, laughing together.

'Lady Carlisle!' Gillespie wrung his hands with typical unctuousness. 'We have returned from our ministrations to offer you and your husband some refreshment.'

I noticed Carlisle answered for his wife at once. 'I can certainly bid them welcome,' he said, smiling at Lady Carlisle and moving to the fireplace. He ignored both myself and Miss Scott entirely. It was as if we were not even there.

A look from Gillespie, however, made it clear I should leave, and I needed no second invitation. Perhaps it might seem like cowardice, but I did not wish to embarrass Miss Scott in any way and reasoned I had no place interrupting a family gathering. After negotiating Carlisle, who gave me a quizzical look, I nodded at the women and withdrew.

Outside, however, I did glance back and saw Sir Henry, Lady Carlisle and Gillespie were talking. It seemed to me that Miss Scott was totally ignored, but then the door was shut.

That afternoon was not so cold as it had been and, rather than go directly home, I wanted to walk and think about this encounter. I was in such a daydream that I hardly noticed where I was heading, and then ahead of me I saw a little cluster of people, mainly traders, with a policeman among them.

Even then I was not alert enough to wonder about this or register who I was. Until my eye was caught by something lying in the gutter. It was a smashed violin.

At once I thought of Samuel and moved quickly through the crowd, for they were gathered around something. I had to push past several people until I came to the front. Samuel's body lay on the cobbled stones before me, utterly stiff and lifeless. The beggar's hand was stretched out as if clawing the pavement and his poor face stared up at the sky just as it had when he played. But now it bore an expression of intense pain, all the features contorted.

I turned away in shock. A policeman stood talking to a grey-suited man, who was evidently a doctor, and I moved quickly to them with my questions.

'See for yourself,' answered the policeman rather impatiently, as if he were discussing a broken horse-trough. 'Old Samuel has had some sort of seizure. Drank far too much than was good for him. They say he was in agony.'

'Aye,' nodded the doctor. 'Alcoholic poisoning is what I surmise. Somebody gave him a bottle.'

'Where is the bottle?' I said abruptly, for I could make no sense of this. My tone evidently irritated the doctor for he spoke quite sharply.

'I don't know. Ask them. They'll know right enough.'

He indicated a group of street-urchins, some quite filthy, who stood laughing across the way. 'But I smell no alcohol,' I said. 'And he was no great drinker. You're sure the death is as you say?'

The policeman stared at me. 'Aye, and what do you ken about it?' he said with an officious air. Behind him the body was at last being decently covered.

I tried to keep calm. 'I do not think it is likely he died from alcohol poisoning and I am a medical student,' I said with as much dignity as I could. But it was a mistake, for both of them smiled.

'Well away and pester someone else,' the police-man said. 'He hasnae been attacked and why would a soul hurt him? They didna even take his pennies.'

He was quite right, for now I saw the beggar's pathetic pile of coins lying on the edge of the pavement. For some reason Samuel had stacked them neatly in a gleaming little pyramid and the urchins were already eyeing them greedily.

The doctor was not to be outdone. 'I advise you to get back to your studies, young man. This is a common enough occurrence. He was just a drunken beggar.'

And they turned away without offering me the chance of another word. I tried appealing to the people around me, especially the nearby stallholder who had served us, who knew quite well Samuel was no drinker. But even he slunk away and I could not blame him. For in those days the minor officials of medicine and justice were frequently peremptory, insular and vindictive. Once Opinion had been issued they would never allow an inferior to challenge it on any grounds. No doubt the stallholder had reasons to avoid the police, and certainly he would not risk his livelihood by opposing them.

Finally, knowing Bell was away examining, I presented myself at the nearest police station and made as much noise as I could about the matter. The old detective with a long moustache and whiskers, who came out to talk to me, was not unsympathetic, writing down my views solemnly in an ancient red notebook. But he was honest enough to admit that he doubted anyone would investigate further.

I returned home, still feeling angry and upset. And in due course, after talking to my mother, a feeling of intense apprehension drew me to my father's study. The kind of death I had witnessed in the street was, after all, the death we all feared most for him: that he would be found in a gutter somewhere with a bottle.

At first I was pleasantly surprised to find my father seated in his chair, a little sleepy it was true, but calm. And he seemed to recognise me. His cup of tea was getting cold before him so I took it to his lips. He drank and, for a wonder, thanked me. But then, as ever, the door opened and Waller was there.

I looked up at him. My father was dozing again. 'He seems better,' I said eagerly. Perhaps I should have known better than to comment, but I had been excited by my father's relative improvement.

'Oh no,' Waller replied with a shake of his fine head. 'I sedated him. That is all.'

As ever the man must have everything under his control. Waller had taken over the supervision of my father's case at the instigation of my mother, but I was quite sure he had no wish whatsoever for his 'patient's' health to improve. How I longed for a day when my father became whole again and sent him packing from the house! Alas I must have known, even then, such a day would probably never come.

Waller was continuing in his clipped nasal tones, '. . . your mother says you were concerning yourself about Samuel. That beggar with the fiddle?'

I was surprised to hear Waller say his name. When describing the incident to my mother, I had never called him Samuel. 'You knew him?' I asked.

'I heard the infernal racket he made. Sad, I suppose, in a way, but are we not better off for the streets being clear of such people? A weak strain will produce weakness.'

His eyes fell on my father, and of course I knew quite well what he was saying to me. But, as ever, his insinuation was veiled so that he could avoid any overt opposition.

'You want me to hear your pathology tonight?'

This last, more civil, remark came, I suppose, because he had noticed my fist clench and thought he might have risked provoking me too far. As it was, I did not dignify him with a reply and left the room.

Later that night I resorted to my friends and several glasses of ale as we lounged on the red leather upholstery of Rutherford's bar. I cannot say I drank excessively as a student for I was poor, and at home each night I faced the living proof of what damage drink could do. But I was by no means totally abstinent. For his part, Neill had independent means from his people in Canada and sometimes, when his money came through, he insisted on buying our beer. On nights like this I was glad of it too for I wanted a diversion. And I also wished to talk to them of Samuel's death.

'But why would anyone wish to harm him?' said Stark after I had explained that the death seemed to me suspicious.

Obviously I had turned this over more than once. 'I do not know enough about the man, but there may have been some quarrel or a debt. I doubt they will make any investigation whatsoever; the bottle he drained has disappeared. It could have contained any kind of poison. But if his body could be exhumed?'

Both of them guffawed at this. 'Doyle!' Stark said. 'Even if you found his grave, how could you persuade them to do that? May I remind you we are not exactly men of influence in our profession!'

Finally I was forced to admit defeat. Even if we

could establish a case, I doubted anyone would listen to us. And so, as will happen late in the evening when undergraduates are drinking, the talk became more abstract. We talked of innocence and goodness (for Samuel was my idea of innocence) and then of evil. And I suddenly remembered with indignation how at my boarding school I was told I would go to hell for playing with a ball in a corridor. 'If that,' I said putting down my glass with finality, 'is what the Jesuits can class as evil, perhaps evil does not truly exist at all?'

'But it does,' said Stark.

'Possibly,' I said gloomily. For I was thinking of Samuel's lifeless body and his staring pain.

'Certainly,' said Neill emphatically. 'Just stand on a high cliff looking down. No death could be worse: you would be crushed on the rocks below; yet something, some imp, still whispers to you to jump. Or let us say you have an important task, something you have to do, you must do, and time is desperately short. Action is essential.' He was almost on his feet himself now, waving his hands, a peculiarity of Neill's when he became excited with some flight of fancy. 'But then something, a lassitude, descends. That same imp is there in your mind, gently, insidiously, whispering delay. You see? Humans somehow desire to do things merely because they *know* they should not.'

Of course I recognised the source of his idea at once, for we had often discussed it: 'The Imp of the Perverse' by Poe, a wonderful story which examines the idea of the human temptation to act against the prevailing good even at our own cost.

'Yet,' I went on, 'that is only one view. And others

have an idea of evil that I could never accept. Look at that madman Crawford. He seems to believe the women who come to our class are evil.'

'It is nonsense,' said Stark.

'But,' said Neill, 'we have to understand that Crawford and his kind call it evil because they are frightened of it, and you know what they are frightened of? I will tell you. It is freedom. That is what the women seek. And it is this message of freedom that terrifies our professors. Yes, it is the message from the New World, from the future! Why, there we had women doctors even before the Civil War!'

This appealed to us greatly, and Stark and I contributed what coins we had to a last round so we could toast the future. Then we left the tavern, reviling our more hidebound teachers and moving on to discuss the better ones like Joseph Bell.

'We know, Doyle,' said Stark, 'you are not so convinced Bell is a charlatan. But what is your opinion of him now?'

Of course I could never reveal to my friends what I knew of the Doctor's investigative activities.

'I think,' I said with careful deliberation and intending to tell the truth, 'that he is decent enough. But also that he can be ruthless.'

'Of course!' Neill said laughing. 'But that is good. Medicine should be a crusade. We fight the army of bacteria as we fight a war. That means to the death, and Bell has the ruthlessness to be a fighter.'

We had turned into a small lane as he spoke and, quite suddenly, ahead of us Stark stopped dead. He was peering forward at the dark empty cobbles and a lantern burning in a window close to an entrance.

Beside me an ancient street sign announced we were somewhere called Jack's Lane. The place was not well lit and there were shadows around us everywhere. We had passed a horse-trough, that seemed to be leaking water, and a little stream of it was at my feet.

When Stark stopped, we had stopped too, and when he turned he was pale. 'Oh no,' he said. 'Wait a minute. I have heard of this place . . .'

'But these are just tales,' said Neill quietly.

I did not know what they were talking about and was about to say so, but Stark seemed truly agitated.

'Move back now,' he said in a low voice. 'And very quietly.'

But even as he spoke, a small smiling figure moved out of the shadowy entrance to a wynd beside the lantern. He had a raised pistol in his hand. 'Hello, gentlemen,' he said softly.

His face was grey in colour, the skin stretched tightly around its features, and his smile was as thin as a knife. We all stood there staring at his pistol while, still smiling, he moved over to inspect us.

'If you would drop your money on the ground, gentlemen?' Of course we had little of it, but I was still so enraged by this that I felt like lunging towards him. Would he really dare to shoot me in the head like a dog? Stark, who was deathly pale, gave me a warning look.

Beside me, I saw Neill had had the same thought yet also calculated that the risk was not worth taking. And so, like a pack of fools, we dropped our wallets and coins on the ground beside him.

The man looked down at his booty. His smile had

gone but his pistol was still trained, his voice firm. 'Now go back where you came.'

We backed away till we were again beside that sign and the man had now disappeared through the entrance by the house, no doubt into the myriad of alleys that threaded back and forth all over this part of the town. Stark was studying the name.

'Yes, I knew I had heard of it,' he said ruefully, as our dejected little group walked back to the busy road from which we had come. It was a relief to rejoin its humanity, hear the sound of the horses' feet and see the bright lamps of the inn we had just left.

Neill looked furious. 'To treat free men in this way,' he said. 'Like we were his playthings. What about the police? Will they do nothing?'

'There is talk that scoundrel has killed two police-men in his time. They don't want to try their luck. Of course he picks his time and his place,' said Stark, 'but most often it is this lane, for you see he can escape from here into a myriad of wynds and they will never dare to follow him. That is why nobody comes this way. We should count ourselves fortunate, gentlemen, we had already drunk our money.'

We were further along the road now, and I was about to express my outrage that the town could effectively give a public lane over to such blatant lawlessness when I saw that Neill and Stark were staring at a cab which had just swept past us and was depositing its occupant in front of a brightly-lit house. I recognised the place at once, for it was the notorious Madame Rose's. Quite often I had stared at its plush red velvet curtains and wondered what occurred inside, but my friends were not looking at it.

Their eyes were fixed on the smart topcoated man who had left his cab and was now walking jauntily up to its entrance. He smiled, turning slightly as the door was opened, and I recognised that smile at once. It was our patron, Sir Henry Carlisle.

The place was said to draw its customers from the wealthier walks of life, but even so I was taken aback. Stark was equally dumbfounded, but Neill claimed to have heard rumours of it before. Carlisle's coterie of admirers was evidently known to snigger over them, for he hinted at such exploits when he took them drinking. 'Oh, yes,' said Neill. 'He may not want women at the university, but I hear he is more than happy with their company in the old town.'

'And this time his wife is naturally left at home,' Stark said. But it was not his wife I was thinking of.

We said our goodbyes and later that night I lay in bed wondering if Miss Elsbeth Scott knew of her brother-in-law's ventures into the brothels of the old town. As I was drifting off to sleep, in that half-state between waking and dreaming, I thought for the last time that I heard old Samuel's ghostly music. I knew it was a kind of guide through a labyrinth, and in my dream I tried to grasp the pattern of these strange scales and arabesques. I wanted to follow its path, but it kept moving further away until I slept.

PART TWO: HIS GAME

The Room of Blood

It was to be ten days before I saw Miss Elsbeth Scott again. The weather had turned for the better, it was a bright spring morning and I was hurrying through the square, which was full of students, and into the corridor leading to Bell's room. I was due to meet the Doctor a quarter of an hour before his lecture in order to receive instructions for preparing the hall when I heard shouting coming from a corridor to my right.

I recognised the voice at once. It was Latimer. 'I have made my position quite clear,' he was yelling at some hapless student. I turned and there, framed in the light from his doorway, was our Professor of Anatomy's fierce red face, mapped with blue veins and crowned by a mop of fiery red hair. 'You will not enter my class,' he shouted and turned away, slamming his door noisily behind him.

It was only then I glimpsed Miss Scott. She had been standing back in the shadows, probably afraid he might strike her. Her fear was not unreasonable for, though I do not think Latimer ever did strike a woman, he would happily lift his hand to anyone he thought was impudent. And his definition of 'impudence' was very wide.

So she had kept her distance. But she was by no means cowed. Indeed she walked back from the door, with her head upright, flushed yet defiant. And then she saw me.

I do not know whether she was embarrassed, but she did not show it as she approached me.

'Latimer has thrown you out of his class?' I asked.

'He refuses to teach us dissection for fear we might see something improper.' Her tone was scornful but I could hear the emotion in her voice. 'His facial expression perhaps?'

I smiled at her joke. 'Blue and deoxygenated, I recall. The man is a pompous clown.'

I expected more banter but to my surprise her face became suddenly quite serious. She paused, as if making up her mind, and then took something from her sleeve. 'One of many,' she said. 'I had this delivered to my lodgings yesterday.'

It was a letter and she handed it to me. The first thing that struck me was the writing which was large and somewhat strange. The letters were huge and scribbled like a child scrawling insults on a blackboard.

'And upon her forehead was a name written: the MOTHER of harlots and ABOMINATION of the earth,' I read. The words 'mother' and 'abomination' were fiercely and madly inked over scores of times. 'Therefore shall her plagues come in one day for she has drunk of the blood of the lamb.'

I knew my Bible well enough to recognise the

phrases from the Book of Revelation, but they were all jumbled. 'You are dealing with illiterates!' I said, handing it back to her. 'This is not even a real quotation. Was there no signature?'

She shook her head. 'But last night I thought someone was following me.'

'Well, it must be Crawford. I saw him threaten you and he used much this kind of language. You must take it to the authorities.'

She started tearing up the letter. 'No,' she said fiercely. 'I am quite aware what would happen. This would just become another excuse to be rid of us. As it is, the author of this rubbish will be crowing to see me banned from the demonstration room. But tell me, you are a clerk, Mr Doyle. Does that mean you have access to Latimer's dissection?'

'Of course,' I said eagerly, seizing on this as a way to extend our acquaintance. 'And it is free at the end of the day.' Then I stopped for I saw the impossibility of the thing. 'But it is no use, for the night-clerk is on duty and would never admit a woman.'

She smiled then, that wonderful, mischievous smile. 'No,' she said. 'But perhaps there is a way if you would help me?'

She was reluctant to elaborate and we agreed a time to meet on the following evening. Then I moved off quickly, aware to my alarm that I was now late for preparing Bell's lecture.

The Doctor was waiting for me in his room, watch in hand, and he did not look at all pleased. 'Thank you for condescending to appear twelve minutes and fifteen seconds after the agreed hour,' he said, putting away his watch. 'Half a minute later and I fear this room would have been empty and your clerkship would have been at an end, for lateness is of no use to me. I have already cancelled the lecture.'

I was dumbfounded and started to apologise, saying I could surely get the hall ready within a few minutes, but he brushed me aside, picking up his cane. 'Doyle, it is cancelled because we are required at once. Fortunately for you the call from Summers only came ten minutes ago and I had arrangements to make so you have only lost me two minutes. But, in a matter like this, two minutes may be critical. Our mystery man has shown himself again.'

I was still amazed by this development, as we strode out of there and a porter told us breathlessly where the cab was waiting. Soon we were moving rapidly through the streets and, within a few moments, we had turned down a thoroughfare I knew well enough, for it was the place where Samuel had played. Almost at once the cab stopped at a large building with tall windows. In the morning sunlight, with people bustling past, it looked so ordinary that I did not at first recognise it. But, as I stepped down from the cab and saw the red drapes, I suddenly realised we were at Madame Rose's.

Naturally the place was not open at half past ten in the morning, but even so I found myself looking round guiltily as the Doctor almost ran up the steps to its door.

It was half open and a woman stood there breathless and worried. She was quite old and, evidently from her dress, a housemaid. 'Oh, thank heaven, are you the police, sir?'

Bell was a little surprised but not, I am sure,

displeased to find they were not yet here. 'No, they are on their way,' he said, 'but evidently delayed. What has happened?'

She led us into a large ornate room with a screen beautifully embroidered in the Japanese manner and several tables and upholstered chairs and sofas. The carpet was of a rich red and the chairs matched it. There was a bar too and, though closed, it looked far better stocked than those I visited with my friends. I had rarely been in so luxurious a refreshment room; evidently no trouble was spared here to put the guests at their ease.

I was reflecting on the contrast with the miserable house we saw by the docks when she led us behind the screen. A woman in her twenties, with exquisitely curled dark hair and blood on her dress lay on a divan, panting for breath and crying. She had her hand to her throat.

Bell went to her at once. 'It is all right,' he said gently, 'I am a doctor.' We could see at once that, despite the blood, the woman – who from her accent was French – was not too hurt. But she was sobbing and finding it hard to speak, making very little sense. The Doctor calmed her a little, as we heard the story from the other woman.

'She was attacked, sir,' the housemaid said. 'I come in to clean and I hear her screaming. She says she had fallen asleep and somebody got her by the neck. She did not see properly. But he must be up there.'

The Doctor started upright. 'Her assailant is still here?'

'Aye, sir. This is why I was so afeared. And there was blood up there, she says.'

Bell was up from the woman in a trice and making for the door. It led to a hall and then stairs which we took at a gallop. The staircase was as plush as the rest of the place with a stained-glass window halfway up which sent somewhat eerie rays on to the dark crimson carpet. We reached a long corridor with many doors leading off it, and the Doctor shouted he would take this floor and I should go for the next.

So I ran on to the top of the house. Here it was a little darker, but another corridor stretched out before me with countless rooms on either side. I flung open the door of the first room and saw very little. The shutters were open and light streamed in to reveal a bed, a basin and chair. I withdrew and tried the one across from it, which was very similar. There were so many doors and rooms that I could see I would have to move swiftly, and I ran on, flinging the doors open as I went. A glance was sufficient to confirm each room I had passed so far was quite empty.

It was very noticeable to me now that the lusher trappings of below had given way to a base functionality. Presumably the owners calculated that, once a man was up here, his thoughts were fully occupied with the activity he desired and he needed no reassurance in soft furnishings. But I was impressed by the sheer scale of the place. These corridors were quite as long and as populated with rooms as any at the university. This surely implied that there must be periods when the custom was very high. How many of the men I knew might supply that custom? I found myself wondering if our 'lodger' Bryan Waller would come here when he went out for

one of his walks. But the idea was so unpleasant that
I left it alone.

I was almost at the end of the corridor when I heard
a sound. It was a little like a door or window closing,
and I thought it must have come from the room
opposite me a little way along. There were about five
more doors on the floor. I approached this one at once
and flung it open.

It was different from all the others, dark and
shuttered. Moreover, by the window a lone candle
flickered. I took a step, trying to make out if there
was anyone there.

At that moment, something came at me out of the
darkness, knocking me to the floor. I was winded and
for a moment could hardly move. Behind me the door
slammed shut. I forced myself to my feet and
staggered to the door, opening it just in time to
glimpse a black figure at the end of the corridor,
moving out of sight. This galvanised me and I ran.

Eventually I reached an alcove with a curtained but
open window. Looking out I could see a roof-ledge
and, beyond it, the same dark caped figure, who had
evidently jumped across to the adjoining roof and was
now clambering into the open window of the building
opposite.

At once I climbed out to follow. The figure had
disappeared inside, but I jumped too. It was a matter
of ease for the distance was only a few feet, but even
so I did not care to look down. And then I was
clambering into the opposite building.

I found myself on a dusty staircase illuminated by
the sunlight from big windows like the one I had used
as an entrance. Perhaps this had once been some kind

of factory but it was certainly empty now. Below me I could hear footsteps but the dust was in any case so thick I could see my quarry's tracks. I took the stairs at speed, and as I neared the bottom, I found the outside door had been flung open.

He could hardly have been very far ahead of me. Thinking I might have trapped him, I ran through it.

And stopped dead. I was right back in the busy street. Before me were a profusion of stalls, beggars, carts and cabs. Thanks to the geography of this labyrinth my assailant had completely outwitted me.

I pushed forward into the seething life of the old town, jostling the crowd as if they had all been involved. A beggar I had noticed before, with a slightly twisted lip, turned towards me, and I attempted to question him, but he just shook his head. The crowd was so thick here anyone might have melted into it unobserved, and I could offer nothing in the way of real description. There were innumerable dark-coated figures and the man I sought could be any of them or none, for by now he had had plenty of time to disappear.

Giving up at last, I decided to retrace my steps. But first I examined the door for I was surprised he had exited so easily from a building that would surely have been locked. As I suspected the bolt had been sheared, something he could not possibly have done while I was behind him. His escape route, right down to the choice of exit and the crowded street, had obviously been prepared with care.

By the time I returned to the deserted corridors of Madame Rose's, Inspector Beecher and Summers, the pathologist whom Bell and I had known from a previous case, were standing with Bell on the top landing. Beecher was looking thoroughly annoyed. He obviously hated being dragged to such a place and Bell's presence there hardly improved his humour.

It turned out that Summers had been at the police station when the message about the mysterious attacker arrived. Knowing of Bell's intense interest in the affair, he had sent the boy on to him but, through no fault of his own, there was some delay reaching Beecher, who was in a meeting with the procurator. This was why we had arrived first and, as a result, Beecher was furious. Indeed, when I reported that I had lost my man in the street, his dark face flushed.

'Yes,' he said. 'This is what occurs when I am delayed. I wish you had left it, gentlemen. We might have had him. Summers should never have sent word to you.'

'At least,' the Doctor responded somewhat drily, 'Doyle has given the man pursuit, which so far as I am aware is more than any policeman has yet managed.'

Summers turned away into another doorway at this, only, I am sure, so that Beecher could not see him smiling.

The Doctor insisted at once on seeing the room where I was attacked, while Summers and a uniformed policeman, who had appeared, went back down to explore any areas that might have been missed. Bell went over every inch of the bedroom where I encountered my assailant though not, that I could observe, with any great success. Now that the shutters were open and light was streaming in, it appeared empty and innocuous.

At last he came back into the corridor, where

Beecher was examining the neighbouring rooms. 'You will find nothing there,' said the Doctor. 'I have looked at them.' He stared along the corridor. 'Indeed I have covered this whole floor bar that one.'

His eye had fallen on an alcove at the end of the corridor where two steps led down to a room, and he moved there now as we followed. Its door, like all the others, was closed. The Doctor flung it open.

At first all I saw was red. A sea of it. But it was not light inside and, for just a moment, I thought perhaps this wash of colour was some kind of mad trick with paint or wallpaper. But then the smell, which had somehow been contained by that stout oak door, reached us and I knew the truth. On every surface there was nothing but blood.

The stuff covered that small and empty room like some kind of obscene soup. It saturated the walls and the door and the ceiling. It even obscured the light from the tiny window.

But the floor was most startling. For, as I stared, and I know this is hard to contemplate, here the blood actually had depth, like water.

In the middle of the room lay some kind of pulpy shape. It was sodden, but you could make out clothes. A coat, and the hem of a skirt.

Beecher was choking but Bell held his ground, though he made no move to enter. The room was, we could all see now, much smaller than any other we had found. Taking his cane, the Doctor leaned forward and poked the horrible object in the centre of the floor. I felt myself almost retching for I assumed it was the body that had been leeched of all this blood. But, as he worked, we soon concluded it was only a pile of women's clothes. The Doctor poked for several moments but could find no evidence of anything else.

Yet there was something more in the room. On a ledge to one side I could see a neat, indeed almost symmetrical, pile of gleaming coins, presumably belonging to the owner of the clothes.

Beside me, Bell used a phial to collect a sample of the blood, taking every care not to step in it as Summers appeared down the corridor. 'Well,' he said, 'we have been through the place from roof to basement. There is nothing that—' He broke off as he saw our expressions and stared in amazement at the chamber. When he noticed the clothes, he assumed the worst until he was told we could find nothing else.

'A room of blood then,' said the Doctor grimly. And he straightened up, putting his sample in his bag.

Once we were sure we had seen all there was to see in that foul room, the Doctor and Beecher closely questioned the two women downstairs. There was not much to learn and, by the time they had finished, Beecher had lost some of his ill temper. Indeed it was Bell who looked concerned. Once again our man seemed to be slipping away into the twilight.

The hysterical woman with blood on her, who had raised the alarm, told us in bad English that she had been sleeping alone in the room where I was attacked. She had been woken in the dark by a sound and started to dress when she felt bloody hands round her neck, hence the stains on her dress. She screamed and ran away downstairs to be greeted by the maid. Neither of them had in effect *seen* anything at all.

Only the room of blood pointed to a serious crime, but whose blood was it?

To make matters worse, the madame of the place, a stout overdressed woman in her fifties, had now arrived. She was courteous enough but said little, and it was soon obvious all she really wanted was for us to leave her place of business. Indeed, if it had not been for the room of blood, I am quite sure she would have blamed it all on her French hireling's imagination.

She was talking quietly in a corner to this woman now, probably telling her to say as little as possible. Meanwhile I stood to one side as the Doctor and Beecher conferred. Summers was still upstairs.

'So, as ever with this mysterious man of yours,' Beecher was saying pointedly, 'we seem to have nothing concrete. Nobody even saw him properly.'

'But we can be sure of one thing,' observed Bell. 'He knows the place intimately.'

'No help there at all,' said Beecher. 'It is true of half the men in the town, yet none will admit it. And, as you know, madame here would probably rather be hanged than betray her custom. I am afraid it may be just another distraction, Bell. These places have their own rough manners, and I prefer to keep out of them.'

This was too much for the Doctor. 'I hardly think, Beecher, even you can describe what we saw in that room up there as rough manners.'

To my surprise Beecher smiled at this. 'We cannot even be sure he had anything to do with that matter. There are other possibilities.'

Bell frowned. 'Perhaps you will be so kind as to suggest one.'

'Well I should wait for Summers, and I put this forward merely as a vague idea. But just suppose,' said Beecher, 'one of the poor wretches who works here slit her wrists. Then she crawled out to die. That would be simple enough, though no doubt you will counter it with some fantastic story.'

To his great irritation, Bell burst out laughing. 'But why should I, when you have done it for me? I realise, Beecher, you would invent almost anything to avoid investigating murder in a city brothel. But if you wish to indulge in ghost stories, then, believe me, with all that blood, I think you would be better off plumping for vampires.'

Beecher was white now. 'What do you talk of?'

'A murder enquiry. Have you any idea,' the Doctor asked leaning forward intensely, 'of the *volume* of blood in that room? Nobody gave that blood and lived to crawl out, I can assure you of that. It has been drained from someone quite recently. It is fresh.'

THE ANATOMY LESSON

It was a very pretty polemic and, though the Doctor had been crudely crushing, I felt little sympathy for his victim. Inspector Beecher was almost a personification of the city's hypocrisy in those days. Here, especially in the city's netherworld, the police always preferred to look the other way. Indeed, as Bell had pointed out when he first introduced me to his private field, the general code was to investigate as little as they could except where a case was so blindingly obvious that success was certain. Such cases, as the Doctor never tired of reminding me, gave comfort to the ignorant while enabling the worst kinds of crime to continue unremarked.

'I will tell you the unwritten code of this town,' the Doctor said ruefully, and not for the first time, as we walked back along the busy street. 'It is to do as little as possible.'

For the rest of that day and into the evening, Bell was intent only on pursuing his chemistry investigations and, after I had helped him set up some of the equipment, he had no further need of me. This was fortunate for I had an appointment I was very anxious to keep.

I had arranged to meet Miss Scott at the entrance of the corridor that led to Latimer's dissection room. She had been mysterious about her intentions but I guessed what she had in mind. Sure enough she was there, waiting in the shadows to one side, in a black coat with a high collar, a scarf and a black hat.

I went over to her at once, uneasily aware that along the corridor the night-clerk was already staring at us. Her eyes were so large and striking that I hoped to heaven he would not see them.

'I will do?' she said softly, looking up at me. Her hair had been pinned up under her hat.

I nodded. But in truth I was starting to wonder if this was madness. 'We must seem to know each other, be old colleagues,' I whispered. 'And don't look anywhere near him.'

'Of course.' She gave a bright confident smile. 'I am ready.'

The sight of that smile once again subdued some of my doubts, which was just as well, for I had begun to realise the true danger of what we were about. If we were stopped and the night-clerk saw she was a woman, no quarter would be given by Latimer or anyone else. Even Bell would be quite powerless to help after such a flagrant breach of the rules: both of us would undoubtedly be flung out of the university, and I could well imagine the sort of gossip that would follow.

We turned to make our way along the corridor. The night-clerk's desk was on my left so I took care to see

Miss Scott was on my right and we started to walk. Ahead of me the night-clerk was writing something, with a pen that he dipped in an inkwell, but we were not yet near him.

Soon we were closer and still he wrote. Perhaps, I thought, this would be relatively easy. After all, he knew me and could have no objection to another student accompanying me. But, just as we came opposite him, he suddenly put down his pen and stared at Miss Scott with such a frown that I felt sure he was going to say something.

Without thinking I began to talk at once, desperately recalling some chat I had heard after an operation the previous day.

'Oh no,' I said, shaking my head at her. 'Walker has a fad about the portio dura, the motor to the face. He thinks paralysis of it comes from a disturbance of the blood supply. Even got it into his head to remove a patient's ear once, which caused a lot of chatter.'

She nodded. The night-clerk was still staring. Of course Miss Scott could not risk speech, that in itself was the problem, but she knew it and gave a little nod and clapped me on the back. 'Yes,' I said, trying to sound amused, 'you remember him?'

We were past him now and I pushed on. 'He always said the first great advance of the human race was when they attained the power of speech. The second was when they learned to control it. Regrettably, according to him, women have not yet attained the second stage.'

With that we turned into the room and I closed the door firmly behind us. Through it I could see that the night-clerk had returned to his writing. We had done it. Miss Scott was almost choking but only with suppressed laughter. 'It is all right,' I said. 'He has gone back to his work.'

Her eyes flashed with humour. 'You are wretched, Mr Doyle,' she said.

'I had to play a part. It was the first that came to me.'

She looked at me. 'You do not believe that, I hope. About women and the power of speech.'

'No,' I said, aware it was the first time since reaching manhood that I had ever been properly alone with a woman of this age. 'But I heard someone say it yesterday and I had to play it as well as I could.'

She turned and I sensed that she too was aware we were alone, but was determined to show no embarrassment. 'Too well for me perhaps. Can we begin? We will not be disturbed in here?'

'I have never known him come in, and so far as I can see there are no other students here.'

I turned up the gaslight. Latimer's dissecting room was a dark, cavernous place with a white skeleton hanging at the far wall who was affectionately known as Jock. Right in the middle were a number of covered tables and, as we approached them, she took off her coat and hat, revealing her beautiful hair. It was so abundant that she could hardly stop it from falling and I remember one of the curls tumbled down around her ear.

I suppose I was just as determined as she was not to be embarrassed, so I removed only the cloth that covered the cadaver's lower legs. 'Yesterday Latimer was dissecting the knee,' I said, exposing both knees. One was intact, the other a mass of muscle and bone.

I pointed to it. 'He used this and said we could continue on the other as we wished.'

She stared down at it and, when she looked back up at me, there was a challenge in her eyes. 'I am not squeamish, Mr Doyle. We do not have to start here.'

I smiled at her doubt. 'I assure you it is what we were doing.'

At last, much to my relief, I could see she believed me, for it was the truth, even if at that point a highly convenient one. So she turned away to pick up a blade and rolled up her sleeves, bending down intently.

Then, after a moment of careful inspection, she made an incision. I watched her face as she worked, for there was something remarkable about the concentration on it. Finally I looked down at her hands and was amazed, for she was moving with a dexterity and speed that would have surely surprised even Latimer.

'It is hard to get at the cruciate ligament,' she said, for she had exposed most of the rest, 'but there . . .'

She found it and I was astonished. 'But . . . we took ten minutes on the other one. You have done dissection before?'

She looked up at me and smiled. 'My father was a doctor. Sometimes he allowed me to assist him.'

'In the hospital?' I had never heard of this happening.

She had gone back to her work. 'And in training. My sister and I were brought up in Cape Town. You can do a huge amount there with very little, and nobody quibbles about being treated by a woman. They need us too badly. Now there is the articular cartilage, I think.'

'I cannot see you need instruction,' I said. And then we both froze, for outside the door there was the sound of heavy footsteps. I felt my heart beating and Miss Scott went quite pale. They were clearly coming straight to this room; there was no other place they could be going. We stood there foolishly waiting for it to open, facing the end of our short careers.

In that instant I suddenly thought of what Neill had said about the imp of the perverse, the serpent of nihilism that somehow weakens your limbs and lulls you into inaction at the moment of maximum danger. Fortunately the thought galvanised me and I raced quickly towards the door, reaching it just in time to pull it open. A labman with red whiskers who worked for Latimer stood there. My heart turned over, for this man was almost as strict as his master.

'Mr Doyle?' he said. 'You work quite late.'

'Yes,' I said, standing as firmly as I could before him, keeping the door half closed and hoping to heaven Miss Scott could not be seen. 'Two of us are completing a dissection. Latimer suggested it himself yesterday.'

I am sure he would have asked me to step aside, but I saw he had a bundle of papers in his hand.

'Oh, I can take these,' I said as airily as I could. 'For I know where they go and my colleague does not wish to be disturbed.'

It was a bold play. This man often showed utter contempt for students, and could have swept past me in a moment to see who this arrogant 'colleague' was. But he also had enormous reverence for the practice of Dissection. That religion had been instilled into him by Latimer who hated any disturbance or noise when he was wielding the knife.

His face was a few inches from mine, scrutinising me. 'Who is it?' he said quietly but rather sharply.

'Douglas,' I said quickly, naming a particularly talented student who was a great favourite of Latimer's.

Again he paused. But in the end, prudence won the day and he handed me the papers. 'They had better be placed correctly or I shall be quite aware who disturbed them,' he said discourteously. And then he withdrew.

I made sure he had gone, closed the door and turned around. Miss Scott emerged from the shadows. We were both overwhelmed by the narrowness of our escape. I told her that Douglas had been here earlier so there seemed little prospect of repercussions, but it was some time before we returned to work.

Slowly we recovered our confidence and I watched as she finished what she had begun, commenting again that she hardly seemed to need the practice.

Miss Scott looked up at this. 'It is more to show myself that I can do it in spite of them all, for I know it would have made my father proud,' she said with feeling. 'In the summer I intend to go back and work in the hospital he helped to found.' She turned back to her work. 'But what of you? Is your father a doctor? Is he proud of you?'

The question was natural enough and yet to me it was a dagger. 'He is not a doctor, no,' I said awkwardly after a moment. But she was so engaged she did not seem to notice.

'Well,' she said as she finished her last incision. 'I am quite sure he is proud of you.' And she covered the cadaver and stood up. It was obvious how pleased she was to have defied the bullying Latimer, for her face had a mischievous expression, perfectly framed in the halo from the gas lamp.

After she had replaced her coat and hat, the walk back along the corridor was uneventful for the night-clerk seemed half asleep. Once we were beyond him she left me to change her outward disguise in the same room where Crawford had once found us. Soon she had let down her hair, packed away the hat and I was escorting her home in a more normal fashion.

I discovered now that her father had died of fever four years ago. Her eyes misted over as she talked of him. 'It was hard to bear,' she said, 'for we hardly knew my mother. She had given me the name Elsbeth but spelled it differently, with a "b" rather than a "p". My father always said it might have been an accident for she was ill when she wrote it down, but he said it made me one of a kind. When I am working, I feel happy and close to him.' I wanted to hear more, but suddenly she seemed to remember herself. 'Like some spy,' she said, 'you ask all the questions. I want to know what makes you happy.'

As she spoke, she studied me closely. I smiled, for it was not easy to answer. And then, for the second time in that memorable evening, she seemed to alight as if by instinct on a delicate subject. 'For example,' she said, 'what about all you do for Dr Bell? Do you enjoy working for him?'

'As his clerk? Yes I do.'

My slip was tiny but she sensed it at once. Her

instinct was extraordinary. 'If not his clerk, what then? I see you must have some other role.'

I did not know what to say for I took her to be serious.

'What else could you be, Mr Doyle, his valet?' she said, smiling.

'Sometimes,' I said ruefully, 'it may seem so. There is a good deal of cleaning.'

And so fortunately the subject was left and all too soon we had arrived at her lodgings, a dreary four-square house with a stone step which looked as if it was scrubbed hourly. This was probably true, for Miss Scott lived in dread of the landlady whose face scowled down at us from a window.

'She is quite as fierce as Edinburgh landladies are reputed to be,' she told me. 'Her house is called Seaview, which is among the grimmer jokes, for the sea feels very far away.'

Neither of us wanted to say goodnight, but it seemed the woman would certainly come down if we lingered any further.

'Perhaps we could meet to arrange another dissection?' I said a little falteringly. 'Next time I will make absolutely sure his labman has departed for the evening. That is, if you wish to continue, for I fear you learned nothing.'

'You are right.' She came closer. 'I learned nothing. About *you*. But next time I will persevere.' We agreed a place to meet and then she turned away and was gone.

I had no lectures the following day and it was not till the afternoon that I entered the Doctor's downstairs room to see if he needed me. The blinds were drawn and the place was in semi-darkness. But I fancied I could hear something, a muttering sound, so I came round the side of the bookcase.

Bell was crouched forward under a flickering gas lamp, staring into a microscope. Around him were a great mass of dirty beakers and test tubes. Evidently many experiments had been tried and, from his pallor, I could see he had been there all night. He glanced up at me but I knew better than to interrupt.

As I watched, he placed a sample of the blood we had found in the room on a slide, adding some acetic acid and a grain of salt before heating it over a Bunsen. Then he squeezed some of his own blood from a small incision in his arm on to another slide and treated it similarly. He examined both of these alternately, but it was obvious the results were far too inexact to satisfy him and finally he pushed them away angrily.

'I am a fool, Doyle, though I cannot yet prove it. Someone is taking me for a fool, and that idiot Beecher will not hesitate to say so. I am surprised he has not sent for us already.'

He got up and opened the blind and, as if in answer to his words, a familiar black carriage could be seen turning into the courtyard.

'Ah, there,' he said. 'Well, we must take our medicine.'

'I do not understand,' I said, for since I had no idea then what Teichmann's test was, I could not know what he meant.

'Nor do I,' said Bell grimly. 'And least of all does he, but I regret to say it will not stop his mockery.'

A short time later we climbed out of the carriage on

a street in the Old Town I did not know but which seemed to lie immediately behind Madame Rose's. As we got out, I saw a number of policemen waiting for us and all were grinning from ear to ear. Inspector Beecher and Summers stood at the back. Summers smirked. Beecher just managed to keep a straight face, but even so I do not think I have ever seen the man so pleased with himself.

He came forward. 'There is good news, Dr Bell. We have found what you were looking for. If you will follow me.'

And with that he strode off round the back of the large building behind him, which was a shared dwelling house. Bell and I followed, as several other policemen kept the pace, and the Doctor was surprised enough by this to stare back at them. 'If only,' he murmured to me, 'they showed similar enthusiasm during their other investigations, half the criminals in the city would be caught.

There was a clump of bushes behind the tenement and Beecher led us through them towards a rather miserable beech tree. I could hear the sound of insects, though the day was not particularly warm.

Beecher had stopped and turned. 'Your victims, Dr Bell,' he said as he folded his arms.

At his feet were two large dead sheep, their throats neatly cut and their eyes removed. The flies were buzzing around but the animals had obviously been drained of blood. 'So I don't think on this occasion,' he continued, 'we need to be worrying ourselves about a murder enquiry.'

Now the reason for all the smiles was obvious. Both Bell and I could sense the eyes of the other police on

our backs. But Bell did not give an inch of ground.
'My congratulations, Inspector,' he said, holding
Beecher's eye. 'And the blood-soaked clothing?'

Beecher shrugged. 'Its owner is an Agnes Walsh.
She worked for a spell at Madame Rose's and left her
coat in that room which was used for storage. No
doubt she will get a shock if she ever comes to reclaim
it. So that would seem to answer that. Someone's
gruesome idea of a prank. All your dramas are, as
before, quite unfounded. I will bid you good day.'

And he left the eyeless sheep and walked back
triumphantly to his grinning colleagues.

The Doctor had been scrutinising the area around
the sheep but now he straightened up. 'One moment,
Inspector?' he said with a careful politeness which I
had learned to distrust. 'If you recall, a woman was
half strangled.'

Beecher turned back. 'A prostitute claimed she was
attacked but she seems perfectly all right. It is hardly
a grievous thing. I dare say the joker did not want his
slaughter interrupted. We will keep our eyes open, if
you will excuse the expression.' There was a guffaw
from one of the policemen. 'But I fear there are other
more pressing matters.'

'Yet none so strange,' the Doctor answered with
derision. 'Do you really suppose the sheep were
slaughtered inside? Of course not.'

He bent down again and pulled out some rope
which had evidently been used to hoist them up and
was still tied to the legs of one. 'No,' said the Doctor,
'they were strung up to drain the blood and then cut
down. The receptacle may even be very near.'

He started rooting through the undergrowth and

suddenly spied something. 'There,' he said, for he had fished out the bloody pail on the end of his cane and held it up.

Of course this did not impress Beecher or his grinning cohorts. 'Mere details, Doctor. But ...' Beecher paused for effect, '. . . if you must reconstruct this terrible crime you have discovered, I strongly suggest you use your own bathroom.'

At this, a great explosion of laughter erupted behind him. I do not think Bell was unpopular with all of them – Summers for one was often his ally – but the Doctor could be severe and proud and it is always amusing to see pride take a fall. Moreover most of the policemen were probably just as relieved as Beecher to avoid an investigation in a leading city brothel, for there was no knowing where such a path might lead.

Beecher beamed and turned away as his little crowd dispersed. Bell was still intensely scrutinising his finds, more interested, as ever, by the details of the case than its politics. 'The laughter of imbeciles,' he muttered to himself as he examined the pail, and then turned his attention to the rope and its knots. 'Probably quite fitting in the circumstances.'

He lingered in that foul place for a long time and, when he was done, he insisted on revisiting Madame Rose's, which was not yet open but showed every sign of preparing itself for customers. Two women were giggling and prettying themselves in a cloakroom by the door, while flowers had been arranged in the main room and refreshments were being laid out.

The Doctor marched right past them to the stairs. At once the madame appeared, looking most uncomfortable, and Bell informed her that he required a few minutes to look again at the room where the blood had been found. She explained anxiously that the place would be receiving guests within the hour, but we were permitted to climb the stairs. There was no sign of anyone, though I heard women's voices, and soon we were back at the end of the top corridor, staring through the open doorway.

At first I thought we were in the wrong room. For the place was utterly transformed. The entire area had been scrubbed from top to bottom, and now that the window was clean, sun shone directly into it, making it look almost cheerful. Of course some staining remained, but that was all, and I could see now how carefully our man had chosen this space, for it was too small to be used as a bedroom and contained no furniture.

Bell stood there staring, his face showing far more open disgust now than it ever had at the blood itself. 'The idiots could not even retain the evidence,' he muttered, moving over to the window and studying it, then turning back to look again at the room. There was no sign of the clothes or the little pile of coins I had seen. Presumably the police had taken them away the day before.

Bell examined every cranny but found little to satisfy him, for there was nothing to find, yet still he lingered, paying attention to the room's corners, to the ledge where the coins were placed, to the window-latch and the floor. I was becoming anxious for I had arranged to meet Miss Scott at six, yet I knew how much he hated to be interrupted in such deliberations. Twice, surreptitiously, while his back was turned, I consulted my pocket watch.

Bell was now at the far corner, bent down at a place where for some reason the stains were more profuse. 'It is singular, Doyle. And I have to say it disturbs me greatly.' He seemed to sink into a trance. But then he continued without changing his tone in any way. 'I think you have about nineteen minutes.'

'What?' I said.

He did not look up. 'Judging by the intervals at which you have consulted your watch, you are meeting someone at six o'clock. I will see you in the morning.'

THE RIOT AND THE PUZZLE

That night Miss Scott's dissection was as expert as before, if less eventful. I had already established that Latimer's labman was away on Tuesdays, and on this occasion the night-clerk turned out to be an ancient short-sighted man who would probably have given almost anyone the benefit of the doubt even at close quarters. Indeed it went so smoothly that Miss Scott began to plan. Perhaps she might even be able enter the place alone on this night of the week and smuggle some colleagues in too.

Afterwards we walked to her lodgings as slowly as we could, taking a roundabout route. During the walk our conversation turned away from science and took on a dreamy, languorous quality. We spoke of favourite poems and favourite books. To my delight she had read a little Poe and we talked excitedly of his stories. Both of us, it seemed, longed to hear the strange music in his work like Roderick Usher's wild and improvised airs on his guitar. I told her how it reminded me of Samuel's violin and went on to describe his death.

As we reluctantly neared her lodgings, I was lamenting how the beggar's death had been ignored because he was poor. Until now the conversation had been a little rhapsodic but here it took another turn. Miss Scott wholeheartedly agreed, telling me her own determination to practice medicine had arisen from observing the conditions in her father's hospital. But then with her lodgings in sight, she turned the tables. 'Now I have told you why I entered medicine, Mr Doyle, but still I know little of you. What is your mission?'

I had not expected this and was left feeling like a fool, for the honest fact was that medicine had not even been my own idea. It had been decided by my mother, at Waller's urging, while I was still away from home. I could hardly tell her this and I was certainly not going to mention Waller's name, but still I was not going to lie. 'I do not appear to have a mission, I am afraid,' I said.

She looked at me intently but then she laughed. 'Well, does it matter? Everyone finds a path.' She became more serious. 'If not medicine, then something else. We all build our castles in the air.'

'Yet, only you could make them sound like an ambition.' These were, I suppose, the first truly personal remarks we had exchanged. 'I never met anyone like you.'

She stared at me. There was obvious emotion in her eyes. She started to speak, and then a window was flung open and a miserable voice with a clear tone of spite called her name. Of course it was her tyrannical landlady.

'There is my demon,' she said. 'I must go.' She

turned and then looked back. 'I still do not even know where you live but you said with your parents.'

I told her it was true, hoping she would not guess that my family's precarious finances made any other arrangement impossible. I added that I would like to walk with her again, perhaps at the weekend and she agreed. If only it had been left there. But she stopped a moment. 'If I could ask you a favour?'

'Anything.'

'When next we walk out, I should like very much to meet your parents. I would take it as an honour, Mr Doyle.'

She turned away then and disappeared. Which was fortunate for I had been smiling hopefully and she had no time to observe how my expression changed to confusion and misery.

My anguish continued as I walked home. How could I tell her about my father? What excuse could I provide? That he was ill? Unfortunately, since she was a medical student, that was out of the question for she would at once ask about his condition. Moreover, if she came to our home it was certainly possible he would scream or cry out from upstairs. Nor could I bear for one instant the notion of her meeting Waller. That was not to be contemplated, for there was no knowing what he might do. If my mother was absent from the room, I could even imagine him laying bare my father's abject condition just to humiliate me.

As if to echo all my worst fears, that night I was awoken out of a fitful sleep by the sound of screaming from below. It was followed by the noise of breaking glass. I dressed rapidly and reached the stairs.

Below me all was chaos. My father was there, fully dressed and in the throes of some kind of violent fit, having smashed plates and a mirror on the wall. My mother and Waller were controlling him with great difficulty and of course Innes and his three sisters had been woken. Ida, who was then three, was crying, the others stared in horror.

I moved at once to help, calming the children and escorting them back to bed. Behind me my father's cries were fading for Waller had forced him to take a draft.

At last he was back in his room and, after doing what we could to clear up the destruction, we repaired miserably to our beds. As might be expected, the episode served as a reinforcement of all my worst fears. Elsbeth Scott was, I acknowledged as I lay there, more important to me than anyone I had ever met, but the risk of seeing her tainted by this horrible house was simply not to be endured. Anything was preferable to that – yes, even not meeting her at all.

It was a cowardly solution, but I am ashamed to say that for a few weeks I stuck to it. I buried myself in my books and my studies, I helped at home, for my father's condition was now so bad that all our energies were needed to hold the house together. I attended few lectures but in any case, when the women were present, they were usually in a large group on the other side of the hall and our paths never crossed. For his part, Bell was engrossed in thought and made poor company. In fact, I suspect he was out of humour.

And then something unexpected happened. It was on the morning I had decided to attend one of Anderson Ritchie's physiology lectures. This course was important for my studies, but it was also true that, by now, I was desperate to see Miss Scott again even if I still had no idea what I would tell her about my home, and could offer little explanation of my withdrawal. I knew that Ritchie admitted women and moreover his hall was small, so there was every chance I would be able to meet her.

The cold weather of some weeks earlier was now a distant memory and we were enjoying an uncommonly mild spring. I noticed a few of the women smiling in the sunshine as they walked across the square to the lecture hall, and I felt suddenly full of hope. Perhaps I would just tell Miss Scott that my parents were away for a few weeks and postpone the evil hour. I did not care for I wanted only to see her, and it was then that I heard the commotion ahead.

There was shouting and someone slammed a door. I noticed a sudden look of alarm on people's faces and I ran forward into the corridor which led to the hall. At the end of it students were milling about a large vaulted area. Now I could see Crawford, his face flushed, his mouth contorted with rage. Beside him were his cohorts, all of them blocking the way to Ritchie's lecture.

The women faced them, their backs rigid, the atmosphere appeared very tense. I could not see Miss Scott and I moved to get closer.

'Someone was in Latimer's laboratory last night,' Crawford was shouting. 'They were not caught, but dissecting work was done and we believe these women are helping themselves to our materials against all the university regulations.'

His words dismayed me, of course, though I marvelled at the man's talent for spying.

Sophia, the most articulate and active of the women, was prepared to challenge him, but kept her distance. 'By all means try and find who entered Latimer's room, but it is nothing to do with this lecture. I would remind you we are permitted to enter the class.'

Crawford sneered at this, frenzied with excitement. 'She does not even deny it,' he yelled to his gang. 'It is written in the Bible what they are.' And he reached into his pocket. For a moment I thought he was about to produce a weapon, but he brought out a fistful of coins and flung them headlong at the women.

One of the coins nearly caught Sophia in the face, but she dodged and the others clattered on the stone. As I stared at them, I was reminded of the pile of coins we had seen in the brothel and something rushed into my mind. But before I could quite fix on it I was delighted to see Neill step forward. 'Whatever your complaint, Crawford, you must let them through,' he shouted and I am glad to say voices were raised in agreement.

All Crawford's attention was still on the women. He was enjoying their terror and his friends were urging him on, roaring and cheering at every remark he made. 'They are such delicate lambs, are they not?' he leered. 'But lambs have blood to shed and who can say what harm may come to them!'

I was close enough to see his face clearly now, and it seemed possessed. His eyes blazed, and there was a fleck of spittle on his lower lip. Its sheer ugliness was too much for me. 'Let them through,' I shouted, and I lunged forward, trying to push him away. 'Are you mad?'

Unfortunately I could not quite reach him among that heaving crowd, but he heard me and laughed. 'Are not all the best doctors mad, Doyle? It is why these women will never qualify, except possibly as wet nurses.'

No doubt this gross insult would have provoked more roars of pleasure from his people except at that moment a woman moved forward from the others, somehow forcing the crowd to part till she was beside him. And, with unexpected speed, the woman brought her knee into his groin. Crawford's face, which had been triumphant, suddenly contorted with pain and he doubled up. But I was not looking at him, I was looking at the figure of his attacker. It was Miss Scott.

Of course Crawford recovered quickly and launched himself after her. He was strong, and no one person could possibly have restrained him in that frenzy. But he was so obviously out of control that even his friends held him back. I clung on to him too.

'I will kill her.' He was screaming. 'You hear me.'

I felt a stern hand on my shoulder and turned to find that several strapping porters had appeared. Behind them was Dr Gillespie who had immediate responsibility for discipline within the university precinct.

The presence of the porters rapidly cooled the passions of the throng, though Crawford was still having to be restrained by his friends.

'This is disgraceful,' Gillespie was shouting to all of

us. 'We cannot possibly tolerate such a bedlam. The lecture is of course cancelled. And the women must stand down for two months.'

There were cries of anger at this injustice, not merely from the women. I doubt it would have had the slightest effect, but Crawford's roar of triumph at this development was so uncontrolled, his frenzy so palpable, that even Gillespie could not ignore him. He turned. 'And you, sir, for three.'

Gillespie moved away, thinking his work done, but I thanked heaven the porters still held Crawford, for now all his attention turned back to Elsbeth, who had moved into the midst of the women. 'This is your doing, Miss Scott,' Crawford screamed at her. 'You will pay for it. As a lamb to the slaughter, and you will not escape me.' For a moment it looked like he might break free, and others, including myself, moved to block him.

At last he subsided, and when I turned round I knew why. The women had gone, and I had lost my chance of talking to her, perhaps for as long as two months. Of course I could try my luck at her lodgings but I knew perfectly well the landlady would never allow a gentleman to call. My only course would be to write a letter and see if she would answer. After all that had happened, including my weeks of silence, it seemed highly doubtful.

With a bitter heart I turned to walk to Bell's room for there was something I wanted urgently to discuss with him. I could find no sign of Bell, but I was told he was in the building, and I wandered around disconsolately for a while until I overheard his voice outside Gillespie's room.

'I incline to think ...' Gillespie's tones were pompous, sonorous.

'Then do so,' came back Bell's voice, obviously angry. 'Of course the safety of these women is our responsibility! And we must accept it!'

With these words he strode out of there so fast that he almost knocked me over. I moved quickly to get out of his way and walked rapidly alongside him. 'Dr Bell, I wanted to discuss a matter with you.'

'If it is about this business with the women, I have already stated my position—'

I interrupted. 'I am glad, and it concerns them in a way.' I struggled to marshal my thoughts for I was about to present the doctor with my own deduction, and I knew it would be subject to ruthless scrutiny. He indicated that I should proceed.

'You recall,' I said, 'that pile of coins in the room where we found the blood?'

He nodded.

'I thought at the time it reminded me of something. Now I know why. It is because there was something very similar beside the beggar who was killed.' I had told the Doctor about Samuel's death and he had lamented that such forensic negligence was nothing unusual.

'Presumably his earnings,' he answered. We were getting close to his rooms.

'Yes, that is what I thought,' I replied eagerly. 'But I felt there was something odd and now I see what it is. Samuel never left his earnings on the street, they were always in his violin case.'

'Perhaps it was overturned,' he said, still without any great interest as we entered between the high

shelves. There was dank water in his tank, no doubt
awaiting some specimen.

'Yes,' I cried. 'That is what I had thought. But now
I see the oddness of it. If it overturned, the coins
would scatter. Yet they were not scattered at all, they
were in a tiny heap exactly as they were in the room.
Samuel would never have bothered to take the
trouble to set them in that way. No beggar would.'

Suddenly the Doctor looked much more engaged.
He sat down at his desk. 'Intriguing. You think there
is a link?'

'I am sure of it,' I went on quickly. 'And not only
that, I have a suspect. There is a fanatical student
called Crawford who persecutes the women.'

The Doctor nodded. 'Yes, I am aware of the man,
he has just been suspended.' He was tapping his right
hand on the polished wood of his desk.

'I believe,' I was keeping my eyes fixed on his for I
desperately wanted to convince him, 'he is responsible for the killing of the sheep. He herded some
sheep into a lecture hall the other day. He constantly
refers to the blood of the lamb. Today I have seen
him throwing coins at the women. The blood, the
coins, maybe these are mad signs he leaves to mark
his crimes.' The Doctor sat there considering my
remarks and foolishly I rushed on. 'Crawford is
obsessed with the women. I fear he may be a serious
danger. They must be protected.'

Of course I had moved from the analytical to the
merely emotional and the Doctor saw it at once.
'From the hooligans certainly, I agree,' he answered
kindly. 'That is what I have just been telling
Gillespie. But in your natural anxiety, Doyle, I very

much fear you are guilty of making connections where none exist. A dead violinist, a room of blood, coins thrown at women, a pile of coins. Some of the facts are suggestive. Your observation about the beggar's money is striking . . .' He paused, thoughtfully, and I felt a glimmer of hope. 'But there is no genuine thread. I am sorry. Until you have that, you have nothing.'

The Problem of Lady Carlisle

I returned home in a state of dejection, with some vague idea of writing out a reasoned argument for my suspicions, but my mother reminded me of an engagement I had forgotten. That afternoon Neill and I were due to play rugby in a friendly game against a Glasgow team so, within an hour, I was on the playing field.

I say 'friendly', but in fact it was one of the least friendly games I ever endured. Our opponents were a huge side, typified by an eighteen-stone forward called Watt who succeeded quite early on in pushing a scrummage over the Edinburgh goal line and grounding the ball, knocking one of our players out cold in the process. A lengthy debate ensued, but the referee had missed Watt's many fouls including his savage treatment of the player who was carried off. So the try was finally allowed and Watt himself converted it to a goal with a gracious kick, and an equally ungracious leer at our side, which naturally left us in a fury, especially when we thought of the man who was injured.

After this, the game degenerated into a heated scrap which was neither enjoyable nor decorous, and our only consolation was that Watt was so ruthlessly marked by our side he never got back into the match and, by the end, was shouting abuse at anyone and everyone like a demented schoolboy.

It was a rather miserable end to a dismal day, and later Neill, Stark and I drowned our sorrows in Rutherford's bar, joined on this occasion by another friend called Cullingworth who had just returned from a time away. For once we did not have to rely on Neill's generosity, as most of the players bought rounds of drinks, and after a time my friends started making conversation with an attractive servant-girl, with lustrous curls and a mischievous expression, whose companion was otherwise occupied.

The girl, who told us her name was Amelia, had a pretty smile and when she laughed her teeth shone like little pearls. But I thought only of Elsbeth laughing, and said little.

Eventually they all chided me for my silence, and I was forced to join in. Amelia seemed most impressed that we were medical students, and that Neill already had a qualification from Montreal. Soon she was describing various conditions and headaches, that struck us all as normal enough, so to shut her up Neill produced a pill from his pocket, telling her it would help her nerves.

Later we tumbled out on to the street, all rather the worse for drink, with Neill complaining bitterly that he had been hoping to see the girl home or he would never have squandered some patent medicine on her. 'Yes,' said Cullingworth, the big-boned son of a borders doctor, 'and now for two months there will be no women at the university. We are cast out of Eden.'

After that we trudged along in search of another bar as the conversation became bawdy. 'Talking of Eden,' said Stark, 'is it not curious that Adam and Eve's knowledge of their own nakedness should be a sin? What is wrong with knowing you are naked?'

'Ah,' said Neill, 'but you miss the point. After they had eaten the apple they wore fig leaves, primitive clothes, because of shame. It is the wearing of clothes themselves which betrays our freedom, the freedom to do what we like with our bodies.'

Sometimes I tired of Neill's wild notions and now I pointed out that clothes had a perfectly valuable function. Not least in a city with the keenest wind in the northern hemisphere.

But Neill lapsed back into rhapsodic bliss over the prettiness of the servant-girl in the bar. 'You know she was the handsomest girl in the place. I would have paid a fortune for her.'

Cullingworth was intrigued by the notion. 'Is it true,' he said, 'that the first thing your cavalry do after they claim a town is send for women?'

'Certainly,' Neill replied as his handsome features broke into an even broader grin. 'Did you never hear of that rogue General Hooker? He would buy women's services by the gross.'

I know the drink was making us loose-tongued, but I had been taught to honour military men, indeed I was brought up with many heroic stories of my great-uncle who led the Scottish Brigade at Waterloo. Not surprisingly therefore, I found this

idea somewhat repellent. 'Your country sounds bar-
baric,' I said.

Neill of course took this as a compliment.
'Gloriously so!' he shouted, clapping me on the back
as his voice echoed along the street.

Stark and Cullingworth were starting to laugh and
I concluded this was surely the silliest discussion I
had ever joined. Soon we were all laughing when
quite suddenly I froze.

For there, marching straight towards me in the
flickering flame of the gas lamp, was the Doctor.
Bell's head was upright, his topcoat buttoned to the
neck, and he gripped his silver-topped cane so tightly
you might have thought it was trying to escape.

At first I could not believe it, but then I recalled
that he made a habit of walking the streets, indeed
the Doctor prided himself on long strolls that took
him into every corner of the city. I had no wish to
meet him, but it was too late. He had stopped and he
was staring straight at me. My companions had seen
him too and they were equally amazed.

'Gentlemen,' he said as he came up beside us.

'Dr Bell!' Stark was literally open-mouthed. 'What
brings you here, sir?'

'Oh, I make it my business to go everywhere.' He
surveyed us without expression. Then he pointed his
cane at me. 'Doyle, you will pardon me if I interrupt
your studies, but I have a patient to visit. You can
accompany me.' And he strode on.

The others were of course consumed with amusement at this turn of events, but there was no choice.
I buttoned up my jacket, ran a hand over my hair and
followed after him.

Already I was feeling a good deal more sober, but he was walking so fast it was hard to keep up. Bell had evidently been on one of his strolls through the city, and now wished to find a cab to take us to his consultation. There was none to be seen for we were not on the main thoroughfare, and he darted forward into a small lane that would take us there as I ran to catch him.

The lane was small with dark cobbles and there was not a soul in it. I was almost beside him when I saw the lantern by the horse-trough and suddenly felt a sickening sense of recognition. I turned, and there was the sign: Jack's Lane.

I cried out for him to come back. But he was already almost halfway along. Finally I caught up with him. 'We must go back!'

He did not stop. 'Why?' he said. But it was too late. Before us a smiling figure had stepped out with a pistol, which he brought up level with the Doctor's chest.

'Hello, gentlemen,' said the man, and I recognised all too well that grey skin and thin smile.

Bell, who had been forced to stop, stared at the figure in front of him.

'Your money, please, or I'll kill you,' said the man, his words all the more threatening for being said with so little emphasis.

Bell just stood there. And his words when they came were equally unemphatic. 'Then do so.' And without hesitation he started to walk on.

The man was a little taken aback, but he raised his gun and his finger tightened on the trigger.

I was terrified. 'You must do as he says, Doctor!' I shouted.

Bell was level with the man now. And to my relief he stopped. 'My money, you say?' He spoke carelessly.

'Now!' said the man with more irritation than before.

'Very well,' the Doctor said, and I thanked God he had seen sense as he put his hand in his pocket. But all he drew out was a handful of pennies.

The man was angry now. 'You've more than that.'

But Bell raised his voice too. 'How could you possibly know? Come, take it. This money is as good as any. See what's here!'

He held his hand up high. I could see that the Doctor's sheer foolhardiness was making the man uneasy. But again his finger was tightening.

I started forward in terror. Bell was holding up the coins now like a madman. 'My money's as good as the next man's, can't you see?'

And he flung the coins hard at the man's eyes. There was a flash and a report as the gun went off, but it was no longer pointed anywhere near the Doctor. Then Bell was on to the man hard, smashing his stick into his legs and sending him flying.

I stood there in open-mouthed amazement, for until then I had had no idea of the wire-like strength of the Doctor when he was seriously enraged, his passions inflamed. At times like this he could look almost crazed.

'I will walk every street in this borough, you understand?' Bell was shouting as he bent over his opponent, administering a series of expert punches. There was only a groan from below. The Doctor picked up the gun and walked on, dusting himself down.

I ran to catch him and soon we were at the end of that horrible lane and had found a cab. But I will admit that I eyed my companion with a new respect as it sped through the streets.

Eventually we entered a smart quarter of the new town and turned into a row of wealthy houses.

'Who is our patient?' I said, for I felt I was entitled to know.

'You will see,' replied Bell. 'I would ask for the utmost discretion.'

The town house into which we were admitted was at that time the richest I had ever entered. There was a marble statuette on one side of the door, which gleamed in the soft light of the lamps, and a palatial central staircase. A smell of good food assailed me as we were ushered into the hall by an elegant butler who evidently knew Bell, but who looked at me with a slight downward curl of his lips.

And then a figure came out in evening dress, his hair as elegant and his smile as wide as when he was telling jokes to his acolytes at the university. Somewhat to my amazement it was our patron, Sir Henry Carlisle.

Carlisle shook hands with the Doctor, ignoring me. 'Thank you so much for coming, Bell, I am sure it is nothing.' And now he dropped his voice a little, glancing at me as I hung back. 'But I wanted her to see someone in the strictest confidence . . .'

'Of course,' said Bell, as unruffled by this challenge as he had been by the man in the lane, and I wondered what Carlisle would think if he knew there was an unloaded pistol in the Doctor's pocket. 'This is my trusted clerk and pupil, Arthur Doyle.

He has torn himself away from his studies to assist me.'

Now at last Carlisle turned properly to look at me. There was just the smallest hint of recognition. I suppose he did recall my encounter with his wife and her sister, but he did not refer to it. He merely shook my hand without the courtesy of a smile, and then led us up that beautiful staircase.

We came to a bedroom at the top which was as ornate as any I had seen, indeed all I could take in at first in the soft light of its lamps were lush green hangings and a tapestry. And then I saw the bed, which was large, though not a four-poster, and in it lay the small, somewhat fragile figure of Lady Sarah Carlisle. She obviously knew Bell but gave a little start of surprised recognition when she observed me. Carlisle had been introducing me as the Doctor's clerk and looked a little taken aback when she smiled at me so warmly. Then of course he was obliged to withdraw.

Bell greeted Lady Sarah kindly and proceeded to his task while I assisted by handing him whatever he required from his bag. He was, I could see, making an extremely thorough examination, but there was not the slightest hint of the imperiousness I knew from the lecture room, indeed he talked to her brightly while he worked. I did not observe all he did, but I saw enough to concern me and, as I closed his bag, I was anxious to hear how he would proceed.

'It is an infection, I am afraid, Lady Sarah,' he said, hardly altering his cheerful tone. 'Though I hope we can be of some use to you in containing it. A circulatory imbalance of the blood, causing inflammation.

I will of course be advising your husband as to the best way forward.'

He was doing his best to offer reassurance, but I have to admit this irritated me, given what I suspected, nor was he entirely successful.

'Please, I beg you, do not alarm him,' she said, and I was sure a shadow of fear crossed her face.

'I promise,' he replied. 'And we will come back again very soon.'

She thanked him, and we were taking our leave when to my surprise she called me back. Bell had already observed that we were acquainted and withdrew tactfully to wait outside.

I moved to the bed. 'My sister speaks very highly of you, though I understand she has not seen you for a time, is that right?'

I was hardly prepared for this. 'No, I have been . . . studying,' I said, aware that it probably sounded unconvincing. 'But I would like very much to see her. Where is she?'

I had been evasive, now I was perhaps revealing too much, but her face softened for I am sure she could read me quite well. 'I can tell you where to find her,' she replied. 'She has not been herself entirely. I know I have worried her, though I must tell you I have concealed some of the symptoms from her. I do not want her concerned.'

She proceeded to tell me where her sister was studying during the day, and soon after that I left her. It was obvious the sisters were close, and a part of me was overjoyed by the luck that had given me this chance to find Miss Scott, but I was also troubled by something else. Bell was waiting patiently on the stairs and said nothing as we descended to the hall where the butler ushered us in to see Carlisle.

He was sitting in a comfortable chair, reading the paper in his ample drawing room, and his manner now was very gracious. 'Ah, doctors,' he said, and then winked at me, 'for even the humblest student deserves the title. You must take some refreshment.' He wandered over to a well-stocked side table. 'It is nothing serious, I trust. I am very hopeful of an heir . . .'

Bell looked a good deal more grave than he had upstairs. 'Oh, I am afraid there can be no possibility of children at present.'

Carlisle had been taking up a decanter of sherry, and now he turned, his expression quite changed as the Doctor continued. 'She has a circulatory imbalance that has been exacerbated by a constitutional infection.' It is lucky Carlisle was not looking at me for he would have seen me react to these words with impatience. But his own reaction was odd, for he showed nothing but anger.

'I have warned her time and again. She was parading around in the cold after church on Sunday . . .' And he strode back to join us, quite forgetting the refreshments in his irritation.

'Tell me,' said Dr Bell softly, 'you have . . . no symptoms yourself?'

Carlisle glared at him. 'Symptoms? Of course not. There is nothing at all wrong with *me*, Doctor. But this is not good news.'

'Well,' said the Doctor, keeping his eyes fixed on him. 'You must be very understanding. It is not a pleasant condition.'

He nodded, I felt somewhat unconvincingly. 'For me,' he said, 'it is a great disappointment.'

I am afraid this was too much for me. Here was Carlisle huffing and puffing about his own disappointment in not getting the heir he required without giving the slightest thought to the pale woman lying upstairs on the bed. All the loathing I had always felt for the man returned to me. 'If she hoped to become a mother,' I said quietly, 'then I imagine her disappointment will be even greater.'

He looked round at me. 'That is hardly your concern, Mr Doyle. You will be back, I take it, Dr Bell?' I was not, it would seem, included in the invitation.

Bell told him he would be calling within the next few days, and shortly afterwards we were shown out. Our cab had been told to wait but there was no sign of it and we walked in silence to the end of the street. It was dark and a little wind had got up but I would not look at the Doctor. In fact I was so angered by all I had seen and heard in that house that I almost walked off in the other direction.

Eventually the sound of our footsteps was interrupted by his voice. 'You have views on the case, I apprehend,' he said drily, for he could see quite well how exercised I was.

And now all my feelings erupted. 'I am sorry, Doctor,' I said with some vehemence. 'A circulatory imbalance that has been exacerbated by a constitutional infection! That is palpable nonsense. You have talked to me about the necessity of precise observation and analysis, of your method. And now here is the result! Not diagnosis, but a cover and a fiction.'

I suppose I expected Bell to rise to my own anger, but he did not. Indeed he seemed almost amused by my outpouring. 'Of course it is,' he replied tersely. 'She has syphilis.'

'And he gave it to her,' I rejoined.

'Probably—'

He was about to go on but I interrupted. 'Certainly. He is a customer of Madame Rose's, I saw him enter the place. I cannot be a party to this. You are colluding with her husband because he is your patron. It is the greatest hypocrisy.'

We were into the next street now under a flickering gas lamp. It was the strongest language I had ever spoken to the Doctor and at last it had its effect. He stopped and turned and, as always with Bell when he was angry, he fixed his gaze on me, his features half in shadow.

'He is not my patron, laddie, and I wouldn't care a ha'penny if he were. You have always doubted my working method, but at least obey one of its more simple rules.' He put his face close to mine, and his voice became a sonorous whisper as it so often did when he was at his most emotional. 'Look at all the facts before drawing conclusions. Yes, "circulatory imbalance" is a crude fiction. But I am hoping her condition improves and it gives me time. You can be sure he will refuse examination. And there is no guarantee he even has symptoms: it is probably dormant in him.'

The idea repelled me. 'But it is still our job to speak out.'

'Why?' he asked.

'Because,' I answered fiercely, 'it is just.'

'Just!' his eyes flashed. A carriage came so close I was frightened he would be clipped by the horse's hooves, but he did not move an inch. 'I will tell you what will happen if we do. Sir Henry will denounce his wife, make public allegations of a vile kind. There are plenty of doctors who would help him commit her to a private asylum. What would they call it? "Moral insanity" or some tripe like that! She would probably be incarcerated for the rest of her life. Is that *just*?'

'No,' I said, appalled and somewhat taken aback but still incensed. 'It is monstrous.'

His tone softened a little. 'Yes, like so much that goes on in our fair city! And we doctors can be as bad as the rest. But some of us, if we have any compassion, try to protect our patients rather than see them crucified. That is our choice, Doyle. And unless you provide irrefutable proof of your suspicion, then I tell you that poor woman's only hope is that you keep it quiet. Surely you must see, judging by what you have told me, that your own family followed exactly this principle. Now I will bid you goodnight.'

The Sign in the Bedroom

Next day I knew what I had to do and felt no hesitation. There were some household chores to complete but no lectures to attend, so by eleven o'clock I was making my way to a small medical library that then lay behind Surgeon's Square.

The place was deserted for it was not much used, and I saw her almost as soon as I entered. She was seated at a small table, head bent down over a textbook, frowning. And I recall the fright her appearance gave me, for she looked pale and troubled.

I walked forward at once and she looked up. If I had expected her to smile I was disappointed, but her face took on a little animation.

'Mr Doyle?' she said. 'You are a stranger.'

'It is the last thing I want to be, I can assure you.' I smiled now, for I wanted to reassure her.

'My sister tells me you were studying.'

So she had visited this morning, but I did not think it wise to talk about her sister.

'Yes, but I wish I had come sooner, and therefore

I must ask your forgiveness. You are making progress?'

She closed the book with a gesture of irritation. 'No, I am not.' And when she looked back up at me her eyes, which were today more green than brown, had softened and I knew she was speaking from the heart. 'I shall not disguise, Mr Doyle, that I had hoped to see you. To tell the truth I have been . . . frightened.'

Now I felt even more foolish and cowardly for staying away. A whole range of awful possibilities presented themselves. 'Is it Crawford?' I said.

Her brow furrowed and she bit her lip a little as she collected herself. 'Sometimes I think I am followed. I do not know if it is him. I saw him once in the street, but I managed to avoid him. Perhaps I am just upset because my sister is unwell. But there is something more . . . I think, Mr Doyle, someone has secretly entered my lodgings, though I have not seen them.'

'So how do you know?'

'It is so stupid. A small thing. I would like to show you, and yet I cannot. For it is in my bedroom. Some coins were placed there.'

Naturally her words shocked me and I told her that, whatever the risk, she must show me exactly what she had found at once. Although Miss Scott did not understand, she saw my determination and agreed.

This was far harder than it sounded. Her landlady would never, under any circumstances, countenance a male friend's presence in the house for any reason whatsoever. However, as I soon established, the woman's rigidity of mind had one advantage: she was obsessed with routine and took a walk each day after lunch at exactly the same hour between three o'clock and three-thirty. Even Miss Scott was not supposed to enter during this time, but she had made an ally of the kitchen maid. This woman would let her in and, after the maid had disappeared back to her duties, I could in turn be admitted.

At the appointed hour we waited around the corner from the house, lurking there like two felons, pretending to be looking in the window of a small grocery shop. It was not an easy task, for the window contained almost nothing of interest at all, and the shopkeeper kept beckoning for us to enter. But three o'clock came, and five minutes went by, and still the landlady did not appear. Fortunately a customer had entered the shop, so its owner's attention was distracted, but the landlady's non-appearance was so unprecedented that, after a few more minutes, Miss Scott began to think something was wrong and we must abandon our plans. At last, after we had been there almost a quarter of an hour, she alerted me and I turned to see that the door of her lodgings had opened and Miss Maitland stood there. She could not see me but, for the first time, I could observe her properly. She wore a long black outdoors dress and her face was quite as mean and tight-lipped as I had expected. Then she turned to the left, as Miss Scott had said she would, and soon she was out of sight.

Without hesitation, for we had already lost valuable time, Miss Scott walked ahead of me to the house and knocked on the front door while I lingered by one of the tiny adjacent front gardens, out of sight. At last it opened, and though I could not see the maid, her voice was quite audible and excited.

'Oh, miss,' she exclaimed, 'you must be careful for she is in a fair temper. It is lucky she did not see you. And it is not my fault, miss, I swear it is not.'

It seemed there had been some accident while the maid had been scraping her employer's boots, and I heard Miss Scott's comforting words as the front door closed. There was a pause, rather longer than I would have liked, while no doubt she heard the story and ensured the maid was safely in the kitchen, for we could hardly risk the woman's employment by involving her, and then the door opened.

I moved along the path as discreetly as I could and entered. Miss Scott was already halfway up the darkened staircase so I closed the front door quietly and followed her. The stairs were shadowy and grim with heavy curtains, and I realised I was in one of those typical Edinburgh households which is permanently arranged on the basis that someone is dying or has just died. Even the blinds were half-drawn.

I walked on tiptoe and reached Miss Scott on the first landing, who was glancing nervously downstairs at the sound of a closing door. Then she led me to the end of the corridor and through a doorway.

Her bedroom was shadowy, but even so it had a much more cheerful air than the rest of the place. There were some personal things: a small picture of a man I took to be her father and some books and letters. Elsbeth turned and gave a little smile, for it was evidently strange for her to see me here. I mouthed a 'thank you' for her courage before she indicated the window sill next to the brass bed.

And I took in a breath. For lying there on the window ledge, was a small, intricately-constructed

pile of coins. They were arranged just as they had
been in the room at Madame Rose's and in the street
by Samuel's corpse. I went as close as I could: there
was copper and some silver, all carefully assembled
into a minute pyramid. I was sure now it was the
same.

'And you woke up to see this?' I whispered. 'You
have not touched it?'

She talked very softly, coming close so I could hear
her. 'I was aghast. Naturally I told Mrs Maitland. She
said I had merely piled up my change and forgotten
it, but I know I had not. It was not there when I went
to sleep. The door was closed.'

I was moving to the window when suddenly we
heard from below the one noise in the world both of
us dreaded: the front door closed with a bang.

Elsbeth jumped, and I turned. 'It is what I feared,'
she said. 'She is so exercised by what happened with
her boots, no doubt she has been to the cobbler and
now wishes to report the damage. Oh, Mr Doyle,
what are we to do?'

I reassured her with more confidence than I felt
that I had my evidence and would leave at once,
taking care I was not seen. We arranged a meeting
place and I was out of the door in a second.

There was another landing above and I wondered
whether to hide there, but in the end decided it was
not worth the risk. Just as I was thinking this a voice
called down from above, a strident female voice.
'Lettie,' it shouted in harsh tones.

At once, dreading the voice would bring Miss
Maitland up the stairs, I moved hurriedly down them.
The hall was empty and now I saw there was another

reason why it seemed so dark, namely the profusion of black wooden furniture, including a forbidding grandfather clock and an equally sombre table.

There were voices from a doorway at the back, and I thought I had better seize my chance. I sprang down the last three steps, but then to my horror a door into the hall was flung open.

It was far too late to open the front door, so I moved into a little alcove to one side of it, where some coats and hats were hung, pressing myself against them.

'Is anyone there?' said a fierce voice which I took to be Miss Maitland's. She turned, evidently to the maid. 'I am quite sure I heard someone on the stairs. Do you think we have someone in here?'

The other answered quietly and neutrally.

Then Miss Maitland's voice sounded again and it was closer. 'Well there is one way to see.'

And I heard the footsteps coming directly to where I was hiding. I pressed myself against the coats and looked desperately round, but there was no exit, not even a window, while the coats afforded no concealment whatsoever.

The footsteps were almost there, then they stopped and I heard a voice I recognised.

'Miss Maitland,' said Miss Scott from the stairs, 'I am so sorry, you heard only me. I had to come back for a book I had forgotten. I went to the park hoping to find you, but there was no sign of you, so I came here and you were not here either.'

'I should think I was not,' came back the sharp voice. 'There has been a famous waste of money, Miss Scott, and you know quite well I do not like my guests in the rooms at this time. But get your book if you must.'

However, now another voice interceded, the voice from upstairs, which I now realised belonged to Miss Maitland's elderly sister. 'Lettie, I believe I have heard voices in Miss Scott's room.'

The silence that greeted this remark was quite horrible and it was quickly followed by another sound. Miss Maitland was mounting the stairs. 'I cannot believe this could be so,' she said in a soft tone that was worse than her loud one. 'I am coming directly.'

Soon I could hear her on the upstairs landing and needed no further prompting. The hall was empty and I came out and made for the front door. Getting it open was by no means as easy as I would have liked for there was a big latch, but I did it noiselessly, and I believe I closed it noiselessly too, though there was a slight creak. Once I was outside my only thought was not to be seen from the window. So I put my head down and walked along the path and, once on the street, I turned the other way. Fortunately I heard no cry of outrage from above.

An hour later Miss Scott arrived breathless and smiling at our appointed meeting place by the university to say that, though both Miss Maitland and her sister had suspicions, they had been unable to confirm any of them, so she had incurred little more than the usual bad temper. And now both of us proceeded to the meeting I had hastily arranged with Dr Bell.

The Doctor was, I must say, at his very best in what followed. I had been able to explain to him all the circumstances. I had already told him of the strange pile of coins Miss Scott had shown me, and how closely it matched the pile we had seen in the room at Madame Rose's and the one beside the dead beggar. To another man the matter might have seemed trivial, but the Doctor knew far better than to ignore details and he saw at once that here was an opportunity for him to assess the evidence for himself.

Indeed the speed with which he acted took both Miss Scott and myself by surprise. After a short chat, in which he was enormously courteous to Miss Scott, and offered her a personal apology for the university's abysmal failure to champion the women's cause, he listened to her story quietly. Gradually, as she talked, I could see his expression becoming more and more serious. When she had finished he got up at once and started putting his coat on, telling us we must both accompany him on what might yet become a serious investigation.

Soon, therefore, the three of us were in front of her lodgings as Bell led us up to the door. Miss Scott looked concerned, but also amazed, to have one of the university's most eminent teachers taking an interest in her affairs.

It was only just beginning to get dark as we arrived, but Bell knocked on the door so loudly you would have thought it was midnight. A few moments later it was opened, not by the maid, but by Miss Maitland herself. She looked angry enough already at the noise but when she saw Elsbeth, myself and then Bell (who was unknown to her), her expression of irritation changed to fury.

'I am afraid we accept no visitors under any

circumstances. This young woman should know far better and moreover I have suspicions—'

But she never completed her sentence, for, to her utter astonishment, Bell merely pushed past her into the hall. 'We are not visitors, madame,' he said in the rapid and disinterested manner he reserved for those who obstructed him. 'I am Dr Joseph Bell, and we are on urgent official business which may affect your whole establishment.'

She stepped a pace back, trying to take this in, and Bell appraised her so swiftly I only just caught it. 'As to the other matters that are exercising you,' the Doctor continued, turning to the stairs, 'the fault is with the mud-scraper rather than the servant. And also with your sewing machine which is mounted four inches too high.'

If Miss Maitland had been thrown out by our visit, now she was staggered. She stared down at her feet and then at her sleeve. 'Official business?' she repeated dazedly, for these were exactly the words to strike terror into her respectable soul.

The Doctor was already at the stairs. 'It need not involve you at this stage. We merely have to make a search of Miss Scott's room.'

And he walked up the stairs, with us following. Miss Maitland still stood there, but I suppose my presence revived her angry spirits a little for she succeeded in glaring at me before I climbed out of view.

'Do you know Miss Maitland?' Miss Scott asked Bell in amazement as we reached the landing. 'Or perhaps Mr Doyle told you of the trouble she had with her servant?'

'Neither,' Bell answered cheerfully, looking around him. 'But I could observe the leather of her boot is scored by three parallel cuts, where a servant-girl has recently scraped off mud with too sharp an implement, while her sleeve shows the heavy imprint of a sewing machine that is improperly positioned. I have made a study of women's sleeves; it is perhaps their most revealing feature, just as in men it is the trouser-knee.'

Miss Scott stared at him, clearly impressed, as we arrived at her bedroom door. Bell took stock of Miss Scott's room at once and advanced on the pile of coins which, fortunately, still lay there untouched. He put his face close to them, then took a step back. And said absolutely nothing. From this I knew at once he found them quite as striking as I did.

Finally he turned and gazed brightly at Miss Scott. 'And they were not there when you went to sleep? Was the door locked?'

'Yes,' Miss Scott answered. 'I always lock it.'

'And your window?' said Bell.

She shook her head. 'I often sleep with it open. I did last night.'

Bell was already there and had opened it. He stared out for a long time. The room was on the street side, but there was a gently sloping roof that extended to all the houses beyond. It would have been a matter of ease to climb along it. After a while Bell closed the window.

'You will close and lock your door and window tonight. Meanwhile we will make certain enquiries and return tomorrow. And you will explain to your landlady that you have assisted me on an important matter but I demand the utmost secrecy. If she wants to know more, she must address all enquiries to me at the university.'

Miss Scott smiled at this for of course it relieved her of a burden, and we left the room. At the bottom of the stairs we encountered Miss Maitland, who was standing there waiting for us. She had evidently regained some of her fighting spirit for she stood bolt upright and her expression was cold. When Bell repeated what he had said to Miss Scott, she replied tartly that there were limits to the intrusion that could be endured upon private premises. However, she agreed not to interfere with his business if he would not interfere with hers.

We quit the premises to find it was almost dark outside now. I was longing to hear what Bell made of the coins, but as soon as we reached the street, he turned and stood staring up at Miss Scott's window. Of course I followed his gaze and could just make out the configuration of roofs, but it told me little more than I had seen from the bedroom. Indeed I was a good deal more worried by my companion's expression. All the cheerfulness he had exhibited in the house had vanished and he looked extremely concerned.

'So,' he said, 'the roofs are interconnecting. Anybody could have reached that window.'

'Yet she was unharmed,' I pointed out.

He turned to me, frowning, and now I knew for sure that his confident manner earlier had been intended principally to boost Miss Scott's spirits. 'I draw no comfort whatsoever from that, Doyle. I am only glad she has agreed to keep her door and windows locked tonight.'

Then he turned back to the street, examining the houses around Seaview. The cab in which we had arrived still waited on the other side, its horse fidgeting a little as the night grew colder. The Doctor once more subsided into thought, but at last, as we moved back to the cab, he turned to me again.

'Yes,' he said, 'that little pyramid is identical to what we both observed at Madame Rose's. It is a sign, and I feel sure now you were right. Your beggar was murdered by our mysterious friend.'

He stopped, his gaze fixed on me in the light of the gas lamp opposite Miss Scott's lodgings. 'I have been mistaken in cases before, Doyle, but I have to tell you this is the first time I have been wrong and someone else has been right. That hurts my pride. A petty feeling, no doubt, but I record it and apologise to you. You may consider yourself fully qualified as my assistant.'

Of course I felt a little surge of pride, but it was small compensation. For I could see quite well how worried he was.

The Lair at Holy Well House

It was now obviously necessary for me to explain my own suspicions to the Doctor while he reflected on every aspect of what had occurred. To this end we returned to the university and he led me upstairs to his private crime room. On this occasion the fire was not lit for he had not expected to be here. I built it myself while I rehearsed all my dealings with Crawford and his cronies down to the smallest detail.

I told him of the man's threats against the women, of how he threw coins at them and denounced them in the language of an Old Testament prophet. I told him, too, of the letter Elsbeth had received. By the time the fire was fully blazing the Doctor had heard everything and I could tell that he wanted to think. So I stared into the flames, trying to take what satisfaction I could from his words of praise (the first I think he ever uttered without irony), and racked my brains to provide him with further insight. But none came and I was wondering whether he wanted me to leave him when his voice suddenly interrupted my thoughts.

'The coins, the sheep's eyes, the blood of the lamb. There is a link here, it is like a message. The references are obviously biblical, if we could find the key. And it must be related to the man we seek.' He had his fingers pressed together and his eyes were closed in concentration.

'Yet,' I said, 'so far we know only of one death.'

'We cannot even be sure of that.' He opened his eyes and looked at me. I am not certain but I believe this was the first time I saw something like fear in those piercing eyes. 'There is an element of playing in this that disturbs me as much as anything I have ever heard of, Doyle. You drew comfort from the fact he chose not to harm Miss Scott. In one way you are right. He strides over the rooftops, comes through the window and is inches from her. What does he do? He arranges a pile of coins. Certainly we must thank God he did not touch her when he could have done anything he wanted. But then is that not part of the message? Like the snip of private hair he took from the girl at the ball. He is saying: I can do anything I like, and is clearly enjoying the sensation. If that develops . . .'

Quite suddenly he got to his feet. 'Well, there is a time for rumination and there is a time for action. We will visit Crawford.'

I was delighted by the plan. The Doctor found it easy enough to obtain an address from his enrolment book. But it turned out that the man lived at his father's home, well outside the city. A cab was ordered and, once we had begun our journey, it took more than an hour to wind our way out of Edinburgh and along the shores of the Forth. At last we were trundling down a densely wooded drive, which eventually came out into parkland, and before us we could see the outline of a large and splendid building lit by torches.

Bell studied this with interest as we drew closer, evidently pleased to be active at last. 'A fine palace for our primary suspect, is it not?' he said with a little more cheer than before.

We were now close to the main door and I could see just how vast this house was. The windows were stone mullion and I counted forty-five of them on the front alone, though more were probably covered by the ivy that grew up the stone. The front entrance, where we alighted from the cab, was huge with an old cast-iron bell to one side. Our driver stared at the place with interest, but seemed perfectly happy to wait, and we walked up a short flight of steps to the door.

Rather to our surprise it was ajar. But though there was light inside we saw no sign of anyone. I tolled the bell twice, and its great low chime echoed loudly all around that grey stone front, but nobody appeared.

Bell looked impatient. 'You would think they are not well staffed. Surely someone would have heard the bell or seen our carriage?'

And so at last he pushed the door open and we entered.

There are many stately homes on the outskirts of Edinburgh but I have often reflected since that Holy Well House, where the Crawford family lived, was one of the strangest. There were few modern comforts here; indeed as we stood in the huge hallway all I could see was the stonework itself and our long shadows, cast by the light of the torches that were placed at head-height along the walls.

Bell advanced halfway down that forbidding hall and shouted another 'hello', but his voice merely echoed around us. We were standing there, wondering what to do, when we heard something. I believe it was Bell who caught it first, for he turned to the right and advanced towards the point where the hall ended in a doorway leading to a corridor. I followed him, and here the noise was quite distinct, a soft chanting.

After a while we could make out the words. 'Let burning coals fall upon them: let them be cast into the fire; into deep pits, that they rise not up again . . .'

It was one of the more gloomy and violent psalms and it was being intoned by many voices with some solemnity. Bell and I walked along the corridor towards a door and all the time it grew louder. We reached the end and there seemed no point in knocking, so Bell pushed the door open and we walked in.

Before us was a baronial hall, with a long table stretching away towards a huge bow window. Standing at this table were about forty people holding open Bibles and chanting the verses. They were all men or women of a good age, and I could see at once they were positioned in order of rank. Nearest to us were some quite elderly women whom I took to be members of the Crawford family (though there was no sign of the man we sought), then came what appeared to be the more experienced indoor servants and next, judging by their ruddy complexion, groundsmen and gamekeepers, followed finally by junior domestic staff.

The chant was being led by a tall man in dark Highland dress, standing bolt upright at the head of the table, with his back to us. 'Let not an evil speaker be established in the earth: evil shall hunt the violent man to overthrow him,' he intoned, and his voice was among the loudest. As we stood there, some of the servants turned to stare at us and in due course others saw them staring and turned their heads too, till at last the man signalled them all to stop.

Now he moved round to face us and he made an imposing figure; in his late fifties but still dark and good-looking, with bright attentive eyes and a cruel mouth which was turned down in disapproval.

Bell at once apologised for the intrusion and explained he was seeking Gordon Crawford.

'You have found him,' the man replied, much to our surprise. 'What business do you have to interrupt our nightly prayers?'

The Doctor stared at him. 'You are Gordon Crawford?'

And now a slight change came over the man. He did not look downcast exactly, it was more of a grimace, almost as if he had smelt something unpleasant. 'Ah, I suppose you want my son.'

'He is not here?' asked Bell.

'He may well be,' said the man with a sombre expression. 'He comes and goes, but if you wish to talk to him, I suspect you will be disappointed.'

With this he gave a commanding glance to a small woman halfway down the table who was obviously a housekeeper of some kind. She put down her Bible at once and scurried over to us, indicating we should follow her.

Behind us the chanting resumed as we came out into the corridor. I could see the Doctor had hoped for some explanation of where we were going, but the woman made a point of keeping her head down and saying absolutely nothing as she led us along the corridor and into another which was smaller and less grand. At the end of this, rather to our bemusement, she took up a torch from one of the brackets, opened a back door and we came out into the grounds at the back of the house.

There were woods here, but in front of them I made out a shed or outhouse, where a light was burning, and she led us directly towards it. The door was open but, as soon as we reached her, she pointed inside and then almost fled away back to the house, evidently quite unwilling to go further.

Bell and I stared after her, and then back at the open door. Her manner certainly did not inspire much enthusiasm for what might be beyond it. Again there seemed no point in knocking so the Doctor pushed it open.

In the feeble lamplight we could at first see only the rubbish on the floor, which was considerable. Books, newspapers, the remains of food and drink, discarded candles and matches. A rat scurried among this heap with little regard to our presence.

I stopped beside Bell, whose attention was focused on the bottles at his feet. I could make out they were medicinal in nature and the dregs of some pink fluid had spilled from one on to the floor. Bell stared at it and then at the dingy furniture.

It was only now I became aware of a shape spread-eagled on a filthy armchair at the opposite end of the room. Slowly it seemed to stir, and then I caught a glimpse of Crawford's head lolling back against the shabby brown upholstery. He looked ghastly, his skin blotchy and a little yellow, his mouth half open, his breathing heavy. Bell had seen him too now, but at this point it seemed he was only dimly aware of us.

'Crawford,' I said, and he looked up. At his elbow was another of these bottles, this one half charged with red liquid. As he stared, he picked it up and smelt it.

'Gentlemen,' he said, and there was a slur in his voice. 'You have no business here, it is my place.'

But then he seemed to recognise me. 'Doyle? How dare you come. Get out!'

The Doctor ignored this and stood right in front of him. 'Mr Crawford,' he said. 'You have been following a woman called Elsbeth Scott?'

The name seemed to galvanise him for suddenly he leered at me. 'Oh yes,' he said. 'I was with her all last night.'

This was too much for me, and I moved forward, longing to shake that horrible grin off his face. But Bell put out an arm to stop me and just as well, for, even in this state, the man was still playing with me. 'In my mind,' he went on, evidently amused by my reaction. And then he picked up the bottle and drank. 'The dreams induced by this tincture are remarkable. She is delicious in her abominations.'

'Then you did not leave here last night?' Bell stood over him, fixing his gaze, obviously determined the man's attention should not wander.

Crawford's hand with the bottle swayed, but he seemed to follow Bell's question. 'Nobody can be absolutely sure, least of all myself. But I am convinced of one thing. You can prove nothing that will incriminate me. And my revenge is sweet-tasting.'

He drank some more of the tincture which was obviously having a drastic effect on his mind. Meanwhile Bell had moved over to the window sill and was occupied in some task, though I could not see what it was. Until he stepped aside to reveal a little pyramid of coins, which glittered in the lamplight. It was almost as neat as the others I had seen. Of course he was scrutinising Crawford's face.

The man looked at it and his lips curled in amusement. 'What have you there, sir?' he said. 'An idol of silver and gold?'

'Have you seen it before?' demanded Bell softly.

But Crawford simply grinned his idiot grin and took some more of his foul drink.

'It is laudanum, Doyle,' said the Doctor as we retraced our steps to the house. 'And laudanum is the worst kind of alibi for our purposes. I do not think he is shamming now, but who can say what he was like last night? His own father admits they keep no track of him.'

We had re-entered the house and the prayers were evidently over for the servants were dispersing. It seemed we were destined to leave as anonymously as we had arrived but, as we approached the front door, a voice rang out from behind. 'So you saw him, gentlemen? What does it say about a man that he can sink so low?' Crawford the senior's tone was sonorous, yet the pleasure he seemed to take in denouncing his own son was deeply unpleasant.

'Beyond the fact his father is a fanatical, self-righteous bully I have absolutely no idea,' said Bell casually without interrupting his path to the exit.

The man looked thunderstruck. 'You will not be welcome here again,' he shouted after us.

'Given your notion of a welcome, I count that as our good fortune,' Bell said with a smile. 'Goodnight, sir.' And we swept from the house as the great door was closed behind us by a servant. 'I have long cherished the notion of a monograph on criminal fathers,' the Doctor confided to me with some enthusiasm. 'That man might well feature prominently if I ever get around to it.' And he climbed with some gusto into our waiting cab.

THE RED CARDBOARD BOX

After that, Bell lapsed into silence as our cab turned back up the drive but, upon reaching the top, it slowed to make way for another grander carriage. Both of us looked at it inquisitively and there was light enough from the driver's torches for us to see the occupant. It was Sir Henry Carlisle.

'Well,' said Bell turning to me, his eyes bright. 'Crawford senior has a visitor, it would seem. I wonder what business the two men could possibly have together. Carlisle does not strike me as the kind of man who attends prayer meetings.' But then he returned to his own reflections and did not say another word until he wished me goodnight.

The following day I had some urgent tasks to perform for my mother, which involved a long trudge through Edinburgh in order to pay some of the household bills. I returned home somewhat wearily in the early afternoon, reflecting on the irony that only criminal matters ever permitted me the luxury of riding in cabs. And to my surprise a message from the Doctor was waiting.

> My dear Doyle,
> There have been some developments at Miss Scott's lodgings which would seem to be linked to this business. She is merely a little frightened but I would ask you to meet me there as soon as you receive this. I suspect now we will have to take further action to protect her.
>
> Bell

Naturally I raced round to the lodgings at once and found Inspector Beecher coming out of the house's front gate with a uniformed policeman. Beecher nodded at me but, when I asked what had happened, he only muttered that I would see soon enough and walked off to confer with his colleague. In my frustration I was about to knock fruitlessly on the door, knowing full well Miss Maitland would never let me in, when a cab arrived and Bell himself climbed out.

'Good afternoon, Beecher, I see you got my message,' he said politely, smiling at me. 'It would seem our young friend at this address is the recipient of further unwanted attentions.'

Beecher responded to his politeness. 'It is a strange business, sir. I doubt it is very grave, though, and for once we may be in agreement for it certainly seems one of the students is behind it.'

Beecher now led us back up to the door which was opened by the maid even before we reached it. Miss Maitland stood in the hall, evidently impressed by the police, but she scowled at me.

'These dreadful things are in the back,' she said, addressing us generally. 'I wish you would take them away altogether. The young lady is upstairs. We are a law-abiding house! In the circumstances I doubt she can continue to stay here very much longer.'

'In the circumstances, madam,' said Bell heartily, 'I doubt she would wish to.'

The landlady led us through a door to the little yard at the back of the house. There was a bench at the end of it and on the bench lay a red cardboard box with brown paper and string. I stared at it. So here were the 'unwanted attentions' Bell had cited. Now he bent down and studied it eagerly without touching anything until finally he sat on the bench beside it and placed it in front of him, staring at the address.

'Well,' he said with all the old enthusiasm I knew so well, 'the string is suggestive. What do you make of it, Beecher?'

'It has been tarred,' the policeman said.

'Precisely, it is tarred twine. You will also see that Miss Scott cut the string with scissors. That is important.'

'I cannot see why, Dr Bell.'

'Because it leaves the knot,' said Bell, who was like a child back in his own favourite playroom. 'Rather a wild and fanciful one, would you not say?'

Now he picked up the wrapping paper. 'Brown paper smelling distinctly of . . . coffee. No postmark, since it was handed to a boy in the grass market around noon. You are sure the boy did not see the man's face?'

'No, the landlady here had the presence of mind to detain him, so we talked to him. The man had a hood and was in a doorway. The boy cannot even say his age.'

Bell was staring at the writing on the paper. 'I see a pencil mark, too, below. Faint, yet the numbers 1 and 1 and a 2 or 3 or 5 are legible, though this forms no part of the address. Which is written with a broad-pointed pen. Miss E. Scott. Box red half-pound. And inside . . .'

He opened it at last. The thing appeared to be full of rough salt. But two pink objects were perched on top. They were human ears.

Of course I had seen such things in the dissecting room, but there was something uniquely repellent about seeing them in an open parcel on a bench in a sunny domestic garden.

'Surely,' said Beecher, 'it is just a vicious practical joke, Bell. Someone has taken human ears from a dissecting room. The women students are constantly the butt of such things.'

Bell was very still now, some of his humour gone. He was staring at the ears. 'Yes,' he said at last. 'This was what I had expected.'

He had taken a pencil from his pocket and was using it to examine the ears. 'But we should never anticipate, Beecher,' he said solemnly. 'How many times do we tell ourselves that, and yet still we do. Bodies in the dissecting room are injected with preservative, but there is no sign of it here. And the infirmary uses rectified spirits, never salt. These things have recently been cut away with a blunt instrument. No, this is not a joke. I have no doubt the owner's body will be found.'

He got to his feet and turned away. Beecher

nodded at the policeman, who proceeded to bundle up the evidence. Bell said nothing as we walked back into the house, but I noticed he was writing something down on a piece of paper. There was no sign of the landlady, but I was relieved to see Miss Scott standing there waiting for us. She looked a little pale but was otherwise in good spirits.

'They have already accused us of entering the dissecting room. This is just more of their stupidity is it not, Dr Bell?'

At this Bell came to life, rewarding her with a gracious smile and handing her a piece of paper. 'I wonder if you would do me the honour, Miss Scott, of having a private lunch with myself and Doyle tomorrow. Here is the address and a note from me with something I want you to consider. It will give us time for a long discussion of these matters, once we have looked into them, for I am quite happy we can resolve them to our satisfaction.'

She smiled back, though of course she was no fool and could see quite well that he had not answered her question. 'I will be delighted.'

'I would be grateful,' he went on, 'if you mention the arrangement to nobody, and I would ask again that you keep your doors and windows firmly locked tonight.'

Later I managed to have a reassuring word with her, pleased not only by her spirit but also by the fact that I would be seeing her properly the following day. Shortly after this Miss Maitland appeared and Bell moved at once to have a quiet talk with her. I could not hear what was said, but clearly some agreement was reached, and soon we were out on the street.

Generally, when Bell wanted to reflect on a case, he preferred either to be alone or to have absolute silence. Today was quite different. He was voluble, questioning, analytical. On our return to the university he did not repair upstairs but stood in his downstairs room among the bookshelves, asking question after question I could not answer. Why the progression? From eyes to blood to coins to ears? Could our man really be so feeble that he thought the box's contents would cause true distress? What was it about Miss Scott that attracted his attention in any case?

I told him that everything pointed to Crawford and he agreed. Finally he asked me to fetch the large Bible that had a special place on his downstairs desk. Now at last he did lapse into silence, and for a long time he turned the pages. And then he gave a cry.

'Yes, here. Psalm 115. "Their idols are silver and gold, the work of men's hands." The coins. "They have mouths but they speak not." The beggar and his shattered violin. "Eyes have they but they see not." The sheep's eyes. "They have ears but they hear not." He is following this psalm, Doyle. That must have been the number on the envelope.'

I rushed over to look at it with him. Both of us stared at the next sentence. 'Neither speak they through their throat.'

The Doctor got to his feet at once and went to put on his coat. 'Well, judging by what we have seen of that household, Master Crawford would be likely to know his psalms. We must pay him another visit. Whatever state he is in, I want to search that den of his.'

In the event, it took longer than we might have liked to find a hansom. And, having alerted the police to our destination, it was mid-afternoon before we were trundling down the drive to Holy Well House. We saw nobody, and this time Bell ignored the front altogether and directed the cab to go round the back. The drive did not extend all the way, but the out-house, where the younger Crawford lived in such squalor, was in sight before it came to a stop.

We climbed down and moved quickly towards the place. Its door was ajar but this hardly helped us to navigate the shadows inside, for there was no lamp now and the windows were small and covered with dirt. Here, it seemed, was one citadel the servants of Holy Well House were either forbidden or unwilling to enter.

Once again I trod carefully over the floor, which was littered with those small and somewhat unnerving pink bottles. A rat jumped back from some dropped food and I noticed the whole place was suffused in a sweet, sweaty odour that must have come partly from the stuff itself and partly from its occupant. We both turned expectantly to the shape on the armchair but it did not stir and, approaching it, I saw we had been deceived. Here was only a pile of filthy blankets. I looked beyond it, fully expecting to find Crawford stretched out on the floor, but there was nothing. The place was empty.

Once sure of this, Bell set to work and began a methodical search. His eyes were remarkable, for I was still looking warily though old newspapers that lay under a plate of congealing food when Bell gave a cry from the fireplace. The ashes were still warm and he pulled out some twine and the remains of something brown and black.

'Here,' he said. 'Half-burned tarred twine, and this paper, too. Good quality.' He held it up. 'Even the coffee smell.' Then he frowned. 'And yet.'

'You think it is not the same?' I asked.

'Oh, I would wager it is precisely the same. But—'

I interrupted him for I had spied something behind one of the bottles and pulled it out. 'A broad-pointed pen.'

Bell took it and stared at it, but he still seemed out of sorts. 'So where is Crawford?'

There was nothing else to see, so we gathered up the evidence and I was very glad to get out of that hellish place into the open air. A police cab had just arrived and a uniformed constable, who evidently knew Bell, came straight to us.

'Dr Bell, you are to come at once, sir. There is a message from Inspector Beecher. A woman's body was found some hours ago. The post-mortem is already in train.'

'As I had expected,' the Doctor said. 'We will be there. Now I wonder if you could do something for us, Constable. It seems to me it would be worth your men checking these woods in the hour or so before darkness just in case there is anything to find.'

I could tell the Doctor was filled with excitement as we made the trek back into town and he fairly raced up the steps into the city morgue, a shadowy building where I had first discovered his strange speciality. Bell stood there impatiently as Summers pulled a sheet off the body of a middle-aged woman. The post-mortem had been thorough but I could still see the body had been in a somewhat desperate condition, skeletally thin with sores. The head was separately covered and Bell leaned forward eagerly as this was removed. The face was a horrible sight. On each side lay reddened stumps and little folds of hanging flesh where the ears had been cut away. The Doctor stared at them.

'As you will observe, Bell,' said Summers, 'we have made the match and there is no doubt these things belong to her. Her name is Ellie Carswell. She lived in poverty in a small room on the grass market, and had not been seen for some days. Her neighbours found her and alerted us.'

Beecher had entered now with a uniformed colleague. Bell was studying the corpse's head, giving all his attention to the somewhat frightful evidence of this callous mutilation.

'So are you content now, Inspector, that crimes have been committed?' he said to Beecher without turning round.

Beecher stepped forward. 'I am,' he said. 'And, moreover, I feel sure young Crawford is the guilty party.' But his face belied what he said, for he was grinning, and Summers – whose relationship with Beecher had its ups and down – again seemed to be sharing the joke. 'But my original observation still applies, gentlemen. These are crimes of a very limited kind.'

I was already sickened by the bloody sight in front of me and this was too much. 'What . . .?'

I would have gone on but the Doctor held up his hand for silence. He was looking at Summers, evidently anticipating something I had missed.

'The post-mortem,' announced Summers, 'showed that this woman died some time ago of heart failure brought on by alcohol poisoning and malnutrition. The mutilation took place after death. There has been no murder.'

The Doctor nodded, his face tense. 'It is as before. He is playing games.'

'But,' said Beecher, 'I have just had some good news, gentlemen. Your player is found. Only he is not about to explain himself to you or anyone else.'

And so it was that a few hours later I stood in the wood behind Holy Well as they cut my fellow student down from the tree, where he had hanged himself, at the back of that great gloomy house. It was quite dark now and torches had been placed all around the clearing in a way that horribly picked out his bulging eyes and the oddly angled head where the neck had broken. Dressed in a filthy red jacket, he looked like some grotesque marionette.

Since he was obviously long dead when they found him, the constable had, greatly to his credit as Bell told him, delayed cutting the corpse down until a proper examination of the site could be made. Bell helped to conduct this himself but could find nothing apart from yet another of those hellish pink bottles, presumably the last that Crawford ever consumed on this earth.

Finally they were ready to lower the body, and two policemen climbed the tree and managed to cut through the rope and get it to the ground. I did not much wish to look at the man again, so I turned away and found myself staring at the spectators instead. All the faces in that clearing were lit by the flickering torches as they stared, and one face in particular showed the utmost misery. It was Crawford's father. He was not crying, indeed he was bolt upright, but he was trembling and pale and all the fight had gone out of him. When he saw my eyes on him he turned away, but it was quite obvious he could not bear to look too closely on his dead son.

I walked back through the trees, hoping only that this business was now at an end. Until I felt a touch on my shoulder. And I turned to see the Doctor, evidently troubled by some strong emotion.

'We are no further forward.'

At first I could not make sense of the words. The evidence, after all, was so overwhelming. 'But we saw what was in the outhouse?'

'Crawford has been dead at least twelve hours, probably far longer. He could not possibly have handed over the parcel. Our man is still at large.' And he turned away to move back to the drive.

It is not easy to think you are at the end of a case and find that you have arrived nowhere at all. My first emotion was, I have to admit, one of indignation. So perhaps the box had not been handed over by Crawford himself. What of it? He might have paid someone to do it and then gone off to hang himself. I simply could not believe that the whole of our carefully contrived case against the man could now be swept away by one scientific observation.

Nor was my mood much improved by the Doctor, who sat in his upstairs room, a watch beside him, endlessly trying to duplicate the pile of coins we had seen. Slowly he became more proficient at building these little pyramids, but he was not satisfied. 'They are not so easy,' he observed quietly. 'I doubt Crawford could ever have managed them in his condition. And to do it quickly with a woman sleeping beside you!'

He swept his latest creation away and the coins fell with a clatter. I tried to control my temper. 'Yet there is so much evidence . . .'

'There is too much evidence!' he retorted. 'It was what irritated me when we found the twine and the paper. For a long time I have been troubled by the neatness of it all. In fact, to be truthful, I doubted Crawford was capable of it. We are dealing with a much more resourceful intelligence.'

'But still you must concede we have built up a case of sorts.' I spoke carefully, wanting to be sure of what evidence we still had after this setback. 'The coins, the psalm, the paper.'

'All intended to lead us to Crawford. He did not wrap or send the parcel, though whoever did wanted us to believe otherwise. And it was a matter of ease for anyone to access his outhouse. I am sorry to tell you, Doyle, this is no more interesting than the waiter with the icicle. There is no case at all.'

I am afraid my anger erupted, for it was only now that I was beginning to grasp the implications for Miss Scott. 'No case!' I got up from the table. 'But surely we were at last reaping the fruit of your so-called method, Doctor. It would be folly to abandon all our painstaking deduction! More likely your timing of his death is wrong. Or Crawford paid someone else to hand over the box.'

As so often, my anger only served to make the Doctor more reflective: his voice became softer. 'You fail to understand still,' he said. 'It is a mental system, Doyle, not a forcing press. If a piece fails, so be it. But once you start to invent connections and the criminal has you! Do you not grasp how lucky we have been today?'

This was too much. 'Lucky?'

'Crawford's suicide. Whoever is behind all this had no idea of it, or the box would never have been sent when it was. We were given the psalm so we could conclude our case, a case that has led us precisely nowhere. It is all a false trail to distract us from the more serious crimes. But at last . . .' And now he too got up. 'At last one mistake has been made. Just one. A single ray of light in the darkness. But in the end, I swear, it will help us to see him.'

PART THREE: HIS MOVE

THE HOUSE ON THE WAVES

The next day I was feeling a little more cheerful as the Doctor and I sat opposite Miss Elsbeth Scott in a well-appointed private dining room in one of the city's travelling hotels. It was an enormous relief to be free of all prying eyes, not least those of her landlady.

The Doctor had, it turned out, once operated successfully on the proprietor's mother and an excellent meal was served, with venison pie as the main course followed by a whole Stilton cheese. Here was a quantity and quality of food I had rarely seen and Miss Scott seemed duly grateful, though she ate only a little as the Doctor engaged us with humorous stories about some of the legendary figures at the university in his earlier teaching days. Clearly they were giants in those times, but highly combative ones like James Syme, an extraordinary surgery teacher, who once threw a student out of the window for impudence. Fortunately it was the ground floor.

Soon the conversation turned to more serious

matters, and she thanked Bell for his letter. 'I have done as you said: nobody knows I am here. Not even my landlady.'

'Good,' said Bell, cutting himself another slice of the cheese. 'I do not wish to alarm you. It may even be, Miss Scott, that though our man is still at large, you have no further part in his scheme. Everything I see tells me his taste is catholic, and I have hopes you were only involved in order to point the finger at Crawford. But I have to be honest and warn you there is something about this man's style which concerns me. That is why I would feel happier if nobody knows your whereabouts. And, in this respect, the suspension may work in our favour. Now, I understand from what you have told me that there is a place near Dunbar where you could study.'

'Yes.' She had finished her meal and was attentive. 'It was left to me and my sister by my father. While we are suspended I would be happy to spend some time there provided you keep me informed of my sister's condition and I can return if she needs me or I wish it. But I have no wish to run away from this, Dr Bell.'

'I assure you it is not running away,' he said firmly. 'But we must not take any risks. That is why I think it should be given out to everyone you are making a visit to London. Is there someone at your cottage to assist you and keep an eye on things?'

'Of course,' she said. 'An excellent woman from the town, Mrs Henderson, has always helped us with the caretaking. Once we send word, she prepares the place and comes in to clean and cook.'

'Excellent,' said Bell. 'If you will inform her you are

coming, I have every hope we can bring this whole affair to a conclusion before the suspension is over.'

And so our plans were laid. The Doctor had already made arrangements for Miss Scott to leave her present lodgings, with its monstrous landlady, and move on to another boarding house that was run on somewhat friendlier lines. This move, however, which was already in train, could only be public and afforded her limited protection. In addition, therefore, it was given out that she had arranged a visit to London commencing almost at once. But she would leave the train at Dunbar, where I would be waiting to transport her up the coast to her cottage.

Naturally I was entranced by the scheme, for it held out the promise of half a day with Miss Scott herself; and perhaps there might indeed be other days, for I had been delegated to bring her news of our progress in the enquiry.

On the appointed morning, which was auspiciously warm and sunny, I travelled to Dunbar by the earliest local train possible. Once there I chatted to the porters and soon established the best and cheapest carrier for Miss Scott and her luggage. Only a few hours later, after her arrival, we were being transported merrily along the coastal road in a fly, driven by a wry old codger with a sweet grey mare, laughing and talking for all the world as if we were on some happy excursion.

When her cottage came into view, the picture was complete. For it was a charming old white-washed building, placed in a jewel-like setting by a sandy bay. Perhaps on a dull day it would not have looked nearly as cheerful, but today it was resplendent.

Her luggage was duly unloaded and afterwards I gave the man his fee which, like my train fare, had been generously provided by the Doctor. Now we were on our own, for Mrs Henderson had left word that she would be there later. I think both of us felt a little strange, and I busied myself with carrying the luggage as she took out her key.

And then she stopped me. 'Mr Doyle?'

I turned. She was smiling. 'I want you to try something. It was what we did when we were children. Try shouting something, anything, as loud as you like.'

I saw at once what she meant. 'Charlatan,' I yelled at the top of my voice, for it was the first thing that came into my head and the word rang around the beach before us. Nobody popped their head up to complain, but we both laughed.

'Do you see?' she said. 'We can say anything we like,' and she called out a slightly peculiar rhyme that was then popular in the faculty, a relic of its body-snatching days.

> Burke's the butcher, Hare's the thief
> And Knox the man who buys the beef

I countered by calling one of the seagulls Latimer. No doubt it was all childish and silly, but at the time I could not quite believe the wonder of having all this space to ourselves. For the first time in my life I was in a place where no words or activity could offend.

Was there also a slight apprehension? After all, I was quite unused to this degree of isolation. Perhaps a little, but I did not dwell on it.

Inside, the cottage was plain enough but quite

comfortable, for Mrs Henderson had bought provisions and made everything ready. It was only now, I
think, that both of us became aware of our physical
proximity here. For this reason we occupied ourselves
with our tasks. I settled her luggage in the rooms
while she tended the stove and prepared to make us
tea. For a time there was silence, broken only by the
most mundane conversation, such as when she asked
me, somewhat gravely, if I took sugar.

Then I went to help her bring down the ancient
cups while she reached for the kettle. And, as is the
way with these things, we brushed against each other.
I felt, I will admit, decidedly awkward and moved
away, with a murmured apology, but I was aware she
had her eyes on me and I turned to face her.

She was smiling at our mutual embarrassment, so I
smiled too and we continued with our chores.

It was then that I found myself face to face with a
framed photograph. Here was a man, handsome
but not impeccable, with more than a hint of amusement, and beside him two little girls, who were
unexpectedly stiff and correct. She saw me looking
at it.

'Oh yes,' she said. 'My father bribed us to sit still
with the promise of jam omelettes. Your bribe is tea
and scones. I am sorry there is no jam.'

I turned to her, for I knew that determined tone.
'My bribe? To sit still?'

'No,' she said pouring the tea. 'To do what you
never do, Mr Doyle. Talk about yourself.'

And so there was no escape, nor to be truthful did
I really want one. I saw she had justice on her side,
and that now, having shared her own personal life to

a degree that in other circumstances would have been utterly impossible, it was time for her to share mine.

At first even now I tried to hide a little of what had happened in our household. I spoke of my father as he had been when I was little, of my pride in him and his design of the zoological memorial. But she saw quickly enough, when she discovered my age at that time, that I was describing the past. And so I was driven to admit that something had happened to him.

She was so sympathetic that I felt no guilt in breaking this confidence. As time wore on and our own confidences brought us closer, I saw how incredibly foolish I had been to imagine that Miss Elsbeth Scott would be in any way distracted or repelled by the circumstances in my home. As to Waller, I mentioned, of course, that we had a lodger who had helped us through these times. Since I had no way of knowing if my very worst suspicions of the man were founded on truth I did not dwell on them. But I had in any case no need to labour the point, for Elsbeth acknowledged at once how difficult Waller's presence must have been for me in these awful circumstances. And we moved back to talking about my father.

'In the end,' I said at last, 'it is as if we have both lost fathers, for I feel as if he is dead, inside a shell.'

She was looking at me with such intensity. 'You think he may come back from it?'

I hesitated to say what I had never said before. 'I always hoped. But my mother . . . endured a great deal while I was away from home. She is always loving to me, but I know her greatest dread. It is that my life will go like his. That I will fail to make anything of it. I share her obvious doubt on the subject . . .'

And so the moment had passed. I had expressed my worst fear and we went out to stroll the dunes. Our talk had brought us together, and in my gratitude and relief we returned to happier topics, and I was marvelling at the wonder of her father's little domain, when she stopped me.

'You have yet,' she said, 'to see the best feature.'

I was about to question her, but she put a finger to her lips and indicated we should walk around the dune. And there it was.

The structure was unique, a cross between a summer house and a tiny pavilion. It was a small white building, elevated from the sand by bricks, but its most remarkable feature was only visible when I stepped inside. Elsbeth had deliberately timed our inspection for high tide, and she made me wait while she removed the shutters. Then she called me in.

The sight was unforgettable. It looked as if she was actually standing in the waves, like some impish goddess, as she removed the dark ribbon from her hair and let the ringlets cascade down around her shoulders. Slowly I grasped that the whole of the front of that little one-room house was glass and the place had been deliberately designed so that, at high tide, the room itself seemed to be almost within the sea.

'Is it not a marvel?' she said, hardly containing her laughter. 'My favourite place on earth. It was once my aunt's folly and since I was a child, I always thought it was a magical place.'

Then she came to me and I held her. I still recall

the sound of the waves and the feeling of her skin and hair and the absolute happiness I felt at that moment. Some would say that this was to take advantage of the situation and exploit my position of trust. I can only laugh at such scruples. She could trust me utterly for I loved her and would stand by her no matter what.

When the moment had passed and we had said what we both felt, she could hardly contain her amazement. 'It is so strange,' she said, her eyes shining, 'because I always believed that anything could happen here.'

'I believe it.' I did.

'But now,' she said, 'I have something more to believe in. You are wrong about yourself. And I want to show you that.'

I kissed her again then, but suddenly we heard voices. And I looked up and saw a group of people walking along the sand: a man and a woman with two young children who cantered around happily. They had not seen us.

'That was always the way,' said Elsbeth. 'We would be alone in the world, weeks could go by without a soul, and then walkers would appear. Well, they are almost gone.'

I do not recall how long we stayed there, but I know we talked a good deal about our feelings for each other, and how for the moment they must remain private but, once the business was finished, we could be a little more open. I told her some of my friends had already guessed we were walking out for they had recalled my great interest in her on our first encounter. Before we left she let me do up her hair again with her ribbon.

And then we went back to the little house to say goodbye. This was not too hard, for both of us were greatly cheered by the thought that I had been delegated to make regular visits and bring news of our enquiries. After my long walk back to the station, I stood dreamily waiting for the train and, as if to complete my memorable day, a porter informed me with due solemnity that I would be travelling the distance to Edinburgh on the London express which stopped here once a day. I climbed aboard, found a window seat and, as we shot clear of the station, I decided that on balance I must certainly be the happiest individual on the entire train. All my problems, even the one in my home, seemed less daunting. I was moving into a new life.

The Nature of Infection

On a late afternoon, two days after my excursion, the Doctor and I sat upstairs in his private room, discussing the various strands of the case left to us now that Crawford was no longer a factor. It was another warm day and, though the conversation was somewhat unproductive following my visit to Dunbar, I was still in a high good humour. I looked around me as we talked and reflected for the first time that Bell's secret room was much better suited to winter than spring. Its high windows filtered the sunshine all too effectively and the dark shelves, on which were placed the Doctor's remarkable collection of criminal artefacts, seemed almost to repel what light there was.

Consequently there was a dimness about the place even in broad daylight, and the walls were so thick that on the hottest days the temperature was not warm. Indeed it sometimes seemed to me that the whole room had a faintly unnatural chill about it, almost as if those objects on the shelves – ordinary

things which had come so close to human cruelty –
created their own grim atmosphere.

'We must at all costs,' the Doctor had his hands
clasped together as he spoke, and was seated under
the window which sent a meagre ray of light slanting
past him on to his precious shelves, 'make the most of
what we have. Our man need not necessarily have
known Crawford well, for Crawford himself was
notorious both in the town and the university. But he
certainly seems to have known someone would follow
his tangle of clues and make the connection to
Crawford. In other words he may know of my interest
in the field.'

'Unfortunately, Doctor,' I shook my head, 'that
knowledge is not so remarkable. Very few people
know of the existence of this room or the time and
effort you have devoted to the study of crime. But a
great many people know of your general interest in
forensic matters. Moreover, the man who was
responsible for molesting these various women could
easily have observed the investigations following his
activities. It would be a useful precaution, and he is
no fool. In which case he could be quite unknown to
either of us and still have made the connection.'

The Doctor sighed. 'Yes,' he said, 'I agree it is not
very much. So let us see what we do have. I would
now discount all the religious imagery. The blood,
the eyes, the psalm. I also believe Samuel's death was
a distraction or a trial. Our man is much more
interested in women, especially fallen women. He
must by all logic be a patron of Madame Rose's for he
knows its geography intimately. But we know also
he patronises other brothels. There, I am sure, is his

weakness, if we can use it. We will start from there.'

The mention of Madame Rose's now reminded me of something. Miss Elsbeth Scott and I had discussed several intimate subjects, and I had been able at last to talk to someone freely and openly about my own family. However, there was one subject we both found difficult and that was the plight of her sister Lady Sarah Carlisle.

Although Elsbeth Scott was desperately anxious about her sister, she knew she could not press me for details, for my own position in the matter was extremely delicate. Essentially I had visited Lady Sarah in my role as Bell's medical clerk, so anything I heard or observed was confidential. As a result the subject was only touched on lightly during our day together at the cottage. But Elsbeth exacted a promise from me shortly before I left her: which was that I would do everything in my power to help her sister. She was not asking me to break any confidence, but she must have first-hand reports, and I was the one to give them.

I told Bell of this now, and he was humane enough to understand, but there were considerable difficulties. Carlisle had not been pleased to see me at the house on the first occasion, and after that Bell always visited alone. 'Of course,' said Bell, 'I would never accept conditions in the treatment of any patient – it is for the doctor to make conditions – but the fact remains he will not admit you. Therefore . . .' He stretched out a languid hand to gather some papers and I half expected him to say it was impossible but I should have known better. 'Therefore,' he repeated, 'we go when he is out.'

We called unannounced at the Carlisles's a few days later when Sir Henry was meeting some London dignitary at the university. I suppose we could have arranged our visit late one evening when Carlisle was off in pursuit of pleasure. But Bell was too proud a doctor to appear clandestine, nor did he wish to alarm Lady Sarah. On this occasion he could not be accused of deviousness, and he had prepared me with a warning. 'There has been a faster deterioration in Lady Sarah's condition than I expected,' he said grimly. 'At first her symptoms improved, giving me hope. Now the omens are far more serious and Carlisle already talks of getting another opinion.'

Carlisle's front door was opened by Drummond, the foppish butler I had disliked from the first. As soon as he saw me, his lips curled in distaste as if he would have liked to block my entry, but he merely bowed to Dr Bell who moved past him with a few words.

Drummond went into Lady Sarah's room ahead of us, announcing Dr Bell but not dignifying me with any description. Lady Sarah exclaimed with pleasure and I entered behind Bell.

He had given me due warning, but even so her appearance was a terrible shock to me. Lady Sarah had never seemed as beautiful as her sister, but she was undoubtedly a handsome woman. Now, however, she looked ten years older. Her skin was wan and yellow. There were great rings under her eyes and, what was worse, she seemed altogether less alert than before while she was also considerably thinner. My one consolation was that she seemed visibly pleased to see me and managed a little smile.

Bell made his examination and talked to her without asking very much. Her replies, when they came, were a little rambling and unclear. She did, however, say she was having trouble eating and, though he was his usual cheerful self, I could tell perfectly well how perplexing he found this. At last he told her he would return the following day but, since she and I might like to converse, he would leave us for a minute or two.

I moved over beside her as he left us. 'Lady Sarah,' I said as positively as I could. 'I am glad to see you.'

She looked at me with emotion. 'Oh, I am not much to see.' There was a pause, and then for a time we talked of Elsbeth and she repeated what she had said on my first visit, namely how her sister thought so highly of me. She understood our acquaintance had been renewed and grown deeper before she left for London, which I was readily able to agree, then suddenly a thought seemed to trouble her. 'Perhaps . . . it is . . . better she is not here for a time. The truth is my husband does not take kindly to her. Once in my hearing he threatened her. Of course she had probably provoked him. I am sorry, my mind is not clear . . .'

I reassured her as well I could, for what she had said was perfectly clear; in fact it startled me and confirmed an old suspicion.

'Mr Doyle,' she said. 'Will you come closer?'

I bent down so she could whisper. How frail she seemed, with none of the life and vigour I had just seen in her sister.

'Elsbeth has said you can be trusted . . .' she went on. And now from her sleeve she produced a little red pill box of distinctive character. Its top was embroidered in scarlet and its sides were smooth. There was something about the design of the thing that unnerved me. Indeed I wanted to see more, but almost as quickly as she had taken it out, she shook her head and put it away again. 'So,' she continued, 'I want you to tell me something. Is it true what Dr Bell says? That this is merely an imbalance, a general infection. Or is there more? Please tell me, for you are the only one I can ask and I know you will speak the truth.'

This was horrible. Was I to tell her what I knew perfectly well? That she was carrying a sexually transmitted disease passed to her by her husband? The more recent symptoms were, it is true, a little puzzling but the original ones made the diagnosis almost certain. All my human and moral instincts told me speaking out would be right. Yet to do so would be a flagrant breach of medical and ethical confidence, and would also betray a man who trusted me. In the end the decision was taken out of my hands but in the worst way imaginable. For the door of the bedroom opened and Sir Henry Carlisle walked in.

Heaven knows what he would have done if he had found us as we were when the door opened, my face so close to hers. But I was quick enough to move away and put a hand on her wrist, pretending to be listening to her pulse.

Even so he stopped dead. 'Mr Doyle? I thought I had made it quite clear that you were not to have any part in my wife's medical supervision.'

His face had reddened, his hands were clenched. All the boyish good humour he paraded before the students was utterly vanished, and I reflected yet again just how very shallow it was. Moreover, there was a slight feverishness in his eyes which I had not seen before and I wondered, not for the first time, what exactly lay at the heart of this man. It was dreadful to think of his dominance over the woman on the bed and I longed with all my heart to oppose him. But I had to keep reminding myself of his power. He needed only denounce me as the mad son of a mad father and I would leave the university in ignominy, breaking my mother's heart in the process.

'Sir, I must take my instructions from Dr Bell,' I said quietly.

He looked scornful. 'Yes, well she may not be Dr Bell's patient for very much longer. Now I will bid you good day.'

I recall the misery in Lady Sarah's face when he said that and I nodded to her, whispering Dr Bell would return. Fortunately Carlisle did not hear it and I left the room as he closed the door behind me.

Bell was standing in the hall downstairs and he indicated that I should leave the house at once and wait for him outside in the cab. It was almost an hour before he emerged and entered the vehicle, instructing the driver to take us back to the university. There had obviously been an argument. He looked tired and preoccupied and for a time, neither of us spoke until at last he turned to me. 'For the moment Carlisle will not force another opinion on his wife. But matters will come to a head very soon, unless we can make more progress.'

'And if he does so?'

'I believe I can guess who will be consulted. If I am right it will be very bad.'

Later, in the privacy of the upstairs room, we discussed the matter in detail. I told him the new information I had discovered, namely the strange box of pills and the fact that Carlisle had threatened Miss Scott.

The Doctor was intrigued. 'Did she say why?'

'No,' I admitted. 'She said her sister had probably provoked him. But do you not see the significance of this? We can establish that he threatened Miss Scott directly. He is a regular customer at Madame Rose's, he was even a visitor to the Crawfords. This makes him a clear suspect, therefore surely we should speak out against him now.'

Bell got up from his chair at once, greatly exercised by my words. 'I have told you the consequences of announcing her condition. They are potentially devastating for the patient. And though I accept Carlisle is a candidate, we can hardly put it more strongly than that.' He went over to his drawer and took out a map. It was a map of Edinburgh on which Bell had marked out the places where we could say for certain our man had been active and drawn a circle around them.

'As you know, Doyle,' Bell said as he pored over it, 'I do not believe in revealing my thoughts before I am ready, but I will make an exception on this occasion. I think there is a pattern to the places he frequents. It is, for example, inconceivable that anyone could have created the room of blood without getting blood on his clothes and person, and yet nobody appears to have noticed. I suggest it is very likely our man lives within this circle, which incidentally would exclude Sir Henry Carlisle.'

I suppose I should have felt privileged. But I kept thinking of the frail and frightened features of Lady Sarah and of Carlisle's cruel manner. 'He could have washed away the traces – Madame Rose's provides every facility – and Carlisle could easily disguise himself in a cape and hood.'

'It is possible. All I am saying is that the evidence cannot yet be considered decisive. We must rely on the principles of deduction and be patient.'

'Even if your method works, Doctor,' I said, 'it is too slow. We cannot simply wait and see this woman suffer. Besides, I have promised her sister otherwise.'·

Bell had returned to his chair, but this made him look up. 'I should be very careful of engaging yourself too personally in this business.' He spoke quickly, his eyes bright and fixed on me. 'From everything I have seen, the man we are seeking has a singular quality. The resolution may not be happy.'

Having issued this warning he returned to his papers, and shortly afterwards I left him. He knew quite well that it was a good deal easier for me to protest than to think of anything practical to do. Of course I could have stormed into the Carlisle household and denounced the man to his wife, but how could I be sure this would have a positive result? And, try as I might, I could think of no way to further my investigation into his activities. Until one night I acted on a reckless impulse.

It was about eight in the evening. I had walked down that familiar street where Samuel used to play and, as so often, I stood before the lighted windows and red curtains of Madame Rose's, desperately wishing there was some way I could share its secrets.

As I stood there, two gaudily dressed, yet not unattractive, women pushed past me, laughing and whispering. They were making for its doorway, and something made me follow.

'Excuse me, madam,' I blurted out at the nearest, who turned round, somewhat surprised and half amused. She had rich dark curls and a pretty mouth.

'Who?' she said. And both of them laughed.

But I had their attention. 'I was wondering,' I said falteringly, 'if you knew a gentleman who sometimes pays a visit to this house. A gentleman of means. His name is Henry.'

They had lost interest now. 'Oh, we have many visitors here,' the woman with the curls said haughtily. I realised now she was French. 'It's a matter for us.' And they turned away.

For a second I was left standing there feeling completely foolish. But I would not let it go and went up the steps after them. 'Of course,' I said quickly, 'it is merely that . . .' They were half inside now and the French woman looked back at me scornfully, preparing to close the door in my face, '. . . that he recommended you.'

The change was spectacular. She smiled broadly, showing a fine set of teeth, and put out an arm to usher me, now a welcome customer, into Madame Rose's.

THE QUEST FOR AGNES WALSH

I felt as if I were in some kind of dream. Fortunately the madame I had met was nowhere in evidence; indeed the hall was relatively empty apart from a discreet servant who guarded the door. My friend, who I gathered was called Marie, suggested we take some refreshment, but this was the last thing I wanted for I dreaded meeting anyone. So I shook my head mutely and she smiled, evidently quite happy to move on to the main agenda.

I was led to the first floor and into one of those utterly mundane rooms I had already seen with a bed, a sofa and a dressing table. I sat on the sofa and gave her all the money I had, ruefully reflecting that I would scarcely be able to eat for the next few days. It was, it seemed, much less than she required but, after a few protests, she seemed happy enough. 'Well, if here is all you have, *chérie*,' she said, 'and you are young. Now do you wish that I prepare?'

I nodded. 'Does he come and see you much?' I said

casually, feeling that now we were friends I was
entitled to this easy conversation.

She laughed. 'Henri. He is a lord, is he not? A tall
man, whiskers, yes?' I nodded, trying to look amused
and disguise my reaction, for I was sure now it was
him.

'I know him, yes,' she said, her accent quite pronounced. 'You are sweet when you say he recom-
mends me but the girl he likes was Agnes. Agnes
Walsh. She would give him what he wanted. I think
sometimes he hurt her. But she is gone.'

I had to look away, trying to contain my excitement. At last we had a serious link. And the name was
familiar. For Agnes Walsh's clothes had been found in
that room of blood. 'Agnes Walsh,' I said. 'She was his
mistress? Where is she?'

'Ah,' she said, taking a little bottle of scent from
her bag and putting it on as she looked in the mirror.
'Nobody knows.'

'And he has not been back?'

'Oh, yes, he is back. He says she may give him
something bad. He is angry. I do not know. But he
does not choose another girl yet. Maybe he will, or
maybe he goes somewhere else.'

This was too much for me and I could no longer
hold back my amazement. 'He did accuse her then?
Of infecting him?'

Of course she turned to me at once and all the
hardness was back in her eyes. 'You did not come here
for yourself, did you?'

It was pointless to deny it. 'Is there no way I can
find her? If I pay you . . .'

She got up at once, evidently aware that she had

said more than she should have. There was a look of spiteful anger on her face now. She was clearly annoyed to have given such secrets of the place away. 'I told you, nobody knows where she went. And nobody will say your friend was here, either, certainly not me. Now please . . . Go! Or I will see you thrown out.'

And she went to the door and flung it open.

I plunged down those stairs and into the street, feeling quite a sense of triumph for I was certain in my own mind that I had discovered the truth. Carlisle was a bully, who enjoyed tormenting women. I could see that even from the way he treated his wife. Eventually he had been infected by a prostitute, Agnes Walsh, and his activities had become even more criminal and bizarre, shown not least in the room of blood with Agnes's own clothes in the middle of it. As a diversion, he had set us on the trail of Crawford, who he knew very well from the university. Indeed Crawford had laughed more heartily at Carlisle's smoking-room anecdotes than anyone.

I was desperate to tell the Doctor, and the following day I went to his rooms, only to find he was out on a visit to the Royal Hospital for Sick Children. At last he returned in good spirits, for it turned out that one of his young patients was making a far better recovery from pleurisy than he had dared to hope. Before I could open my mouth he took one look at me and said, 'You have found something out, I see.'

I explained all that I had heard. He was impressed, and also, thank heavens, tactful. I told him I had gathered the information on the street, and I am sure he disbelieved me, but he did not ask for details.

'Carlisle is, I fear, like many men of our age, a gross hypocrite,' he said. 'As yet I cannot finally accept you have proved he is a murderer, but . . .' and he raised his hand, anticipating my objection, 'but the facts you have uncovered are very suggestive indeed. At last we have a serious link to the room of blood. There is a web here, and I am quite sure Carlisle is part of that web.'

All our attention was now centred on the missing Agnes Walsh. 'Since,' the Doctor continued, with a mercifully small hint of irony, 'you have been so successful gathering information on the street, I suggest you gather some more for me. You must find out from your sources if there is any news of this Agnes Walsh. Some of these women will have seen her. And I really believe, Doyle, it is possible that if we find her, and help her, we will be within sight of the solution to this whole business.'

I was greatly heartened by his response but, after I left him, my excitement diminished a little. For I had to face the bald truth that my source would provide nothing more, indeed she would not even speak to me. In the end I decided the best course was to enlist my own friends. Together we could cover more ground, and I could still keep the real reason for the enquiry a secret.

Stark and Neill were loafing around Surgeon's Square in the sunshine, lamenting the absence of the women. We agreed to meet in Rutherford's that night and, after we had sat down together in that bustling panelled bar, I waited to let the conversation take its course. All of us were amused by the fact that a first-year man had fainted away outright at an operation the previous day and, after the topic of operations had fizzled out, I launched into my story.

I told them that a relative had got in touch with our family, anxious to make contact with an Agnes Walsh, an old acquaintance who it seemed had fallen on hard times in Edinburgh, possibly even working on the streets. My relative wanted to help her and was very anxious to make contact discreetly for that purpose.

Neither Stark nor Neill had ever visited my home, so they had no way of disproving the lie. They were well aware that I had little money, but Neill always put this down to the strictness of my parents, comparing it to the penury of our hero Poe who constantly quarrelled with his wealthy stepfather. So with only a little embroidery, my tale excited the imagination of both of them. Stark concluded that my relative was wealthy and the poor waif would be transformed at a stroke into a princess, while Neill loved the idea of a charitable mission into the stews of the old city. The division between rich and poor, he often said, was the nearest thing our country had to a frontier.

And so we set out into the streets, full of enthusiasm for the quest to redeem Agnes Walsh. I suppose I should have felt some guilt about the subterfuge. But I reasoned that, if we found Agnes, she would indeed be helped, for the Doctor had already indicated he would offer medical care. I had, of course, no intention of revealing Bell's role in the business, and if my friends discovered it I would merely say I had consulted him on the matter.

In the event, none of these precautions proved remotely necessary. We started the proceedings optimistically enough, with Neill whistling merrily as we turned into the street where most women were to be seen, hanging out of their windows and sometimes standing in doorways. Our first encounter was with a small fair-haired woman who stood in an alley and smiled warmly at us as we passed. When we told her we were searching for Agnes Walsh she looked blank.

But the next experience was very different. We had arrived at one of the smaller houses of assignation which flourished in the town at that time. It was run by a matronly dame in middle age, who greeted us warmly and invited us in.

Neill smiled at her as he stepped forward. 'We are hopeful of finding a Miss Agnes Walsh or anyone who has news of her.'

The effect on the woman was dramatic. The smile left her face and she moved back at once, slamming the door in all our faces. Stark and Neill were as aghast as I was.

'What has she done, this Agnes Walsh?' said Stark. 'Did she strangle one of these girls?'

'I do not understand,' I said, pretending innocence but thinking fast. The woman had looked angry but also frightened. Were they aware of the trouble Agnes had brought on them? We went on down that street passing two young women who stood arm in arm smiling at us in front of a window. This time I took the lead and asked politely if they had any knowledge of the whereabouts of Agnes Walsh, but at this they merely shook their heads curtly and tried to interest us in coming inside.

That reaction was the most typical, a sullen denial. But none of us could forget the slamming door and, an hour or so later, after we had received further rebuffs, my companions were becoming bemused, if not irritated.

Neill still had the greatest spirit and decided to prevail on a woman standing beside a lamp-post. He did a twirl around it and kissed her delicately on the cheek, making her laugh. But once again, when he asked his question, we could see her head shaking, and he came back to us mournfully.

'She has never heard of your mystery woman,' he said. 'Perhaps your relative will be disappointed.'

'If it is a relative,' said Stark impudently. 'By the by, what in the world has happened to your Miss Scott? We thought you were walking out with her, and now the women I see at the library say she has gone to London.'

'I believe she has,' I said.

'But Doyle,' said Neill, 'you must tell us, is it true you had trysts in Latimer's lab?'

'A strange kind of tryst,' I said quickly. 'The women only needed to practice their dissection and I offered help. Now, what of our quest for Agnes?'

But we were already footsore and exhausted. Neill saw some women's heads peering out of another house of assignation a little way down. He called at them, 'Agnes Walsh?'

As always they shook their heads.

'Well,' said Neill, grinning, 'let us try something more exciting.' And to my amazement he whooped and yelled out, 'Jesse James! John Wesley Harding!'

The women laughed at these antics.

'Who in the world are they?' I asked.

'They are Western heroes,' said Stark. 'He was telling me about them today.'

'Yes,' said Neill, excitedly. 'Harding has a notch on his gun for every kill, and he's rumoured to have twenty-three. Jesse James is a Christian gentleman who robbed a train in Iowa and gave three million dollars to a Southern school. The place is so vast. You could search for years and not find a man. And think of how hard we have found it tonight in just one small town. Come on, let us return to Rutherford's. We are doing ourselves no good at all here.'

The memory of that fruitless evening quest for Agnes Walsh colours all the days and weeks that came after it. For now, just at the moment I so desperately needed to pursue the case against our mysterious assailant, it seemed to come to a complete standstill. The Doctor was gracious enough when I told him I could make no headway in my search for Agnes Walsh, but I could see he was frustrated. And his frustration grew as week followed week with no new development.

But none of this affected my mood on the days I visited Elsbeth. Mrs Henderson turned out to be a small, exceedingly friendly woman of tidy habits. But quite soon she went to St Andrews for her annual holiday fortnight, leaving us alone to walk among the dunes or sit in that beautiful beach hut, staring out at the water. It was, I think, on my third visit that she broached the subject of Sir Henry Carlisle. We were sitting in the tiny kitchen, it was cloudy outside, and Elsbeth had been a little quieter than usual, absently kneading the blue scarf she was wearing with her hand. No doubt she was wrestling with her conscience, for she knew the question she wanted to ask was inviting a breach of confidence. But in the end her natural sympathy for her sister overcame any scruples.

I was discussing Lady Sarah's condition and had laid out the matter delicately yet I hope reasonably clearly. I never specified the infection, for Bell was adamant I should not, but I felt it only fair to provide enough indications so she could reach her own conclusions.

'Tell me,' she said, 'this infection . . . you are in a position of confidence and I do not press you for a final diagnosis, but I wish to know one aspect, which is this. Was it passed by her husband?'

And she looked at me with eyes that held so much quiet feeling, waiting for an answer.

Of course I had to give her one and in the end common sense triumphed over medical etiquette. 'I believe so,' I said.

She nodded. 'In which case,' she said very quietly, 'I would very much like to kill him.'

The softness of her tone in no way detracted from its passion. I stared at her and she nodded.

'It is why, as you may have noticed, I never speak of him.' She was trembling now and my heart ached for her. 'You see before you a woman doctor with means and with motive. The act could perhaps be disguised as part of something else. His nocturnal habits seem promising.' And then some of the spirit went out of her and she turned away. 'But do not worry,' she spoke haltingly, the tears welling up in her eyes. 'Unfortunately the scheme has a flaw. Even now, after all that has happened, I am persuaded my poor sister actually loves him.'

I took her in my arms then and she wept. Of course

I could not tell her what I suspected. Until I had conclusive evidence, it would only be terrifying her with my own notions. And the last thing I wanted was for her to come running back to Edinburgh where she was surely most at risk. I thanked God that here she at least was away from him. If only we could help her sister to escape.

Sometime later that afternoon the sun came out and we went to the beach house and perhaps, because of this confidence, something had changed. Our manner together was slower, more languid, as if we were both in a kind of dream. We started to talk of Africa and her memories of it.

'Have you ever thought,' she said, as we stared out, 'that we do not know what we will remember? Now I think I will recall this beach and this hut and both of us here and the things we have said.' She turned. 'And your eyes reflecting the colour of the sand. But who knows? Perhaps I will only remember the dull book I read before you came.'

The words made a big impression on me. I wanted so much to give her things she would remember. And so in reply to this, without any preparation, I asked her to marry me.

For a moment she looked shocked. We had an understanding, but I had not before thought it right to introduce the subject formally. She moved back and away from me. 'Do not mock me,' she said.

But I put my arms round her, and she knew it was true. The next few hours were full of plans and kisses and laughter and fevered talk. And later, for some reason, as we were walking on the beach, she sang a song under her breath.

And one could whistle
And one could sing
And one could play on the violin
Such joy there was at my wedding
On Christmas day in the morning

My heart pounded with excitement as I rode the train back to Edinburgh, but there was news awaiting me. Bell had been to see Lady Sarah and found her feverish and agitated, while Carlisle had almost made up his mind to seek a second opinion. No final decision had been taken, but the Doctor felt it would only be a matter of days. If there was further deterioration, Elsbeth must be informed at once, and no doubt Sir Henry would bring in a doctor more to his liking, one who would essentially act as his lackey. After such a wonderful day, I dreaded the prospect of returning to Dunbar with news of this kind.

Of course, I wanted to see Lady Sarah but Bell counselled against it, for we both knew how her husband would react. The next day I found the very idea of going to lectures intolerable. I wanted to act. After pacing the university in a state of agitation, I decided I had to do something and so, without much hope, I set out once again through the city to try and find word of Agnes Walsh.

After visiting the usual streets with absolutely no result, I was soon searching further afield. As before I received only blank glances and shaking heads, but one woman who was cleaning her step, not so far from the dockside brothel I had once explored with Bell, went rapidly inside and slammed the door.

Yet I felt I must persevere, and the memory of that day fades into others like it. At night I made frantic notes on the case, striving for a way through, looking for some connection I had missed. Some weeks earlier my father had, for the first time, been taken to an asylum and I found some solace of a self-pitying kind standing in his now abandoned study, staring forlornly at the odd paintings, wondering if he would ever return to us and to his room. During the day and evening I continued to roam the streets.

Eventually, having failed so miserably to extract any information from the women I approached, one windy afternoon I turned to other sources and started asking among the beggars who congregated on the corner where poor Samuel had fallen. They at least talked to me, but it was clear they had never heard of Agnes Walsh. At last I gave up and had started on my way home in a dejected state, when suddenly from behind me there came a great cry. 'Please, help, oh, please, sir.'

I whirled around to see a woman running after me. She was wearing bright clothes but her face was pale and frightened and she looked quite distraught. 'Sir,' she said, 'I have seen you here before, sir. You said you were medical. You were asking for Agnes, sir. Agnes Walsh.'

It was the first time any of these women had ever mentioned the name aloud. I was amazed.

'Yes,' I said at once as she came up to me panting for breath. 'I have been trying to trace her. Do you know where she is?'

'No.' The woman looked at me beseechingly. 'But

I know someone who knew her. And, sir, if you are
medical, we are in need of a doctor. My friend, she
is taken very ill. She is near, sir, please, will you
come?'

The Strange Medicine

We hurried down a side street, then a wynd and into a small rooming establishment. I had never seen it before but it was the kind of place we had tried so often when seeking an answer to our puzzle. She led me at once to a small untidy sitting room, which smelt foul, and here all was commotion. A woman in a purple dress was holding another, who was bent double and vomiting into a yellow ceramic basin. The invalid was wrapped in a blanket but a nightgown lay on the floor beside them.

'This man will help,' said my guide, and the woman in purple turned and I saw her look of fear. 'Oh please, sir, she is taken so poorly.'

I moved quickly to the other woman, who was still retching. Some of the filthy water slopped out on to me but I felt her forehead, which was cool, and her pulse was steady.

'You're not feverish,' I said. She retched again but nothing came. 'I am only a student doctor, but it is something you have eaten.'

'It is something she has eaten all right,' said the woman in purple, who had dark hair and dark eyes.

And now the poor girl who was so afflicted straightened up, breathing heavily. She was very pale, staggered a little, but managed to reach a chair and sat down in it with a great groan of relief. 'Oh,' she exclaimed. 'Oh. Ah . . . Ah feel a wee bit better. But I thought it wouldna stop.'

I could see the worst had passed. 'You will feel very weak, you must sit quietly.'

'Aye, I will, sir. Thank you. Aye, I feel better now. It was like it would go on for ever.'

'What was it you ate?' I asked. 'For we should make sure nobody else takes it.'

The dark woman in purple gave a bitter smile at that. 'Aye, we should that. You'd better tell the truth, Kate.'

Now Kate, who had been sick, looked away from me, still giving little gasps for air. But her friend put a hand on her, half of comfort and half remonstrance.

'Come on, you must,' she urged.

'Yes, please tell me.' For I had caught the eye of the woman who brought me here and recalled her tantalising words. 'I would like to hear. What has done this?'

Kate looked up and the woman in purple pointed at the nightgown lying on the floor. Kate nodded. I was baffled until the woman went over to it and took something out that had been lying underneath. I stared in astonishment.

For she was holding a little red box, its top embroidered in scarlet. It reminded me of nothing so much as the box Lady Sarah had been holding in her bedroom, though I had only seen that briefly. I took it from her eagerly and opened it. It was a pill box, but to my disappointment it was empty.

'Where did you get this?' I asked Kate, making an effort to sound less excited than I was.

Kate didn't answer for a long time, though some of her colour was returning. 'A gentleman,' she said at last. 'He was a gentleman.'

'She has the rest of the pills, sir, but she has hidden them,' said the woman in purple to me before turning back to Kate. 'You must give them up now.'

'She is right, Kate,' I said but I spoke gently. I hardly wanted to scare the girl at this stage. 'Did you know this gentleman?'

Kate nodded. 'Aye, sir, I kent him from afore. I used to work at the madame's and he would come there a good deal once.'

'At Madame Rose's?' I felt slightly giddy, as if I had gulped a glass of water and found it was brandy.

She nodded. 'He is a good-looking gentleman. Some said he was a lord. We had not seen him for a while. Since his particular friend left.'

'And that friend,' I said, 'his friend was Agnes Walsh?'

There was a palpable reaction in the room to the name. Both women fixed their eyes on Kate.

'Aye, sir. But she had left. We never speak o' her, but ah ken where the grave is. Near Greyfriars.'

'Her grave?' I could not restrain my excitement now. 'So she is dead?'

The woman who had brought me here nodded. 'She died some months ago, but nobody talks of her for she had the pox and she brought us all bad luck.'

Naturally I asked how she died, but here there was only confusion. Kate supposed Agnes had drowned herself, but the woman in purple contradicted her and said she had died of her own disease. Clearly Agnes Walsh had become something of an outcast in her last weeks, her condition was hardly something these other women wished to advertise. I asked them again about the mysterious man who had liked her. Kate was the one who knew him best, but she had not seen him since she had left Madame Rose's, and then, by chance, they had met last night when he stepped out of a hansom. She had been standing, hoping to attract some custom, and she thought he must have stopped for her.

'He asked if I was clean. And I said I was. Then he come here and paid and we lay on that bed, sir. He talked to another girl here too. Harriet. I think he likes her, but she's no here. Then after we got up, I said how I felt a little poorly, and he tells me he knows doctors. And he gave me the pills. Said it was for my liver, sir.'

Evidently she had held back from taking one until earlier that day, then had taken only a small amount, yet its effect had been dramatic as I saw. Now I begged Kate to give me the pills, but for some reason this seemed to frighten her. 'You are a student, sir.' I cursed the fact I had told them this. She shook her head. 'It is the business of a doctor, sir. A proper doctor.'

The other women remonstrated with her, but Kate was adamant, for, as her strength returned, so did her anxiety. At once I told them I would return with one of the most distinguished doctors of the town, and on no account must she touch the pills before then.

As luck would have it, Bell was not in his room but in the square outside, where I saw him striding with his retinue, towards one of the larger lecture halls. I managed to reach him almost as he entered.

'Dr Bell! I must talk to you.' He turned and I saw his reaction. It was only now that I realised what a sight I was. Not only had I been running: my shirt and jacket showed abundant traces of the foul contents of Kate's basin.

But Bell came over to me. 'Later,' he said. 'I have a lecture to give.' The other doctors were waiting by the entrance, obviously perplexed, but they could not hear us.

'It *is* Carlisle. I am sure of it. He has killed twice. Another woman has been very nearly poisoned today. And he may yet kill his wife.'

I produced that sinister red box from my pocket as I spoke. Bell stared at it. I had described the box I saw at Lady Sarah's to him and he was quick enough to make the connection. There was just a moment's pause and then he turned and made his way back to the other doctors. 'I am afraid,' he informed them with due gravity, 'I have an urgent medical case that cannot wait. You will have to step in for me, gentlemen.'

As a hansom drove us back through the narrow streets to Kate's little dwelling, the Doctor sat back, eyes closed, listening to my story. He opened them only to study the pill box which I had shown him. For some reason he was particularly interested by the inside lining and smelt it judiciously.

I suppose I had expected praise, but none was

forthcoming. He merely remarked that it was fortunate I had caught him before the lecture and soon we were back in the wynd, rapping on the door. Fortunately Kate herself answered, and at once the Doctor exuded charm and authority. 'I am Dr Bell,' he said, smiling. 'The Professor of Operative Surgery. And I understand you have been ill, madam?' Kate, who looked much better, was so impressed by this imposing figure in black hat and coat that she could not quite bring herself to answer, but simply nodded and curtsied and led him once again into that little room.

It was tidier now, and, though still cramped, the basin was nowhere to be seen. Bell made her sit down and sat close beside her, talking in a low voice as he enquired diligently into her symptoms. When he was quite satisfied she was over the worst, he proceeded to hear her story much as I had heard it. But he remained utterly patient, asking only the occasional question about the man's appearance which elicited little except that he was good-looking with thick dark hair.

At last, he told her gravely that it was essential that he saw what remained of the pills she had been given. She nodded and turned away from us. I still do not know quite where she had them, perhaps in some pocket, but when she turned back she was holding four pills.

The Doctor took them eagerly in the palm of his hand and smelt them.

'Now,' he said, 'Kate. I am glad to see you are stronger. But you will tell me exactly what he said to do and what you did and when.'

'Yes, sir,' said the girl, who I was beginning to admire a little. There was clarity in her blue eyes and a certain determination in her face. In fact, I reflected ruefully, she had probably been quite right to reserve her pills for someone who wielded more authority than I did. 'He said to take the three, sir. But I didn't take them till this morning. I was going to do as he said but the smell of them put me off, sir . . .'

The Doctor leaned forward. 'So what did you take?'

'I only took a bit of one.' She kept her eyes on him, a little frightened now as if he would scold her.

'You are sensible, then,' said the Doctor. 'What happened to the rest of that one?'

'I put it in the gutter, sir, when I slopped out my bowl.'

I am sure Bell was disappointed but he did not show it.

'Now you may take these, sir,' she went on, 'but I'm nae wantin' to talk to no one else, sir. I'll say no more to no one.'

Bell looked at her thoughtfully. 'I agree to that. But I may well come back to see you for there will be other questions I need to ask.

It was not in fact till the next morning that Bell and I finally discovered the semi-derelict graveyard where Agnes Walsh was buried. It was situated off Keir Street only a short distance from Greyfriars Church. The place was grim, with weeds and trees and rubbish from the nearby Cattle Market strewn among the headstones. Not that there were many of these, for most of the graves were barely marked. It took an hour for us to find the tiny cross stuck hastily in one corner by a low wall amidst some sacks and other rubbish. I say a cross, but it was scarcely more than a piece of wood sticking out of the ground with hastily carved initials.

AW

Something about that piece of scratched wood in all that dereliction spoke poignantly enough of human waste, and we stared down at it silently. The Doctor had, in any case, said little since our talk with Kate.

Eventually we found a cab at the end of Keir Street, and once we were in it and had turned south, the Doctor removed a piece of paper from his coat pocket. I stared at the slanted official writing. It was a report by the physician who had examined Agnes Walsh on her death bed.

'As with your beggar, the doctor thought it was alcoholic poisoning,' said Bell as he took out that horrible red box I had obtained from Kate, now once again containing the pills.

'Whatever these contain,' he continued gravely, 'and I have no doubt it is lethal, I ought to warn you that we are still on very treacherous ground. Our mysterious man appears to poison prostitutes and itinerants. No wonder he thought that implicating Crawford would prove a wonderful distraction. But the only witness has refused to speak out and, in any case, would never be believed. You can be sure nobody will go on oath to admit Carlisle visited loose women. They have their businesses to protect. As for

Lady Sarah, well perhaps it was some patent medicine you saw. Can you be absolutely sure that the box
was the same? Think very hard, it may be critical.'

I took the box from him and stared at it. Of course
I could not be absolutely certain, but there was
something about that plush red upholstered lining
which repelled me.

'Of course,' I said, weighing my words judiciously,
'I only caught a glimpse, but even so the similarity
seems striking. And is there not something horrible
about it?' Bell nodded and looked at me with his
hooded eyes. 'Has Lady Sarah been sick in such a
way?' I said.

'Yes,' he agreed. 'At times, and it was something
that puzzled me greatly. Poison would explain a great
deal and offer hope for her. We will go there directly.'

I looked somewhat amazed. 'Of course I will need
you, for you saw it and I did not. In any case I am
quite sure I have only a day or so left in charge of her
case so we need hardly stand on ceremony.'

I was pleased by his tenacity, but I hated to
imagine the kind of doctor who would be appointed
in Bell's place, someone who would do Carlisle's
bidding, perhaps even shut her away. In that
eventuality, I knew too Elsbeth would insist on
returning at once, while Carlisle would do everything
in his power to stop me seeing either sister.

Carlisle's repellent manservant Drummond was
surprised to see us. 'Sir Henry is not in, Doctor Bell,'
he intoned without the trace of any greeting.

'That is no matter,' said the Doctor, who had the
measure of the man. 'I merely wish to attend to my
patient.'

Drummond could hardly oppose this and stepped back to let us in, but he managed a scowl at me.

I hung back a little, while Bell made his entrance, so Lady Sarah did not see me at first. But I could observe her and was horrified by what I saw. The room was not light, for its blinds were closed, but a few rays of sunlight shone down on that large bed and in it was a figure I barely recognised. The skin was stretched over Lady Sarah's face, the colour of her hair was faded, even her lips were hardly red. Her breathing at least was normal, and Bell took her pulse and commented it was strong, but even so I knew I would have to convey this change to Elsbeth, who would surely insist on returning.

I stood there, trying to contain my alarm and watched as she spoke, noticing that her voice was weaker. 'I know my husband is considering a second opinion, Dr Bell.' She said. 'I do not at all wish it.'

'Thank you,' said the Doctor graciously. 'It is his right.'

At this, I put on my bravest face and moved forward into her vision. I was touched by the fact that she managed a little smile. 'Mr Doyle. I am glad you are here.'

I greeted her as warmly as I could, but there seemed no point in delaying. 'Lady Carlisle,' I said, trying to be as gentle as possible. 'Do you recall when we met here last? You had some medicine. I think you were going to ask me about it, but you changed your mind.' She did not reply, but she stared at me. 'Do you know what I describe? It was a little red box. I wonder if you still have it.'

She shook her head, biting her lip.

'Well, perhaps you can tell us what was in it?' I stumbled on.

'A patent remedy, I believe. It is unimportant.' The anxiety she was showing utterly belied her words.

'But who gave it to you?' I asked.

She was trembling now, quite obviously frightened. 'As I say, I think it contained a patent remedy. It is of no consequence.'

Out of the corner of my eye I saw the Doctor was about to stop me, but I knew I had achieved nothing. 'Was this remedy given to you by your husband?' I pressed on.

She was almost in tears. 'I . . . I do not wish to be questioned in this way.'

Bell glared at me but I could not leave it there. 'I think it was,' I continued. 'The pills have made you worse, you have taken only tiny amounts, but pretend to take more. You are even starting to suspect your husband is trying to poison you, is that not true?'

She was crying now, little sobs. I suppose my tone was bullying, yet I was so sure I was right. I felt the firm grip of the Doctor's arm on me. 'We must stop there, Doyle.' His voice made it clear I had gone too far.

Lady Sarah continued to sob. 'Please go away. Go away. I do not know what you talk of.' And she turned from us. There was no more we could do. Bell merely told her he would visit her next day, and to forget what we had said, but I do not think it brought much reassurance.

I suppose, once we left the house, I expected a rebuke, but the Doctor merely reiterated that time was short. It was obvious he had no wish to talk and not another word passed between us until he looked up from some new chemistry apparatus in his downstairs room. He had placed one of the pills in a glass phial, mixing it with a compound of his own election. Now he stared as it changed colour.

'Yes,' he said, as much to himself as to me. 'This is arsenic. But some of these have traces of other poisons including strychnine. Whoever he is, this man is generous with his favours.' He turned and stared at me, taking in my presence properly. 'Well, we must find Inspector Beecher, Doyle.'

The interview with Beecher was conducted in North Bank Street where he had been discussing the security arrangements of the Scottish bank. This appeared to be something he enjoyed and he was not at all pleased to see us. Indeed, rather than use one of the bank's ample offices, he insisted on walking hastily down to the street and talking to us there.

'The key to the matter will lie in Agnes Walsh's grave,' said Bell at the end of his account, ignoring the fact that Beecher's lips were curled in obvious disapproval. 'I want you to apply for an emergency exhumation.'

At this Beecher almost laughed out loud. 'An emergency exhumation?' he said, his mutton whiskers quivering with such scorn you would have thought the Doctor was asking him to dig up the castle mound. 'For a known prostitute? And little enough evidence.'

Bell was very still, refusing to be drawn. 'You are quite aware of how I work,' he said almost inaudibly. 'You have seen my results.'

'This is just speculation,' said Beecher. 'It would need an order from the procurator fiscal.'

'And he will give it,' said Bell, 'if you say allegations of a very serious kind have been made.'

Now a gleam came into Beecher's eye, and I am sure he did not care if we noticed, for he had seen his opportunity.

'Doctor,' he said, 'you have helped me out once this year. But I need hardly point out that most of your speculations since have been wild in the extreme. I can try and obtain this but, if you are wrong, your association with the police would be at an end. I should not be calling you again.'

'So be it,' said the Doctor indifferently. And, strange to relate, it was only in this moment that I saw how high the stakes had risen. Blinded by my own personal involvement, I had not realised that for Bell this was far from being an ordinary case. The very idea that he was willing to risk the work he loved in order to pursue this man was a revelation to me. For the first time I saw how much the quest meant to him.

He turned away now as Beecher moved back to the bank, and there was anger in his eyes. 'Stuffed-up pen-pusher,' he exclaimed. 'Knows little, understands less.' But his expression changed as he saw someone pushing themselves through the crowd towards us. 'Ah,' said the Doctor, 'I always thought that Carlisle's footman was a very resourceful young fellow. He has tracked us down here and I have no doubt we are about to pay the price for our earlier visit.'

Sure enough it was Carlisle's footman who had

been dispatched with an urgent message for the Doctor. 'Well,' he said, opening it as the man moved away. 'You are honoured, Doyle. He has summoned us both for an interview. The fact that you are included tells us the state of his temper. I think we might as well go there and take our medicine.'

Even without Bell's warning, there was something ominously polite in the way Drummond greeted us at Carlisle's door. Unlike the last time, when we had taken him by surprise, now he was smiling unctuously.

Carlisle was seated at his desk as we entered, but was obviously fully prepared for the interview. He shook hands with Bell, refusing even to look at me.

'I am glad you have called,' he said in a businesslike tone, directly engaging the Doctor's eye. 'Doyle is here because he expressly disobeyed my wishes by coming today. I therefore wished to make the position absolutely clear to both of you, which is that from this point on neither of you will be welcome in this house on any pretext whatsoever. Dr Gillespie will be taking over my wife's case.'

Of course it would be Gillespie. That fawning, slippery figure would not lift a finger to help Lady Sarah but would do everything in his power to accommodate Carlisle. I dreaded to think what that could mean.

'That is your right, Sir Henry,' said Bell without emotion. 'But I have something else to discuss with you. Did you ever know a woman called Agnes Walsh?'

The man did not start or react at all. He was far too good a performer for that, but I was sure there was guilt in the way his expression changed so rapidly to blankness like some experienced rider who quickly pulls his horse around a pothole. 'Not that I can remember,' he said indifferently. 'Why?'

'I have reason to believe,' said the Doctor studying his face, 'that you visited her from time to time in the old town.'

Carlisle did not like that reference to the old town. 'Yes, I sometimes visit the old town. What of it?' he said, pursing his lips in irritation. 'My work as a member of parliament takes me all over the city. But I do not recall the woman.'

Since I knew this to be a blatant lie I fear I could not let it go. 'I have seen you myself. At an establishment called Madame Rose's.'

Now he did react. His expression was seriously angry and somehow it goaded me on. 'Which is why your wife is suffering from syphilis.'

I suppose I knew as soon as I said it that it was foolish. Far better to have let him give full vent to his rage. Now he merely turned back to Bell, refusing to talk to me. 'Dr Bell,' he said quietly, 'this is an outrage.'

Bell kept his eyes fixed on him. 'It seems likely the diagnosis is correct.'

'Then,' said Carlisle, 'I have all the more need of Gillespie, who will tell me the truth. I suspected my wife had strayed and he will have to act. Now I would like you to leave.'

Bell's tone softened a little, as it always did when he was moving for the jugular. 'I am sorry Sir Henry.' He spoke almost sweetly. 'You see, you do not quite grasp the seriousness of the situation. You have been witnessed at the establishment in question, you are almost certainly the one who was infected by this disease and you passed it on to your wife.'

This really did get to him. His teeth clenched momentarily and there was fury in his face. How I wished all those students who laughed at his stupid self-serving jokes in Bennett's Bar could see their man now. 'You can prove none of these vile accusations,' he said. 'No court in the land would accept such women as witnesses any more than I would.'

I do not know how Bell would have handled this. Perhaps he would have reminded Carlisle gently of his reputation, and indeed this might have been a highly profitable approach. But I was determined that the main charge should be aired. 'It is even more serious than that,' I said. 'There is evidence that you administered poison to a woman who is still living and could identify you.'

'Now listen to me.' Carlisle's eyes were blazing and he moved over to his bell-pull and rang for Drummond. 'You can prove none of these disgusting inventions. But I intend to pursue your malicious behaviour with the proper authorities.' He was regaining composure now, for he was doing what he enjoyed best, contemplating his power. 'I will destroy you, Doyle. And you are not immune, Dr Bell, whatever you may think.'

The door opened and I expected to see Drummond there, but to my amazement Lady Sarah herself tottered on the threshold. She could stand up, but she had to lean against the frame of the door and trembled a little, having been drawn by the sound of the loud argument.

'Henry?' she said, befuddled. 'I heard voices. Are they here still?'

'The doctors are leaving now,' he said. 'You must go back to your room. If you heard any of this nonsense, you can ignore it. But I fear your sister may well be involved and she will not return to this house again.'

That got through to her and it probably triggered my own angry response. For, if Elsbeth was to be shut out, what hope did this frail figure have once we too had left? 'Not before we have told her the truth,' I said, moving quickly to her side. 'Lady Sarah your condition is a venereal disease passed on from your husband to you. He contracted it from a woman called Agnes Walsh.'

I know she took this in. Indeed she stared at me and then at her husband. But now the hateful Drummond was there behind her.

'Drummond!' said Carlisle savagely. 'Show these people out at once.' He turned to his wife but his expression was hardly more encouraging. 'We have wasted enough time with these quacks, my dear. Another doctor will make the diagnosis. And we will get to the bottom of everything, I promise you.'

There was nothing I could do to help her. Drummond was herding us out and two burly footmen had appeared to help him. I am sure the man would have loved the excuse to manhandle me out of the place, so I kept my dignity.

But I did manage to look back as we went out of the door, and was appalled by what I saw. Carlisle had taken his wife's arm in a way that suggested absolute ownership and his expression was by no means kindly. Over his shoulder she cast a swift glance at me and tears were rolling down her cheek. It was obvious that she at least knew the truth of what had been said.

I had been spared the Doctor's rebuke, when we last visited Carlisle's house, but I was not to be spared it now. He was as angry with me as he had ever been.

'It was folly to say that to her,' he said with some intensity as we walked down the street, for of course no cab had been summoned.

'It was the truth,' I replied, refusing to be intimidated by anyone, even him.

'Oh yes,' he said grimly. 'And we happen to live in a society which suppresses such truths! Once they are out, people look for victims. Lacking any support for your case, that is precisely what you have made her.'

Returning home in a black mood, I stared disconsolately at my medical books, wondering if I would ever need them again. Carlisle, I knew, was quite certainly in a position to see me expelled. I attempted to pen a letter to Elsbeth, for above all I wanted to see her, yet it was only sensible and fair to know exactly how things stood before I did. At last I decided I would find some consolation in my father's old study. There was a lamp burning in it as I walked down the corridor and entered.

I stopped in shock. The room was transformed, immaculately neat and tidy. All the paintings and pipes and photographic plates were gone. Medical papers filled the shelves, there was a couch I am sure I had never seen before and a framed degree that had nothing to do with our family.

A figure turned from where he was hanging something in the corner. It was Bryan Waller, smiling at me as smugly as ever. 'Well now,' he said, 'does that not look better? It makes a very fine consulting room. You may sit in sometimes if you wish.'

I could not bear to look at him and a few minutes later I was remonstrating bitterly with my mother in the kitchen. 'Arthur,' she said in her most conciliatory tone. 'I understand, but the fact is the doctor needs a room.'

'Of course,' I spoke with vehemence. 'After all, he has paid for it. Money and respectability, an excellent way to cover all the lies and hypocrisy.'

This really hurt her, I could see as much. 'What has happened to you?' she said with tears in her eyes. 'You tell me nothing of your life, but to hear you speak with so little generosity! Your father will be back.'

'But when?' I said, close to crying myself.

She shook her head. 'You know . . .' she said, taking my hand. 'You know how nearly we came to the end.'

Eventually we embraced, for I loved her and what else could I do? But I still feel the bitterness of the transformation of that room to this day. And, despite my mother's reassurance, it never was restored, indeed my father's illness worsened. But sometimes in my mind I still return to his study just as it was with all its profusion of drawings and papers. The fire is lit, the door stands open and I feel a miraculous little tug of certainty that its owner is about to return, as he was, not as he became.

The Exhumation

Next morning was a hot, humid day and I was hurrying to Bell's room when I encountered Stark crossing the square. I smiled at him but he looked concerned.

'What is going on, Doyle?' he said.

My heart sank at this. 'Why?'

'We were told you were leaving us. Gillespie said so. Is it true?'

'Possibly,' I said, seeing that events were moving ahead as fast as I feared. 'And have you heard about Carlisle's wife?' Stark added.

'What of her?' I said with some dread. Around us the square was filling up with students who had emerged from one of Latimer's lectures.

'Evidently Gillespie has diagnosed moral insanity. They are trying to find two doctors to have her committed. What has the woman been doing?'

So Bell's worst fears were proved right. And if anyone was responsible for the dreadful speed of events it was me. I did not answer him but turned away and pushed past two students, who stood in my way, for I had to see Bell.

I found him in his room, bent over a huge bath of rectifying fluid and he turned, looking surprisingly cheerful. 'Good morning! Your career is at an end. And mine hangs by a thread.'

I did not know whether to laugh or cry – there was something so admirable about his stoical amusement at such a dreadful time. But though there was little hope for me, I could not believe they would unseat him, and said so.

'Oh,' he replied. 'They must placate Sir Henry at all costs. He has accused me of a vicious slander. However, as long as you go, I am probably safe.'

I wondered if he was serious. 'But we cannot abandon it now. Lady Sarah is to be committed.'

'That is so.' He turned back to the bath. 'And just as I predicted. Gillespie was there early this morning.'

For an awful moment, I wondered if I had misjudged Bell. I knew he would never stop searching for his prey but perhaps, now that he was faced with a potential scandal which risked his status and his occupation, he was prepared to make a temporary retreat into his little world of scientific exploration.

'So we have failed?' I said bitterly as he finished his measurements.

He straightened up with daunting speed and strode back towards me. 'Failed?' he said contemptuously. 'Your emotions lead you again, despite all my attempts at instruction. I failed once a long time ago, Doyle. The rest is shooting in the dark. There are other paths to this case and you may be surprised where they lead us. In the meantime I am making preparations here, for there is one other small piece of news and we will have to make good use of it.'

He handed me an official paper that had been lying on his desk. 'Our exhumation order.'

The Doctor pointed out that, although we both knew time was short, we must now proceed with the utmost care, which was why he was making such elaborate preparations. He intended to conduct the autopsy himself, but it was vital that the official pathologist, Summers, who was a far more broad-minded man than Beecher, worked alongside him. We would need Summers's support to persuade Beecher to take up the case.

Summers was not available until the evening, so the Doctor and I spent some time preparing a room not far from his own where the autopsy might take place. On those rare occasions, when the Doctor undertook such work himself, he always preferred this somewhat unorthodox procedure for he liked to have all his laboratory equipment close by.

Next I was given the task of recruiting diggers for the exhumation. This was not difficult, but the Doctor remained insistent that not one spade of earth should be turned until Summers arrived so that he could be a witness to every stage. Fortunately the weather was warm, but lamps were procured, for it was almost dark by the time we started.

Our first problem was that, in such a place as this, there was no reason to suppose the grave had been marked with any great accuracy. But here its miserable position helped us, for there were no others near that dismal spot. The diggers therefore marked out a broad band of territory where she might lie, cleared away the rubbish, and then proceeded to dig in a line right down the middle of it.

It was hard work as I can testify for I assisted them. The ground was hard for there had been little rain, and almost at once we thought we had struck something which turned out to be a stone. The Doctor and Summers followed our progress closely and, looking round, I could see what an odd sight we made for our lanterns gave us long flickering shadows which reached almost the length of the place.

For a time we could find nothing at all and, though the Doctor stood there immovably in his black coat and hat, I knew he was becoming impatient.

Then the man beside me gave a shout and I saw he had hit something. At once Bell sprang forward, signalling that we should stop. He crouched down and put his hand on what looked less like a coffin than a box.

'Yes, it is barely more than paper, but it is dry, thank God. We will have to be very careful. We must work around and under it.' From here he meticulously directed the digging. Eventually, with some care, we managed to reveal a long and horribly slender container which, as he said, looked hardly thicker than cardboard.

Now we were told to dig carefully around it. Until, at last, under the Doctor's direction, came the moment when the six of us were able to get underneath. Slowly and with great caution we hoisted it to the surface, though at every moment I could see Bell was worried it would fracture, especially since a little night rain had started to fall.

Once we laid it down, the Doctor took up a lantern and then, with Summers, he lifted a flap of the thing. I could see almost nothing, but the two of them seemed satisfied even as they replaced the flap. Now orders were issued for it to be transported, with extreme diligence, to the police cab Summers had at his disposal.

The three diggers seemed to have developed a great respect for Bell in the course of these operations, and proceeded with the utmost delicacy under his close direction, as Summers and I followed. We were, I suppose, a very strange spectacle, as we strode behind this respectful procession in the gleaming rain, our lanterns held aloft. All that was needed to complete the scene was a regimental piper, for our pace and solemnity must have made it look as if we were honouring a dead hero. Agnes Walsh, I reflected, had found some respect at the last.

The autopsy that night was as thorough and meticulous as any I have ever known. I was not present when they placed Agnes Walsh's body on the table of the room we had prepared. But I entered shortly after and, despite all my curiosity, I had to force myself to look. Rotted decaying blotches covered what remained of her face, and in some places bone was clearly visible through the skin. There was something hideous about the ungainly way that bag of bones and skin lay on the table, but the two doctors were beaming with delight. 'It is much better than I feared,' said Bell.

'Yes, the state of preservation is remarkable,' said Summers. 'We are very fortunate there has been no rain.'

'Now,' said Bell, 'it will take us well into tomorrow and it is not by any means easy. My ultimate intention will be to remove the internal organs, dissolve them in methylated spirits and to boil, cool and filter the residue. I will start with the viscera.'

It was, as he said, a long and arduous task, and I saw little of it for I was involved largely as a dogsbody and messenger, not to mention cleaner, fetcher and carrier. Soon I was having to transport much of Bell's chemistry equipment to the other room for he preferred to keep all his tasks in one place. As a result I had little idea of what was taking place, and noted only the grim concentration on their faces when I re-entered. Indeed, as the night wore on, I became somewhat concerned, for their faces were long and by no means as happy as when they had begun. I decided this might only be exhaustion, but I was tired too and it preyed on my mind.

By the time dawn had come both men's attention had transferred from the corpse itself to the chemistry experiments they were conducting, but their faces were even grimmer and they said little.

My mood was hardly improved an hour or so later when I was taking a bucket of waste to the disposal area across the corridor and encountered a group of students, Neill among them.

'Doyle,' he said eagerly. 'Did you hear? It is all around the place. Carlisle's wife is to be committed tonight. They have found a second doctor to sign the papers.'

I merely nodded miserably and went on with my tasks.

When I came back to the autopsy, I was

determined to ask how they had fared, and I had my opportunity for Bell was there alone, heating a solution which was turning purple. He looked round at me, his face pale with exhaustion.

'It seems certain,' he said, 'that she was suffering from the advanced stages of syphilis.'

This was hardly major news. 'And?' I asked, for I was really anxious now.

'There is no arsenic. Not a trace of it anywhere.'

Here was the news I dreaded. We had exerted every effort, and we had failed.

'No,' said the Doctor, 'it was strychnine.'

At first I could hardly take this in.

'In quantity,' he added, pointing at a frog which had been a living sample an hour earlier and was now dead. 'A few drops were enough to kill it. Moreover, I matched the poison to traces in the pills Kate was given. He is obviously fond of both compounds. But the strychnine is faster.'

A door opened and Summers re-entered, looking more refreshed as he beamed at me.

'There is no question!' he said. 'The woman was brutally poisoned.'

The Doctor rolled up his sleeves, and moved to the basin to wash, but I could not contain my excitement. 'Thank God! We have been lucky.'

'Luck had absolutely nothing to do with it, Doyle,' said Bell as he scrubbed. 'The doctor who wrote Agnes Walsh's death report was a fool, but the symptoms he described were as clear as day. Tetanic convulsions of the arms and legs. Unmistakable. And your beggar was probably the same. Now I am delighted to say that, given the circumstances,

Summers here has agreed to persuade Beecher to accompany us on a visit to the house from which we were summarily ejected thirty-six hours ago. Let us see how Carlisle enjoys being the centre of attention when the reason is a murder enquiry.'

THE CARLISLE FAMILY SECRET

I will never forget the face of the repellent butler, Drummond, as he opened Sir Henry's front door that afternoon and found myself and Bell on the threshold. I have no doubt he would have stood in our way, but then he saw the figures behind us – including Summers, Inspector Beecher and a uniformed policeman – and his face dropped. Meanwhile Bell pushed past him and came face to face with the unctuous Dr Gillespie, who was putting on his greatcoat. Gillespie stared somewhat offensively.

'What on earth are you doing here, Bell?' he asked. 'I await another doctor. Surely you must know I have taken over this case.'

Bell smiled back at him. 'Ah, but I am afraid it is a murder case now.' He scarcely needed to say more, for we had all followed him into the house.

'He is perfectly correct, Dr Gillespie,' said Beecher, 'and we need to speak to Sir Henry.'

Gillespie was obviously staggered but he recovered smartly. 'Well, naturally I have no wish to stand in the way of your business, Inspector. Nonetheless I have a patient in this house who is suffering from a deplorable malady, one she has brought on herself. We have decided on a course of action. I will return to conclude it a little later. Good afternoon.'

And so with an odious little smile he turned to leave us. Of course we all knew what he meant. He was serving notice that he would stay on the side of the more powerful man until he judged it likely we would bring him down. And whenever I hear the expression about rats and a sinking ship, it is Gillespie's whiskered face I see.

We were shown into the sitting room at once, and soon Carlisle entered, smiling pleasantly. I have no doubt he had been watching us from the stairs and prepared his most polished performance. Somewhat laboriously, Inspector Beecher pointed out that he had heard allegations of an association between Carlisle and an Agnes Walsh.

'Yes, Inspector Beecher,' said Carlisle assuming a grave expression and ignoring myself and Bell completely. 'I am aware of these men's allegations. And you should know that I deny any associations of the kind they suggest.'

It was a cool enough performance, but Beecher continued doggedly. 'Perhaps, but I fear it is beyond that now, sir. There is clear evidence that a woman has been killed.'

I found myself marvelling now at the way Bell had succeeded against all odds in drawing Beecher into this case. By enlisting Summers, he had placed the Inspector in a position where he could not deny a murder had occurred. His hand was forced, and so he had to face Sir Henry, a task he manifestly loathed.

'That may be so, Inspector,' Carlisle agreed. 'But it has nothing to do with me.'

'So,' said Beecher, 'you absolutely deny contact of any kind with this Agnes Walsh?'

'I have never heard of her,' Carlisle said bluntly. He must have been aware nobody could say otherwise.

'Then can you tell us, sir, why such stories arose in the first place?' Beecher asked. It was, I reflected, a good question, for Carlisle must have been furiously thinking whether it was still possible we might find a witness. He would have known the chances were slight, yet he needed to open up another front. And so he made a move that was as unexpected as it was cowardly.

'I'm afraid,' he said, 'I can. My wife is to be committed to an asylum. I am told she has strayed into bad company and might have spread any story, possibly even arranged a blackmail. I cannot now be answerable for anything she says or does.'

He looked every inch the suffering victim and, much to my dread, Beecher seemed impressed. But I also noticed the door was ajar, and yet I was sure Carlisle had closed it behind him.

'So therefore I would ask you to leave this sad house,' he said. 'I am having to try and get through this. And, as you can see, there is nothing else for you to find here.'

While he was speaking, the door of the room slowly started to move. At first the effect was a little uncanny, for we could see nothing beyond it. And then Lady Sarah came into view. She was dreadfully pale and thin, wearing a nightdress, but I recall that, even so, she appeared stronger than when we had last seen her. Her eyes were clear, and she was not trembling.

'They will find this,' she whispered, as she turned to me and now I saw the red box in her hand. 'You were right, Mr Doyle. My husband asked me to take these. They kept making me sick, but he persisted and I had to pretend, taking only tiny doses, hiding what was left. But I stopped yesterday, and feel stronger.'

Carlisle now looked truly worried and moved towards her. 'Sarah, you have no business . . . These are a harmless herbal remedy that—'

Quick as a flash the Doctor stepped forward and intercepted him, taking the box of pills and smelling them. 'Yes, I see, Sir Henry. Perfectly harmless.' His voice was gossamer soft.

'Certainly,' said Carlisle.

The Doctor shook out two pills and held them out.

'Then will you be so kind as to swallow two for us now?'

You would have thought from the gentleness of his tone that he was offering Carlisle a glass of brandy. We all stared. Sir Henry looked round, then back at the pills.

'And I will at once withdraw all accusations,' Bell continued in his soothing manner.

I could see Carlisle's mind working but he could find no easy way out. Nobody in the room moved, all our eyes were on him. Lady Sarah was watching him too, yet I am sure I saw a flash of sadness in her.

'I do not think,' began Carlisle rather feebly.

'Consider it,' interrupted Bell, 'as merely a quick and easy way to resolve the matter.' And now he held the pills to Sir Henry's mouth. 'Continue. We are waiting.'

Carlisle was actually perspiring a little now. His eyes were locked with Bell's and he was trembling. 'Take them,' said Bell firmly.

Carlisle put his hand up. But only to push them away. 'I will not,' he said with angry defiance.

'You are very wise,' said Bell. 'From the smell, I would say these are strychnine, similar to what was found in Agnes Walsh's body. And also administered to another woman who could identify her supplier. I have long been baffled by your wife's case, for though it seemed at first to be venereal I soon began to suspect the infection had not been serious and was something else. Then, just as matters appeared to be improving, she started to become sicker and weaker. Now of course I see why.'

We all turned to Carlisle, and I will admit I was shocked by the transformation of the man. He had almost crumpled into a chair. As he sat there, all his arrogance and authority seemed to melt away before our eyes. He was trembling uncontrollably and, as I watched him, I suddenly felt that I knew what lay beneath that bluff exterior and also what had caused the strange feverishness I once saw in his eyes. In his heart the man was a coward with not the slightest true belief in himself or his abilities. Little wonder he had curried favour with the students to boost his fragile ego, little wonder he bullied his wife and put her away from him when she presented any kind of problem or challenge. Beneath the surface manner, there was only weakness and self-doubt.

'But I was given them!' he was murmuring. 'A man gave them to me. I met him at Rose's, but I swear I never gave them to Agnes.'

'You admit relations with her?' the Doctor asked quickly.

He nodded mutely.

'So your wife is not responsible for any infection?' I added.

Carlisle did not look at me, his face was downcast. 'No, if she had it, it was me. But I have had no symptoms. I was told this would prevent her contagion. And I believed it. I hoped so much it would go away but it only seemed to get worse.'

He was crying now and it was his wife who went to him, putting a hand on his. 'Please, that is enough. I do not wish my husband's admission to be public, Inspector.'

Carlisle's cowardice and weakness I believed. As to this explanation and the remorse that went with it, I was not so sure. But I marvelled at the sight of Lady Sarah's compassion for a man, who one hour earlier, would have seen her dismissed to an asylum. The marks of her own suffering were still on her; indeed she looked positively saintly as she stood over him, her head bowed.

Carlisle was given time to prepare himself and say his goodbyes. There would be many questions about the poison in his possession and, I hoped fervently, other matters too. He did not look me in the eye as he left the room to make ready, but I knew that in a whispered conversation with his wife he had consented to our reinstatement as her doctors. Indeed, after this, Bell had time for a quick word with his patient, confirming to her that as long as she rested and kept to a diet he would prescribe, she would surely shake off the rest of her symptoms for it seemed the infection had not been as we, and her husband, feared. That much I heard, but when she asked anxiously about her husband's legal position he dropped his voice and I learned no more.

And so a short time later, as dusk was falling, Sir Henry was led from his house. I was at the rear as we came out and I was delighted to see Gillespie ushering another doctor out of a cab. Both of them looked utterly amazed at the sight that met their eyes and, somewhat mischievously, Bell refused to have any dealings with them, suggesting I convey the news instead. This I did, taking a particular pleasure in it too. 'Sir Henry has discharged you,' I told them. 'And I think you can see, gentlemen,' I added venomously, nodding at the bowed figure between the policemen, 'that he has no further need of you.'

The Figure in the Upstairs Room

I returned to the police cab and, rather to my surprise, found Beecher and Bell were still beside it, locked in animated conversation. Beecher nodded a few times and then at last he signalled for the cab to pull out, taking Carlisle with it.

Later, Bell and I climbed into another hansom and the Doctor settled himself beside me with some satisfaction. 'Well, Doyle,' he said. 'At least a little justice has been done tonight.'

'A little!' I remonstrated. 'You are too modest.'

But even as I spoke, I noticed that our cab was not following theirs. It had turned off in a completely different direction, and the Doctor was looking at me in the way I knew so well.

'I fear not,' he said. 'It was necessary to succeed here for the sake of natural justice and the wife Sir Henry barely deserves. It will, I am glad to say, be a long time before he can hold his head up and brag of his exploits to his students again. But I must dash some of your hopes. For I have every reason to believe that what he said about the poison is true.'

'But he knew it was poison. You showed us that much.'

'Yes,' said Bell, and the lights of the city played on his hawk-like face as we bumped over the cobblestones. 'He suspected it was poison, but only, I believe, quite recently. And, once both of them suspected this, it altered the stakes for she had hidden them and only had to produce them to expose him. But you saw quite well, Doyle, that she does not truly believe her husband was a murderer, and nor do I. A liar, a coward and a fool, yes, but not a murderer. Now she has finished with the pills, I believe it is more than possible that she will recover.'

This was some relief and it was cheering to think of Carlisle humbled. But I reflected gloomily that it also meant we were no nearer the solution, and said as much. The Doctor looked at me.

'You are wrong,' he said, staring out of the carriage though it was now pitch black since the back streets we were traversing had few lights. 'We are nearer than we have ever been. It was vital to solve the mystery of Agnes Walsh, not only because it linked directly to our case, but also in order to save Lady Sarah and bring Beecher into the fray. That is important because tonight, in two hours' time, there is an assignation for which I have been planning. It should tell us most of what we need to know. It has been the most desperate case I have known, Doyle, and I doubt the final unravelling will be pleasant, but we are close to it, I am certain.'

I knew there was no point in asking further

questions and I stared through the window eagerly, hoping for a clue to our destination, but I could make out nothing. Quite soon the cab stopped in an alley I did not recognise.

As we got out, the Doctor discharged the cab and it trundled away, leaving us in near darkness. There was nobody about, but the Doctor seemed to know where he was. He led the way down a narrow wynd till he came to what I took to be the side door of a building. It was open and we entered a passage.

I could just make out that we were in a dull, utterly undistinguished corridor. There was a door at the end and we moved to it. As we came through it into a passageway, I saw another door across from it. 'We go in here,' whispered Bell. 'I would like to have been here sooner but we should be in good time. Keep your voice down.'

I was becoming impatient with all this mystery. 'Where the devil are we?' I whispered.

'You will recognise it shortly,' said Bell. He pushed the door open and struck a light.

Before me was a tiny sitting room with bedding. I could just make out a moth-eaten chair, a washstand and a small bed. The arrangement seemed familiar, and soon I realised we were in the room where I had seen poor Kate vomiting. The entire building, I recalled, was a warren at the best of times and the Doctor had approached it by its most obscure entrance.

But even as my eyes grew more accustomed to the near darkness, I began to see something was wrong. A basin had been overturned and reddish water shimmered in the light of the candle. Elsewhere another chair lay on its side. The Doctor looked shocked and worried, darting forward to examine the wreckage more closely.

We heard a groan from the shadows behind the chair, and, moving forward, we both made out Kate lying there in the light of the candle. Her cheek was discoloured, her lip swollen.

The Doctor bent down and eased her up a little, taking a cushion. I could see how upset he was. 'Kate! What has happened? He was not due.'

Her face was bruised but she seemed not to be seriously hurt, for she spoke, though it was painful. 'Aye, sir,' she said thickly through those hurt lips, 'but his plans are changed, he says. I think he had wind o' something, sir, for he was in a fair taking. Asked for the pills.'

The Doctor looked deeply concerned as he bent to make a proper examination. One of her arms looked fractured. 'There must be someone else in the house, Doyle. Go up and get help.'

I did as he said while he tried to ease Kate into a better position. Outside the room, in the darkness, I turned towards the main door, for I knew opposite it were stairs leading to other rooms used by other women. Sure enough I found them and there seemed to be some light above.

I climbed for a while and the first landing seemed lifeless. Of course I was aware that Kate's assailant might be anywhere, but I called out anyway. My voice echoed up the staircase. Nobody answered.

So I took it at a run until I came to the door where I could indeed make out a light, and flung it open.

I will never forget the sight I witnessed. A fire of

newspapers was burning on the hearth in front of the grate. The flames sent flickering shadows around the walls and gave the whole room a hellish hue. They also picked out a glass jam jar which lay beside the bed and contained something dark and crimson.

On the bed lay a pretty, fair-faced woman who I had passed several times on the street, and who had once kissed me in an attempt to make me go with her.

Now she was sprawled on sheets which were sticky and wet with clear viscous liquid which smelt like chloroform. Her nightdress was jaggedly slashed open, as if by a knife, and she seemed to be breathing, though there were some smaller cuts on her. It took a little while before I saw the second slash in her nightdress below her waist and the redness under it. Yet this was merely another of his deceits which I would soon learn were just as prolific as the atrocities. For the redness was natural, obscene only in its flagrant display of her most personal features. It had been cut here to make just this display – and there was more. For mad ink writing was on the skin beside the exposed thigh and what was above. One word was 'come' and I think the other 'in'. A twisted scrolled arrow of ink pointed up beside it.

I saw him as I saw the writing. He was crouched to one side of her, a knife in one hand, the other dipped in a small basin. And now he turned and he grinned at me. As I saw him my legs almost seemed to give way under me and I swayed a little.

For here smiling up at me was my best friend, my fellow lover of Poe, the smiling, mischievous American who I had always known as Neill. I never used his full name, but it would eventually be emblazoned on newspapers all over the British Isles as Dr Thomas Neill Cream.

He arched his eyebrows and nodded at the woman below him. 'Doyle!' he said in friendly tones but with a slight slur. 'I recommend Harriet. She's not as dirty as most of them.'

I couldn't say anything, for my mind was still reeling. I looked again at the woman on the bed for I was only now making sense of her appearance. 'She's only asleep,' he added playfully. 'I think.' But seeing my reaction he laughed. 'No, I assure you. I gave her something to make her sleep. I had a little myself.'

So it was certain. And suddenly I remembered something. 'Of course,' I said. 'You gave a woman a pill in front of my eyes. Did you give them to Sir Henry too?'

Neill had got to his feet lethargically but there was something lucid and fierce in his eyes. I did not think for a minute that he was incapacitated.

'Oh.' He looked amused. 'I am sure he'd have loved his wife to die. I was glad you and Bell chased Crawford, thanks to my mumbo-jumbo. A shame the fool strung himself up. I had already disposed of poxy Agnes and a few others. Samuel spoke so often of another world that I sent him there.' And now he laughed with his usual good spirits as he used to laugh while we were drinking together at Rutherford's. 'Sometimes I was sure you would guess. I even thought you might share it. The women especially.'

I was judging the distance between us now. But one thing still haunted me. 'Why?' I said.

He seemed amazed. 'But we have spoken of it so

often.' He raised his hands in his old exuberant gesture. 'And still you do not know the meaning of the future and what it offers. It is true carriers of germs such as Agnes who should be killed, but that is only a part of it. There is far more.' He waved his hands in excitement. 'And that is the New World's real freedom. To do what you will because you can. Here is the message of the future just as I told you. Evil *is* freedom.'

Of course I had heard his talk before but now I stood there, realising all that had been concealed and the full extent of the betrayal. This man, who I had taken as a friend, actually *meant* it. He actually believed in his right to behave like the hero of Poe's 'The Black Cat', who cut out his beloved cat's eyes with a penknife and stuck his axe in his wife's brain purely in order to prove *he was able* to do so. I stared at Neill with utter loathing now. He had twisted all of our reflections and thoughts – imaginings that I had thought to be wholly innocent – into the most absurd and monstrous belief of all. That of pure self-gratification. 'Freedom!' I said with contempt.

I suppose I would have closed with him then, but there was a sound from the door and we both turned. Bell appeared there and I have never been so pleased to see him. The Doctor stood in the doorway, blocking Neill's way, his hand tightly grasped round his metal-topped cane. Nor was there the slightest surprise in his face. I do not think he knew who his man was before this moment but, now he faced him, he recognised him at once.

Heartened by Bell's presence I moved forward but Neill was quicker, turning to the window with

an agility that surprised both of us and jumping
from it.

We ran over to it and could see a broad roof with
chimneys and a ledge below it. Neill was already on
the next floor down. As in Madame Rose's he had
obviously mapped out his path of escape. Bell
shouted that he would sound the alert below as I
followed Neill.

It was easy enough to move to the next floor, but
he was already well below me and – as I jumped to a
lower roof – I very nearly missed my footing. As
before, Neill had the advantage of proper knowledge
and no doubt had tried the descent a few times. For
when I straightened up, he was already on the ground
clapping ironically.

'Bravo, Doyle,' he shouted. 'I have left a message
for you too even though we will not see each other for
a little while.'

I heard this, and all the time I was descending,
praying only that his vanity would delay him long
enough for me to wring his neck. But when I reached
the bottom I was in a well at the back of the building
and there was no trace of him.

I started towards the street, unsure which way to
go for he had deliberately slipped into the shadows,
taking no obvious direction. Suddenly a figure
appeared round the building, but it was Bell.

'He is not in the street, Beecher was there.' As he
spoke I saw figures behind.

'Round the back then,' I said desperately, and we
ran down a lane only to be met by a maze of empty
alleys. There was no sign or sound of anyone.

'Beecher's men must comb these alleys,' said Bell,

'for I suspect time is very short. We must get to his lodgings at once.'

I had never entered Neill's lodgings, but I knew they were in a close off Guthrie Street, which put them just inside the circle on the map that the Doctor had drawn. Bell turned back urgently to Beecher now who nodded and shouted instructions to his men. But I could see the Inspector looked less conciliatory than he had earlier.

'Very well,' he was saying as I reached them. 'I am going along with you but I cannot yet see the point of all this. The man who gave Sir Henry the pills could have been anyone. It is all circumstantial.'

'Then will you do me a favour?' said Dr Bell. 'Go into that house and take a statement from the woman you find there. She had the pills too. And see what has been done to her friend upstairs. Now come, Doyle.'

Beecher did not look very happy but he agreed while Bell and I ran round to the front. The Doctor had made sure a police cab would be at our disposal, but now the most maddening problem of the night occurred, yet one that in its way was typical. The driver had been given conflicting instructions and would not set off until he had personal authorisation from Beecher. In vain Bell and I threatened, cajoled and remonstrated. The man was adamant. At one point I thought Bell might have pushed him off and driven the thing himself, but in the end caution prevailed, for not only would this have hurt our case with Beecher, but the police horse was a surly black brute and the initiative would probably have ended in greater delay than ever. At last the policeman who had gone in search of Beecher returned to confirm his agreement and we set off.

I was just as anxious as the Doctor as the cab drove through the streets. I felt a perfect fool for not having read any of the signs that might have led to Neill. And what kind of message was he leaving? To the driver's credit we were in Guthrie Street in a matter of minutes. Once I had shown Bell the house, the door was opened by a startled landlady with a rosy complexion who would probably have slammed it shut if she had not seen the police cab. She led us through a bare and unwelcoming hall to a door, but it was locked. Her tenant, she said, was out, indeed he was leaving, and she had not seen him for a day. The Doctor demanded the key at once.

'That is not possible, sir,' she said with the satisfaction some citizens of Edinburgh take in petty obstruction. 'The keys are the property of the owner who—'

She broke off with a scream for Bell had taken a small sharp implement from his coat pocket and was inserting it smartly into the lock. I heard the sound of splintering wood as the lock yielded, and the door was open. We were inside.

There was no shortage of light for the hall outside was well lit but what we saw was desperately disappointing. The room was almost bare. I could not even see much furniture, just a bed and chair. But Bell quickly discovered the marks of trunks, boxes and recently moved furniture. The landlady followed the Doctor about in a kind of daze, having obviously decided she had underestimated his importance, and she was able to confirm that Neill's things had been collected earlier in the day while she was out.

Bell made a further examination of the room and then demanded to know more about the collection. Who had supervised it? We were taken to the chamber of a flustered maid with red hair who had evidently been about to go to bed. She confirmed there had been a lot of fetching and carrying in the morning though Mr Neill himself was not present.

'So surely,' Bell appealed to them, 'if they took away these boxes they would have issued a bill of receipt, and you say your tenant was not here, so where is it?'

The maid looked a little panicked but led us back down to the front room where she went to a little secretary on a table. She opened its top drawer and took out a shopping list and then something else below. I could see it was indeed a bill of receipt and Bell seized it eagerly. 'The *May Day*,' he said to me with some agitation as she looked on uncomprehendingly. 'It is a passenger ship.'

Within a few moments we were back in the police cab racing to the docks, the Doctor's eyes fixed anxiously on the dark streets as if willing it to go faster. Once again our driver showed his mettle, riding at maximum speed and only narrowly avoiding a collision with another cab. Even so it seemed like an eternity till we at last approached the Victoria dock. This was ominously deserted, yet our spirits lifted when we were told nothing had yet sailed. And then we discovered the mistake. The *May Day* was indeed sailing that night, but not from here. It had been tied at Granton more than two miles to the west.

The cab did its best and indeed as we reached Granton pier there was some evidence of life but little enough of any vessel. At last we found an ancient clerk in one of the offices, who was unwrapping some sweetmeats to eat before he left for home, and looked at us quizzically, brightening when we mentioned the *May Day*.

'Oh yes, sir, I saw them off myself about thirty minutes ago.'

This was bad news and our hopes were dashed further when Bell offered him the name of Neill Cream. 'Yes, of course, sir, an American gentleman. He was last on. Cut it very fine, he did, but he had cabled us to wait if we could and he was fortunate. She sailed on the tide, sir. For Dartmouth.'

'Dartmouth?' I said eagerly with visions of greeting the boat in Devon. 'When do they dock?'

'About three weeks, sir. The *May Day* is bound for Canada, sir. Dartmouth, Nova Scotia.' And he took a small bite of his pastry.

THE WRITING ON THE SAND

There was only one place I wanted to be now. That was in Dunbar, and the Doctor agreed to help me travel there as fast as possible. Apart from being frustrated, both of us were also a little unnerved by the way our actions had been anticipated. It is true we had come close. But in the end he had eluded us and it was obvious that the recklessness of the man masked an ingenious talent. He would take risks, yes, but they were calculated ones. Bell's trap had both enticed and alerted Neill. He had obviously calculated that it was now too risky for him to remain in the town, and his escape route had been carefully prepared.

But at least, I said to the Doctor as we retraced our steps to the cab, we now knew exactly where he was. It seems he had not allowed for that and could we not arrange to have him arrested when he docked in Nova Scotia?

Bell turned to me and there was a despondency in his eyes. 'Of course we will try what we can, but I very much fear, Doyle, that we do not have the police forces of the world at our disposal. It is, as you can see, hard enough to rouse our own constabulary.'

The bleak truth of his words came home to me then. But at least, I told myself, there was one good, for I no longer had any reason to fear for Elsbeth.

The trains had all departed and it took some ingenuity to arrange road transport that would take us up to Dunbar, but we found it in the end. The fact that Bell had agreed to undertake the considerable cost involved in the interests of speed at first cheered me. But then it aroused the faintest spectre of anxiety.

As we rode through the night, Bell began to talk about the case and its stranger aspects, explaining some of his deductions. Evidently he had added a little tracing dye which told him the pills were mixed in the hospital laboratory. Once he had nearly caught his suspect there, but his man had been scared off by a porter before Bell could reach him. 'However,' he told me, his eyes fixed on the road ahead as if he could increase our reckless pace by sheer concentration, 'I became sure the criminal was a student of high self-regard who would not enjoy failure, and therefore his unsuccessful attempt to kill Kate would prey on him. Surely, then, I reasoned, he would wish to retrieve the evidence. Yet I admit, Doyle, that Sir Henry's role in the matter was highly perplexing. I did not truly believe he was more than a callous husband, but there was the strange twist of the pills. I even began to wonder if he was acting in concert with our man. Thanks largely to your work, we resolved that difficulty and meanwhile I had word from Kate he would be there. I was more than two hours ahead of the time he stated but it was not enough. I should have allowed more. He is clever. He anticipated me and I should have gone one further and anticipated him. It was, I very much fear, a crucial error.'

The Doctor was unusually voluble and I wondered if he was trying to calm the slight apprehension I was beginning to feel. In the end I voiced it directly. 'He knew of my regard for Elsbeth, so his persecution of her may have been aimed at me. Could he have guessed where she was? Some of the women knew of the place. Perhaps we should have come here directly we found him at Kate's.'

Bell turned to me, his face oddly impassive. 'We know he went directly to the ship. He may be devious, but even he could not suddenly arrange another passenger to impersonate him.' I agreed with that and it brought me comfort, but I noticed he had not directly answered my question. Of course I had never revealed my close association with Bell to Neill, but it seemed to come as no surprise to him. Had he been spying on us?

Dunbar was barely waking up as we trotted through its streets at dawn. Bell wondered if Mrs Henderson would be out at the cottage, for sometimes she arrived there early, but I told him she was still on holiday.

The cottage looked resplendent in the morning light and my heart could not help leaping at the sight. The place certainly looked like a haven of peace and tranquillity compared to the foul stews of the city we had left and that desperate room where I had found him.

As we stepped up to the front door, the cab disappeared back along that little road, for we had no intention of returning with Elsbeth in so uncomfortable a fashion. There was, as yet, no sign of anyone, but as usual the door was not locked and I opened it.

The snug little room inside was much as I had last seen it. Neat and tidy, the book she had thought 'dull' on the table, a bowl of flowers. Perfectly welcoming, as were the other rooms. But nobody was in them.

Moving back to the main room I noticed a page of writing propped on a side table and picked it up. I knew the hand, of course, for I treasured every letter she had sent me.

'"I am sorry but I cannot maintain the deception."' I read aloud. '"I wish to put an end to it . . ."' So she has gone back.' It was the only way I could interpret this note, left, perhaps, in case I arrived unexpectedly.

The Doctor looked far from happy. 'But this is only a fragment of a letter. And all her things are here.'

I turned now to see if anything else had been left. Through the window the beach house gleamed in the morning sunshine. But almost instinctively, a part of me registered that there was something different in the view. It did not take long to see what it was. In front of the beach house there was a mound of sand.

The Doctor must have observed this at much the same time I did, for both of us moved to the door and we started towards it. I am now sure I had stopped thinking rationally. But I reached it before Bell and found only a large rectangular bank of damp sand which had been packed hard. On it was writing. Judging by the erosion, it had been there about a day. Some of the letters had crumbled while others were readable.

The Doctor was beside me now and tried to make them out as I did, reciting them quickly. *Here*, the writing began, *is the message from the future*.

The words froze my blood. My legs swayed but I forced myself on.

What followed was a D, but the rest of the letters had crumbled. *Doyle?* Beside me the Doctor was also studying it with a ferocious intensity.

The freedom is a freedom to commit any act. All your methods useless against . . . Again missing words, but it resumed, *Pure and shining without motive from the New World to which I return* . . .

There was a little more, but I had had enough.

'What in the name of the devil is this?' I fell on my knees and moved to claw the sand away, to obliterate that obscenity and uncover whatever was buried beneath it.

'No, Doyle,' the Doctor shouted as I have never heard him shout. 'If we destroy this, it is what he—'

But he was too late, for that foul writing was gone and I was tearing away at the sand, dreading what I would find. And then I saw the arm of Elsbeth's red coat, one she had worn when we first came here, and I pulled at it.

The coat came out with some sand but there was nothing else I could see. Desperately I dug on, clawing at the ground. At last both of us had dug below and around where it lay until the Doctor restrained me. There was nothing else at all in that hellish pit.

And we raced on to the beach house itself. I do not even know who opened the door. It may have been me. All I know is what I saw there.

She lay in front of that beautiful window. So peaceful that for one tiny moment I thought she was asleep. The tide before it was again high and the waves almost seemed to be lapping around her head.

I went to her and her expression was serene. I have often wondered how that could be, but it was the only miracle God granted me that day, though I prayed for so many more. There was a pallor in her cheek and I put out my hand to her face and it was cold.

And then I held her in my arms and wept. I felt her presence and yet her absence. Her skin was like marble as I kissed her face and the waves seemed to lap around us.

After that there is much I cannot remember clearly. I know Dr Bell must have come beside me for I was aware of a hand on my shoulder, and also, I suppose because of its import, I have a vague memory of seeing Bell through my tears, examining a cup and saucer on a table in the corner and a small bottle lying beside them, but the image is a blur.

I know too that I must have held her tightly and long. I have no memory at all of leaving her. I think I must have refused for some time and I am sure Bell did not coerce me. We have never talked about it and never will, but I always suspected that at the last he might have pulled me away, and I was by then so numb inside I doubt I would have resisted.

In my next clear memory I am outside on the sand and by then the sea had receded a little and I imagine it was early afternoon. I was simply staring into the waves lapping around my feet. I could write, I suppose, that I was thinking of drowning myself, but it was far less rational and deliberate than that. In fact I just wanted the ceaseless activity of that churning sea to take me over so that I would not have to think. And then (an hour later, three hours?) Bell was beside me. He said something about 'moving' or 'movement' but I hardly took it in. And then afterwards I was alone again.

At last I remember I did look back at the beach house and I was surprised to find how far away it was. So I had followed the tide out. But there was activity of some kind there. Figures entering. As I have said, the Doctor and I never discuss the events of that day but, shortly after we found her, I suppose he must have walked into Dunbar and alerted the authorities, sending word to Beecher. I had been trying to drown my pain in blank refusal but it was still there, only now it had more concrete form. And the sight of other people at the beach house made me think I must go back, for I felt it was wrong for them to be there.

On the walk back up the sand I began to think more coherently again. I knew that Neill had murdered Elsbeth, poisoned her I suppose. That he had discovered where she was hardly surprised me. Some of the women knew she had a house and he must have guessed she had been sent away to frustrate his harassment. The motive for this insane act and the harassment was altogether more difficult to fathom. But then the motives for all his acts were

in that category. It was part of his madness, though I
could not in my heart think 'madness' the right term.
Would I have to return to his own one: 'evil'? These
were only the tiniest beginnings of the endless and
agonised thoughts I would have on this subject, and
here was something Bell and I did discuss, for he was
just as concerned to understand it as I was.

Strangely the beach house looked exactly as it had
before: white and innocent in the sun. This was
wrong, I thought, though I could hear raised voices
from inside which seemed more fitting. A uniformed
policeman stood to one side of the door and he would
not look at me. Nor do I blame him, for what is death
to those who have no part in it but a burden and an
embarrassment?

The voices were louder as I entered. Dr Bell stood
at the back wall, Inspector Beecher was near the
window. Elsbeth had gone. No, she was there, but
she was covered. The person who had been private
and intimate to me, my friend and love, yes, even
while she was lying here dead, was now merely an
artefact to be discussed and covered and uncovered
and soon no doubt dissected.

As I entered, Beecher was speaking and did not
see me. 'You cannot,' he was saying. 'You cannot use
that superior tone now. That is all there is. And you
know it.'

'So,' said Bell whose fists were clenched but whose
face I could not see, 'you say not even the procurator
will—' And then he broke off, for Beecher observed
me and Bell saw his expression and turned too. It was
only now that I realised there were others here, a
second uniformed policeman at the far side of the

window and the pathologist, Summers. They had obviously been waiting to remove her.

The Doctor looked extremely concerned at my appearance and moved away from Beecher to me, making it quite clear that their discussion had ended.

Beecher looked sombre too. 'A terrible business, Mr Doyle,' he said solemnly. 'My sympathies.'

I said nothing, for I was beginning to reflect on what I had heard and it puzzled me. Beecher too looked as if he wanted to say more and my silence gave him the opportunity. 'We think it fairly clear . . .' he started.

But the Doctor interrupted him, looking more troubled than ever.

'I think we should leave that now.' His eyes fairly blazed at Beecher. 'It is not the place—'

Even here in such a setting Beecher clearly did not like being overruled by the Doctor and he stuck his thumbs in his lapels, still looking sombre but every inch the authority. 'Yes, of course, Dr Bell. It is sad. But we can have no reason for concealment. The matter here is straightforward.'

I could not entirely understand what he meant. Beside me two more uniformed police had entered, carrying something. They were about to take her out. This realisation did not help what I heard next.

'We have the note she left. I recall she was thought unstable at the university where there had been trouble. The poison came from there. It is clearly suicide. There is no evidence anyone else was even here.'

Even now the words did not quite have their full impact, for I could not entirely believe them. But I did take a pace towards him and I uttered only one word, 'Neill.'

It came out very soft but he heard it.

'Ah, well, Mr Neill. I have told Bell here that I entered that house and none of the women would say a word against the man. The woman at the top was awake and one of her customers had roughed her up, but she remembered nothing. Hardly surprising, for she had taken a drug.'

Summers took up the same song. 'We understand what you have been through, sir, but there is no case of any substance against the man.'

'Certainly not here,' Beecher went on. 'Yes, Bell has his theory . . . but all he could show for it is a pile of sand.'

This was too much for me. It was as if they had all conspired in this, and Beecher was enjoying the detail of it. Yet all the time I knew quite well the man would kill again. This was what I shouted as I lunged forward at Beecher and I got my hands round his throat and pressed as hard as I could until his head cracked against the wall. I managed to pull forward and repeat the action even harder before the police-man and Summers (and Bell too for all I know) were on me. But I would not let go until they had almost snapped my arms and pinned them down and hauled me away.

Even now I struggled to be free as Inspector Beecher got to his feet, breathing heavily. It was fortunate for him that he had a head like a small ox. And to my great irritation there was only kindness in his eyes. 'Of course the poor boy is not of right mind. Take him out. Give him some air.'

It must have been the uniformed policemen who hauled me out of that place and only released me when I was several yards down the beach, once more facing the sea.

Again there is a gap of time here. For I had a new horror to wrestle with. She was not to be avenged, but to have the stupid indignity of a suicide. A suicide! With all her love and all her confidence! The idea was a travesty and one of his devising. That much was certain.

Now Bell was beside me again and I turned to remonstrate with him. 'But there must be evidence!'

His gaze on me was fierce. 'Only what we ourselves destroyed, as he knew we would. There are not even footprints, for I have searched. He must have walked by the shoreline and lured her down here so that he never crossed from sand to house. Later he returned by road to use the letter she was drafting to you. There he was lucky, but even without it he would have constructed some forgery and Beecher would have accepted it.'

I could just about take this in but it only emphasised our uselessness. There was movement behind us and I looked back to see that the covered body was being carried out, held high.

I turned back to Bell. 'I only wish,' I said bitterly, 'we had never met. He kills her and escapes and you can do nothing. Your method is shown as a pitiful lie.'

Bell's eyes sparkled with anger. 'No.' He raised his hand as he indicated the beach house. 'No, *that* is the lie. There is no possible reason for the crime. No gain,

no profit. Not even wicked pleasure. It is meaning-
less. On behalf of all that is decent in this age, I tell
you if that is the future, if that is the "new world",
then I reject it utterly and with contempt.' I have
rarely seen him so ferocious and for a moment it took
me away from dwelling on my own grief. 'Perhaps,' he
went on, 'when men commit murder for no reason,
my methods are useless, objective deduction useless.
Very well then! We will find new!'

'But you can do nothing,' I said.

He stared at me. 'On the contrary, I will do everything in my power. And if it takes years, we will trace
him. Our crusade is personal now. I want you to see
something, Doyle. If he uses the sand to mark this, so
will we.'

And he bent forward with his cane, which looked
like a great staff, its silver top gleaming in the sun,
and dragged it through the sand. Between us now
there was a solid line. 'Here. . .' Bell said. 'Here the
line is drawn against his world. If it means we fight
the future, so be it! For we will, on into the next
century if we have to.'

I was still numb but I could not help being affected
by the declaration, a declaration of war.

'Perhaps,' he said more quietly, 'the disease will
prove ineradicable. But it will still be fought.'

And now he stood on the other side of the line and
looked at me, and for the first time I saw not just the
rage and frustration but also the sorrow in his eyes.
'Will you come?' he asked.

I must have stood there for a long time. I was
looking down at the line and all my old numbness
seemed to descend on me. And then as I looked I saw

to my surprise that something was wound around my wrist. It was Elsbeth's black velvet ribbon, the ribbon I so often used to tie for her. I had no memory of taking it but, in my shock, I must have seized on it and tied it there.

I traced it with the other hand. It was soft to the touch. And I felt a jolt of realisation. For it seemed to me then that this was a message, and some of my numbness lifted. What was the use of wallowing in my own agony? It would not help my beloved now, or any of the others he would kill. Or those who others like him might kill.

I untied the ribbon carefully and held it at one end so that it fluttered in the sea breeze like a flag. If I opened my hand it would fly away, and I could turn from the Doctor and try to forget. Or I could follow him and keep this as her last wish that I help avenge her.

All this time the Doctor stood there observing me, presumably guessing with his old intuition some of these tortured thoughts. Slowly I placed the thing carefully in my pocket. Then I walked across the line to where he stood.

After a time we moved away up the beach. No words were spoken at first. But then he broke the silence. 'I never told you,' he said, 'that my wife died. Before I began this work. It was of peritonitis. A single night. She was gone. And just like you now, I could do nothing. Such things can never be elementary. I am sorry.'

The hardest thing of all, even harder than crossing his line, was moving from the sand of that beach to the solid ground, for it was solid ground I would never again share with her. It was not hers any more. And in a way, therefore, I hated it.

I think I closed my eyes. And then I opened them and saw my feet were on the grass. But I never looked back.

THE DEAD TIME

It is not easy for me to describe in sequence what happened after I stepped off that beach. That is not because my memory of the days and weeks that followed is blank in the same way that it was in the hours after I found her. In the immediate shock of her discovery, I actually did, mercifully, have gaps of darkness. But in the weeks and months after that day there are no such lapses in my memory. I did not lose time, it was more as if I gained it. The days and weeks and months hung heavily on me and in the end they seemed to bleed into each other, linked only by a numb pain in my heart.

I know that Bell had requested, probably on the very night of the tragedy, to talk to my mother about what had happened. But I obdurately refused. Perhaps this was not rational but it was my wish, and so it was that I returned home without anyone in the house knowing of the events. I was fortunate that night, for I have a memory that young Innes had developed a fever, which proved to last only a night and a day but which kept the entire household so occupied that it was a little time before the change in me was recognised, and then my mother merely assumed that I had exhausted myself by his bedside. It was true that I had spent hours with him for it was easier than facing other people and also helped to disguise the oddness of my own behaviour. But once he was well, my mother saw the change in me.

And now Bell was to play a part. I had been so reluctant to reveal my feelings to my mother that I made a point of going into the university almost at once but, as soon as Bell saw me, he insisted I should return home. Moreover, he came with me, and on this occasion I allowed him to talk to my mother on condition that the true circumstances were not mentioned. It seems he explained to her in no uncertain terms that I was suffering from intense fatigue, brought about by too much study. He also indicated tactfully that some private disappointment of the heart could well have contributed to my mood. Using this strategy, he urged her to let me rest and on no account to trouble me with questions. Best of all, he was adamant that Dr Waller should have nothing to do with my case for Bell himself would supervise it, though he did not anticipate that much medical visiting would be necessary.

In one way this was my salvation as, for several days, I was allowed to rest in my tiny room at the top of the house. Afterwards the romantic disappointment was always alluded to with the greatest delicacy by my family which, in a strange way, I found comforting. For, while I was glad of their sympathy, I was equally glad they had no idea of the miserable circumstances.

But there was to be another, perhaps inevitable, effect of the Doctor's words and I was so caught up in my grief that the full force of it only dawned on me later. The moment of realisation came one selfish morning when I was very low and did not feel like talking to anyone in the world. My mother had insisted on bringing me some tea and, as ever, was discreetly encouraging. But, as she turned away, I caught a glimpse of an emotion in her eyes that I have never forgotten. It is best described as a suppressed terror, and even in my numbness the cause of this terror was quite obvious to me.

In her face, quite plain to see, was the dread, which of course she had always harboured, that I had inherited my father's affliction. I would like to say that, once I recognised this, I was able to offer her reassurance. In fact I was still not strong enough, but I believe that, after a time, the memory of her expression did galvanise me and helped to prevent me giving in to my own sense of desolation.

And so eventually I forced myself up and entered into the life of the household again with a semblance of normality that was partly real and partly feigned. Gradually I was lifted a little out of the mental abyss by my own activity, and my reward for this was the vast and visible relief that it afforded my mother. I wish I could write here that I have never again suffered such a mental paralysis of mind and body as I did in those weeks after Elsbeth's death. In fact there have been two other occasions when it returned, both no doubt because of a strong mental association with the time I now describe. In such periods it is as if the mind enters a long and dark railway tunnel, full of incomprehensible sounds and possibly imminent danger. The hapless passenger awaits the light and sometimes it is a long while coming.

But, as I have described, it did come to an end now, partly helped by the look I had seen on my mother's face. Not that the world I re-entered was exactly the same as I had left – how could it be? – but it was the world all the same, and I had to live in it.

I suppose that in certain respects, given my youth, my illness was an even grimmer household secret than that of my father. Fortunately Waller kept out of the way completely, and in the worst week I believe the family told anyone who enquired that I was away in London. Later, after my 'return', Bell welcomed me back with some kindness and I learned the news that our strange campaign had begun with a highly unsatisfactory inquest.

A CRIMINAL RECTITUDE

It was true then, as it still is today, that the word 'suicide' was literally unspeakable in a reputable family in Edinburgh. There was such a stigma attached to the thing, that even the inquests in such cases were quite often little more than a sham. Dunbar had been far enough away, and small enough in size, for Carlisle to exercise every ounce of undetected influence to avoid the dreaded verdict. With the help of a local doctor, who I am sure meant well, it was given out that Elsbeth had been struck by a sudden outburst of the fever that had killed her father and that, in the throes of her delirium, she had made the tragic mistake of swallowing an excessive amount of a purgative. That her death, in other words, was merely a tragic accident.

Of course this meant ignoring the supposed 'note', the oddity of the circumstances, the absence of any direct evidence of fever and many other things, but as a medical student I had heard of far more flagrant distortions. Not many years earlier a philosophy lecturer had hanged himself from the beams of his bedroom, but the rope was destroyed and it was given out that he had broken his neck falling downstairs. Out of sympathy for the family, the police and the doctors were often expected to collude in such things.

On this occasion, though, it meant that Bell was placed in an utterly invidious position. 'Suicide' had become the dark secret and Beecher spelled out his own position to Bell in no uncertain terms. Out of the kindness of his heart, he was prepared to help the family in their difficulty by supporting the fiction of an accident. But if Bell tried to peddle his own theory of murder, then the police would not hesitate to produce the note and admit what they considered to be the truth: namely that she had killed herself.

I still remember the pent-up frustration in the Doctor's face as he sat in his upstairs room, many weeks after Elsbeth's death, telling me about this conundrum. Even as he described it, his features were white with rage. 'I can fight one lie, Doyle, but this was a wilderness of them – a twisted travesty of justice. Many nights I debated the matter with myself. You might say it was my obligation to bring out the truth at any cost. And in some respects so it was. But I lacked the evidence I needed, while I also knew Lady Sarah's condition was still delicate. And finally I was forced to concede that my intervention would only have achieved the opposite of what I intended. No doubt, once the note was produced, "suicide" would become the popular wisdom, and probably the verdict too.'

In private of course he had continued to make

every effort to persuade the authorities of what had happened. Ultimately he put his case to Carlisle, who was still genuinely chastened by his own skirmish with the law and treated him civilly, responding to the story not with his old arrogance but with unusual candour and dignity. He accepted that Bell had been right about such things before and was prepared to believe he might be right about such a fantastic hypothesis now, even though the police took the view the pills he had given his wife, and which had come from a man he met only fleetingly at Madame Rose's, were the result of some chemist's mistake. But, he continued, there were other considerations too. Even in the unlikely event that the police were persuaded of Bell's theory, there seemed little prospect of finding the criminal. Meanwhile Lady Sarah – now making an excellent recovery under Bell's own care – firmly believed in the story of her sister's fever, and any mention of Bell's theory would revive in public the question of suicide, which might affect her badly. It was why, Sir Henry said, he had undertaken such efforts to avoid it.

Naturally I was indignant and wished I had witnessed this interview myself. I pointed out that Cream was probably the last person on earth Carlisle wished to bring before the public eye, given his unfortunate association with the man. But Bell was convinced Carlisle was genuine. He certainly no longer exercised the same power over his wife as he had done, and to prove it Bell had every intention of taking me to visit her.

We made that visit shortly after I returned to the university. I freely confess my heart quailed a little to find myself back in front of Carlisle's great door with its brass handle. By mutual agreement, Sir Henry had arranged to be absent, yet I dreaded seeing Lady Sarah almost more, for her face alone would trigger memories. But Bell, I am sure, felt that since I would have to make the visit at some point, it was better to be done with it. And perhaps too he had another motive.

At least, as I was aware almost immediately, everything had changed in that once dreadful house. The hateful manservant, for example, was nowhere to be seen, for we were ushered in by a friendly young housemaid. I learned later that the butler had quit the house in a show of moral indignation, but actually because he knew quite well that Lady Sarah wished to be rid of him. This maid curtsied charmingly and showed us into the drawing room, which had lost all its overheated air and had fresh flowers in two vases. We waited only a moment and then the door opened and she entered.

Lady Sarah had certainly aged a little. Her face was lined and there was a new sadness in her eyes but she had lost all the weakness that once caused us so much anxiety. Now, evidently in command of herself and of her household, she seemed to have made what was nearly a full recovery, despite her loss.

She smiled with great happiness to see Bell and then she saw me. For just a moment both of us exchanged a flash of such pain that I had to look away. When I turned back I could see that, like me, she had tears in her eyes and she clasped my hand and said only, 'I am so glad you came. I very much wished to see you.'

Rather to my surprise the Doctor now excused himself. 'I am quite sure the two of you would like to talk alone,' he said, smiling. 'I told the cab to wait and I will return in an hour or so.' And, as no doubt had always been his plan, he withdrew.

Yet soon I was glad he did, for now that I was in Lady Sarah's presence, I found that I badly wanted to tell her, not of the end, but how happy Elsbeth had been when I last saw her.

And that indeed is largely what we talked about. I described the last day I had spent with Elsbeth, and others as well – the jokes we shared, the walks we took, the things we said. I did not mention my marriage proposal for, even if it were not a private thing, it would have been unnecessary. Lady Sarah understood quite well what I was saying and it obviously pleased her. Indeed soon she joined in, offering stories of Elsbeth that she alone knew: of little things the two sisters had done together, of games they had played as children and their private ways.

We were even able to become quite merry until it so happened that almost at the same time we both found ourselves mentioning her sister's unruly hair and the trouble she had with it. It was as if a chill had suddenly entered the room, for we felt again the physical sense of our deprivation and all the joy went out of us. From somewhere in the room a clock struck the hour and it acted as a kind of signal.

'Mr Doyle,' she said, and I knew at once what was coming. 'Since you were last to see her, I think I would like you to confirm my view. I am sure you will share it, but I have to put it to you for there are stupid rumours she would take her own life. Elsbeth's death was a tragedy, but it was an accidental one. That is so, is it not?'

I do not know how long I waited. I was wrestling with my own conscience, aware that to tell her what I knew would cause extraordinary pain, but nonetheless desperately reluctant to collude in the web of lies. In the end, and it may be that this was cowardly, I found I was asking Elsbeth herself what I should do and the words came then quick enough. 'I do not believe so,' I said.

The effect was so dramatic that I wondered if I had made the most terrible mistake. It was as if the woman in front of me had been physically struck. I found myself recalling at once how desperately frail and ill Lady Sarah had looked not so long ago when she was being slowly poisoned. And would not the Doctor have been frank with her if he had thought it was worth the risk? Once again, was I simply allowing my own feelings to overwhelm my common sense? At last she spoke.

'I knew that there had been a rumour it was suicide. Now your words confirm it. And as you see . . .' For a moment her lips worked and nothing came out. 'I just find this so hard to bear and very hard to believe.'

'But it was certainly not suicide,' I exclaimed. 'That was what was used to cover the truth. You can put it entirely from your mind. The police believed so only because it was convenient for them not to pursue the matter.'

Her expression changed again. There was shock but some of the absolute distress left her. 'But if not, then what are you saying?'

'That I believe, both Bell and I believe, that it was deliberate.'

She was clasping her hands now. 'That is horrifying, but the evidence—'

'There is little, I must warn you.'

Her tone became vehement. 'Yet even so this is still more intelligible than almost anything I have heard to date. What I could never bear, Mr Doyle, is the utterly incredible notion that my sister would take her own life. And the accident therefore was the only other explanation. But in itself it seemed hard to believe. And you say the police do not accept your theory?'

'That is so. And it is why the Doctor did not wish to air it for he was concerned—'

'—that the idea of suicide would be believed before an unknown murderer.' She completed the thought and I was struck by the firmness of her tone now. 'Yes, and I feel sure he was right and I am grateful to him for that. I would ask you to convey that gratitude. The worst of all for me would be for Elsbeth's name to be tainted by an act she never would or could have committed in a thousand years. Now you must tell me what you believe. Leave nothing out.'

I cannot pretend I obeyed her injunction. I did not for a minute wish to paint Neill in his true and terrifying light for, while this might disturb and horrify her, it would hardly help her to understand. And it was now obvious to me that, after her torture of doubt, to understand was what she wished most of all. I told her therefore that someone Elsbeth and I both knew, an American called Thomas Neill Cream, had proved in our eyes to be criminally insane. The word was one that Bell and I would often argue about, and not one that satisfied either of us, but it was convenient now for, I added, there was little point in analysing his motives. We believed he had deliberately poisoned Elsbeth but he had now left the country for good and would not be back.

She was silent for a time, thinking over my account. 'If it is so strange as that—' she said after a time, and though there were tears in her eyes she was still fully in command of herself, 'for, Mr Doyle, though I believe you and Bell and know from experience that I should believe you, it *is* strange – then I can understand why the police fell back on their stupid belief. Thank you for telling me. I assume there is little prospect of persuading them to act against this individual.'

'We have, as yet, insufficient evidence,' I said, choosing my words carefully. 'Though every day we hope—'

'But you,' she said, 'you and the Doctor will try to find him?'

'The Doctor has pledged as much. He swore it on the day she was found.'

'Well, then I believe that you will,' she replied. 'For I have great faith in him. There is no point in talking of this to others, Mr Doyle, apart from those who can help us. I will say nothing of it except in that respect. But I trust you to find him. I know you will do that for her.'

Shortly after this Bell returned to find us taking tea. We were talking about nothing in particular by then, but a single glance told him that the visit had achieved what he had hoped and he sat down affably beside us.

Afterwards I told him what had occurred and he thought for a little. 'Well, we have another person who seeks justice. It is not much, Doyle. There are only three of us. But it is something.'

THE GIFT FROM THE LABYRINTH

At the time I write my mother and my siblings were still making very occasional visits to my father, though it was a long enough trek for us. He was in Fordoun House in the little town of Fordoun, which was nearly a hundred miles away to the north along the east coast past even Montrose. I had always protested that it seemed monstrous for him to be so far away, but, as ever, Waller had made it his business to find a secluded asylum which, he said, would suit the patient. For my part I wondered who exactly it suited? The distance made regular visiting an impossibility, but no doubt there was less risk of local gossip about my father when he was at such a distance.

A few days after my talk with Lady Sarah, it had been arranged that our family would go to see him. At the time it seemed only a distraction and I had little idea of how important the visit would prove to be. It was then impossible to make the journey by rail, for there was no railway bridge over the Forth, though it was much discussed. So on the day in question, my small brother, my twelve-year-old sister Lottie, my mother and I took a ferry over the Forth, and from there we boarded a train north. My other sisters stayed with a neighbour, while Waller was in the south, attending to some business at his estate in Masongill.

The excitement of the journey was to travel over the new Tay Bridge into Dundee, which had been opened only a few weeks earlier, and I still recall our awed silence as our little compartment trundled over the lattice girders supported by massive but slender cast-iron columns. Little did I know then that the bridge would play such a terrible part in another of Bell's investigations in the Christmas of 1879. On this occasion, as we crossed the Tay, it was a grey, windy day and we peered down at the dank, slate-grey water below us plumed with choppy waves. Even then I thought how horrible it would be to plunge into that torrent.

In a short time we were in Dundee, but there was still much ground to cover. It was not till late afternoon that our train travel ended and we were making the journey by road out of Montrose to the asylum. In my mind now, as I look back, Fordoun House itself somehow takes on the form of a grim, grey, gothic castle with turrets and high windows beside a belt of ash trees. In reality it was much more mundane, a miserably drab three-storey building with hideously yellow blinds on the upstairs rooms that seemed always to be half closed. I have seen the same thing in many houses in Scotland and for me it always signals gloom and oppression.

At last we were shown to my father's room by a formidable head nurse with iron-grey hair and my heart leapt for he was sitting drawing. But then he turned and stared at us. And I saw that, though his beard was tidier and his expression less anguished, he was still not properly there.

We went to greet him, and his eyes filled with tears and he asked plaintively if we had come to give him deliverance. But there was little hope in the question. And soon his head lolled back in his chair and he hardly seemed to notice us for a time as he clicked his tongue and hummed a little. I have strong suspicions now that my father was heavily sedated for these visits and that this was one reason for the sheer horror of them. Privately I was furious at how little we saw him, but I cannot pretend there was anything but sadness when we did. How I wish that in those early days I had found some way of visiting unexpectedly and alone, for I feel sure I would have been astonished and probably shocked at what I found. Perhaps then the scales would have fallen from my eyes and I would have seen that the man needed no more than some real care and affection. But, by the time I did visit him in that way, matters had changed.

On the occasion I am describing, after a few hours of torment, we left to spend the night at some lodgings. In the morning we always visited him again before starting (with some feeling of relief) on our way home. The ritual is not, in fact, one I take any pleasure in rehearsing, but I do so now because it was on the following morning of this visit that events took an unexpected turn.

Fortunately my mother and the children had gone

ahead to his room, while I sought a word with the head nurse (for in those days the doctors in such places did pretty much what they liked and were rarely present). I knew well enough that there was little real hope of discussing my father's condition with this woman, for she was a disciplinarian of the old school who brushed aside medical talk. So I was somewhat surprised to be greeted not with the usual raised eyebrow and abrupt words, but with the news that she wished to talk to me.

'Of course,' I said with pleasure as I entered her spartan little corner. 'I am sure we can help him more than we are at present.'

'Oh no,' she said, her eyes severe. 'It is not of that I wish to speak, Mr Doyle. I had intended to ask for an interview this morning to inform you that we do not enjoy being treated as a parcel service.'

My mouth must have dropped open and I stared at her.

'Of course the patients receive some letters,' she went on, 'but we have always made it clear we prefer parcels to be brought on visits and not posted. We have to open them and we have nowhere to store them before we do. That is bad enough, but I had not thought you would expect us to hold parcels for the relatives of our patients. It is an absurd misuse of these premises and a waste of our time and yours.'

'But what parcel do you mean?' I said, almost stammering for, though I was more perplexed than anything, I felt a sudden small alarm.

She went to a locked cupboard and opened it and took out a package about the size of a book. 'I am quite sure you know exactly what I mean. And, if it happens again, I can assure you we will merely destroy it.'

I took the wretched brown parcel from her and stared at the writing.

MR ARTHUR DOYLE

Then came the address of Fordoun House in large letters and the following, heavily scored:

TO AWAIT HIS ARRIVAL

Of course I knew the writing, and my legs were trembling, as was my hand, but I had to try to stay calm. 'Thank you,' I muttered.

'I repeat, if anything else arrives we will destroy it. Those are the rules.' And she turned on her heel.

It is fortunate she did for it gave me a chance to collect myself. How in heaven's name had he known? He had not to my knowledge been in our house. But, I reflected, it would have been easy to discover where I lived and, from there, to spy. In this way he must have discovered all he wanted to know. It came to me now that though I had never breathed a word of my father's condition to anyone except Elsbeth and the Doctor, I *had* discussed asylums with Neill and Stark, and especially those with inebriate inmates. Stark knew of Fordoun House for he lived in Dundee. Neill may well have noticed my interest in the place. And, if he already knew of my father's condition, it would be simple for him to deduce the reason for that interest. As for confirming that my father was a patient here, that was the easiest thing in the world.

He only had to send some circular letter and, if it was not returned, he could be sure he was right.

I stared at the postmark, and the word Aberdeen jumped out at me. My hands clenched. But then I saw my foolishness: the full postmark was Aberdeen, North Dakota. It had been posted in America.

I still do not know how I contained myself, for I had no idea what could be in the package. But I could not open it there, nor could I let my mother have the slightest inkling of what had happened. I concealed it in my jacket and later transferred it unseen to my bag.

The return to Edinburgh seemed endless, but we were there in late afternoon. My mother had matters to settle so I was able to get away, and by luck the Doctor was in his room. As soon as I told him what had occurred, and produced the parcel, he took it from me with unbridled zeal.

'I can only thank heaven you did not open it,' he said. 'There are plenty of tales of murder by the post. I have heard of poisoned springs attached to the inside of an envelope, and there is the famous case in Russia where a man was sent a box with the sharpest of steel blades placed just where he was directed to open it. We must take every precaution.'

I was glad of this activity for it helped to deaden my own pain and alarm. We could be quite certain now that the man I sought was intent on tormenting us both. In the privacy of his upstairs room, the Doctor placed the parcel on a broad table. He took a magnifying glass and, without touching it again, studied it for a long time, poring over the writing and the address and the postmark. Finally he took a long-handled knife and, standing well back, he pierced the paper at a corner, peeling it away. We could see bright colours and print. He studied it. 'A map,' he said. 'So far as I can see, quite an ordinary one.'

Now, once again using the long knife, he tore a deep slit in the thick brown paper till we could both see the contents. It was indeed a half-folded map of America and another oddly shaped object wrapped in tissue paper. The map had writing scrawled across it, the same wild erratic letters.

HERE BUT YOU WILL NEVER FIND ME!

My mind flashed back at once to my conversations with him. Neill had often pointed out to me that America enabled freedom and evil to flourish in tandem because of its size. Men could commit a crime in one state and move hundreds of miles away to another, leaving the authorities impotent and useless. Now I saw that, with his mad vanity, here was yet another way in which he had been telling me something about himself.

Bell picked up the map now, satisfied that it was free of any taint, and spread it out. There before us was the full continent of America in all its dispiriting vastness. 'The idea then,' I said 'is not a physical torture but a mental one. He wants us to feel dwarfed by his new world. But there is more writing here.'

As I struggled to decipher it, for it was much smaller, Bell used his knife to slice the tissue paper around the other object. Of all things, what stood before us was a pair of opera glasses. We both stared at them. And he lifted them slowly but nothing happened. Meanwhile I had made out the writing.

But I am fair I give you a single clue. Use the glasses.

Bell was holding the glasses, which seemed innocent enough. 'There is a clue,' I said eagerly, staring at the map. I pored over it for a long time. 'But I can see no more writing.'

Bell, who had put down the glasses, was looking too, but he shook his head, unable to make anything of it.

'Well perhaps it is these.' I took up the glasses in one movement and put them to my eyes. There was nothing at all to see, simply darkness. 'Perhaps if we train them on the map,' I said as my hand moved to adjust the focus.

There was a piercing cry from Bell and his fist came down jarringly on my wrist, causing a great stab of pain. My hand dropped away, and the glasses too but, as the focus mechanism engaged, there was a click and two eight-inch spikes of steel erupted from the lenses.

I stared at the murderous things in horror.

Bell took them now and examined them while I stood there, shaken by the narrowness of the escape. 'He is a student,' said Bell, examining the spikes and the trap. Pressing them down on the table he was able to push them back and release them again. 'Of that there is no doubt. I believe he borrowed this from a very famous case in Trieste in the 1850s. But if I am not mistaken he, or perhaps someone he employed, has improved on the original mechanism.'

He turned and remembered me. 'My dear fellow, I am sorry,' he said. 'Sit down, and I will get you some water. It is not a pretty prospect, for they would have drilled right into your brain. Death would be more instantaneous than any poison. We are certainly fortunate you were not visiting your father alone. That is probably what he hoped, for then you might have opened it without guidance on the journey home.'

Once I had recovered I sat a long time in Bell's room that day. And now indeed was the first time, since the events on the beach, that Bell and I together actually reflected on the nature of our foe and of the task ahead of us.

'We cannot even be quite sure he is in America,' said Bell. 'It is the overwhelming probability, but I will take no single clue offered by the man at face value. I am sure he would like nothing more than for you to embark on some fatuous voyage there in pursuit of him, which would quickly see you out of funds and in despair. But you were right about one thing, Doyle. He is playing a mental game and with me as well as you. If you had opened these yourself, I would of course have been brought in and found the American clue, which would certainly have goaded me unendurably after those spikes had found their mark in your skull.'

'At least, thanks to you, they did not,' I said. 'So we have frustrated him in one endeavour.' I was struggling not to dwell on the matter in which we failed to frustrate him. 'But I still find it hard to understand his intentions. I know he truly believes in his idea of evil and I know he is cruel and enjoys his murderous games with women. From them he gains power and excitement. But why is he so concerned with me?'

To my surprise my companion, who was still seated at the table, suddenly looked downcast. 'It is my belief that you pricked his vanity and he saw your discussions as a challenge. You were a friend who became, for him, an intense rival. This can happen. But I very much fear what has magnified it in his eyes, what has driven it to this length of obsession is your association with me.'

This had not occurred to me. 'Oh yes,' said the Doctor gloomily. 'We know that he observed us and was aware of my activities. He knew you would come to me and I am sure he saw my skills as a direct challenge to his. That message in the sand expressed it clearly enough. What did he say? That all our methods were useless against something, perhaps the purity of his will? And at times too, do not forget, we had the better of him. Even the fact that we finally forced an end to his activities here must have rankled. For now he is filled with a competitive loathing and you, his former friend, are right at the centre of it. In goading you, he plays with me. But we will have him, Doyle. Make no mistake. We must protect our age from this. I ask you to take my pledge seriously.'

I knew enough to take it seriously. But I still felt my old ambivalence about his method. For in the end it had not protected the one thing in the world I treasured above all others.

'How long?' I said at last.

He cocked one eyebrow as if he had been expecting the question. Then he fixed his glance upon me. 'It is, I fear, a long game. Perhaps years.'

I stood up in anger and frustration, nearly knocking

my chair to the ground as I did so. 'But how can we let
it go so long? Others will be killed. He will be there
laughing at us, exulting in his power to do so. We
must find some way to reach him sooner.'

'No,' said the Doctor. 'We work within the con-
fines of possibilities. There is no point in making wild
promises and attempting reckless strokes. The only
thing we have at our aid now, Doyle, is what he
lacks: namely patience, perseverance, dedication,
diligence, toil. In the end his own arrogance will lead
us to him or him to us. But I cannot know when that
will be and nothing must be done to prevent it.'

'Prevent it! Good God, what do you counsel? That
we sit here in armchairs deliberating until he comes
through that door with a bottle of chloroform and a
blade?'

Bell got to his feet. 'No, I am not suggesting
inaction. I counsel purpose, thought and deliberation.' He looked for a moment at the map Neill had
sent and pushed it away. 'That is a poor thing. As
perhaps he intended. I can do much better.' He went
to the corner where there was a large chest I had not
seen him use before. Inside was much correspondence, and many other papers, but he ignored these
and took out a map of America which he unfurled on
the table. I saw that already there were marks on it,
with a prominent circle around Dartmouth, Nova
Scotia.

The Doctor pointed at Dartmouth on the eastern-
most tip of Nova Scotia. 'The *May Day* docked here
some seven weeks ago,' he said. His finger moved
west along a path outlined in pencil. 'There was no
prospect of our man staying there. But he needed

time to make the journey back through Newfoundland and Quebec. His qualification was from Montreal but I believe, from everything I have been able to glean so far, which is not much, that his stamping ground is not there or Quebec but in this circle here.'

The Doctor's hand covered a broad area around Lake Michigan which included Toronto and Chicago. Then he pointed to the postmark. 'This postmark does nothing to change my mind. Nothing could be easier than to move off west for a day or so to North Dakota with the express intention of irritating and frustrating us. Of course I have said he may be bluffing, but on balance I believe this area is where we will find him. And I intend to commence my search there.'

I was amazed. 'You seriously intend to follow him there?'

'Oh no,' he shook his head impatiently. 'Of course, as I have said, he would like nothing better than to have us both disrupt our careers, spend any savings we may possess and embark on a wild goose chase which would have absolutely no result. And, Doyle, even in the enormously unlikely event that some connection was made, what would you propose then? Hand-to-hand combat? The chances are that, with the help of his friends and his knowledge of the ground, he would come out well ahead of either of us even in that eventuality. No, I propose to make what study of him I can. I have told you, perseverance is our only asset.'

I turned away, for, though I saw the logic of what he said, it did not help my mood.

The Doctor disregarded me and started to remove papers from his case, talking as he did so. 'The steamship company was relatively helpful, the Canadian and American authorities not at all. I was forcibly reminded of my observation to you, Doyle, that we are medical men, who cannot expect to find the police forces of the world at our disposal, so I have resolved to concentrate on the advantages of my profession rather than its weaknesses, and there has been one piece of luck.'

He had now unpacked most of the contents of his case, and I was amazed to see that on the table was a mass of correspondence. Bell had been as good as his word. There were letters and cables, it seemed, from hospitals, doctors, surgeons and even medical orderlies in Canada and America.

'You have found a trace of him?' I said.

'Undoubtedly,' he said.

I came forward. 'Where is he?'

He smiled at me then. 'I said a trace, Doyle. I have told you this will take time. It comes from before we knew him.'

I was disappointed but still engaged. He handed me a letter with pages of nearly indecipherable handwriting.

'A Dr Andrez who works in the hospital in Quebec was extremely helpful. It transpires Cream was run out of the town as an abortionist in 1876. He is not a wanted man, but it was made clear to him he would not be welcomed back there. It is why I believe he has moved on from Canada.'

'And will this Dr Andrez let you know if he has news of him?'

'Of course, of course,' said Bell. 'Every one of these new-found correspondents has agreed to alert me in confidence if they receive news. But I doubt it will be Dr Andrez. As I say, Thomas Neill Cream avoids Quebec now. It may be some time before he emerges. But, if he is not arrested, you can be sure of one thing, Doyle. We will see him again. Perhaps, if we are not careful, it will be when least expected.'

Of course I was impressed by the Doctor's industry, but it still seemed only a meagre consolation for the enormity of the acts we had endured.

'But would he not laugh at this,' I protested, 'when our only weapon is letters and correspondence!'

The Doctor stopped then, reflecting. 'Oh yes, undoubtedly he would laugh. That is precisely my hope. For so long as he enjoys himself he will be less guarded and I can surely gather in the end what I need.'

'And then?'

'It will depend solely on him. But I have told you I am confident.'

'I wish I could say the same,' I said. And I left him shortly afterwards.

Over the next few weeks I did not see so much of Bell, for I was still sunk in a degree of gloomy apathy. Sometimes I would wander by the docks, staring at the boats bound for the great American and Canadian ports, wondering if I would be able to stow away or work my passage. Once I even made enquiries and it was brought home to me that, while the arctic whalers were often in need of a ship's doctor, and would therefore bend the rules, all boats heading out for the New World could afford to insist that their ship's doctors were fully qualified. And of course a paid passage was out of the question.

In any case, I was not so foolish as to forget the Doctor's word of warning. A futile excursion to America would, even I had to acknowledge, be quite likely to yield no results whatsoever except for transforming me into a purposeless vagrant. Yet most evenings I took out her ribbon and touched it, renewing my vow to find justice.

After a time I made some attempt to continue my studies and carry on what routine I had. I cannot truly say that there was much lessening of the pain, but I was in a more balanced state of mind and aware now that, while I would never give up the quest for justice, I must at the same time try to get on with my life. During the year that followed I had the distraction of two further cases with the Doctor, climaxing in the extraordinary Christmas of 1879 when the Tensmuir railway disappearances were resolved. The matter concentrated my mind and acted as a diversion from my grief, yet by the start of 1880 I was again grimly aware of all the time that had elapsed since Elsbeth's death, and still we had no further news.

The Doctor naturally reminded me that he had never expected anything else. But I was finding it very hard indeed to settle down, and when a fellow student called Charles Augustus Currie asked me to take his place as a ship's doctor on an arctic whaler out of Peterhead called *The Hope*, I decided to accept.

We sailed north in the last week of February in 1880, and there was plenty of time for reflection in the extraordinary eternal day of the arctic summer. When I came back to Edinburgh in September, I knew I was in some way changed. It was not that I was reconciled, but physically I was more robust and I took pride in being able to hand my mother fifty gold pieces, knowing that at last, for the first time ever, I had made some real difference to the household accounts.

Bell had only one serious piece of news, namely that Neill Cream had been practising in London, Ontario. We had been sitting by the fire of his upstairs room and I remember jumping to my feet as soon as I heard this. 'Then we must detain him. I will go there . . .'

'There would be no purpose in it,' he said sadly. 'He has moved on. A chambermaid called Kate Gardener was asphyxiated by chloroform. Some suspicion attached to Cream, but not enough to arrest him. And so he left hurriedly.'

'When?' I asked.

'Six months ago. They have no idea where he has gone.'

I brought my hand down on his mantelpiece in despair. 'What is the use of it then? We will always hear when it is too late.'

He pointed out that we had little alternative, and in one sense we were getting closer, but I will not disguise the sheer bitterness I felt in that moment. To think of this monster moving remorselessly through North America, already having killed again and probably more than once, while we were left with nothing, was hard to bear. On the basis of this new case, Bell had in my absence applied to the authorities again, but they were just as uninterested as before. He had also proceeded to write directly to law enforcement officers in Ontario but received only bland unforthcoming replies.

And so, as before, I stared with utter frustration at the map which the Doctor had placed in a prominent position on his wall, with its carefully pencilled line marking our foe's known movements. As I stared at the outline of that great continent, what struck me again was the enormity of it all. The land was, in the end, so large. Town after town, city after city, state after state, each with hundreds and hundreds of communities.

'Yes,' said Bell, reading my thoughts. 'A man might lose himself there easily. It is the ultimate labyrinth.'

The ultimate labyrinth. I suppose these, more than any other, were the words that stayed with me. How long would it be before the beast appeared from that labyrinth to claim more lives, perhaps here, or more likely in London? For I knew quite well that Neill had come to Edinburgh from the capital and often spoke of it with interest and excitement.

It was with a heavy heart that I returned home from that reunion with the Doctor and contemplated the future. The sea voyage had made it imperative that I must now apply myself to my studies for the final examination. The prospect held little appeal, but I could hardly let my people down, and it was what Elsbeth would have wanted. Also, I knew that I would have more chance of finding justice as a doctor than as an impecunious student. And so it was I spent that last winter at university in furious study, attempting to make up all the work I had lost, and passed my Final Examination with no great distinction in the spring of 1881.

It would be nice to be able to write here that the Doctor was pleased by my results, and that we came together in muted celebration at the end of my training to make further plans in our quest for justice. But it would not be the truth.

In fact, I saw less and less of him as that last year progressed. And, looking back, I suppose it may even be that I had taken my berth on the arctic whaler to get away from him. This change of heart might seem puzzling for at first, it is true, Elsbeth's death had brought the two of us closer, and the bond stayed strong when we were active. But during most of 1880 there was almost nothing else for us to dwell on except the failure to find Cream. Inevitably, I fear, this impasse brought all of my old reservations about the Doctor and his method flooding back.

During my last term, an unspoken understanding was reached that neither he nor I would mention our unfinished business unless there was news. This meant that our meetings began to have a strained air and our final encounter as teacher and pupil took place, shortly after my graduation, when I came to his room to say farewell. By accident we met, not in his domain, but outside in the square.

The sun was going down, sending shadows on to the old flagstones, and there was a chill in the air. He clasped my hand and there was a slight twinkle in his eye, but I remember thinking somewhat sadly as I walked away how utterly unremarkable any listener would have found that conversation: just a desultory farewell between a student and a teacher. It seemed an odd and diminished climax to all that had happened between us. But I had decided that the Doctor's painstaking hunt was proving useless and that I must make my own way and wait until I had the resources to do better. Then, no matter what the cost, I would see justice.

PART FOUR: HIS HELL

THE MURDER ROOM

The weather in London in the late autumn of 1883 was of a kind I had not known before. It was dank and cold with a drifting directionless wind which could not finally penetrate the thick fog. *The Times* indeed wrote of the 'weight' of fog which enveloped the streets every day like a thick blanket of green and grey. Normally you would equate fog with stillness, but this was quite the opposite for in other respects the weather was unsettled and stormy.

Two years had elapsed since I left Edinburgh and, without giving up any of my unfinished business, I had been struggling to establish myself as a doctor on the south coast of England. My Uncle Richard, a wealthy and successful London illustrator, who I used to visit as a child, became aware of my financial difficulties and sent me several letters of intro-duction including one to the Roman Catholic Bishop of Portsmouth. This might have helped but in the end I burned it for, though I had not abandoned a religion of some kind, I could not honestly claim to be a Catholic. I was aware that this attitude had not pleased my uncle, but shortly afterwards, to my pleasure and surprise, I received another offer. A London doctor of his acquaintance called Small (who was no Catholic but a Quaker) wished to visit his sister in Egypt and wrote asking if I would be interested in taking his place at a wealthy riverside practice in Ponsonby Place near Vauxhall Bridge. It was only five weeks and I suppose most doctors would have regarded the fixture as too short to be worthwhile. But I soon calculated that the weekly salary I would earn was ten times more than I could possibly hope to make in Southsea. Moreover some friends and patients of Dr Small had agreed to lodge me at a modest rate, so almost every penny of my wage could be saved against the future.

There was no difficulty in arranging for my practice to be covered by a neighbouring doctor, fortunately one who would not poach my meagre list for he was on the point of retirement. And so it was that I found myself trudging through the London fog that damp November, little knowing the immense significance of my visit.

The house where I was billeted turned out to be a small place in a tiny street called Esher quite close to the river and not very far from the Royal Aquarium. Martin Morland, who lived there with his wife Sally and their two small children, was from Wales, where he had been brought up in the countryside. He had come to London in the 1860s to work for a publisher in Chandos Street and prospered at first, rising to become principal private secretary to the firm, but the business had done badly in the stagnation of the

1870s and he was forced to obtain a humbler post elsewhere as a senior clerk in a company that made calendars.

Morland, who was in his mid-thirties, could be moody but essentially he was kind, and welcomed my presence just as eagerly as the money it brought to his home. His wife Sally (for as soon as they saw my youth they had insisted on Christian names) had fair hair and the most exquisitely pixie-like ears I have ever seen in a woman, and the ears somehow seemed to mirror her nature. I knew that as soon as I set eyes on her, and it delighted me that she took me up as a friend who she could trust.

No doubt partly because she was married, Sally, who was some years younger than her husband, was the first woman since Elsbeth with whom I enjoyed a simple affection. The fact of her marriage made her safe, and yet, if I am absolutely honest, it also awoke an old sadness in me. After one recent mistake, I was now absolutely sure that if I were ever to pick up the pieces of my life successfully (which no doubt is what Elsbeth would have wanted), it would be with someone like Sally Morland. But she was just as unattainable as my long lost love.

Sally's nature was generous, her spirits high and much of her delight was in her children; Lucy, then starting her letters, and Will, who was three. She would pick them up like skittles and sit them on her knee and read them silly rhymes and fables till they were bursting with laughter and merriment, and all I wished was to sit quietly in the corner, hoping that nobody would notice me.

But Sally was never the kind to exclude anyone,

and soon enough she would look over her three-year-old son's shoulder at me and chide me for not joining them, and the children would reach out and call me to come. At once I would be exhorted to tell them of skeletons and prescribing and dead men's bones and all manner of doctor's lore which they seemed to find highly ridiculous as indeed, when you reflect, it certainly is.

After such times, when the little cook who helped with the meals had begun preparing the dinner, I would slip away and undertake one of my long evening walks of exploration. Most often I trudged down Romney Street and others till I reached the Thames and turned left to walk for about a mile till I came to that extraordinary maze of little ways and lanes on the north side of the Strand which reminded me of Edinburgh. I was particularly struck by Holy Well Street, a name that always gave me a secret amusement because the thoroughfare was so far from Holy and so unlike the house of the same name I had known before. It might once have been smart but now it had become a dingy place where the less reputable booksellers offered guinea sets of dubious engravings imported from Paris.

There is a story about this area of the city which seemed to me then a wonderfully pointed reflection of the feeling of those endless streets. It relates that a young man from the country found himself lost here one winter's night but took courage from the fact that he was only a few yards from the light and safety of the Strand. The boy set off with a brave heart but kept returning to the point where he had started until he was completely adrift in the stifling courts, yards and alleys without light or air until he died of exhaustion.

I thought of this often as I walked through that warren, sometimes myself fearing I would never emerge into the light. And then, just as I was giving up hope, I would make out the 'Chocolate in Spain' shop on the corner of the Strand, where the chocolate was strong and thick and came with a goblet of ice-cold water, and my heart would lift. At other times I would cross Waterloo Bridge and walk east to stare at the teeming dock-life of the city, dimly aware that London itself was working deeply on my senses. And then I would walk back the way I had come to the little house near the Vauxhall Road where Sally would greet me with a smile and an offer of tea, Martin would look up from the fire with a wave, and I would sit down and hear about the day.

Sometimes the two of them would talk of their circle, which seemed highly exotic to me for, though the family often had to struggle financially, they were on friendly terms with a number of illustrious neighbours. There was Macandrew, the marine scientist, who was well known for his inventions and marvels at the Royal Polytechnic Institution and had a house near Timber Wharf. There was Guthrie Johnstone, an obscure artist who specialised in somewhat eerie moonlit scenes. I say obscure because he never found fame, but I recall, when I was a child, my Uncle Richard once mentioned his name in a whisper as if its very syllables might contaminate me. The children also talked much of their Uncle Tim from New York who had visited the previous year with an Aladdin's cave of treasures; indeed their eyes grew wide even at the mention of this relative. And of course there were also the doctors from my practice, who often visited.

It was evident to me that Dr Small, the Quaker, must have taken up the family and introduced them to a whole series of people, though I must confess I was slightly baffled as to how he had made the connection to me. Undoubtedly the subject must have arisen at the Athenaeum, where I knew he met my Uncle Richard, but the latter was so annoyed that I had accepted what he regarded as a puny engagement, rather than the grander introduction to the Bishop, that he would not discuss the matter and showed no interest at all in my visit.

It may, I suppose, sound from these new excitements as if I had put the thought of justice behind me. It was not so. My mind returned to it every day, indeed I recall wondering, as the Morlands told me of their circle, if there was any hope I might find someone there who could help me more than Doctor Bell. Of course this was only wishful thinking, for it seems obvious to me now that I could have moved through every corner of London society for a hundred years without meeting anyone else quite like the Doctor.

Shortly after my arrival at the Morlands's, one night I had a toothache and took a draft of laudanum. I do not in my heart believe I ever used the drug to excess but I admit that, following my experiments with gelsemium as a reliever of pain, I had resorted to it on occasion.

It might have been the reason for my dream. But I am more inclined to the view that exploring those teeming streets of London had stirred something in me. For they could hardly help reminding me of the terrain *he* liked best, of the women he liked to prey on, of the desires and weaknesses he chose to manipulate. The labyrinth of streets at the back of the Strand often recalled for me their counterparts in Edinburgh, though here there was more of everything, including people, and the lanes and wynds seemed unending.

In my dream, I was walking urgently through them with a sense of expectation. I would hurry on, hoping to arrive I do not know where when suddenly I saw a familiar figure. For *he* was striding along ahead of me, his face shining in a broad luminous smile, glorying in the muck and lust and misery around him. He looked a little older, and in some ways his figure seemed almost like some evil parody of the Doctor for he held a cane too. But, unlike Bell's smart silver-top, his was a cruel-looking black rod and he did not hesitate to use it to sweep people out of his way. That was bad enough, but in the dream I had an overpowering, if indefinable, feeling that his black cane had known far more disgusting and lecherous uses. Was it a prophecy of what was about to happen? I do not know. I think the influence of the city would have acted on my memories in this way even if there had been no sequel. But it came.

Every Friday afternoon it so happened that Sally Morland's children went to visit their aunt in Turnham Green, which was then a place of many amenities with fields and gardens and lawns. Once I had done my rounds, my Friday afternoons were often free. This allowed Sally Morland and I to take excursions together, for she was as anxious as any hostess to ensure I saw the sights. And one afternoon, quite soon after I arrived, we paid a visit to the famous waxworks exhibition, then situated on Baker Street, called Madame Tussaud's.

I had first been enthralled by this display of waxworks and other oddities when I was a young boy visiting my Uncle Richard in London. Then I thought it utterly magical to come out of the London cold and the bustling streets with their hansoms and enter a great hall where you were suddenly transported by the faces and scenes of a bygone age. As a boy I spent hours staring in particular at the heroic figures of chivalry, especially the likeness of the Duke of Wellington. Sally Morland was amused to hear of this as we stood before the Duke again, but I will admit some of the magic of the illusion had faded. Now I could not help noticing that the colour of the skin, which I had once ignored, was hardly flesh-like, while the hands looked more like grey gloves than limbs. And I said as much to my guide.

'Well, Arthur,' she replied, and I had come to love the ease with which she spoke my name. 'Perhaps it is sad the Duke has lost a little of his lustre for you. When we next come I think I will get Martin to dress up in his jacket and stand here and you will recapture all the old magic.'

I told her that he would make a first-class Duke, and we walked on, soon finding ourselves in what is now, thanks to *Punch*, generally known as 'The Chamber of Horrors', but was then the 'Hall of Murderers', or sometimes, (in a phrase that reminded me at once of Dr Bell) the 'Murder Room'. Compared with the Doctor's collection of crimes, much of this was not so grisly. There were, it is true, waxworks of various executions and tortures, many dating from the origins of the exhibition in the French Revolution, and also figures of various murderers through the ages, starting with a waxwork of the Scottish cannibal Sawney Bean. Elsewhere we passed the French 'Bluebeard', Gilles de Rais, and the more local figure of Sweeney Todd, the demon barber of Fleet Street.

My companion took a lively interest in the barber and his hellish shop but I was more intrigued by the collection of ancient police papers and old newspaper reports adorning one wall. There was even a reference here to the famous Abbey Mill murderer Ian Coatley, whose 1870s exploits had impinged in a most unfortunate manner on the last case and my patient Heather Grace. This had at least reunited me with Bell but I knew rather more of the facts than were set down here, and I was moving on quickly to the report of an Irish highwayman's infamous deeds when my eye fell on a police artist's ink drawing above it.

My reaction was instantaneous. It was something about the posture, something about the hair, something almost, above all, about the room in which the figure crouched over his victim with its large red and heavy curtains. My eyes went at once to the writing beside the drawing.

Portrait of an Unknown Poisoner

On 11 November 1882, Lizzie Norton, resident of Cheapside, but employed in an establishment near the Strand, was given a lethal cordial by a gentleman who had offered her hospitality and claimed to have knowledge of chemistry and medicine. The gentleman, who was evidently a man of means, insisted she drink it and would have stayed with her, had he not been interrupted by a chance disturbance in the next room. At once he removed himself from the premises and was not seen again, while Miss Norton became violently ill. A doctor was called who pronounced Miss Norton had been poisoned with strychnine, and would certainly have perished if she had taken the full draft. Upon her recovery the fortunate young lady was able to help a police artist to complete this sketch of the man who she thought was from the colonies. Enquiries were set in train but he has not been seen again.

It was fortunate for me that my companion was still mesmerised by the waxwork of Sweeney Todd. No doubt the idea of a man who claimed children among his victims was particularly dreadful to her, and it gave me time to compose myself. I read the details again quickly, making sure I had really seen the devastating phrase 'from the colonies', and then turned away to gather my wits. Even so, as soon as she came over to me, Sally noticed the change in my mood. I tried to divert her with some foolish question or other, but she looked at me closely.

'Arthur,' she said, 'are you quite well? You are pale.'

There was little I could say at first. 'I am perfectly well,' I replied. 'It is only that I was reminded of a sad memory, that is all.'

She looked at me gravely. Fortunately I had moved

far away from the 'Portrait of an Unknown Poisoner', and behind me were some ancient newspaper reports about London riots and the violence of the mob. Even so, her eyes turned to them quickly and then back to mine. And I believe she was quick enough to understand that, whatever I had seen, I had no wish for her to share it.

'Have you been the victim of a crime, Arthur?' I know it was her innate sympathy that made her say it, and she added quickly, 'I promise I will not ask you more.'

'No,' I said, feeling I should tell her something. 'It was someone I was once close to.'

'I see,' she said. 'Well, I have said I will not ask more. Let us leave the room and go back to the generals and admirals.'

I nodded gratefully, and Sally Morland never impressed me more than she did for the rest of that day. For she contrived to ask questions and make comments that piqued my interest and attention, keeping up our spirits. And slowly, with difficulty she dragged my mind away from what I had seen. Yet all the time, too, she succeeded in showing she had not forgotten what had happened, and was strongly sympathetic.

Perhaps fortunately, then, it was not until I lay in bed that night that I was able to reflect sensibly on what I had seen. Was it possible, I now wondered, that the picture was just a coincidence? Perhaps it was, but even so I had no intention of leaving the matter there. In the light of my dream I could only feel I was being led back to Cream. And I had to seek the Doctor's opinion.

We were due to meet in any case the following week. Examination duties were taking Bell to London quite regularly at this time, and on the appointed Saturday I found him curled up in an armchair before a roaring fire in the large railway hotel he favoured. He looked a picture of health, his silver hair glowing in the firelight, his hawk-like features animated with excited interest for he was giving his attention both to a treatise on the properties of sympathetic ink and to the observation of his fellow guests.

At once he sprang up with a great smile to shake my hand, his energy as boundless as ever, and waved me into the other chair. 'You lodge with a publisher, I perceive,' he said as we sat down.

I looked at my hands and my clothes to see if there was anything that could possibly have told him this, but there was not. 'Do you know the Morlands?' I said with a little amazement, for I had mentioned the name only in passing.

'Of course not,' he said, holding up my letter to him. 'This was written from your lodgings – see how dark the ink is? It is genuine Indian ink, rubbed up perfectly black, which is difficult to get hold of but essential for publisher's drawings. I therefore deduce you sat at your host's desk to write it.'

This led us naturally enough on to the monograph he was reading until at last I started to tell him about what I had seen. I sensed his excitement growing and I had not got very far before he put up a hand to interrupt my account. 'Forgive me, Doyle,' he said, 'this is no criticism of you but I would much prefer that you do not prejudice my own judgement further until I see it at first hand for myself.' He glanced at his watch. 'Yes, there will be plenty of time to attend to our lunch afterwards. If you find me a cab, I will collect my coat.'

The day was cold and the streets were empty so the doorman found a cab without difficulty and we were on our way. Since I had suspected the Doctor might dismiss my account, I could certainly have no complaint about the attention he was paying to it. As soon as we had reached the exhibition and entered its 'Hall of Murderers', he gave a single cursory and uninterested glance at his surroundings before we moved on to the wall of papers and newspaper reports. Soon, without my prompting, he had seen the sketch and walked directly to it.

I did not look at my watch but I am fairly sure the Doctor must have stared at the drawing, and the accompanying text below it, for fully thirty minutes. Occasionally, during this time, he would walk away a few paces, reflecting, but always he would move back, studying it again with the same rapt attention.

Finally he was finished and we walked out together though I said nothing for I could see he was still deep in thought. We had our lunch back at the hotel but neither of us did any justice to the game pie and trifle that was provided. In fact we barely said a word until the meal was over.

At last he came to the point, admitting that the thing had had almost as much impact upon him as it had upon me. 'But in the end,' he said with sudden passion, 'we cannot be sure if it is chance. If not for the mention of the colonies I would certainly presume it was. For I place little value in such vague and sensational reports, and even less in the so-called doctor's diagnosis. It does not even sound like strychnine. It is just that the mention of the colonies is so suggestive. Yet even *that*, Doyle,' and he slapped his hand on the table in frustration, 'is so vague a term.'

'But I have been feeling an intimation of something for days. Before I even saw this I had a dream that he was here.'

'You are not asking me to deduce anything from that, I assume?' he said. 'London is a city that feeds the imagination as you have no doubt observed.'

'Is it not worth trying to talk to the girl?' I asked, for I knew the Doctor had some distant connections within the local force and was occasionally called for forensic advice.

Bell shook his head. 'After a year, there is little chance they will even know where she is. Of course I will try to make enquiries. But my honest advice for now would be that you assume it is coincidence. If you do not, then you will see him everywhere.' Now he turned and gave me a searching look. 'And you are not sleeping so well, I determine.'

I knew what he was thinking. The Doctor had more than once strongly expressed his disapproval when I took stimulants to alleviate the mental anguish that sometimes returned. He was wondering now if I had reverted to the habit.

'It is hardly surprising. The sight of this had an effect.'

'If you are taking something to dull it, Doyle, I counsel you to reconsider. I would hate old memories to be reignited in any fanciful way.'

I assured him my only draft had been for a toothache, and eventually we parted with a vague proposal
to reunite at some point during the rest of my stay. As
I walked back to the Morlands's, I will confess I was
slightly irritated by his final words on the subject.
There were, I thought, rather more important things
to discuss than my self-prescribing habits. And, while
I was grateful he had given the subject his attention,
surely he must know that, in asking me to ignore it,
he was recommending a course of action that was not
merely difficult but practically impossible. That
night, as I lay in bed, I noticed, for the first time, that
the street light outside my window sent a shadow on
to the ceiling above me. The longer I studied it, the
more I saw that it formed the outline of a figure,
crouched and predatory, with a black rod clutched in
one arm. It was some time before I slept.

The Den at Reheboth Chapel

On the Sunday following my meeting with Bell, the Morland family had arranged for me to come with them to visit the scientist Colin Macandrew. His place was only a short distance away, but there was a world of difference between their little street and his off the Grosvenor Road which was broad and light with painted doors and elegant stonework. These houses, moreover, had backs which looked directly on to the river and the Morland children, who had been many times before, were in a fair state of excitement even before we rapped on the gleaming silver knocker. I had had enough of grand houses to last me a little while, so I was pleasantly surprised when Macandrew himself answered, explaining that his manservant was indisposed. He proved to be a youthful enthusiastic man with a ruddy face and long red hair who shook me firmly by the hand as soon as we were inside. Then he ushered the delighted children directly to where they longed to go, namely the maritime laboratory in his basement.

This sounded so grand that I fully expected to see a huge flooded tank with a diving bell just as I knew Macandrew had demonstrated in the Royal Polytechnic exhibition. In the event the place was more modest, but there was a small tank with subaqueous plants and fish which the children loved to observe. Beyond it stood a dissecting table, two large basins with running water and some other intriguing items of scientific equipment including a microscope which magnified the tiniest marine creatures into huge monsters.

Macandrew presided over these with a manic energy, sometimes giggling at the children's endless questions and pushing his hand through his hair. 'These are the toys,' he cried. 'And toys should be played with. Ah Will,' he said, ruffling the little boy's hair. 'People say a boy should not pull the wings off flies. Quite right. He should pull the heads and legs off as well for then he will be called an anatomist, and soon the school will be putting up a plaque in his honour!' And he laughed heartily.

Of course Will had no idea what he was talking about but laughed too, and the demonstration continued. At one point, while Sally was lingering by the tank with her children, I asked Macandrew with interest about the dissecting table and the man leaned against it, drumming his long fingers on it as he talked.

'Oh,' he said in answer to my question. 'I am a toiler. One recent area I have been exploring is the exact nature of the human lungs during and after drowning. It is my conviction that the doctors could learn far more from the other sciences than they do. What is the human body but a machine? If we could better understand the lung's susceptibility to water there might even be a way of strengthening them.'

'You could hardly make us amphibious?' said Martin, joining us.

'Yet once we may have been.' Macandrew raised his hand as if to begin a lecture on evolution but then seemed to think better of it. 'No, my hope was that there might be a way of delaying the effect of drowning. It became quite an obsession, but so far it is a forlorn one. Another was the state of the body after heart failure. Again, the heart is just a pump, sometimes not a very efficient one. Is there no way of improving it?'

'But surely that is not your main work?' I asked.

'Oh no, it is a sideline, Dr Doyle.' He turned to me, studying my features. 'You must have a special hobby in your medical practice. What is it? Let me guess? The facial muscles? Perhaps blood temperature?'

I felt more foolish than anything for I had no real answer. 'I have done some study of the eye but I am only just starting out. Tell me, did you not make the diving bell?' I was keen to get the subject away from me.

'Oh yes,' he said, 'I study all aspects of oceanography, and I helped to design the diving bell among other things.'

At this point the children came running over. 'The tunnel! The tunnel!' they chanted.

Macandrew picked up Will with a genial air. 'Well, I can hardly refuse so strident a request, and I have made preparations,' he said, handing the boy back to his mother and leading us over to a door on the other side of the room.

We all followed expectantly as the door opened on to a stone staircase with a black railing beside it which went down to a sub-basement level. The workshop had been lit by gas, but below us there was dim light from what I took to be carbon filaments, and somewhere I could hear the hum of a motor.

'Macandrew was at the Munich exhibition of electricity this year,' said Martin. 'He knows a deal about it.'

'Be careful now,' said Macandrew, 'for sometimes the stairs get a little wet.' We proceeded slowly down, with Sally keeping a close hand on both her children. The electrical illumination did not flicker as a candle would but nor was it very bright, casting a suffused and rather ugly red glow on us as we descended.

Soon we were in a damp stone corridor which led south, though as the children had said it was more like a tunnel than anything else. The air was a little stuffy and I noticed a puddle of water beside one door, but we walked on past it for several yards until we had to crouch low, and finally the space came to an abrupt end with a single light hung dimly above us. Ahead was a small square of wood, but otherwise nothing.

'Well, where are we?' said Macandrew to the children as we stood there in that damp space.

'We are under the river,' they said with whispered awe.

'Quite right,' said Macandrew, 'and to prove it . . .' He turned and removed the wooden lid from the wall ahead and I could see a tap with a wooden mug beside it. He turned this and water came spilling out, which Macandrew used to fill the mug, raising it to his lips. 'I always toast my guests in the water of the river.'

Soon it was my turn and I wet my lips in the liquid which was not particularly appetising but not foul either. Evidently Macandrew was able to purify it for I did not like to imagine how such a draft might taste otherwise, containing as it would all manner of noxious things. But there was something strange in knowing the river was above this space, and I hardly wondered the air was a little dank.

On the way back another wonder was in store, for Macandrew opened the waterproof portholed door we had passed earlier which led to a small chamber. All I could see inside was some kind of closed vent on the floor and a large opening in the wall. The children, who knew it well, were again full of excitement. 'This is the flood chamber,' he told me, pointing to a large wheel in the wall outside. 'If you open the vent, it fills with water in twenty minutes or so. I test models of much of the equipment here and sometimes the apparatus itself.' As soon as we were outside, and the door was sealed, Macandrew turned the wheel and, for just a few seconds, water flooded into the small space. Then he pulled a handle and much to the children's glee it drained away.

Once we were upstairs again, the children rushed over to look at the magnifying apparatus. While they squealed and laughed and took turns with their parents, Macandrew questioned me about my training and experience. 'I am sure Edinburgh is all very well in its way,' he said. 'But of course the larger teaching hospitals here see a far greater variety of patients, meaning their experience is unrivalled. In the end we cannot escape the fact that London is the empire's heart. The rest are all outposts.'

It was not a point I had much interest in contesting, especially with a man who had evidently studied biology and engineering rather than medicine. But I could see quite well now that, behind his easy manner, Macandrew was intensely competitive, and I also had to recognise, though it was not very enjoyable to do so, that here was the reason why a man, only a few years my senior, had reached a position of some eminence while I was a struggling junior doctor.

Of course, I was careful not to let the Morlands sense I had any reservations about the visit, and that evening I talked animatedly to Sally about all we had seen. She was not, I had already noticed, as enthusiastic about Macandrew as Martin but I was surprised now to notice a slight anxiousness in her. She kept looking worriedly at her husband, who sat staring gloomily into the fire. I was well aware that he sometimes found work a burden, so I could only conclude he was dreading another week making calendars. Feeling that I was in the way, I thanked them for the outing and retired to bed. But, even as I said goodnight, Martin barely stirred from where he sat.

The start of the following week was, for me, very busy, too busy even to spend much time dwelling on the matter of the sketch in the 'Hall of Murderers'. One of the partners in the medical practice had sprained an ankle getting out of a cab, while another was suffering from a chest cold. Consequently there was more work for all of us and it was not until Wednesday, when another doctor had agreed to cover some of our patients, that things became a little easier. Even so I did not return to the Morlands till well after nine that evening, having sent word that I had already dined, though in truth I had only managed to take something from a pastry cook's stall I passed while out on my calls.

I had seen little of the Morlands all week and was looking forward to their company as I took off my coat, so I was, I must confess, a little surprised when the cook appeared to inform me with a slight air of agitation that Mr Morland was not at home. I went straight to the drawing room at once. Sally stood at the fireplace with her back to me.

'Well, I am sorry to be such an absent guest . . .' I began as cheerfully as I could, for I was remembering the low spirits of the previous Sunday night, when she turned and I saw to my astonishment that she was crying.

The sight was so heart-rending that my words died away and I took a pace towards her. But she put up a hand to stop me.

'Of course,' I said. 'I am sorry to intrude, I will go.'

'No,' she said, and her voice was unsure but she had contained her tears. 'Please, the truth is, Arthur, I have been waiting for you.'

At this I did come forward to face her. It was strange to stand so close to her and she did not look away, though the sadness in her was all too apparent. Of course it brought back memories and I reflected

that, though I had been mistaken about someone else
not so long before, in Sally there could be no mistake.
Her lack of guile, her instinctive kindness were there
so visibly before your eyes.

'You know I would do anything to help you,' I said.
Since there was not and never could be the slightest
impropriety in my relationship with Sally, I saw no
reason to conceal the fact that I admired her.

She nodded and looked down. 'I am asking a favour
of you, Arthur, and I am not sure I could ask it of
anyone else in the world other than my husband,
whom it concerns.'

I waited. I could see her lips tremble as she
summoned up the courage to tell me.

'I have not seen him since yesterday morning.'

I was amazed and almost exclaimed aloud, but
fortunately realised in time how little help that
would be. 'And you have no idea?' I said as
unemphatically as I could.

'Why, I have every idea,' she cried. 'You think
otherwise I could have borne it? But to go to the
police is only to get him into further trouble. And I
would never be admitted without . . .' She was
wringing her hands so tightly I thought the finger-
nails would pierce the skin. I led her to a chair and
made her sit down.

'Sally, we will get him back. You must just tell me
where to go.'

Now I saw the hope in her eyes. 'You must not
blame him, he has had such worries. We had hoped,
but . . .' The tears welled up but she collected herself
again. 'Sometimes when he is so cast down and can
see no way out, when he is in a black mood, he wishes

only to escape in this way. Once before he was there a whole night, but never two. I cannot bear to wait and worry about what might happen to him.'

It was not easy, but gradually I had the story. Sally Morland was sure that her husband was in an opium den in the dockland south of the river and, though she could not name it, she believed she could describe its precise location. It was in a small alley not far from the long and rather forbidding street known as Shad Thames, an area, one social reformer described as 'the most out-of-the-world and low-lived corner of London', that was mainly notable for its warehouses and its crime. The alley was almost at the eastern extremity of Shad Thames, near Gainsford Street. Fortunately she had made Martin tell her this after the first occasion, precisely because she dreaded it might happen again. But now, after hours and hours of waiting, poor Sally Morland hardly knew which was more unendurable: the fear that her husband was still there, and had been for a night and a day, or that something even worse had befallen him.

At first she was utterly determined to come with me and, for all my protests, I believe she would have insisted, except that upstairs Will woke up from a dream and cried out for his mother. Here was my opportunity: I told her she must go to her son and meanwhile promised her faithfully I would set out to try to find Martin in the place she described.

I took a hansom across the river, discharged the driver near Curlew Street, which was more respectable, and then walked without any problems a little way up to the warehouses of Shad Thames. I had been told the place I sought lay well past Butler's

Wharf towards Landell's Wharf and that the alley lay between a shop and a tavern called the Lord Lovat. As I moved further east I had two frights, the first when three men came out of a slop house and stopped, staring at me and whispering among themselves, obviously debating whether to come after me. I doubled my pace.

But there was worse to come on Shad Thames itself. I was walking in the darkest part of the road between two gas lamps when suddenly a shape reared up from a doorway to my right and a hand clamped my arm. The old man had a crutch but his hand gripped like a vice. 'You have pennies for me, sir,' he muttered.

I was fumbling for a coin but his grip only tightened. There was a movement behind him and suddenly I saw other shapes as the glimpse of a blade flashed in the dismal light. My fear gave me strength and I managed to snatch back my arm and I ran. Fortunately nobody followed.

At last I reached the ale house, which was doing noisy business, and a few people sat drunkenly on the corner beside it. A sign on the side of the tavern pointed up the alley and read, 'Reheboth Chapel'. To this day I have never discovered exactly where or what the chapel was and sometimes wonder if it ever existed, except as a false reassurance of virtue in such a dismal place.

The alley was short but also very narrow, and soon I recognised the steps Sally had described, leading down under the light of a flickering oil lamp to a strange little maze of a building. Of course there was no sign. Years later when I used the den in a story, I called it the Bar of Gold but this was a romance for it was hardly the kind of establishment that boasted a proper title. The sailors and everyone else referred to it as 'Ah Sing's' or 'Sing's', after a Chinese who had started it, but nobody of that name was connected to it now.

I ventured down the steps and, through the half-open door, into the darkness and silence. I was trying to take some comfort from Sally's insistence that gentlemen from the more fashionable regions of the city had been known to make the pilgrimage here for a pipe. But in truth it was not easy to imagine, for the interior now was absolutely pitch black.

I called out with no result. Was there no one here at all? Then I heard a noise and a light became visible somewhere below me, an oil lamp which threw my own flickering shadow on the exposed wood and plaster behind me. I could hear the slosh of water from somewhere below and supposed there must be a way down to the river at the bottom of the place.

A figure shuffled up a flight of stairs. The lamp drew closer, at last reaching my level, and I glimpsed the face above it.

Of course I expected the face to be foreign, even Oriental, for Sally had indicated as much, but it was English and belonged to a small lean woman in a cotton gown which hung awkwardly over her sharp shoulders. Her skin was pale and tightly drawn.

'You come for pipe, sir, you can,' she said. 'But my man isna here, he back soon.' She spoke with an accent I have never heard before or since, an odd mixture of cockney and Chinese, for it turned out her husband was the Oriental and she had spent years in the East.

I took out some money and her eyes fairly gleamed. 'I do not wish a pipe,' I said, handing her a coin, 'but I am in search of a friend who may be here.'

She took the coin eagerly. 'A sailor, sir?'

'No, a gentleman. English.' She was about to shake her head but I caught just a glimpse of something else in her eyes and at once I felt a flash of hope. Of course they would hardly wish to lose a good customer so easily. Quickly I gave her another coin. 'Please, it is very important. You will get a little more if I find him.'

I could see at once that I had been right for she fingered the coin and deliberated.

'Business very bad. Few ships come, but we had a party of gentlemen last night, sir. All have left but one. And he is wanting another pipe soon. That is money in the bank for us.'

'Show me,' I said, taking out the largest coin I dared and holding it up.

That was enough. She led me along the dark, dusty passage, bearing her lamp high, until we ascended a few steps at the end of the corridor. Below I heard again a splash of water and saw another corridor running off to the right. I was only just starting to have some idea what a warren the place was as she opened a door.

The stench assaulted me at once. The fumes that wafted out of the room smelt like treacle melted with glue over an open fire and then flavoured with singeing horse hair. The one source of light was a glowing fire, but the woman held up the lamp and soon I was able to make out the interior. It was only about fourteen feet long and not much wider. There was a small table and three chairs, a few gaudy prints on the walls and a mantelshelf of Chinese ornaments.

But these were mere details for the only thing that really struck you was the bed. This was so large that there was but a yard or so of space between it and the fireplace, and it was covered not by a counterpane but by a huge breadth of fine Chinese matting with a long bolster, making enough room for three people to lie on it in a kind of horrible comfort.

That was the number before me now. The nearest was certainly foreign with thick matted hair, but his face was turned away so I could not make out much of him except that I felt sure he was a seaman. Past him lay a pale figure, tossing even as I watched, and as he showed his face to me I saw it was Martin, his eyes starting to blink in the light.

At once I turned to the woman. 'This is the man. Give me the light, I will wake him and we will be gone.' I was already beginning to appreciate my luck in dealing with her, rather than her husband, and had no wish to wait for the man's return. She started to protest but I handed her the coin and took the light and she muttered something and scuttled out.

Quickly I brought the light so it shone full into Martin Morland's face. 'Martin,' I called. 'Martin, we must go from here.'

He blinked more and stared. Now I saw he was covered in perspiration and he seemed frightened of me. 'Who's there?' he muttered, obviously imagining he was in a dream.

'It is Arthur. Arthur Doyle. I have come to take you home.'

'Arthur?' he said in wonder, and I could see he was

coming awake. I seized my advantage and put the
light down on the table, placing my hand under his
and urging him to get up. He took a few moments but
then he seemed to understand and started to do so,
rubbing his eyes as he looked at me.

'Is it very late?' he muttered. 'Is Sally worried?'

'It is not merely late,' I said. 'You have been here a
day and a night. It is Wednesday.'

I could see a wave of fear wash over him at that. He
was properly awake, but now I could hear something
on the floor below us. Steps. 'Come, man, we must go
now,' I whispered. 'This moment.'

Fortunately the other, nearest, sleeper was still
utterly stupefied as Morland staggered to his feet.
'Wednesday? How can it be Wednesday? I had taken
some ale with a few people I met, we decided to
come here. Oh, Arthur, for God's sake tell me it is not
Wednesday.'

'We will have time to discuss it, but now we must
go.' And I took him by the hand and pulled him to the
door.

We opened it and, fortunately as it turned out,
found ourselves in total darkness. I had quite forgotten to take the light but there was no time for it
now. I heard a voice somewhere below, a thick
guttural voice raised in anger and another voice, the
woman's, protesting.

'Follow me,' I said, gripping Morland's hand and
moving as quietly as I could down the few steps. To
my great relief the conversation came not from this
level but down the stairs from where the woman had
first appeared. I knew the light would have attracted
attention at once and was glad to be rid of it. Our only

hope now was to get out without being heard.

Gripping his hand with my left and using my right to grope my way back in the direction of the door, we made a little progress. I remembered the corridor was straight, and some way ahead I could make out shards of light which I took to come from the doorway to the steps leading up to the alley. Below me somewhere I heard the sound of coins flung down and suddenly there were voices again, only louder. The first was the man's I had heard before, and now I realised it was Oriental. 'Why we only waited for him to take a few pipes more. Why did you not call me?'

The woman's came back shrill, but she was interrupted by a new voice, one I liked even less. It was hardly more than a whisper with a touch of the West Country, yet there was a power about it. 'Come, the box is warm. And two's good.'

Then I heard footsteps on the stairs.

There was no time to grope our way now – I was sure I could make out the light of the alley ahead. I pulled Morland along behind me even as I saw someone carrying a lamp coming rapidly up the staircase. In itself that told me where the door was and I reached it, pulled it open and faced the steps. 'Now run,' I said.

I held on to him as fast as I could as we stumbled up those steps. Morland nearly fell twice and I could hear him gasping. Thank heaven they were not so steep and we reached the top, but there was shouting behind and I felt no safer.

I pulled him on down the alley and soon we were by the Lord Lovat. Fortunately there was light and quite a number of people were milling about here.

Some were seamen but there was also a group of workers from the warehouses, who must have just come off their shift, and who looked at us curiously. I was glad of their curiosity for I doubted even our charming hosts at Sing's would take on both of us in full view of all of them. So I risked a glance back.

Sure enough two men stood in the alley, having mounted the top of the steps that led up from the den. They stared in our direction but did not look as though they meant to follow. One was Chinese with a pigtail, old but strong. The other, no doubt the owner of the West Country voice, unnerved me more. He was a large man, with big limbs, and yet his face was small, active and intelligent in a way that reminded me of a gargoyle on a church I had once visited in Southsea. And now that face was staring directly at me, not with menace, which I might have preferred, but with a small smile, the smile of a man who pats you on the back and sticks a blade between your shoulders. As I watched, he said something and turned away and I saw a mark on his neck which was long, red and ugly, a rope burn presumably for I had seen similar marks among sailors. And then the two of them went back down the steps.

Morland and I did not take a hansom. Finding one might have proved difficult in any case, but I judged that he would be far better to walk. We kept to the main thoroughfares, finally reaching London Bridge and starting to trudge back along Upper Thames Street. I could only thank heaven for my timing. If I had arrived when he had just taken a pipe, I could never have got him home without help. But, as it was, the exercise quickly returned blood to his cheeks and energy to his limbs and by the time we had travelled less than a half a mile he was walking well and talking like himself.

It transpired he had got himself in debt, had been forced to accept charitable loans from some philanthropic society and now found himself unable to repay them. Sometimes, he told me as we walked, when he thought of the happiness of his early marriage and the worry he was inflicting on his wife, he found the burden of guilt unendurable. It was at such times that he had recourse to drink and on rare occasions to the pipe. But he insisted that he would never have gone back to the den if he had not already been intoxicated and in the wrong company.

It was hardly my place to lecture him. I could understand his emotions all too well, so I merely observed that I thought Sally was better able to bear the difficulty of debt than she was to bear the agony of his absence. He agreed with this and even shook my hand vigorously, for his strength was fully returning. 'I am so grateful, Doyle. I long to be home.'

To keep up our spirits on that long tramp I turned the talk to other matters, notably London, for Morland never tired of the subject. And it emerged he had a fund of stories about the den and its customers. 'I will never go back there,' he swore, 'but I tell you, Doyle, there is a whole folklore to that dockside and you would be amazed by some of the things I have heard.'

'But they are the fantasies of the pipe, I take it?'

'Oh, I do not mean merely from the opium smokers, but others. Some of it is very strange.'

Of course I told him I was interested in such things

and asked him to continue. Many of the tales he recounted were familiar: sea serpents and ghostly ships. But one was not and it certainly intrigued me.

'There is talk,' Morland said, 'of a man down the docks, who keeps something quite horrible which gives him power. A head that has been severed.'

I nodded. 'Shrunken heads are not unheard of.'

'No, not shrunken,' said Morland vehemently. 'I thought so at first, but it is nothing like that. The thing is said to be large and it is alive. Some talk of it as a female head.'

This was certainly something different from the usual legends, and he was very animated.

'But there is more,' he went on. 'The mouth has a sting in it. That is always repeated. But one touch and its victims may live for ever.'

It was an odd tale. 'The idea of living on after death?' I said. 'Perhaps these stories come from the Penny Dreadfuls. *Varney the Vampire* and such like. In those, corpses are revived and live.'

'I do not think it is the same,' said Morland. 'It may well be folly, but it is frightening, for I have spoken to people who genuinely believe in the thing. One woman said she had seen it but absolutely refused to talk about it.'

There the conversation ended, for, as we reached Vauxhall Bridge we were suddenly interrupted by a flare going up from the river. Drawing closer, we could see there was some alarm on the far shore where it appeared a boat had got into difficulties. Several police craft were there and Martin was so restored that it was all I could do to restrain him from swimming over to help. It must, I reflected, have been this impetuousness that caused him some of his troubles, yet it was a likeable enough quality.

Finally we reached his house and Sally was overjoyed to see us, behaving quite as if we were indeed rescuing heroes of the river rather than fugitives from a criminal drug den. She hugged him for minutes and then gave me a sisterly hug too. 'I will never forget what you have done for us, Arthur. Never.' And it was time for me to leave them.

When I reached my bed at last that night, I noticed with pleasure that the shadow on my wall had become just a shadow. And I found myself reflecting on the strange events of the day. Of course they had made a deep and lasting impression, and I suppose my apprehension of London around this time inspired some of the images and episodes later employed in my stories. Yet it is certainly not the case that the stories were ever transcribed facts; the truth was quite the opposite. The Bar of Gold opium den in 'The Man with the Twisted Lip' bears only the smallest resemblance to Sing's. Sometimes it is true (as in 'The Speckled Band' and 'The Copper Beeches') that I played with some facts and characters from cases I had known; 'The Final Problem' was certainly intimately personal, but in other respects they were always essentially fiction.

That was one reason why, even from the beginning of my fictional detective's fame, I never thought it necessary to deny the role Dr Bell had played and indeed made a public point of acknowledging my debt. What *was* held back, quite ruthlessly, was all the detail – much of it so sensitive and personal – of the matters we investigated and of our association. As I slept peacefully in the Morlands's small guest bedroom that night, I had no idea of how brutally that association was about to be tested.

The Body of Harriet Lowther

I did not see Morland the following morning. He had left the house before I came down, and the children were playing upstairs. Sally Morland therefore sat alone at the breakfast table and, though she was composed, some of the elation I had witnessed the night before had gone. She smiled and bid me good morning, but her hand was twisted tightly around the handle of her teacup.

She was quick enough to register my look. 'Yes, I am being glum again, Arthur,' she said. 'What is it about we poor humans that after one prayer is granted, another rushes to fill its place. I am glad Martin is not like me – he was humming a tune as he set off for work.'

'I am glad to hear it,' I said. 'But what is your new prayer?'

She smiled and took a sip of tea as I started to eat. It was a fine morning and the sun shone prettily on the table, but the dappled light served only to underline the worry I saw in her face.

'It is what he told you. The money he owes. We have applied to the League, that is the charity that has assisted us – the League of Hope and Sorrow – to defray it. How I so wish we had the means to settle!'

'But surely they will take every care to help in such circumstances,' I said. 'Thank heaven you are dealing with a philanthropic society and not a usurer. It might take time, you might have to rein in, but at least you need fear no worse than that.'

Her face brightened at this. 'Yes, you are right,' she said, bobbing her head up as her spirits visibly lifted. 'I must be tired after last night.' She looked across at me passionately. 'He promised me he would never return there, and this time it was quite different from before. I believe him and I resolve to spend no more time moping, Dr Doyle.' And she went off to her children.

The day at the practice began normally enough until the police sent word that they needed extra medical help at a riverside morgue near St Saviours in connection with the river accident that Morland and I had witnessed the previous night.

It was not a long walk to this large and somewhat dingy grey building of two storeys. I was accompanied by Dr Baird, the senior partner who had been delegated to oversee my work. Baird, with his eyeglasses and whiskers, was a slightly pompous practitioner of the old school and he chatted amiably as we went along, though clouds were gathering and the early sunshine had quite disappeared. Evidently he had heard from Dr Small in Egypt and had written back to him, commenting favourably on my presence at the practice. This pleased me, for there was every chance I would need the good word of these people if I ever sought to join a large practice in the future.

'Who was it recommended you for the locum, a friend of the Morlands, is that right?' Baird was saying.

Slightly taken aback, and wondering why my Uncle Richard should be so reticent about his hand in the matter, I told him I did not know the Morlands before and it was my uncle, Dr Small's fellow member of the Athenaeum. But I saw he was hardly listening, for by then we had entered the building.

It was dark, and smelt of soap, and our footsteps clattered on the flagstones as we came to a little room where a rather lugubrious clerk with red cheeks made a note in a great register of everybody that was admitted. We were of course anxious to help any victims who had survived the tragedy. But he raised his eyebrows and I saw at once there had been some error. He pointed out of his window to the opposite shore.

'I believe,' he said, sucking his cheeks, 'that they have all the medical help they require.'

Naturally, Dr Baird became rather indignant, and the clerk eventually recalled that a general alert had been sent out earlier to nearby practices which had then been countermanded.

'I am very sorry you have been inconvenienced, doctors, but I will make enquiries just in case I am in the wrong.' And he made a careful note of our names and left the room.

Dr Baird continued to look annoyed. 'We should charge them for our time, Doyle,' he said. 'It is not as if they can just summon us hither and thither like errand boys.'

After only a few minutes, a more senior policeman in plain clothes entered, introducing himself as Inspector Miller. He was a quiet, stocky man, but when he spoke he looked you straight in the eye.

'Pardon me, doctors, we are very sorry indeed about this mistake,' he said. 'We will not detain you both any longer, but since you are here I wonder if you, Dr Doyle, sir, could help us with a minor matter that demands medical advice? Would you spare him, Dr Baird?'

'But why?' said my colleague, rather irritated. 'You are aware Dr Doyle is our locum?'

'Ah and this is very trivial. Which is why we would not want to take up any more of your time, Dr Baird.'

Baird was still not entirely satisfied. 'Very well, but we have our patients to consider and it has proved rather inconvenient to come over here on a fool's errand. I suppose there has been some injury to a member of the force?'

'Yes, it is nothing,' said Miller. 'One of the constables who was assisting in the rescue has done some mischief to his knee, and as you know, our usual men are all busy. You may certainly submit a bill, and I offer you our humble apologies for the incon-venience we have caused you. We always make a point of recommending your practice.'

Baird was better pleased by this and could afford to be magnanimous. 'Ah, no, we like to help where we can. Are you sure you do not wish me to look at it?'

I could have sworn that a look of genuine anxiety passed over Miller's face, but he covered well and Baird did not seem to notice. 'No, no,' he said. 'We would not wish to hold up a senior doctor for any longer. I could not hear of it.'

He was fortunate, for it was nearly one o'clock and I knew Baird liked his lunch. 'Very well,' said Baird, 'Doyle will assist you, and the knowledge that you recommend our practice to the public is quite enough remuneration. Keep Doyle as long as you like until your own man returns.'

He said goodbye to me and left us as the policeman led me out of the room and up a winding staircase. We walked down a stone corridor and he pointed to a door at the end. 'If you go through there, sir. You are awaited.' And rather to my surprise he left me.

I opened the door expecting, I suppose, to find myself in some cheerful office where a burly constable would have his foot resting on a chair. Instead I was in near darkness. As the air was slightly damp and I stood on stone, I was fairly sure I was in one of the building's windowless central mortuaries. Slowly my eyes became accustomed to the gloomy light. There was a lamp to my right, and I turned towards it.

Soon I made out what it was illuminating: the half-covered body of a woman on a large stone slab. She had lustrous dark hair but her teeth were set in an expression of pain and she lay very rigid indeed. I could not understand why I had been directed here, but I supposed the constable was waiting somewhere for me. So I moved nearer to the lamp and peered down at the body.

'An odd sight, is she not?'

I whirled round.

Bell was sitting on a bench in an alcove, half in shadow, staring at me. I had not seen him before because the alcove was flanked by great stone pillars. In the shadowy lamplight his face looked like a death's head.

'Doctor?' I said. 'But where is the injured policeman?'

'Oh there is none, but I am helping the chief pathologist here, an old colleague who has asked my advice with what you see before you. It has some notable features and it occurred to me you might be of assistance, hence the imaginary summons. Her name is Harriet Lowther and she was found in her rooms yesterday. There were some signs of violence in the place, but not a trace of it on her. Unless you count this.' He pointed to a patch of redness around her fingers. I raised my eyebrows for the skin was not even broken. 'Yes,' he said, acknowledging my scepticism, 'and otherwise you will find not a mark. So there is much to consider.' And he moved forward in that way I knew so well and peered down intently at the corpse.

'There will be an autopsy?'

'Certainly,' he said as he stared into the left eye. 'And I feel sure that heart failure will be their final conclusion.' He straightened up with a smile. 'Now I see no harm in our imaginary constable being a little more hurt than you had expected. We have to return to Miss Lowther's lodgings and I would be very glad if you would accompany me.'

I was perfectly happy with this subterfuge for I too was supposed to have a lunch hour, and soon we were rattling through the dull but busy morning streets in a hansom to an address on the other side of the river, indeed part of the journey took us east in the same direction I had walked the night before. But, on reaching the docks, we turned not towards Shad Thames but into the more respectable area of Queen Elizabeth Street, where there were small dwelling houses. At one of these a policeman waited, and he greeted us as we got down.

We were led inside a clean hallway and up a narrow flight of stairs to Miss Lowther's quarters. The Doctor thanked the man and he tactfully withdrew. I looked around me but there was not a great deal to see in that modest room, which was evidently like scores of others rented out to those who made a living from the dockside. Bell picked his way desultorily over a carpet past a stove. The window was small and, the day being what it was, he soon enlisted a tiny and badly trimmed oil lamp to give us more light.

The place had been left as it was found. In the flickering illumination of the lamp I stared at an overturned chair, a broken cup, and the space on the carpet where Harriet Lowther's body had fallen. It seemed she made her living by cooking pies and selling them round the local dockland streets, where she and her filled basket were well known.

Bell stood staring a long time at the spot where she died and then, as if remembering himself, told me the circumstances. 'It seems, Doyle, that the woman was in financial difficulties because of her precarious employment.' He spoke slowly as if assessing each fact anew. 'She returned to this room unexpectedly with her basket at around three yesterday. The lodger downstairs, a ship's carpenter, was just going out and noticed the victim was a little flustered. She told him someone was coming to show her something, but seemed mysterious. Later another tenant, an old woman who lives above here, heard footsteps on the stairs and then voices. There was some noise, including the sound of the chair falling, but it was not followed by anything and nobody bothered to come and look. The body was eventually found by the landlord yesterday evening when he arrived to collect her rent. It seems there had been a struggle, but the rent money was untouched and she had been dead some hours, almost certainly from the time the visitor was here.'

I stared at the place where the body was found, but Bell now showed more interest in a curious mark on the carpet a few feet away. It looked like something had rested here, a table perhaps. 'Could she have quarrelled with someone who threatened her,' I ventured, 'and then suffered some excitation of the heart which killed her? In such circumstances the attacker might well run off.'

'Quarrelled? But what about? Certainly not money for none was taken. Moreover the marks you saw on her were recent, but I cannot imagine they were the work of an assailant. Accidental perhaps, but odd, even so. Another point. Perhaps strangest of all. The room was very cold, the fire out, yet she was warm to the touch.'

This was curious and there seemed nothing in the room whatsoever to explain it. The Doctor stood there musing for several minutes.

'There is something else,' he said at last. 'A

curiosity. The docks here breed all kinds of legends, as you know. There are tales of priceless treasure buried out near Blackwell Point, of a sacred monkey on a ship encrusted with fabulous jewels, of fruit brought from the East that will destroy your mind with a single bite. But there is one that is very odd and evidently Harriet Lowther took an interest in it. The story tells of a sailor from the West Indies who has a severed head, some say human, some say a giant animal, of horrifying power. The thing is disgustingly ugly and its mouth stings, yet the story goes that, beyond the pain and horror, to some it gives immortal life.'

I exclaimed aloud. 'I have heard it.'

'Yes,' said Bell. 'It is pervasive, but as with all these stories you can never find out a proper source. The odd thing is that Harriet Lowther became particularly exercised about it in the last few days of her life. She was excited about this severed head, talking of it to many people. A few even believed she might have some idea where the thing was.'

'You do not take that seriously?' I asked.

'I take everything seriously, as you know,' said the Doctor. 'It is certainly curious, not that it seems to lead anywhere. Now we must go through all that is here.'

The two of us went through all the belongings in that room but found no object that would enlighten us. The rent money had been carefully placed to one side, her savings were untouched. Without motive, means or even the absolute certainty that any crime had been committed, it seemed to me more and more hopeless to expect a solution.

A small bag lay at the back of a drawer which seemed to contain her best things. This was of good quality, which suggested it was reserved for special occasions, and without much hope I looked through it. There was almost nothing inside: a comb, a handkerchief, and a little card which I took out. On it was printed, in firm respectable letters:

THE LEAGUE OF HOPE AND SORROW

'The League!' I exclaimed, for the words triggered a memory as I turned the card over and read the back.

Charitable loans and services provided in confidence to those who are in need.

The Doctor was beside me in a moment. 'What is it?' he asked.

'I believe I have heard of it. It is a philanthropical society which arranges loans for those who are in need of them. The Morlands have taken their charity.'

Bell took the card and stared at it. 'There is an address here, but only a forwarding agent by the look of it. Well, perhaps it is worth further study. Your Morlands may help us to decide.'

Soon after that we left and, as we made our way back along the street, I had of necessity to explain to the Doctor that the matter of Morlands's debt was a sensitive one. I went on to describe my adventure in the opium den and how I had found him there. In some respects this was breaking a confidence, but I was sure it was the best course, for I had always trusted Bell implicitly in such matters.

The Doctor showed a very lively interest in my story, asking all manner of questions. He insisted on hearing everything else I had seen and heard. And then, with typical impetuosity, he declared that he would like to walk up to Shad Thames and see the alley for himself. In daylight it seemed we could hardly be in danger, and so we made our way north, turned up that forbidding street and soon stood before the Lord Lovat.

There was not much to see, the tavern was doing only modest business and the alley had not a soul in it. At my insistence we went only a short way along but Bell stared with enormous interest at the steps and the den itself. At any moment I dreaded to see one of the two figures I had glimpsed the previous evening, and I was glad when he turned away.

Bell was thoughtful on the journey home. 'Geography,' he said at last, 'has never been a major interest of mine, Doyle, as you once deduced from my library. But even so I have always wanted to write a treatise on its connection to crime. I am convinced it is not a fanciful subject. What is it that makes some places indefinable in their darkness? Would we feel the same thing on a mountain where many explorers had died? Their bodies would, after all, be perfectly preserved, for beyond a certain altitude they could not be buried or even carried down. They must lie there as you climb past them.'

I told him the idea was horrible.

'And yet,' he said, 'that alley has something of the flavour. A tavern beside it and yet so empty. Did you smell anything?'

I shook my head.

'Well,' he answered, 'it is more of an instinct than anything else. But in our own way we are explorers and I have a feeling we will be visiting it again.'

THE MESSAGE FROM HELL

The following week I had a message from Bell, telling me his investigation had not progressed very satisfactorily. As expected, the pathologist had decided Harriet Lowther died of a heart attack, a verdict with which he was most unhappy. My days were busy and I saw only a little of the Morlands but sensed their worry. Martin was working long hours to make up for the time he had missed. Sally, meanwhile, did her best to keep a brave face and never talked again about the debt, so I hardly liked to return to the question of the League, even though I knew Bell wished to hear more.

And then one morning at breakfast Sally was talking of her longing for a garden like the one at Turnham Green when she smiled and exclaimed, 'I nearly forgot, you have a letter.' She handed me an envelope. 'And now I can hear the children are thumping on the floor, which usually means they are getting too excited, so I will leave you to enjoy it in peace.'

I glanced without much interest at the envelope before me. It had, as I observed at once, been forwarded from my home in Southsea in a plain packet. A bill seemed the most likely content. When I took out the envelope inside, I saw that the writing was plain and clear. Yet any clerk could write like this so it hardly seemed important and I opened the envelope with no great trepidation.

Inside were four closely written pages in much the same style. There was no greeting, no address, but just a heading. It read:

A DAY OF LITTLE ACTIVITY

This meant nothing at all to me. I wondered if it was some mistake. Perhaps my colleague in Southsea had somehow confused it with another letter yet this seemed unlikely, so I started to read.

I decided I would today try Jones Street, for it was a rough place not far from the port and one thoroughfare of that kind I had not enjoyed before. I had risen late, spent some time over my lunch, and then walked out, reaching it by the middle of the afternoon when I was amused to see already women were standing in the doorways, for all the doors in that street lay back about eight feet between area railings.

I chose a well-built woman with bright dark eyes who smiled out at me from one of them. I made sure the street was empty and then approached her, merely nodding my head. Soon I had gone up with her to a small and disappointingly bare room and she started to take her clothes off. I allowed her to do so and then made her sit

down and told her I was a doctor who would examine
her . . .

Despite the broad, neutral handwriting, this narrative had begun to alarm me almost immediately, and at the word 'doctor', my heart missed a beat.

Her form was not a bad one, but after an insertion, using my stick, which in her ignorance she accepted as a medical instrument, I saw she was suffering from some inflammation so I could not conscientiously enjoy her. Instead I pretended I was satisfied but wanted to wait a little. Then I produced my flask and said we should enjoy a drink together. She seemed quite happy with this but I insisted she bring glasses and with some reluctance she procured some from a room opposite. I poured out two generous portions of drink and as I was about to swallow mine, I drew her attention to a mark on the wall behind her. Most of my glass went into hers and the rest on to the rug. They can find it there but I doubt they will even look.

She turned now and I pretended to have just swallowed the last, but she was a little quicker than I would have liked and chided me for the largeness of her portion. Even so she drank, and the sweet brandy drowned out the taste, at least long enough for her to drink it down.

I looked at her then, marvelling that her fate was sealed. No man would ever enter her again, indeed she would not even drink again. When I told her she was about to die, she laughed, but then I think she felt the first stirrings because her laughter died and she whimpered a little and said, 'What have you done?' I watched the rest quietly, it was not much of a show for which you must accept my apologies. There was little vomiting but the stuff could not in any case, as I knew, be brought up. She barely managed to get to her feet, choking and staggering, though to my amazement she did manage a look of baffled reproach.

This is unusual: I suspect she had considerable will-power. 'You are dying,' I observed. She had ceased to listen now but I continued. 'You gave yourself to me,' I said softly. 'All of you for me to consume as I wished. You made yourself worthless. And I am only doing what I enjoy, taking all of you.'

She had collapsed back on the bed and there was the rattling rasping noise that sometimes comes in their throats and her limbs flailed and the eyeballs bulged until after a time she was utterly still. That was the first of the day.

I went to a coffee shop in good humour and had some refreshment and then a safe distance away once it was dark I chose another. Fair-haired and well fed. This one was excited and voluptuous and seemed clean enough so I took her but was interrupted when a child cried out below. The child saved her life for it stirred others in the house and I had to leave but I may go back there and finish it, perhaps this evening . . .

I had had to force myself to keep reading to this point where the narrative broke off. Now I put the letter down. Just a few sentences were left, but they were clearly different from the rest, some wild scrawled capitals, and I had no stomach for them yet.

I found I was pushing my hands down on the table, for my senses were swimming. I feared I might faint but, as some clarity returned, I thanked heaven that I had read the letter while I was alone. Above me, like some mocking contrast to this ghastly narration, I could hear the domestic sounds of the house. Sally Morland was laughing with her children and I found myself thinking how dreadful it would be if she read these words. And I made a kind of stumbling vow then that nothing of him, not even his reported deeds, would ever enter this house. The letter must be concealed where nobody, except of course the Doctor, would ever see it.

The reader may find it strange that it was only now that I properly scrutinised the postmark, but I had assumed the contents would reveal the sender. In the event it was faint and difficult to read but I could see it was foreign, and once under the light, the words were decipherable.

Chicago,
Illinois.

This, then, was something, and I returned quickly to the end of the letter only to find it was as if he had read my mind.

TRAVELLED A LONG WAY TO MAIL THIS SO HAVE NO WORRIES YOU WILL FIND ME HERE. GO INSTEAD AS SOON AS YOU CAN TO ELSIE OR JENNY IN WYCH STREET AFTER THE BUTCHER THEY EXPECT YOU

I could not at first take this in, but I stared back at it with dawning apprehension that was no less intense than my disgust at what I had read before. Was this a trap of some kind? In any case how could the writer of a letter, posted some weeks before in Chicago, have any recent knowledge of Wych Street, which I was dimly aware lay north of the Strand? My mind raced with wild speculation. Was it even possible he was here? And of course I thought again of the drawing in Tussaud's.

I sat there, trying to take in what I had read, attempting to analyse the position as the Doctor would. This letter was surely evidence of a kind, evidence of cold-blooded, disgusting murder. Yet, though I knew its author, it was signed with no name and it was perfectly possible the street names were disguised. Nor did I even know what city contained this 'Jones Street', for Chicago seemed to be ruled out.

My mind turned to the message at the end. I knew I would feel no rest until I had acted, and therefore I must do so at once. In the first place I would cable the Doctor's hotel, though he was an early riser and I knew there was little hope of finding him there at this time in the morning. Then I would try and uncover what this last sentence meant. I was aware I must proceed cautiously, for I had not forgotten the opera glasses. But delay was not to be borne. This was, after all, my first real trace of the man who had killed Elsbeth. And besides, even if Cream was waiting to make some murderous attack upon me (though the letter's postmark made this seem improbable), I would relish the chance to lay my hands on him.

Of course a reader, who has appraised these pages

with any care, will be aware that a murderous attack of a straightforward kind was hardly my enemy's style. But he should also understand how desperately I had longed for avenging action ever since the murder and here, at last, even though on his own terms, was something I could do.

I memorised the exact wording at the end of that foul note and then set about carefully concealing the letter about my person, even though I knew nobody in that house would ever spy on my personal correspondence. After this was done, I went through to where Sally and the children were looking at a storybook.

She turned with a smile to greet me and I smiled back but I should have known there would be no concealing my mood from her. 'Why, Arthur,' she said, 'what is the matter, you look flushed!'

'Only because I ran up the stairs,' I lied. 'But the truth is I have had some news. Nothing too serious, but an old friend is ill and I want to visit him. I will send a message to the practice. Fortunately they are fully handed again and I feel sure they can spare me for an hour or so.'

'Of course they can,' she said, looking at me intently. 'Is your friend very ill?'

'No, it is not so bad,' I said, turning away. 'But I want to go at once. I will see you tonight as ever and tell you more.' And I waved at the children and retreated before she could ask me further questions.

After sending a cable to Bell announcing I had heard from Cream, I was in the Strand about half an hour later. Wych was one of a wilderness of intersecting streets to the north crossing Newcastle

Street, Drury Lane and several others. I had never been here so early before but it was no brighter or happier than in the early evening. There was a stench of human waste in the roads, and most of the thoroughfares were very narrow, with tall cramped houses that seemed almost to overhang the pavements.

Soon I reached Wych and stopped by the Olympic Theatre, which was the only semi-respectable landmark in the area, turning over the words of the letter in my head. *Go . . . to Elsie or Jenny . . . after the butcher.* There had been some sunshine that morning but it had now clouded over, and I stared through the gloom without seeing anything like a butcher's shop.

As I walked away from the theatre and the street curved round, it seemed more and more as if the houses were leaning out above me to cover the sky. There were a few dingy shops, some children ran about and I saw two men lounging in a doorway. Perhaps, I thought, the butcher was a nickname of some kind, but I might as well walk the street before I started to ask. I trudged on past a narrow grimy courtyard, trying to avoid the mud thrown up by a cart.

And then I saw the sign. It was so dirty I was barely able to read it but I could be quite sure it was a butcher from the meagre display of hung meat. I walked into the close and came past the shop to a crumbling brown four-storey dwelling with a peeling dark green door which was half open.

'An early one, are you?' The gruff voice came from beside me and I turned and saw a swarthy butcher in his apron. He winked and I realised he had been watching me with amusement as I studied the house.

I hated his leer, but I went on at once, walking straight into the place without looking back, for no doubt if I hesitated I would face even more derision. The hall of the house was dark and dingy, but I could hear shouting and noise from a room at the back and what sounded like an argument between two women. I called out and a haggard woman with grey hair appeared and stared at me.

'Is Elsie here?' I asked.

She took a step forward, still staring. 'Elsie Farr? Of course but she's sleeping it off, you want to come back later.'

'No,' I said. 'I wish to talk to her.'

She burst out laughing. 'A strange kind of talk. Well, I suppose a few coins will wake her up.' And she pointed at a door up the stairs on the next landing. 'Shall I go out to fetch something?'

'No, there is no need,' I answered quickly and began to climb the filthy steps. The woman glared at me rudely from below, and I suppose she was displeased because sending her out for beer or food was part of the accepted practice of the house. But soon she disappeared.

I reached the door, which had some old bottles beside it, and knocked firmly. There was no reply. Rather than stand there, I opened it and went in.

The room was in near darkness, or so it seemed at first. I waited where I stood, trying to make something out. There was a hanging on my left over the window, so I moved it slightly and a little murky light filtered through.

Now I could make out that I was standing in a

good-sized and not uncomfortable bedroom. There was, it is true, a faded screen to one side of me and the place was hung about with cheap flimsy material. But the mantelpiece had crockery, ornaments and a rosewood-framed mirror while the bed in the corner looked crisp and clean. A woman lay in it but she was not sleeping soundly. And as the light came into the room, her eyes opened and she looked around and saw me. I suppose I expected her to be startled but she merely eyed me curiously. She had goldenish hair and pretty features, though her face was sallow.

'You are Elsie?' I asked.

She sat up slowly in a long cream chemise that must have been chosen to show off her charms.

'Yes, and who are you?'

'You know someone called Jenny?'

'Of course,' she was wide awake. 'What has she done?'

So I had found them. 'Nothing, I just had to be sure there was no mistake. I wish to ask you something, Elsie. Do you know any medical men? Any doctors?'

I had hoped this would alert her but it seemed to mean nothing. 'Oh, Lord, I see a lot of men, and they don't always tell me much either. What do you want?'

'You never see an American gentleman?'

Again this brought no reaction. 'Why do you want to know anyway?' she asked. And then her expression changed and a look came into her eyes, a little smile. 'Ah, wait now, if you look for a doctor. Are you yourself a medical man?'

I nodded.

'Then will you come here, sir?'

I hesitated and then went over to her bedside.

She lay looking up at me and I saw I had under-estimated her appearance. She may have used herself badly but she was still lovely, her hair long and golden, her features pert, her lips full, her eyes wide. In Edinburgh, while I searched for Agnes Walsh, I had seen many women who gave themselves for money and some at Madame Rose's were undoubtedly handsome, but I had never met one as fair as this. It was a wonder, with looks like hers, that she had come to the profession at all, but no doubt there was a reason.

'I do not know why you are here, sir,' she said in a friendly tone, looking up at me and smiling, and I saw that her little teeth were very white against her red lips. 'But it is my good luck for I have a condition and I wish you to give me your opinion, sir.' She spoke very sweetly.

'I will do that if you wish,' I replied, 'but you must help me first. You have no idea of an American gentleman?'

'None at all,' she said. 'Perhaps you should ask Jenny, but she is not here now and has not been for a few days. Now, sir, can I show you.'

'No, just tell me where the pain is.'

Her face was suddenly concerned. 'It is a swelling,' she said. 'You will have to feel to understand. I am so fortunate to meet you, sir. Perhaps we can be friends.' And she looked up imploringly.

Standing over her there, I felt a little giddy. I had had nothing to eat or drink since waking, but had come directly here as soon as I read the letter. Now I was staring down at a woman who was sweet and voluptuous, a fact which no doubt accounted for her success on the streets and for the butcher's leer. I took a breath, forcing my head to clear.

'Will you just give an opinion, sir? It is all I ask.' She threw back her hand to look up at me, squirming a little as she did so, and I wondered if she was indeed in pain.

I collected my thoughts. There could be no harm, but I must not linger. I wanted to try to find the other girl.

So I nodded, bending forward, and she took my hand and with her other hand pulled down the bedclothes. The chemise did not extend below her waist, her legs were sprawled open and without any hesitation she placed my hand firmly just inside the full moist lips of her pudenda, arching her back and pressing me into her.

Stupidly I had been taken by surprise. My hand lay there and I could feel her breath on my neck as her other hand sought to pull me down to kiss these bright red lips. It had been so long since I had had physical intimacy of any kind at all with a woman that of course I felt desire and a sudden longing. What man would not? My whole body responded and there was a moment when I felt I might succumb, a moment I am sure she recognised, for she pushed my hand further in and gave a great sigh of pleasure. But also, fortunately, in that same instant, I thought of how I had resolved I would be prepared and felt a sudden fury and revulsion at myself for being so easily deceived. With an effort I pulled back. She was still trying to excite me, lying languorously back to show me as much of her as possible.

But I simply pulled the covers over her and stepped away.

'I would never tell a soul, Dr Doyle,' she murmured.

At this I reacted and even looked around, half expecting Neill himself to step out, laughing, but at least I had made sure the room was empty. 'How do you know my name?'

Her guile left her almost as rapidly as it had begun and she started to look irritable. 'Will you not take some pleasure in me? You have paid, sir. Though we hoped to get a little more.'

'I have not paid,' I said. 'I never saw you before.'

'You must ask Jenny. She knows more of it.'

'But you do not know where she is?' I felt foolish and compromised, which was no doubt what was intended.

'Not for days, sir. I have not seen her. Nor has anyone.'

'Very well,' I said, gathering my thoughts. 'You must tell me everything you know. It is a criminal matter and there will be serious trouble if you do not.'

'Oh, Lord, I cannot see how,' she said, turning around to get more comfortable, again an expression of irritation on her. 'A gentleman's game is nawt to do with us.' But she had heard the urgency and impatience of my tone and continued. 'For that is all I know, sir. A gentleman paid for me to do this. Not one I ever set eyes on. But Jenny says she has and he gave money to her and me and says if a medical man comes calling, we were to treat him extra well. And, if we did, there might be more for us then.'

'Who was this man?' I said.

'I have told you I know nothing of him. And I have told you all she told me.' She was losing interest. 'You will have to find her. But I cannot see that you will.'

'But when?' I asked desperately. 'When did she give you the money? How long have you waited?'

She screwed up her face. 'Some weeks ago I think, sir. It has been a little while.'

Of course I asked a dozen questions more but she seemed to have told me everything she knew. The missing Jenny, whose full name it seemed was Jenny Galton, had told her little beyond the fact that she had met a man who gave her money: the condition was that she and Elsie were to look out for a medical man called Doyle. And if they treated him 'extra well' there might be more, though how or why there would be more, the elusive Jenny never said. Even her meeting with the man lay in question, for Elsie seemed to recall her saying something of a message, as if perhaps the man had sent a letter or a note possibly via someone else. The more I asked, the less clear it became, but finally I was convinced I knew all that Elsie knew.

The practice, I fear, saw little of me that day. It was spent in a hunt for Jenny Galton which proved just as fruitless as Elsie claimed. None of her regular haunts had seen her for at least a week, not that this was considered unusual. At times she might go off with a gentleman friend for as much as a month or more. It seemed she had two lodgings, including the place I had visited, but at each the story was the same. And even her meagre belongings seemed to be absent from both.

In the late afternoon I returned to Bell's hotel,

where I found him awaiting me in his sitting room, having received my telegram about an hour earlier. He was far from pleased. 'I wish you had waited,' were almost his first words. I was pent up enough to say something I might well regret, so I said nothing and I believe he saw this and relented. 'I am sorry, Doyle,' he went on more softly, 'but the matter needs to be taken step by step. You have the letter?'

I nodded and handed it to him.

He sat reading it in silence, saying nothing. And then he got to his feet. 'Very well, I will study it further, but you must tell me everything that has happened to you as we travel to Wych Street.'

A hansom was summoned instantly by the hotel porter and we were on our way, but I found it far harder than I had foreseen to give Bell a full account of my day. When I reached the most delicate part of the story, I said merely that Elsie had attempted to seduce me, and tried to describe all that had happened since. He listened carefully and then returned to the letter. Finally he handed it back. 'So it is dated only a few weeks ago?'

'That is only one reason I believe he is here. And has been for some time,' I said. 'The letter could easily have been sent to a friend in America and sent back to me. That is simpler than anything else.'

'It may also be what he wishes you to think, Doyle. Nothing would give Cream greater pleasure than for you to see his shadow everywhere. If he is here, why need he conceal it? But to play this game from Chicago, all he needed was knowledge of these women and their address, which from your description is notorious. As to how? There are, it seems to

me, a number of ways. Imagine, for example, that he
fell into the company of travellers from London who
like to discuss such conquests. This is by no means
improbable given his tastes. At once he sees his
chance and charges one of them with the paid
commission to bribe these women to seduce you.
Your Elsie is muddled, but she seems to recall hearing
of a message or a letter brought via another man.'

'Yes, it is possible,' I granted. 'But how much easier
if he were here himself. For otherwise how could he
be sure with such a transient trade that these women
would still be here?'

'Exactly,' the Doctor came back quickly. 'That was
indeed his risk and you will note one of them is not.'

'But in all of this there is such a sense of his
presence!'

'Which is exactly what he intends,' said Bell. 'Of
course he would like nothing more than for you to
descend into this twilight world and spend your time
in futile searching. I want you to promise you will be
cautious, but before we go further let me make this
visit to Wych Street and also put the word out for
Jenny Galton.'

At first I suppose I felt a little relieved that the
matter was in his hands, but I cannot say the rest of
that day was remotely productive. Elsie had gone
out so much time was spent in waiting. When she
returned, she was the worse for drink and in a foul
temper which did not improve when she saw me. It
is true that, using all his authority, Bell managed to
make her answer his questions seriously, but even
so he heard nothing more from her than I had.
And, after this, our energies were expended on a

second hunt for Jenny Galton which proved utterly fruitless.

I have rarely seen Bell looking so tired and demoralised as he did after we gave it up and journeyed back. 'I am afraid,' he said at last, 'today confirms all my worst fears. You are being tempted into a search for a will o' the wisp that is almost certainly not here at all.'

Of course I knew there was some sense in his words, even though I was not yet prepared to be convinced. But before he got down from the cab that was taking me on to the Morlands's, he was kind enough to clasp my hand.

'Please, Doyle,' he said, 'try to rein in your thoughts of him as far as you can. You will come and dine with me tomorrow night and we will talk it over.'

I must have looked an exhausted and dispirited figure when I finally returned to my lodgings, inventing a story that my 'friend' had proved more ill than I expected, but had rallied, and was now out of danger. I had already sent another message to the practice and Sally told me they were sympathetic, but I could see that she was not wholly satisfied by my explanation. However, she asked no further questions.

Perhaps it was the fruitlessness of the day, perhaps the accumulated shock of *his* return into my life. I only know that what followed was easily the worst night I had spent since I arrived. A fierce storm arose in the late hours to rattle the roofs and chimneys, making matters worse. Utterly unable to sleep, as the hours wore on I was by turns anxious, apprehensive and, I will admit, frightened.

That monstrous letter had confirmed in a dramatic fashion just how spectacularly Neill was transformed from the person I had once known. Even at university he had concealed so much from us, pretending merely to be a spirited rebel and carefully hiding the extent of his appetites. But now it seemed he had indulged these appetites and diversions to a point where he was a wholly different person, one who seemed capable of innumerable horrors and would justify them by a rhetoric of nihilistic madness.

If Cream were truly in London, as I believed in my heart he was, I dreaded to think of what he would do next. It had evidently taken him only a little research to discover my practice in Southsea. If he applied there, he would be given my forwarding address at the Morlands's. It was now too late to avoid this. And then what would amuse him? A crude physical attack was unlikely. It would be something far worse. Perhaps he would turn up on the doorstep in the dead of night with some subterfuge of his own devising that would terrify the entire household. My imagination began to work itself into such a state that I almost thought I could hear his footsteps on the pavement outside or on the stairs leading to my room.

Finally I could bear it no longer and got up and went to my bag and took a small dose of an opiate. But I fear it only served to give me a series of terrifying dreams. In many of them, Cream's head – severed from his body – towered grotesquely above me, boasting of monstrous crimes. And I believe there was a horrible nightmare before dawn in which he menaced Sally and her children, but fortunately I awoke and could not remember it.

THE LEAGUE OF HOPE AND SORROW

The morning brought a little relief from these night phantoms, but I was still flushed and tired and the storm continued unabated outside. I decided to avoid breakfast and left a note for the Morlands saying I had made an early start. Fortunately the day that followed was quiet, perhaps because our patients were deterred by the weather, and most of my time was spent on calls in the neighbourhood. But I know I was not entirely myself and was quite sure that Baird and some of the other doctors saw it. Around five o'clock I told Dr Baird I feared I was going down with a cold and he seemed a little relieved, advising me not to come in the next morning, which was in any case a Saturday when duties were generally light. That would afford me two days to try to weather it.

As I entered her sitting room, Sally Morland looked up from her embroidery and her smile turned to concern. 'You look tired, Arthur and I am sure you have had nothing all day.'

'That is not true,' I said, 'but in fact I came to tell

you I have a dining engagement with an old friend.'

'It is just as well, for there will be little good company here,' she said gloomily. 'Martin should be home shortly but will have to go out again at eight, for he is making a further application to the League tonight. I just pray they will agree.'

'The League of Hope and Sorrow?' I asked, remembering the card in Harriet Lowther's room.

'Yes,' she said, 'Hope and Sorrow. And I know they mean well, but sometimes I wonder if there is not more of the latter than the former.'

'Where do they meet?' I asked, aware that Bell would like to know.

'Oh, in different places, I believe. They must keep the meetings private for their business is highly confidential and they help people from all walks of life. Martin said tonight it is in some church hall, although not for once across the river. But why do you ask?'

I told her I thought I had read about them, and we changed the subject for it turned out Sally and her children had one piece of good news at least. Their Uncle Tim had written to say he might pay a surprise visit within the next month and I found myself wondering if this splendid uncle – though it seemed he was a friend rather than a relative – would not be able to help the Morlands with their pecuniary difficulties.

When I reached the hotel, Dr Bell was seated in exactly the same armchair beside the fire in the public room where I had first encountered him, but his greeting was very different. Then he had sprung up to shake my hand, now he merely scrutinised me intently as I walked towards him and waved me into a chair.

'You have had another bad night, I perceive?' he said.

There was no point in denying it; his eye was far too acute for that. 'I admit you are right,' I said, sitting down. The fire was bright but the cheerful room of armchairs was almost entirely empty apart from a family gathering up their things to leave.

His eye was still fixed on me. 'He wants to stir your imagination and I fear he is succeeding all too well. You took something last night?'

I was a little irritated by this interrogation, for my health was hardly a major issue considering all we faced. 'Is it important?'

'An opiate?'

'A small quantity only,' I said.

'Of laudanum, I assume. I recall your experiments with gelsemium. And you really think it is worth putting that kind of burden on your system at this time?' He was leaning towards me, his eyes still on mine.

The room was now empty and I raised my voice. 'Doctor, I do not seriously think . . .'

But he interrupted me, speaking quickly, a finger raised. 'Do you not *see* how he would rejoice if it took hold. And even in minor drafts it may affect your judgement, Doyle! No doubt you do dream of him under its influence. And it may also explain your sense of his presence.'

I could hardly disguise my anger at this. Perhaps I felt vulnerable about my occasional use of the drug, but surely he must see my consumption was in no way comparable to the kind of excessive use we had witnessed in others. 'I can reassure you without qualification.' I said tersely. 'Yes I have taken laudanum from time to time. It is not something I generally prescribe, but I find it can be effective. So please disregard that possibility. I may be wrong but I still implore you to believe me when I say that I sense him.'

'Well,' he said, after looking at me, 'it is not my place to legislate on such things for you now.' And then he fell to examining Cream's letter again. After a time, he told me he was even more firmly inclined to the view that it was part of a game being played from a distance. 'And one we should be extremely cautious about playing. For he means only to distract and discompose us, so I promise you there will be no genuine clues. Of course I am using all the means at my disposal, including the redoubtable Inspector Miller, to pursue Jenny Galton but in the meantime I urge you not to return to Wych Street.'

I could assure him of that for it was certainly not my intention, and the mention of Miller returned us to the case of Harriet Lowther. The Doctor asked if, as requested, I had sounded out the Morlands about the League of Hope and Sorrow? I started to tell him what I knew but, as soon as I mentioned Martin Morland's meeting that night, he jumped to his feet. 'Then why are we sitting here? The more we can learn of it, the greater the chance of discovering if the card has any importance to the case.'

'But they will never admit us,' I said without moving, for not only did I think it was an irrelevance but, after all that had happened the day before, I had little appetite to leave this safe haven for the rain and wind of the streets.

'Of course not,' said Bell, turning to seize his coat, 'which is why we must follow him.'

The plan was concocted in a hansom that Bell had instructed to drop us close by my lodgings. 'I suggest,' he said, leaning forward eagerly, obviously glad to be doing something, 'that we follow Morland separately rather than together. If he sees you, you can make up some explanation, but with any luck he will not see me.'

In truth I could not at all understand why he thought this mission important, especially at so critical a time in my own affairs. I was still smarting, too, from his words about my mental reliability in the hotel.

'But Doctor, this is surely a fool's errand?' I said, turning to him to give my words greater emphasis. 'I cannot see what you hope to achieve. The League is evidently some philanthropic society which administers loans to the needy. Sally Morland indicated that they have many clients from all walks of life. Perhaps Harriet Lowther herself hoped to secure a loan. But why is that of any importance to you?'

'Possibly it is not,' he said holding his cane and looking straight ahead as he was wont to do when he was thinking. The flare from the gas lamps we passed in the rain illuminated odd corners of his face and he rocked slightly with the motion of the cab. 'But how could I know that until I have discovered more? I have learned from long experience, Doyle, that need and debt often have a bearing on a crime. And in a case as odd as Miss Lowther's I am more than happy to follow any divergent path which presents itself.' Then he did turn to me, and I sensed the frustration he always felt when he was short of material. 'We are not, you will agree, exactly presented with a surfeit of clues in her case.' By this time we were already close by the lodgings and Bell leaned forward to tell our driver to stop.

Within a few minutes we were huddled in a doorway round the corner from Esher Street. It was still raining and I was struggling to think what to say if Sally Morland walked past and saw us. However, there was not long to wait for Morland came out at twenty minutes to the hour, dressed in a heavy overcoat against the weather, and turned away towards the Vauxhall Bridge Road.

We had agreed to scout him separately, and so, after a judicious interval, I moved off to follow. In the unlikely event that he stopped and saw me, I would have to pretend to be on some errand. But soon he was walking so rapidly there seemed little chance of this and I smartened my pace to keep up with him, reflecting that the Doctor would probably have to rely on me for his bearings. Indeed when I glanced back to where Bell had been, there was no sign of him at all.

Spurred on by the fact that he seemed to have left the field entirely to me, and might even have some other plan afoot, I hurried after Morland's figure. The rain and wind was an aid to me now, for I attracted little notice in these dark streets, and the man ahead of me was clearly in no mood to look round.

He turned into Chapter Street, and I hung back as

he crossed over but came closer to him again as he weaved through an endless series of residential roads. Soon we found ourselves close to the river by Fire Wood Wharf, where the water was choppy and an old trading boat rocked angrily back and forth on its moorings. Here I stopped and pretended to stare at it till he was almost out of sight, then followed on. He passed Pimlico Pier and trudged on down Grosvenor Road until at last he came to a great old stone church just within sight of Grosvenor Bridge.

Here, then, was the place of the meeting. The door of the church hall was, I saw, opened to Martin by a dark-suited man with a beard, who closed it again firmly as I passed by on the other side, taking care he did not see me.

I saw no way I could obtain admission, and I cursed Bell for sending me on this fool's errand, which I noted the Doctor himself seemed to have abandoned. But I could hardly give up now, and my only hope was to try to find some way in through the church itself.

I circled round to the back of it, where there was nobody to be seen, and stared up through the rain at the tower and a huge stained-glass bow window. Finally I arrived at a large oak door and, after yet again ascertaining that nobody was on the street, I turned the handle, only to establish that it was locked fast. This was poor luck, but I guessed that the League had made sure of it. Perhaps the meeting was destined to go unobserved, but, whatever my feelings about this mission, I did not much care for the idea of abject failure.

I walked on round the side of the building which took me behind a clump of bushes that marked the small graveyard. There was little light here, but in the furthest corner I saw an outline of something in the stone. Coming closer, I made out it was an old vestry door, evidently little used. Here was my last opportunity and I tried the handle, but it too was locked. I was about to turn away, but, after some reflection, I gave it one more try, applying more pressure. Now I felt some movement. I pushed again. This time it definitely yielded a few inches. Unlike the other, this was not locked at all, it was merely sealed by disuse.

Before me all was dark and I had to push the door further in order to squeeze myself through. There was noise as it scraped the stone floor, but I doubted anybody would hear, for I must be some way from the hall.

I groped my way into a dusty room and pushed the door shut behind me, glad at least to be out of the weather. I could still see nothing, but I felt mouldy piles of paper and boxes and it seemed certain I was in some semi-abandoned storeroom. Feeling my way round the wall, I made a complete circle and yet found no door of any kind. Could it be that there was no exit from this place into the church? It seemed unlikely. There had to be a door, so I raised the level of my arms and tried again. This time I was rewarded with the touch of something metal jutting out from the stone, a handle and beside it a latch. The reason the door was so high, and I had missed it, was because it led up from a couple of stone steps that I had mistaken for an alcove. I climbed these carefully and then negotiated the latch, and the door opened without much noise.

I was looking out at the body of the church, which was shadowy and empty. But there was light from somewhere and I could hear voices. I stepped out of the doorway and moved slowly and stealthily in the direction of the sound. The church was large and well kept, its pews gleaming in a flickering light whose source I still could not properly see.

At last I came to a side aisle and, beyond it, was a wooden partition wall with a curtained door, separating the hall from the church. This was better luck than I could have anticipated. I heard the voices quite distinctly now and, peering through the curtain, I found I was at the back of a hall where the meeting was in full progress.

The place was lit by large lamps, set in the walls, and I soon saw that the building was in fact less like a hall than a side-wing of the church, which is what it must once have been. There was another stained-glass window and rows of seats, mostly empty, although Martin Morland sat nervously at the front of them.

Facing him on a dais sat five men and one woman in front of a long table, which contained an enormous ledger, various papers and a great box which obviously held money.

These must be the dignitaries of the League, and as soon as I saw them my heart went out to Martin. I had no idea what the elders of a philanthropic society should look like but, as I studied the pinched faces ranged along that dais, with their stony expressions and cold eyes, I felt I had never before in my life seen such a collective absence of humanity. It was easy enough now to understand Morland's attraction to the opium den if he knew he had to come before these people to plead for charity. Even their clothes were so sombre that they could have been mistaken for a party of undertakers.

At first I was surprised to see the meeting was in full progress, but it soon became clear that they had been taking clients at short intervals and Martin's appointment at eight was the last of the night. As a result there was only one other person present, a riverman in a coat nearly worn down to its threads, who was apparently applying to this unholy jury for a loan of twenty pounds.

'And you have work on the river?' said a man with red cheeks at the centre of the group, holding his quill pen above the ledger as if it were a badge of his estate.

'Aye I have, sir. Yes. But they will not pay before the end of next week.'

'I see, and can you sign your name?'

'I can, sir,' said the riverman proudly.

'We will always support honest thrift,' said the man with the pen, obviously the bookkeeper. 'And we will charge you a modest rate of interest. Let us say thirty per cent per week. Back the sum of twenty pounds.'

'Back the sum,' intoned a sonorous grey-haired man as he proceeded to open the cash box. But I barely watched him for I was still reeling from the interest figure that had been quoted. Thirty per cent a week? At that rate, given the slightest problem, how could the man ever repay it? Was it possible that Martin Morland had been mad enough to accept such terms? And from people such as these whose guise as philanthropists seemed about as threadbare as the riverman's coat? Whatever the detail, it certainly seemed that my friend's situation was far more serious than he had ever presented to me.

The answer to my questions came soon enough for, as the riverman sat down at a little table to put his name to these pernicious documents, Martin was called. I noticed that the man with a quill seemed almost to sneer as he said his name and took out some loose documents which were evidently the papers he had signed.

'So you are here before us again, Mr Morland?' he said when Martin rose. 'We have asked you to come at the close of our business. Are you still unable to pay?'

I was pleased to see Martin Morland adopt a dignified tone in reply. 'I accept I have reasons to be contrite and also that we are anxious to be quit of each other's company,' he said. 'We have exchanged harsh words in the past and, as you know, if I had not been the worse for drink I would never have signed your papers. But then one of you met me with a kind smile in a tavern, not at a gathering such as this.'

'We are well aware of the circumstances,' said the man with the quill. 'And your rate of interest was exceedingly generous.'

'Certainly better . . .' But Martin broke off, eyeing the poor riverman who did not even look up from where he was busy signing away his life. 'Well, I shall not say more, and I beg the committee's grateful pardon, but I will, I must, have more time. I have paid off a little.'

'That was some weeks ago,' said the man with the quill.

'And I cannot pay more for at least a month or—'

'Impossible,' said the man, putting down his quill with a defining movement. 'Utterly, rankly, impossible.'

His words were echoed by others.

'We made it quite clear when you last appeared here,' the book-keeper went on.

But Morland did not seem to hear him and continued unflinchingly in words I found horrifying, for I believed them. 'You must, for you are meant to give hope and the alternative is too dreadful. If I were to pay you, my wife and children would starve. I need my income for them and I cannot give it all to you. I will never make such a mistake again . . .'

'I fear it is too late for that. Indeed we have already decided,' said the book-keeper, who had clasped his hands in front of him on the table. And now I could swear I saw a brightness in his eyes, which had until now been so cold. I was sure that I recognised it too. It was pleasure. And, looking along that ugly group I could see the same vicious little glow in several of the faces staring down at Morland.

The book-keeper continued, 'We will apply for a public order for all your possessions which will not, however, I am sure, meet the full sum owing. I am afraid, therefore, it is the workhouse.'

The words sent a chill of fear through me. I expected Martin to shout back at them, for surely they could not hound him in this way. But to my horror he merely flinched and his eyes filled with tears. And then I knew for sure that he had never allowed to anyone, not even his wife, how bad things were. The meeting was at an end.

I did not know what to do. The idea of that little family being destroyed was more than I could bear. Should I intervene? Yet I had not the money to help them. I sat there paralysed by a storm of opposing thoughts, when a sudden noise came from the side of the hall.

A figure had stepped out from somewhere and one of the chairs in its path went over with a clatter as he came forward.

'I am afraid these proceedings cannot be allowed to continue,' pronounced the Doctor, his eyes locked on the astonished committee as he strode towards them. He must have been behind a pillar and, even from where I was, I could see the rage on his face.

The riverman stared up from his papers with amazement at this spectacle. Morland looked a little puzzled, but it was obvious he could hardly take it in for the weight of his sorrow still gripped him.

'You have no business interrupting us,' said the book-keeper, who had taken up his quill again, no doubt to give himself a more official air. 'This is a private meeting of a private charitable society.'

'It is nothing of the kind,' said Bell. 'But I little wonder that you care to keep it quiet. You are practising extortion masquerading as respectable charity and neither the press nor the courts would view it as anything else.' He turned to the riverman. 'This man could obtain more generous terms from the worst magsman in Seven Dials.'

The riverman could not follow but I was pleased to see a flicker of doubt cross some of the faces on the dais. And the red-cheeked book-keeper had certainly heard more than he liked.

'I have no idea who you are, sir, but your presence and manner are highly offensive. If you have any complaint against us, I suggest you apply to law.'

'Yes,' echoed the grey-haired man with the money, 'we are careful to abide by it.'

Now Bell hesitated for just a fraction of a second as he decided on his tactic. Nobody else there would have registered the pause, but it told me what I suspected: namely that he had stormed out of his hiding place driven by his own sense of justice without seriously planning how he would or could proceed. 'So you will consent to have your books examined?' he said.

It was the best he could do and it worried them, for their books would certainly have made shameful reading. But the man with the quill sensed his opening. 'Not by you, sir. But we have nothing to hide. Now shall we throw him out?'

As he rose to his feet, he seemed to unwind, and for the first time I saw how very tall he was, at least six and a half feet. Other men got up from the table too.

With a silent prayer I pulled the curtain aside. 'Then perhaps,' I shouted, 'you will consent to their examination by my constabulary.'

There was confusion and I moved quickly forward, desperately praying I could capitalise on it. 'This man you scorn has been assisting us in our enquiries into the more fraudulent lending societies. We now wish to impound your books and papers, pending possible prosecution.'

The Doctor was smiling at me, which was a good sign. I did not dare to look at Morland. Instead I walked to the table, delighted to see my presence had caused even more consternation than Bell's. Perhaps I was still a little flushed, but they had probably never seen a plain-clothes policeman in their lives and now everyone had sat down except the book-keeper, who eyed me with what I hoped was anxiety.

'But why do you think we have broken the law?' he said.

'By charging terms,' Bell said quickly, 'that cannot possibly be met and plainly exceed those stipulated in the Act of 1871.' He had come back without a pause, which was just as well for I had almost nothing to say. 'It may well be prison for most of you. We have more men outside.'

This caused a real ripple of anguish around the table. There were yelps of horror as those pompous, self-regarding people contemplated a wholly new prospect. The only woman gasped.

'You should have told us, Jim,' said the sonorous man with grey hair to the tall book-keeper. 'This is your fault, not ours. You said the terms were up to us. I am prepared to swear it.'

The tall man opened his mouth to reply. He was the one I feared most and I was sure the best course was to help him. 'No, I am afraid if the decision is made to take this forward, it is not just one but all who will be liable,' I said.

The book-keeper evidently saw his chance. 'If we agreed to close our books now, shut down new business, would you consider leaving it at that?'

I turned to Bell, who of course deferred to me. I turned back to the man, praying I would not overplay my hand.

'You must destroy the books and write off all outstanding debts.'

The man opened his mouth to protest, so I leaned forward as if to take the money. 'Well, it is all the same, but if we go forward, all of this is the property of the Crown till the matter is resolved.'

The idea of their money being confiscated was enough. 'Yes!' the grey-haired man shouted. 'We will write off the debts. Jim, tell him.'

'Very well,' said the book-keeper with obvious pain. 'If no more is said.'

Now I risked a look at Morland. The hope in his eyes gave me new zeal. I went to the table, passing the box with the money, and laid my hand down firmly on the ledger and the pile of signed loan papers, including his own, which was on the top 'These will be destroyed. You may take your money and do with it what you will.'

The riverman had been watching everything, his eyes fairly popping out of his head.

'The League is therefore dissolved,' Bell intoned, turning to join me in this happy destruction. 'None of its customers will hear of it again. All the papers are forfeit.'

And with this, he snatched the astonished seaman's signed papers and tore them up. 'These are of no value now, sir, you may take your money and go.'

The man was speechless but needed no further encouragement. He got up, clutching his money, barely able to believe his luck that what had been a loan was suddenly a gift, and almost ran from the place. The book-keeper's face was now a picture of horror at seeing his latest victim leave with twenty pounds and no debt. Meanwhile Bell had turned to Morland, who was on his feet. 'Your business with these people is at an end, sir,' said the Doctor with just the hint of a gracious smile. Morland nodded and left too, taking care to avoid my eye.

But all the tall book-keeper's suspicions had been reawakened, indeed he was enraged. 'This is all a sham,' he cried suddenly, trying to snatch the papers from me, although I held them firmly now and had taken the additional precaution of pocketing Morland's document. 'How do we know they are who they say?'

Fortunately for us he had left his move too late. His colleagues were only concerned with their share of the remaining money, and his remonstrances were drowned out by their squabbling, as they attempted to extract what each felt was rightfully theirs from the box. Meanwhile, as Bell seized a list of the League's debtors from the table, in case of a mention of Harriet Lowther, I was taking a candle to the papers and the ledger itself. The pages burned quickly and merrily, and I rejoiced to see them do so, knowing justice was being done and the poor people in that book would never hear from the League again.

Bell was at my side now. 'I have the list,' he said quietly. 'And if the rest is quite done, I think we are probably best served by leaving matters there. Our friend is becoming bolder.'

The book-keeper was now hovering angrily nearby, increasingly dubious of our authority. If he had had the slightest support from his cohorts, I am sure he would have challenged us by force if necessary, but their thoughts were still on the money. He glared angrily enough as we left and I was glad Bell had made up the story of the policemen outside for, though he was not completely convinced, it was enough to stop him following. There was, I am sure, nothing in the world any of those priggish tyrants feared as much as the ignominy of being arrested by a group of uniformed policemen.

Soon we were quite clear, and the Doctor was in high spirits as we moved briskly through the rain. 'Well, Doyle, I think you may discharge your men and let them go home to bed. Indeed it would seem you have already done so, which is excellent for they have performed sterling work this evening.'

'Just so long,' I said, 'as the gentlemen of the League do not find out our true identities, for then surely they might take some kind of action.'

'My dear Doyle,' said Bell, clearly amused and caring not one jot for the wild weather. 'Why do you suppose they conducted their affairs in such secrecy and with such a ludicrous show of pious rectitude? For the same reason we found it so easy to panic them. My Act of 1871 was a fiction, but they knew quite well in their hearts that the full exposure of their terms would have made them infamous, even a laughing stock. No, they will scurry back to their boroughs and we may rejoice to be rid of them.'

I never saw the Morlands more happy than they were that night. Bell was given a hero's welcome, and Morland had all the glow of a man from whom a terrible weight has been lifted.

Sally could not at first quite believe he was free of what had been such a foolish debt. I think she half expected the horrible tall man to come knocking on the door. But Bell assured her that even that vicious book-keeper could not try to collect money without any documentation proving that it had been lent. We let her see the loan paper with her husband's signature on it. And there was great rejoicing in that house as it was flung on the fire.

Once Bell had established that there was no mention of Harriet Lowther in any of the League's records, he showed Morland the card he had found in her bag and asked him if he had ever seen anything similar.

'Yes indeed,' said Morland. 'I had one just like it and wrote to the address. Subsequently a meeting was arranged in a tavern.'

'But where did you obtain the card?' said Bell eagerly.

Morland struggled to recall but Sally had no difficulty. 'I know,' she said, 'for I was there and I often wished you had never taken it. It was when we were visiting Macandrew's diving bell at the Royal Polytechnic Exhibition.'

Bell determined at once that we should make a visit there the following Sunday. 'For,' he said as I showed him out, 'I intend to keep you occupied, Doyle, and I also want to know why Harriet Lowther had it. It is not as if her name is on the League's books. What or who was her connection to those people?'

After he had gone I looked back into the drawing room once more to say goodnight. The children were by now peacefully sleepy as they snuggled into their parents on the hearth, while Martin and Sally sat framed by the firelight in a wonderful tableau, holding each other with a breathless kind of joy.

I had been so taken up by the events of the evening that, as Bell had no doubt intended, my mind had been freed of my own problems. I had even been quite elated. But now, as I watched the family unseen, a terrible pang assailed me.

> And one could whistle
> And one could sing
> And one could play on the violin
> Such joy there was at my wedding
> On Christmas day in the morning

The tune seemed a good one for the happy couple, if not for me. I made no sound to disturb them but turned to walk up the stairs, pledging silently that at least my darkness would never harm these people. I would rather die than be a source of harm to Sally Morland or those she loved.

THE NIGHT CALLS

I had visited the Royal Polytechnic Exhibition before, as well as its rival the National Gallery of Popular Science in Adelaide Street, and had been duly impressed by their scientific wonders, which could be sampled for the cost of a shilling.

I had a special fondness for the Gallery's great steam gun, an apparatus that fired seventy balls against a target in four seconds, but overall the Polytechnic seemed to be the more spectacular of the two. For, among its crowning attractions, was the diving bell and tank which had caused quite a sensation, especially among the young. Little wonder that the Morland children had been so excited to visit the home of Colin Macandrew, for he was already famous as one of the bell's designers.

That Sunday afternoon the Polytechnic was filled with people as Bell and I entered the great hall, lit up everywhere by its glowing filaments. That blaze of light contributed greatly to the sense of the marvellous, as did the water troughs on either side of

the entrance which were charged with electricity.
People would trail their hands in the water and laugh
with amazement as they felt the strange tingling it
produced.

Bell studied the effect with interest before we
began our enquiries about the League. There had
indeed, it transpired, been a small stand, not far from
the main exhibition, where the League's cards could
be picked up by anyone who passed. We reached the
place quickly enough, but the table was quite empty
and a helpful official, standing nearby, told us he had
removed all the cards because a message had arrived
to say that the League was no more. In other
circumstances the news might have been gratifying,
but it hardly helped the Doctor's mood. For it was
obvious now that Harriet Lowther could, like any
other Londoner, have passed by here, taking one of
the cards, and then perhaps forgotten all about it. If
this was indeed the case, the card revealed absolutely
nothing about her or her murder and we were on a
fool's errand.

After a few minutes we moved on and eventually
came to the main exhibit, the tank and diving bell.
Here I almost laughed, for the Doctor stared at that
great splendid construction with such blank indif-
ference that it might have been some dreary article in
a newspaper. However, I already knew from the
Morlands that today Macandrew himself was likely to
be present, for the Polytechnic always promoted
itself as a genuine scientific laboratory. And I caught
sight of him almost immediately, stepping out of his
huge bell. In his hand was some magnifying tool he
had been using to inspect its condition.

As we approached, he recognised me and also seemed delighted when I introduced him to the Doctor. 'Why, of course I have heard of you,' he said, shaking Bell's hand almost too vigorously. 'Your work on the human eye precedes you, sir. I presume you have come to the capital to take your research further.'

The Doctor was cordial enough, but I could see his mind was on other things. 'No, I am quite capable of finding all the specimens I want in Edinburgh,' he said, and at this point Macandrew was called away for the bell was about to be lowered.

I am sure the Doctor would now have walked on but, fortunately as it turned out, I insisted on staying to watch. The sound of the motor which powered the hoist reverberated through the hall, and the cable around the bell tautened and slowly lifted that great orb as it swung away over our heads towards the tank. The sight of it suspended in the air above us was extraordinary and I turned to the Doctor to say as much. But he was not even watching. There was no point in remonstrating with him so I moved away to get a better view and, in that moment, my eye fell on the small enclosure where Macandrew stood, surrounded by a considerable quantity of scientific equipment.

Several of the pieces were heavy and cumbersome so it was natural that labourers were employed to carry them back and forth. And one of them was at that moment carrying a large box towards a door. As he reached it, he put it down and turned in my direction. The sight of that small gargoyle-like face awoke an immediate memory of fear in me. I saw, too, the red mark on his neck. There could be no doubt it was the same man who was in the opium den. I must have flinched and, when I looked back, the man was gone. But Bell happened to notice my reaction and came over to me. As soon as I told him the reason, he was transformed. 'Show me exactly where you saw the man,' he said, gripping my arm.

I led him to the spot and we moved through the door. Beyond it was a staircase which gave on to the street but it was empty.

'No matter,' said the Doctor, 'I am far more interested to know what he was doing here than where he is going.' And for the next few minutes Bell questioned me mercilessly on all the details of the man's appearance and how he might be described. After that he watched other workers carrying scientific equipment, and studied Macandrew as he answered the public's questions about his diving bell. And then, when the audience was all but over, the Doctor made a point of speaking again to Macandrew and this time his manner was exceedingly flattering.

'It has been fascinating,' said the Doctor. 'You must be very proud of your achievements.'

Macandrew beamed at this and I wondered how he would react if he had actually witnessed Bell's cursory glance at the wonders of oceanic exploration, a glance lasting at my estimate about five seconds. 'Well, Dr Bell,' replied Macandrew with obvious pleasure, 'as you of all people will be aware it is always satisfying to convey knowledge as well as accumulate it.'

Having prepared his ground, the Doctor now continued. 'But the truth is I have some other business here beyond mere pleasure and enlightenment. I am engaged in a forensic investigation. A woman has been murdered whose name was Harriet Lowther.'

He watched Macandrew closely, but Harriet Lowther's name clearly meant nothing at all to him, indeed he looked quite surprised by this development. 'Is that so?' he replied. 'I can well imagine the police would be grateful for your help, but how can I be of service?'

'Oh,' said Bell casually, 'there are a number of odd avenues we are exploring. At this stage, who can tell where they will lead. But perhaps you can help us to identify a working man who I believe assists you with these displays? He was here until just after you began, when he carried out some materials. A large man with a red mark on his neck. A rope burn I would think.'

Macandrew thought for a moment. 'That sounds like Hanbury, Charles Hanbury. Powerfully built? I can't claim to know him well but he has made himself very useful. Sometimes he helps me here if I am short-handed. I hope he is in no trouble, for I could ill afford to lose him.'

'None so far as we know,' said Bell. 'Do you use him as a porter?'

'Oh no,' said Macandrew, 'Hanbury has a small boatyard down the river at Landell's Wharf. Charlie was a seaman and he is quite a wonder in bringing me materials I might need. The Thames is my laboratory, Dr Bell, and I have need of a man who knows it as he does. That is all I can tell you. Except . . .' And he looked at me with a smile. 'Well, it is true I have one regret as far as Hanbury is concerned and young Doyle knows all about it, for it involves a friend.'

I was taken aback, not merely by his somewhat patronising tone but also by the way he smiled so secretively at me, even though I had no idea what he could possibly mean. My frown made him smile all the more. 'I will explain,' he said, 'though this is in confidence. Hanbury's yard is only a short distance from one of the most notorious dives of its kind in London, a place called Sing's. You will find scarcely a sailor from the East who does not know the place, for it is a centre for opium worshippers. But I believe many gentlemen have occasionally chased the dragon there as part of an evening's entertainment. Out of a scientific interest, I got Charlie to point it out and visited once myself though I did not care for it all. But on that occasion I was stupid enough to introduce a mutual friend to its delights, which is something I now regret. His name, as Doyle will now realise, is Martin Morland.'

Of course I reacted now and he saw my reaction. 'Oh yes, Doyle,' he said. 'And he confided to me your recent adventure. It is just as well and I think we can be hopeful he never returns to the place.'

I nodded politely but also somewhat curtly, for I will admit I disliked the fact that this man was so complacent in his admission of a circumstance which had cost my friends the Morlands so dearly. But Bell was obviously extraordinarily interested. 'So does Charles Hanbury have a connection to the den?' he asked.

'Why, the man has a finger in so many pies on that part of the river, it is entirely possible,' said Macandrew. 'But it is run by a Chinaman. A pretty rum customer too.'

'Thank you,' said Bell. 'You have been candid and helpful.'

'Well, if I can be of any further assistance, I would be delighted,' Macandrew said. 'And will you not come around to my laboratory while you are here, Dr Bell? Doyle knows where it is.' It was petty, I admit, but I could not help noticing that, while Macandrew always respectfully awarded Bell the title 'Doctor', he took no such trouble to prefix it to my name.

'I would enjoy that greatly,' said Bell. 'Oh, there is one more thing. Do you know anything about this?' And he took out the card of the League.

Macandrew squinted at it. 'Why, I have seen this before, yes,' he said. 'Hanbury showed it to me.'

'Why was that?' said Bell with a casualness that did not deceive me for a second.

'Oh, he is always looking for opportunities. He came across those cards here some time ago and took a pile of them, for he said he knew so many needy people he could find a hundred customers for the League down by the docks. He asked me if I thought the League would give him something in return for his trouble. I told him they might. In fact he was quite put out to hear they are no more.'

'Of course he would be,' said Bell cordially, 'if he has gone to that trouble. Once again my heartiest thanks, Mr Macandrew. We would indeed be delighted to call upon you at some point.' And with that we left him.

I have often written that the Doctor could be silent when he was contemplating a problem. That was his norm, but he had other modes. Quite often he liked to trawl through possibilities and there were even occasions, generally, I admit of a simpler kind, when he was positively bubbling with observations. I could see, as we left the hall, that this was one of them.

'I tell you, Doyle,' he said excitedly, pushing the door ahead of us open with his cane, 'there are cases when a mountain of suggestive evidence leads to not one single opening, not one useful avenue! And others where the tiniest nothing will suddenly sprout into a great oak tree of suggestive fact! Fortunately this appears to be the latter species. An hour ago, we were in a fog with only that card as a guide. By chance, it is true, it helped us come to the aid of your friend Morland, but by then I was already sure the late and unlamented League had no direct bearing on this business. And now, by following that card, just consider what we have been able to establish.'

We had reached the streets and we were searching for a cab as the Doctor brandished his cane to itemise the points of advance. 'Firstly, we make a link between Macandrew and one of the rogues you encountered that night. Second and best of all, the card offers a clear and possible connection between that same rogue and the murdered woman, a link which, given the character of the man, may prove very valuable.'

We entered a muddy hansom, which Bell directed to Landell's Wharf. 'But,' I said, anxious to make the most of the fact that he was sharing his deductions with me, 'your victim Harriet Lowther could still have had the card in her bag from the exhibition stand. Think of the crowds that passed it.'

'I will admit,' said Bell, losing none of his animation, 'that is possible. But probability is against it.

For we have no evidence that Harriet Lowther ever ventured near the Polytechnic. That shilling's admission would have been a lot for her to afford, especially if she was in financial difficulties. However, we do know for sure that every day she wandered all around the area where Hanbury's boatyard stands. It was her business to do so, for she sold her pastries to the people working in the surrounding streets. And we also know that Hanbury, a man who never missed an opportunity, expressly declared the intention of handing out these cards to people in his locality who might be in need of a loan. Would not Harriet Lowther, who was in financial difficulties, be likely to fit the description? And Macandrew also told us something else. That Hanbury liked to have a finger in every pie on that part of the waterfront. No, in the circumstances I think we can be fairly safe in the supposition that Hanbury gave Harriet Lowther a card because he knew her and, moreover, knew she was in need of money. At this point the card itself ceases to interest me, and the association between Hanbury and Lowther must command all our thought and attention.' And with that, he lapsed into a satisfied silence.

It was still early afternoon when the cab turned into the less oppressive end of Shad Thames, which was yet to take on its night-time dangers. Children played merrily with a rag-like object, men stood and drank outside the ale houses, a woman with washing wrestled with a water pump. The hansom set us down at Landell's Wharf and we could see at once that it was only a short walk from here to Harriet

Lowther's rooming house. Indeed, given her occupation, taking pastries along the river, it was probably a journey she would make every day. Soon enough, with the help of a friendly shopkeeper, we were able to identify Hanbury's tiny boatyard which had a dark, shed-like dwelling attached to it.

I have no idea if Bell intended to interview the man, and I would not have relished the prospect, but in any case the place was locked and silent, with almost nothing to see other than a few timbers lying in the yard. Even so, the Doctor stopped for a long inspection, perhaps pondering how little evidence there was of honest trade in the place; certainly no boats.

After that, we chose one of the more savoury public houses where we were served beer by a pleasant landlord with a bald head who took us to be the usual gentlemen on some dubious excursion and laughed at almost everything we said. Though whether this was because he found us genuinely funny, or because he was hoping to keep us there as long as possible, I could not say.

In the midst of the conversation Bell was able to establish that the man had known Harriet Lowther and that the public house she frequented was the Lord Lovat. 'So,' said Bell to me quietly after the landlord had gone to serve another customer, 'Harriet moves closer and closer to your den and to Hanbury.'

The Lord Lovat was less welcoming, and as we supped our brandy and water, I was aware of some of the other customers staring at us with suspicion. There was at that time I am sure a better prospect of a working man sneaking successfully into a dowager's ball than of a gentleman going unnoticed in a dockside public house. No doubt in a story we would have donned some handy disguise, but in reality such a strategy would have been not only ineffectual but positively dangerous. What could possibly be the point of putting on ragged clothing and cloth caps when any publican worth his salt, and most of his clientele too, would see through the disguise at once? They would, moreover, certainly deduce you were a police spy and then mere indignity would be replaced by serious risk.

So Bell and I adopted the best method we could, which was to be friendly but also very subdued, and to make it clear who we were and why we were asking for advice. Bell approached the task with his usual skill, indicating that he was a doctor from Edinburgh with a great love of the capital who enjoyed collecting its stories and exploring its streets, after which he introduced me as his nephew. It was easily the best solution to our predicament, for we could not be caught out by questions, and soon we had struck up an acquaintance with the publican – who had a bushy beard and almost no teeth – and a tallow man, originally from Newcastle, who worked on the wharf.

After a decent interval, talking of all manner of things, Bell indicated that he had heard of the death of Harriet Lowther and not long afterwards we had our second real piece of luck of the day. The tallow man knew Harriet and had in fact seen her on the day she died. She had been in the pub in perfectly high spirits and, at first, alone. But later she had been in conversation with one of her customers, though he heard little of what they were saying except it seemed to concern money. 'And ahm nae askin' either,' he said with a smile, allowing Bell to smile back with just the right knowing air. 'He's a boatyard along from here and nae a man to cross.'

Shortly after that, the Doctor obviously judged we had all we could possibly have hoped for and he changed the subject and talked happily of the man's aches and pains and bruises, and of how he had inherited his red face from his mother, for fully half an hour, before we bade him a cheery farewell.

Outside I noticed the air was becoming colder again. Hanbury's boatyard was still dark and uninhabited as we passed, and the Doctor only glanced at it. 'We have what we came for, Doyle,' he said, doing up his top button against the chill. 'Our oak tree is grown and in just a day of work. When we return here I think it may well be with the police.'

He left me shortly afterwards, saying there were matters he wished to follow up, and I assumed he would have a talk with the police. Meanwhile I returned home quite pleased with these developments, little knowing that the main events of my day were only now about to begin.

The Morland family was still out, but as soon as I opened the door the little servant handed me a note. 'It came at lunchtime, sir. A boy brought it. I had no idea where to find you.'

I thanked her and took the note to my bedroom, where I opened it. There were only a very few words in poor writing.

8 Cole Lane by Halloes Pier

*Please cum fast Sirr for me to tel you what you must
no I am so feard of the head Jen Galton*

I stared at this. The handwriting was hard to decipher
but the street name was clear enough, though a
glance at a map the Morlands kept in their drawing
room told me it was in one of the meanest of all the
riverside areas, near London Bridge, where I had
never before ventured. The number of the house
looked like an 8 but might too have been a 6. Was this
then where Jenny Galton had been hiding and
waiting to contact me? Did she truly have the news I
was so desperate to discover? And why did she
mention the tale of the head?

Bell had made it clear he was not going to his hotel.
I did not have the slightest inkling of where he would
be now, and it might be hours before he returned.
Already this message had lain here unread for half the
day and how could I be sure whether Jenny Galton
might not disappear again as rapidly as she had
emerged? Already I could hear the Doctor's rebuke,
but there was no alternative. I must go alone.

I have already pointed out the impossibility of
disguise in such places, but equally there was no
sense in attracting attention. So I donned my oldest
coat and ventured out. Soon I found a cab which took
me east along the Strand and on into dreary Cannon
Street. Past here the roads were dirty and strewn
with refuse, while the buildings pressed in around us
even more darkly than they did in Wych Street, an
effect not helped by the fading light and rapidly

increasing cold. I asked the cabman to drive down to All Hallows Pier by the South Eastern Railway bridge and soon found myself in the most miserable area of the city I had yet seen. Yes, Shad Thames and its streets were menacing at night and certainly a haunt of criminals, but they were also working places for the people of the docks. But here, even though it was on the north side and nearer to the heart of the city, you felt that even work and labour had been left behind. Across by a miserable pier, a fire had been lit under the hulk of a lighter boat and a few bedraggled people were crouched in the gathering darkness. Looking back to the streets heading north, I found they were dark, filthy and, because of the increasing cold, almost uncannily empty.

As I got out and the cab turned back the way it had come, I could see the entrance to Cole Lane, which was so narrow no hansom could possibly have traversed it. I forced myself to turn up it and moved along quickly, thankful for a gas lamp at the entrance of the street. But, as I walked, the light of the gas threw my shadow before me and I found I was hatefully reminded of my dream of Cream, striding down streets and lanes such as these.

Some of the buildings near the river were semi-derelict and, even further on, where they were more substantial, the road had no shops or alehouses, just a series of dark, forbidding rooming houses. Number eight was halfway along, a tall thin structure with peeling paint and, unusually in this street, an ancient knocker on the door. I rapped twice. After only a short time it opened and much to my amazement a middle-aged woman greeted me as if I were expected.

'Now come in, sir,' she said. 'Come in out of the dark.' She bobbed and smiled at me, but there was a tightness about her smile which I did not like. 'And what do you wish, sir?' She wrung her hands together as she spoke.

'I am looking for Jenny,' I said.

She smiled again. 'Ah, and you are in time, for she has been waiting for a gentleman and was about to go home. We like to see gentlemen here,' she said. 'The more discerning find us out.'

I said nothing to this as she led me up a rickety ancient staircase that creaked on every step. At last we reached a door at the top of the house, and she called out, 'A gentleman is here for you.' Then she gave a little smile which was almost a leer and turned away.

I waited till she had descended, and opened the door.

The first thing I saw was a fire, which was burning quite brightly. There was no other light, but the rest of the room was clearly illuminated by the flames. It was not untidy, from what I could see. Opposite me was a bed, and sitting on it was a rather short woman with dark hair in a long nightgown, her eyes modestly cast down at the floor.

'You are Jenny?' I said.

'I am any name, sir,' she said, turning her head up to me. And to my horror I was looking at a child.

I felt such a conflict of emotions that I stood there immobile. There was horror, pity, some rage (for I supposed this was another of his tricks), but I also felt as if I bore all the shame of the men who had come here before me. Was it then so easy to be consumed with pleasure that you would happily corrupt a child? I thought of the woman's smile as she led me up. What was it she had said. 'The more discerning gentlemen find us out!' Discerning!

All of this went through my mind as the girl still sat there simply, her hands on her knees, no longer staring at me and no doubt waiting for matters to proceed in the usual way.

I walked quickly into the room, taking care not to go near her, but staying by the fire and looking at her with as kindly an expression as I could muster. She was probably no more than ten. She had brown hair and a sweet face, though I could not really see her eyes and for the moment was glad of it.

'So Jenny is not your name?' I said.

She shook her head. 'They call me Hettie. But the gentlemen here knows what they will get.'

She had an accent I could not place, but even so she spoke well and must at some time have had some education. 'Hettie,' I said, 'I do not wish to have anything from you. Can you read?'

She nodded. I brought out the note. 'Have you seen this?'

She took it, somewhat puzzled, and glanced at it. 'But,' she said, 'I believe there is a girl next door and she could have that name for I heard the mam say.'

It was only now that I remembered the illegibility of the street number. I had thought it an 8 but 6 was possible. The house next door was 6. Perhaps the writing had misled me. Or was the deception deliberate?

'Hettie,' I said, 'I would like to help you. Do you live here?'

She shook her head.

'Is the woman your mother?'

Again she shook her head, this time even more vehemently.

'When do you next come here?'

'Tomorrow, sir, at three.'

'Very well,' I said. 'I will wait a few moments and then I will tell the mam, as you call her, that you have proved exactly what I required, and that I am returning tomorrow at three o'clock. If she asks, just say I was like the others. But tomorrow I will try and bring help to you. Would you like to get away from here? And not wait on men?'

Her little face was blank at first but then behind the mask I saw just a flicker of something as if she did not quite dare to believe I was telling the truth.

'Am I not young, sir?' she said doubtfully.

'Hettie,' I said, 'you are very young, and you should not be here but with other children like yourself, doing what you would like.' I do not know if she took this in, for she looked a little puzzled, but at least I could see she was happy enough not to have to endure my attentions. I leaned over and rumpled the bedclothes, for I could not afford to arouse the woman's suspicion, and I gave her a coin and told her to hide it and keep it for herself, and finally I left her.

Almost as soon as I reached the hall downstairs a candle appeared and the woman was there smiling at me and demanding a considerable sum. I thought it better not to challenge this, indeed, it was fortunate that my weekly wage from Friday was still in my wallet or I could never have met the demand.

'So our little Hettie was to your taste, was she, sir?' she said, slightly smacking her lips and looking almost demonic in the flickering candlelight.

I never in my life felt more like hitting a woman than I did at that moment, but I controlled myself. 'Perfect,' I said, trying to keep my face in the shadows. 'I wish to see her as soon as she is next here.'

'Why, of course, sir. We will look forward to that. I take her now for we are shutting up shop, but she will return at three o'clock tomorrow. You can make a special appointment if you wish. I shall keep her free.'

'I most certainly do,' I said with force. And I longed to see this woman's face when she opened the door at the appointed hour.

As soon as I was in the street, I moved along past a yard entrance to the next door which indeed bore the number six. There was less sign of habitation here, and not even a candle flickered in the window. Taking out my note to show it to whoever opened the door, I gave a loud knock – for there was no knocker – glad that a lane separated it from its neighbour. As I waited, I reflected that I still had no idea whether my encounter with Hettie was an accident. For was it not exactly the kind of joke *he* would have loved to perpetrate? Yet perhaps Bell was right and I was seeing his hand even where it had no place.

There was no answer to my knocking, so I tried the door and it opened just as I heard the door of the other house open and the sound of that hateful woman's voice. I entered quickly and closed it behind me.

Standing in that cold hallway I listened as

footsteps came out of the other entrance and went off down the street in the direction of the river. The house before me was silent. As my eyes grew accustomed to the dark I could see the place was clean but with little furniture. I moved to the stair-case and thought I could just make out a flicker of light at the top. I did not want to call out, so I started to mount the stairs.

I was on the first landing, moving as quietly as I could, when I heard the noise. It was not very loud, a scraping sound. I waited, but there was nothing more. I debated going to look in one of the rooms, but all were pitch-black, so I climbed on.

At last I reached the top and turned towards the light source, which turned out to be a half-gutted candle standing on a bench at the far end of the landing beside an open door. It illuminated a bare corridor. And the house seemed quite empty. So who had lit it and why?

I advanced along the corridor and picked the candle up. Thinking perhaps there was someone in the room beyond, I held it high so I could see through the door.

There in its guttering light was the outstretched corpse of a woman. It lay on a table, almost like some dreadful embryo. The limbs were curled, the mouth was wrenched open in shock and the eyes seemed to push forward out of their sockets.

I had seen bodies enough but none like this, for the effect was so uncanny that I almost let go of the candle. It took every shred of my medical training to move towards her. I now realised even the corpse's hair was standing on end and I put out a hand to touch her fingers, trying as I did so not to look at her face. The fingers were rigid, which I would have expected, yet they had a horrifying quality I had never before encountered, a clammy warmth that made them slither away from me.

As I recoiled, I must have pushed the corpse's shoulder for it seemed to quiver and I heard its teeth suddenly grind down and air came from the larynx almost as if it were starting to retch. There was something so horribly animated about this body, something so indefinably repellent, that I could bear no more. I dropped the candle and moved away back down the stairs, wanting only to get out of that house.

As I reached the first landing I thought I heard something and I looked down at the floor. The figure was crouched on its belly below me where it had been waiting. I caught just a glimpse of skin and hair and then it was rearing up towards me, and I felt the terrible pain as it struck out. It was fortunate for me I had twisted round even as I saw it, for the sharp object stabbed into my arm not my heart, and I recoiled with the blow and half fell, half ran down the stairs.

Behind me I knew it had sprung up but I never looked back, desperately staggering on, my arm almost useless to me now. At last I reached the door, managing to fumble it open even as I felt movement behind me. Then I was out in the night, pulling the door closed. In the dim light of the gas I could see a few figures up the street by the river, and wondered if I could get help. But it seemed doubtful so I moved in the opposite direction and slipped inside a doorway.

Beside me my assailant was out of the door almost at once. I could see little enough of him, but, now that I was clear of that house of darkness, at least I made out a male figure. Clearly he supposed I would make for the lights of the river and as soon as he saw signs of people, he started in that direction. So I used the darkness, which I would once have feared but now welcomed, to move stealthily up the street away from him. Soon I had reached St James's Church and was almost in Cannon Street.

Here it became busier, in spite of the cold, and I welcomed the crowd, even if my torn coat and wounded arm made me an object of curiosity. Eventually a bored hansom driver spotted me as he came down Queen Victoria Street on his way to the West End, and asked if I wanted a lift. He stared at me oddly when he saw the wound but I merely gave him directions to Bell's hotel and lay back against the cushioned seat, breathing heavily and trying to decide if I had imagined the dark blotch of colour on my pursuer's neck.

I drew many stares as I entered the hotel. I had wrapped a bloody handkerchief round my wound, my coat was torn and I was shivering from pain and cold. There was no way on earth they would have allowed me to proceed and I stood leaning against the porter's desk while the Doctor was summoned. Luckily he came down quickly enough, took one glance at me, nodded at the porter and within a few minutes he was bandaging my wound in his room.

As he did so, I told him of everything that had happened, uneasily aware of how little I had to show for my adventure. Even the letter was gone, for I dropped it in my flight. But I was emphatic that the body I saw must have been Jenny Galton.

'Well, you have lost blood but your wound is not so bad,' the Doctor announced, 'and I can give you a spare coat. Once you have thawed out we must return to the house at once, only of course with company.'

Since Bell was already working on the Lowther case, assistance came quickly and within about an hour we were in a police cab alongside Inspector Miller and his two uniformed assistants. Miller, a quiet and sensible policeman, was already aware from Bell how anxious we were to contact the missing Jenny Galton, though the Doctor had not explained the real reason why, merely stating that he had grounds for thinking she might offer evidence of an important kind.

Nor did Miller show much surprise when I told him, as cogently as I could in my somewhat exhausted state, of my earlier experience in the house next door; indeed he was sympathetic.

'I am glad to have the information, Dr Doyle,' he said, taking out a notebook and making a record of the address as the cab rattled along Cannon Street. 'I admit much of it goes on but we will try to ensure that particular business closes for good when we call upon it at three tomorrow. There is a charity I know which secures homes for the victims of such places.'

The word 'charity' made me think at once of the League, and he must have seen my expression.

'No, Sir, you need not fear for the child. I talk of a real charity run by women who are genuinely kind, not at all the type who believe they are doing their charges a great favour. I have three children of my own and know the difference.'

I was pleased by this, but it was to be the only satisfaction remaining to me that evening. Armed with lamps, we soon found ourselves before that house in Cole Lane. I felt a little tremor of fear as they opened the door, but I need not have worried, for the place was not merely orderly but entirely empty. There was no sign of anyone, least of all a corpse.

Bell could not find a single spot of blood on the landing where I had been stabbed. When we reached the top of the house the table was still there as I had seen it, but nothing lay on it. In vain I held the lamp high and searched for a piece of hair or a flake of skin or even the candle I had dropped. The shining wood of the table gleamed innocently back at me in the lamplight.

I was glad of Bell's presence for, with the best will in the world, it was a highly embarrassing situation. A corpse that seemed to move, but which had now completely disappeared. A figure that was nowhere to be seen. A mysterious letter which I no longer possessed. And now a house that, even to eyes as sharp as the Doctor's, offered up not the slightest clue. All that was left was my wound, which of course could have been picked up in any street brawl. One of the uniformed policemen, who wore a long moustache and whiskers, had looked away with a smirk as I described the house next door, and by the end of our search I am sure he thought I had gone out looking for a little lechery, been beaten and robbed in the usual way and was now concocting a feeble story to save my honour.

In the circumstances even I began to wonder if my mind had played tricks on me in the darkness of that house. But then, I reasoned to myself, was it not possible that what I saw here *explained* my lucky escape? Perhaps my assailant had not bothered to follow me very zealously because he was more concerned to remove all the evidence as quickly as possible. I made some attempt to explain this point to the others, but by now I was too bewildered and exhausted to be remotely convincing. The expression on the moustached policeman's face grew more and more incredulous as the night wore on. Even Miller's patience was not inexhaustible, and if Bell had not been involved, I strongly suspect I would have been rebuked for wasting their time.

To his credit the Doctor never uttered a word of doubt in their presence. But on the way home, when they had left us, he did ask me one question I could have done without. 'Tell me,' he said, putting his fingertips together in that way he had and looking out of the police cab at the dark streets. 'When you went home today after our work in Shad Thames, did you take a draft of any kind, Doyle?'

The implication infuriated me. 'You mean laudanum,' I said. 'Of course not. I was only at home for a few minutes and went straight out again.'

'Very well,' he said, and shortly afterwards we parted.

I travelled on in the cab to my lodgings alone, feeling deeply dispirited if not angry with the whole world. As we turned down Page Street into Esher, I was sure I could make out a figure standing on the pavement opposite the Morland house looking up at

something. But I was in no mood to trust my judgement that night and, to my relief, when we stopped,
there was no sign of it.

THE WAREHOUSE TO ANOTHER WORLD

The next day, Monday, dawned bitterly cold and there was no possibility of avoiding my work for the practice. Fortunately my wound was easily coverable, and it was healing too, but my arm ached terribly when it was used for any but the easiest of tasks. In normal circumstances I would have taken something to alleviate the pain, but after Bell's question the previous evening I was determined to avoid that. I felt his suspicions were deeply unjust, and a part of me burned at the injustice. One day, I reflected, I might take an amount of the stuff just to spite him, but not now.

I was brooding on this as I spent an arduous few hours in the surgery, hoping my patients would not notice me wincing whenever I was required to apply pressure with my left hand. The weather outside was still freezing cold, but at least the surgery was warm and, as I worked, the events of the previous evening stayed unpleasantly in my mind. In particular I wondered again if my visit to the house next door had been accidental. To the police I had pretended so, but in my heart there was real doubt. I could almost sense *his* amusement at the thought of it: my entrance to the room, my shock as I saw that little shape on the bed. It was his notion, I was sure, of corrupting me.

'Doctor, is it done?' said a voice. And I found I was staring down at a bandage I had just applied to the arm of a local horse dealer.

'Ah, yes,' I said quickly. 'I just wished to be sure it was not too tight, but it is fine.' I quickly straightened myself up and was pleased to see he lost his puzzled expression and beamed happily.

As I showed him out, I reflected that it was not worth telling Bell of such suspicions. It was hard enough even to convince the police I had seen a body. Indeed, I am convinced now that, if matters had continued to stand as they did that morning, then within a short time the Doctor and I would have gone our separate ways.

But a few minutes later, after I had finished the surgery and earned some time for lunch, I was handed a telegram.

I opened it as I walked out on to the street. The message was terse but I understood it immediately.

She is found in the river. Come at once. Bell.

The address was the morgue I had visited before and, when I reached there, the bewhiskered police-man from the previous day – now, I noticed with pleasure, utterly straight-faced – showed me up to Bell in the large and gloomy mortuary where we had stood in perplexity over Harriet Lowther.

The Doctor was just inside the door of that place, his hand beating a rhythm on the nearest workbench, and there was nothing perplexed about him now. Later I learned he had been up most of the night, with no thought for the freezing cold, and had even spent a part of it watching the opium den and Hanbury's boatyard. But, far from seeming tired, his fund of energy was stronger than ever and, as the policeman disappeared, he walked me over to a slab in the corner, pulling off the sheet.

Staring up at me was the body I had seen in the house. The face was unmistakable, its mouth still gaping in that horrible rictus of agony, the eyes starting forward out of their sockets. But the hair no longer stood on end for the corpse had been in the river and bore all the marks of it.

'It has been a very busy night, Doyle,' said the Doctor intently, studying the body with obvious satisfaction. 'She was found close by Swan Pier, only a short distance from Cole Lane, in the early hours of this morning. Because of your story, Miller had her brought here, and we have not been idle. Two hours ago she was positively identified by Elsie Farr. It is indeed Jenny Galton. And I would stake my life she did not drown.'

Of course he saw the look of relief on my face. 'Oh yes. You are entirely vindicated. Now, I am intending to undertake the post-mortem myself. For protocol's sake I cannot ask you to join me, since I must work alongside their own pathologist, but I am hopeful he will confirm my suspicions.'

'Suspicions?'

Suddenly he was serious. 'Yes, I am very much afraid those strange stories of the river have a serious foundation. She was killed by the foul thing they call the 'head' and we may have a grim night ahead of us. I suggest you get something to eat and finish your day's labours in good time.'

My mind was in a whirl for the rest of the day which, fortunately, was not arduous, and I was able to get home to the Morlands in late afternoon. There was nobody at home so, before I set out, I sat down in the drawing room to write a message that they should not expect me back for some time. As I was writing I recalled that at breakfast that day Sally Morland had said something about a surprise for me that night. So I added a line, expressing the hope that I would see them later in the evening.

It was nearing five, and still just as cold outside as it had been all day, when I reached the morgue. The post-mortem was complete and I found Bell sitting alone in the clerk's office writing up his notes, if anything even more excited than before.

'It is, I would say, Doyle,' he said, looking up from his labours, 'the most exciting autopsy I have ever performed.'

'And what did you find?' I asked with enormous curiosity.

'Not a great deal,' he replied without the slightest acknowledgement that this appeared to be a flat contradiction of his previous statement. 'And I am sorry to say the pathologist made even less of it. As we knew, Jenny Galton did not drown, but rigor mortis was very marked indeed. The blood in her heart was extremely fluid, more so than I have ever seen, even the right heart was free from clotting. Her pupils were enlarged, and we concluded that she suffered from primary heart failure. That was the sum of it.'

'Then I find it hard to see why you found it so exciting.'

'But you will,' he said. 'Now, as to our plans. From my own observation, our best chance of finding the truth lies in Sing's establishment. I am convinced there will be little of use in Hanbury's boathouse. We must therefore get into Sing's, but as I have told Miller, I am extremely wary of a police raid. In such an area, things have a habit of getting out and, moreover, all the evidence we might hope to find would probably end up at the bottom of the Thames. So for the moment I am falling back on our own devices.' He studied me for a moment. At his suggestion I was dressed against the cold and wore a dark, heavy overcoat. 'Good,' he said, 'that will suit us, for it is already freezing outside. Now I must myself change, so you will come to the hotel. I have already asked them to lay out a buffet, so I hope some cold roast pheasant and oysters will suit you.' And, with that, he dashed off a signature to the report he had been writing and got to his feet.

Later the Doctor was silent as we consumed our meal in the hotel, and I was a little surprised that Inspector Miller was nowhere to be seen. 'He is talking to Macandrew,' Bell replied in answer to my question, looking up from his pheasant without expression. 'But I have asked his men to stand by and he should be with us later.'

'Macandrew?' I said with surprise. 'Why?'

'Because I suggested he did,' said Bell, taking a last

mouthful and glancing at the window. 'Good, it is time for us to go.'

Bell was extremely specific in his request to the cab driver, directing him not to the alley or Shad Thames but to Charles Street, a more respectable thoroughfare well to the south.

We stepped out of the cab into a freezing night, lit by a huge moon. The cold was dry and bracing, and we walked up into Shad Thames, sticking to the shadows and keeping a wary eye for any trouble, but the weather was keeping people off the streets. When we reached the Lord Lovat, Bell did not venture into the alley. Instead he walked on, glancing only once at the place as he did so.

As soon as we were past it, he turned into a little path between the houses that was strewn with stones and ashes. At the end of this, I saw at once he had discovered another way of getting down to the level of the den without using the steps, for you could clamber down a muddy bank that now lay in front of us and get across a narrow gully on to the broad timber ledge that surrounded the whole building. And there was enough rubbish on the bank, including some half-rotten barrels, to provide concealment. Looking down I could not make out what lay at the bottom of the gully itself: the river, perhaps, or a mudflat.

It was so cold that we were having to thrust our gloved hands in our overcoats to stop them from freezing. As we surveyed the place, away to our left its main door opened and a man tottered out. I heard him stumbling up the steps and then he was gone. The Doctor waited out of sight in the moonlight, till there was no sound of him, and then scrambled down the bank as I followed. Close to the edge, he took the easiest distance across and jumped with customary agility, landing on the ledge that surrounded the structure in front of us.

It was broad and he moved along it to leave room for me to join him. Perhaps partly because of the doubt he had shown in me, and also out of athletic conceit, I took a far longer leap than he did. Of course I cleared the distance with ease, but it was very foolish for I had failed to anticipate that the ledge would be icy. My foot slipped and I went over with a bump, clutching out to stop me falling. There was no real danger of going over, but the Doctor stood stock-still in case we had been heard. I was ashamed of my stupidity and I dreaded to see someone appearing from the door or hear the noise of a shutter opening on the side of the building. Fortunately it did not happen. The only sound came from the slight lapping of water below, so I clambered to my feet and we started to edge our way cautiously along towards the back of the building.

Bell ignored the first shutter that presented itself, assuming, I suppose, that it was too near the front, but he stopped at the next one. We were now almost at the back corner of the place and, beyond it, I could make out a stone wall. Already the cold was starting to ice up my hands, even inside the gloves, and, thanks to my folly over the jump, some of the pain had returned to my arm.

The Doctor turned half back towards me and the moonlight picked out his hooded eagle's eyes, a picture of concentration, as he listened with his ear close to the shutter. Evidently he heard nothing, for he put out a gloved hand and applied some pressure to see if it would open. It did not move a fraction; clearly the frame was held fast by a catch. With a deft movement, he took some instrument out of his pocket and slid it through the crack at the centre of the shutter, levering it upwards, and I heard a tiny click. Then Bell pulled again and the shutter opened quite easily. But he did not pull very far, only a few inches, evidently in order to see if there was any light in the room beyond him. All was dark, so he opened it wider.

The window before us had several small panes but there was a large hinged one at the centre of it. It too was closed but again Bell's implement went to work. This time I could see he found it much harder – he had to press down and apply force to try and lift the catch. Evidently it was barely used, and even in that cold there was perspiration on the Doctor's face as he pushed, and pushed again, and nothing happened. But finally it sprang back with a sudden grating noise which made him instantly withdraw the tool and put out his hand to steady the window.

I am sure both of us were eager to get in, for it was all I could do on that moonlit ledge to stop shivering. But once again we waited, motionless. The Doctor peered into the darkness of the room, yet nobody came and we saw no light. At last, after what was, I am sure, a full minute, Bell reached out and opened the large central pane as far as it would go, which allowed just enough room to climb through. He entered first and was soon on the ledge at the other side. After a few seconds, surveying what was below him, he disappeared down into the darkness and I had the easy task of following.

It was not particularly warm inside, but at least we were out of the frosty air. The ledge was dusty and, though it was still difficult to make much out, the room I climbed into felt damp and ill-used. The Doctor was staring down at something, and I soon saw what: a pile of clothes. He took a pace and lifted a few up. There were coats and hats and waistcoats but also women's clothes too: skirts, petticoats and bodices. A few were of a good cloth; most were shabby.

I walked to the back of the room and here was another pile with a little shawl on the top. There was something so indefinably pitiful about the whole collection that I hated to look at it, for it was obvious that these could not possibly belong to one person or even a family. Yet it seemed hard to believe it could be the proceeds of crime either. Who would bother to rob a man of his clothes? And both our victims had been fully dressed.

But something was wrong here and I could not help noticing that Bell was equally concerned. Looking round, he had found another heap in the corner and was sifting through it with anxiety.

At last he gave up and turned to the closed door at the opposite corner of the room from the window, indicating I should follow. He removed his gloves and I did the same. At the door he listened again, and then with a painstakingly slow movement he turned the handle.

It opened silently and, beyond, all was still dark. Both of us moved out stealthily and waited. There was light from somewhere to the right of us and I could make out that we were in a corridor. Presumably, if we turned to our left we would arrive at the front of the den and the entrance. I assumed Bell would go in that direction, for the stairs down to the bottom level were there, but he did no such thing.

Instead he turned right and began to move towards the light at the back of the building. I could only assume that, with Miller's help, he had established that the place had once been a warehouse of some kind with a back staircase. The corridor was bare and dirty and there was still not much we could see, but soon it veered to the left and I made out light coming from an entrance a little way down. The Doctor headed for this at once and, as I reached him, he turned to me and nodded. We were at the top of a flight of stone steps.

We moved slowly down the winding stairs and the light below us grew brighter.

Bell was ahead of me but, as we descended, I noticed him looking anxiously back the way we had come. His face told me he was concerned that we might be surprised from that direction, and he whispered to me to keep a watch behind.

After a few turns of the steps, we reached the floor below. Before us was a short passage piled with boxes, and at the end of it an old curtain of Oriental design. Beyond the curtain was the source of light, and I could make out the sound of voices. Slowly and quietly we inched forward. Soon we were at the curtain itself, which was so torn and old that it was possible to see into the room ahead.

Through the cracks I made out a large space, rather

like the cabin of a ship, with some rudimentary furniture: a table was close by us with two upright lighted candles which illuminated a desk, a threadbare armchair, cushions, a stove, and some objects, associated with the opium trade. The sound of the river was stronger and it was not hard to see why. This part of the structure must have stood above one of the numerous inlets, and in the far corner a trap door stood propped open.

I took all of this in at once, but most of my attention was on the table and the two men close by it. Standing with his back to us was Hanbury. I could not see his face, but I recognised not only the burn on his neck but the whole bearing of the man. He stood laughing, one meaty hand on the wooden table before him, the other in his pocket. In front of him, facing us, was a pale thin waif of a man, though he was by no means young. His hair was lank and silver-grey, his eyes red, presumably from the effects of the pipe, and his hands shook. Yet he was not unhappy; he was laughing at something Hanbury had said. Therefore I assumed he was a confederate and wondered why Hanbury would be interested in using someone so evidently frail and feeble.

'You saw them – what a pack of fools,' Hanbury repeated, still evidently seized by the humour of something.

'The Old Chink,' the older man was wheezing. 'The Old Chink, he has a devil of a pipe. Why, my feet are blocks of wood. And did you see the sailor, he's under the bed now, and will be there till morning.'

'Let him lie,' said Hanbury.

'Aye,' said the other. 'But the sailor will be rank.' He laughed and the other joined him. 'The stench up there is already foul.'

'They can roll in it for all I care.' Hanbury banged a hand on the table. He seemed to me to be indulging the older man in a way that was unnerving. 'But you are to have a private pipe here with me, so why do you stand there? You say you want to see something?'

'Aye,' said the silver-haired man, his face glinting craftily in the candlelight. 'I have heard what you have. Your head. Your live head.'

Behind the curtain I heard Bell take in a breath at the mention of this.

'What head?' said Hanbury scornfully, and then his manner changed a little. 'Ah well, if you have heard of it, somebody has said what they should not.'

'Yes,' said the silver-haired man, lolling forward, 'the Chink's wife was full of it. It came from the East. She said it is alive? A female head. A dragon's head?'

'Not a dragon, though they say it lives for ever, but nobody should talk of such things for it is devilish ugly and it stings,' said Hanbury. 'You do not want to see the head.'

'Show me,' said the man recklessly, for it was obvious that opium had dulled his fear into a sort of thrilling pleasure.

'Well,' said Hanbury, 'you are a help to me, so I will grant you if you wish. But only a little turn before our pipe. And you will not touch?'

'Ah, no,' said the silver-haired man.

At this, Hanbury went over to a large storage cupboard. For a few moments he could not be seen, though I thought I heard a noise of some kind. And then he reappeared with an old and bulky black box which he carried over to the table. There was something very ugly about this box. He dusted it off as the silver-haired man leaned forward eagerly. Beside me, I sensed the Doctor too crouching forward.

'That is it?' said the silver-haired man.

Hanbury nodded and put his hand on the box which stood on the table between them. 'So you are ready to see it?' he said.

The silver-haired man nodded and made some noises of assent. Because of the drug, I take it, he had not much control, and his curiosity was making him almost slobber. But Hanbury merely smiled and stood erect and put two hands on either side of the box. The man was bent down in expectation and, as he watched, Hanbury slowly lifted the great lid.

Of course, from where we stood we could see nothing of what was inside, but now a shaft of light fell on the silver-haired man's face, and his mouth opened wide and his eyes bulged with wonder as he stared at its contents.

'The head.' He spoke in a reverent whisper. 'The damned head.'

His hand beside him was quivering and came a little closer.

'She says there is nothing like the touch of it,' he whispered. 'It will give you more than twenty pipes, more than a woman, more than anything else.'

I expected Hanbury to slam the lid down at this contradiction of his warning, but his tone had changed and his eye was fixed on the silver-haired man. 'Go on then, Ben,' he said with unexpected recklessness, 'you have earned it, I suppose.'

And the silver-haired man put out his hand.

All this time I had sensed Bell's growing tension beside me. Now the Doctor suddenly erupted. For he flung himself forward through the curtain with a great shout.

Hanbury whirled with a furious look. The silver-haired man hesitated – but he was too late, for his hand had connected with the head, or whatever it was, and it must have bitten out at him. Now his hand was caught fast and he was quivering with pain which, from his expression, was as acute as any I had ever witnessed. His mouth stretched in a frenzy, his face contorted, the terror and agony in him was so great that he could not even scream out.

But Bell had lost not a second. He sprang across the room, raising his cane, and flung it with all the force at his command at the man's arm. The impact was enough to tear his limb away from whatever was in that box, but the Doctor's effort was in vain for the man slumped lifeless on the floor not far from the trap, and I could see from his posture that he was dead.

Hanbury turned on the Doctor now, his face full of fury, catching up a short, ugly-looking staff from the table. I stepped forward at once, but even as I did so something brushed past my hair, and my neck was suddenly jerked back with horrible force as a cord was slipped round it and pulled tight.

I cursed my stupidity, for I had been so transfixed by what was happening in the room that I had utterly failed to heed the Doctor's last warning. Behind me, as I twisted back, I caught just a glimpse of the Chinese I had seen before, his face murderous as he pulled the cord taut, choking the life out of me. And even as I struggled, events in the room before me were taking a terrible turn. Having no weapon, Bell had tried to sidestep Hanbury's blow, but the man was quick and the stave smashed into the Doctor's neck, sending him reeling.

In a trice Hanbury had pinned Bell's arms and was dragging him half-conscious towards the table where the box lay. But that was all I saw. The cord was so tight now that my senses were swimming. My hands scrabbled uselessly at my neck trying to free it, but it was already cutting into my throat and my senses blurred.

THE HEAD

I could feel my legs were about to give way, and my eyes were closed. But a part of my mind knew that if I fell now, I would die.

And it was then, in the extremity of pain, that I registered that my hands, so uselessly fumbling at my neck, had found something soft. It must be the hair of my attacker, whose head was therefore close to mine. With a great effort I brought my hands up high and clamped them round his scalp, pulling it forward. It was a last play – in another instant I would have gone into the darkness – but I gave it every ounce of strength I had. And in response I felt the cord round my neck slacken slightly, and was able to take a few gasps of air, for the Chinese could not possibly keep the cord tight as he struggled to free himself from my grip.

This gave me more strength and a sudden idea. With a quick movement, I flexed my knee, dipping a little and then, releasing my hands, I brought my head hard back into his. There was a crack as the back of his skull hit the stone of the wall, and the cord was looser still. Before he had time to recover I repeated the action to even better effect. I felt his body sag.

I was able to turn now and tear the cord from my neck. The Chinese had crumpled to the floor and I staggered round and moved forward through the curtain into the room.

A dreadful spectacle was before me. The Doctor was slumped in a chair, still obviously greatly weakened by the blows he had sustained, and Hanbury was crouched over him beside that horrible box. At first I could not make out exactly what Hanbury was doing until I saw he had tied a strip of cloth round Bell's right wrist and was carefully and gleefully forcing the Doctor's hand directly into the open box and whatever hellish thing it contained.

Bell's face was ashen but there was nothing at all he could do, for Hanbury had used wire to tie him to the chair. The body of the silver-haired man itself was nowhere to be seen. I was still a little dazed but I ran forward, seizing one of the metal candlesticks on the table. Hanbury was so intent on what he was doing that he never turned, and I brought it down hard on his head.

But I was too late. For even as he fell, the Doctor's hand was already in that box and in the light of the one remaining candle Bell's mouth opened, his hair fluttered up and he cried out in deadly pain.

I moved to him but, before I could come round the table, his cry stopped and his expression changed. He even smiled, and then, for a wonder he withdrew his hand, turning to me. 'I suppose the Chinese detained you,' he said, closing the box.

'You are all right?' I said with wonder as I untied the wire and helped him to his feet.

'I believe so,' he said, putting up a hand to smooth his hair and then moving to retrieve his silver-topped cane. 'There are limits to even Hanbury's devilry, I am glad to say. He has put one corpse down his trap tonight and I am pleased not to be another. I once told you I smelt an air of death about this place.' Although still weak, he examined Hanbury and then looked through the curtain at the Chinese, who was as he had been.

'Well done, Doyle,' he said. 'I am grateful, but I must ask another favour. As you know, I did not want suspicions aroused, but the police are not far away. Go to the end of the alley past the Lord Lovat and stand under the gas lamp. Wait a few minutes and they will be with you. I can keep a watch over things here. I suggest you take the main staircase out, it is more direct. You may see the Chinaman's wife, but I do not think she will offer any resistance.'

I was concerned about leaving him but he insisted there could be no delay so I ran up the straight staircase at the front which I had seen on my first visit. It was dark at the top, but I knew the main door was almost opposite and found it without difficulty.

Then I was out on those steps in the cold and moving quickly down the alley. It was so icy that few were on the streets, even by the public house ahead of me, and my mind kept thinking what it must be like to fall down Hanbury's trapdoor into the black freezing water beyond. Perhaps it was merciful that his victim was dead before he went through it.

Reaching the end of the alley, I slackened my pace,

having no wish to appear suspicious, and passed the
Lord Lovat. There were people here and I weaved
around them until finally I reached the next street
and stopped at the gas lamp. I had been told to wait
a few minutes, which was not an appealing prospect
in this setting, but I did my best to observe it. A
couple of people stared at me, but then went on their
way. Eventually I felt sure something must have gone
wrong with the plan. Then I saw men emerging from
the warehouse doorways up towards Shad Thames.
And soon Inspector Miller was beside me, closely
followed by three other police, including my sceptical
friend with the moustache. 'Is the Doctor all right?'
were Miller's first words.

I told them he was but he needed their help at
once. We went into the alley and took the place's
steps at a run, for my commission had taken far longer
than I would have liked. Soon we were inside the den,
trying to get our eyes accustomed to the darkness as
we stumbled towards the front staircase.

My worst fears seemed to be realised when there
was noise, and I heard a shout from the space below
where I had left Bell. I could see a figure was at the
bottom, but from the size of it I knew at once that it
was not Bell and I cried out. Hanbury took one look
at the police behind me and turned to go the other
way. We managed the stairs at a run and reached the
floor below where, to my enormous relief, I saw Bell
on his feet before the curtain. In his hand was his
cane and he was blocking Hanbury's escape.

'Hanbury, give it up,' Miller shouted but the man
obviously thought he could take Bell easily and
advanced towards him. There was a gleam of

vengefulness in the Doctor's eye, for some of his strength had evidently returned and he probably relished the chance to make a better showing of himself than he had last time. I could see Hanbury had not the slightest idea of the Doctor's agility, obviously assuming, from all he had seen so far, that his opponent was a weak old man. For this reason, he moved recklessly within range of the cane without the slightest hesitation, but the Doctor was ready and swung it directly at Hanbury's head. Too late the man saw his danger and put up a hand, but the metal tip hit him a mighty crack under his ear and he staggered back across the room.

The Doctor shouted out, for the trapdoor was right behind him. But Hanbury was still reeling from the second blow he had sustained that night, stepped back over it, failed to find his footing and lost his balance, falling backwards right into the dark space.

I ran to it and saw a white splash about ten feet below as he entered the freezing water. It was inky black and, though we watched, there was no sign of him. I was wondering, not, I will admit very decisively, if we should attempt a rescue when I felt the Doctor's restraining hand on my shoulder. He pointed out that on a night like this nobody was likely to come out of there alive. 'He follows his victim, Doyle, and judging by that pitiful room of clothes upstairs, God knows how many more.'

Inspector Miller had come to stare into the water too, though the other police were almost more amazed by the Doctor's appearance. Bell was still pale and there was a cut on his right temple, but even so he glowed with a fierce kind of energy. 'My apologies, Inspector,' he said. 'While Doyle was fetching you I became so absorbed by the contents of this room,' here he waved at a pile of papers he had pulled out of a drawer, 'and also by that box, that I neglected to check the Chinese Doyle encountered. It was too long before I went through the curtain to look for him and of course he had gone. While I was looking, Hanbury must have got up.'

'My only regret is that we were not here to help,' said Miller, withdrawing his eyes with difficulty from the trap. 'But you seem to have done well enough. Hanbury was the important one. The Chinese was hardly more than his servant. But we will find him.' And he turned to issue instructions to his men to search the rest of the premises.

'I rather doubt that,' said Bell as the uniformed men dispersed. 'He and his wife will scuttle back into some other dive, but from what I can see they were mainly involved in the supply of opium. It was Hanbury who used this place for what it was, and I very much fear his main victims were derelicts.'

'Ah, yes, and on that I have to tell you, sir,' said Miller, looking with some fascination at the objects in the room, 'that I had a most interesting discussion tonight with the scientist Macandrew. Of course he was utterly horrified to think the cadavers Hanbury provided were not legitimately obtained. He paid Hanbury handsomely for them, and the man even provided paperwork showing that relatives had agreed the usage.'

'They were fraudulent, of course,' said Bell.

'Perhaps,' said Inspector Miller, 'but they seemed genuine enough.'

Bell nodded. 'Very well. Of course I would like to have a chat with Macandrew myself to inform him of what we have found here.'

'But now . . . .' Miller was advancing eagerly towards the box . . . 'you must tell us exactly what was done and why, and of course what is in here.'

The box was still on the table, but Bell stepped between him and it. 'Ah, yes. It is better to be careful.'

'Still, you must open it,' Inspector Miller demanded eagerly. 'Is it some kind of snake?'

'Far deadlier,' said the Doctor, laying his hand on the top.

'Then how did you survive it?' I asked, staring at him. I was still far from clear about the details of the crimes Miller and Bell were discussing but, more than anything else, I wanted to know what was in the box and what had happened in that awful moment when for a few seconds I was sure the Doctor was a dead man.

'I was lucky,' he said, 'although to tell the truth I had some slight hope I would be. Now I would ask you both to stand before it, just as Doyle and I saw that poor man stand earlier.'

We did so. Bell placed a hand on either side of the box, watching our faces. He waited, and then very slowly he pulled it open.

A ghastly illumination started to shine out. Of course I had heard stories of creatures emanating their own light – large dragonflies, glow-worms and so forth – but they hardly prepared me for what I saw now.

The light was a sickly green and it was blinding. Then, as my eyes slowly adjusted, I made out something through it. A great swollen shape of almost the same colour. It had malevolent hideous eyes, a stretched scaly green skin and a massive fanged mouth. This was a reptile's head of some kind, that was certain, but far bigger than any I had ever seen or knew to exist. And it pulsed with a disgusting energy, which trapped the eye. I could understand now the source of all those stories. Anyone seeing this would undoubtedly believe they had witnessed something unnatural. The wide fanged mouth seemed to entice you, but there was no body.

'What in heaven's name is it?' I exclaimed, putting out my hand to feel the glow.

'No,' said Bell. 'Do not go near it.' And he slammed the lid of the box shut with such force that I had to snatch my hand back.

'But you touched it,' I said.

'And it hurt too. But very fortunately its power was waning. Since then I have examined it and restored it, so it is now almost as potent as when it last killed.'

Both Miller and I looked at him, baffled.

'I will show you,' he said. And from a compartment in the base of the box he took out a long metal handle. He placed it in an aperture in the side and slowly at first, but then more quickly he began to turn it. 'Now observe,' he said. 'I will demonstrate the full extent for you, but please do not even lift your hand.' And once again he opened the box.

The horrible head was still there but a remarkable thing was happening. For as Bell turned the handle, the light inside was getting brighter and brighter. Soon it was dazzlingly bright and we had almost to shield our eyes.

'There is nothing alive here,' said Bell. 'At least in any conventional sense. Take away the trappings, which are in their way extraordinary, and you will find a dynamo, to which Hanbury gained access through Macandrew. Indeed you saw him carry it out of the Polytechnic exhibition, Doyle. The head you see is the preserved head of a reticulated python, no doubt bought from a sailor.'

'You are not saying he did this with Macandrew's knowledge?' said Miller.

Bell hesitated. 'No, I suppose I am persuaded the scientist could not have known. Inside the head you will find an electric contact which can convey up to three hundred and fifty watts of what is called alternating current, wrapped in a lethal wire. This is originated when you turn the handle, but the power is also stored and augmented by a powerful battery. Here is what killed Jenny Galton and made her corpse so strange to Doyle. It also did for Harriet Lowther when Hanbury transported it to her room. In her constant toings and froings on the dockside she had no doubt seen far more of what went on in this den than Hanbury liked. The poor woman thought she could get money from him but he lured her with the prospect of seeing the fabulous head. And she saw it all right, just like the legion of people whose clothes are upstairs. Dozens of intoxicated opium seekers were seen off here, all valuables stripped from them before being dumped through that hatch. Many were picked up a day or so later by Hanbury on the river and went to Macandrew as raw materials for his investigations. But whenever these poor victims were dragged out of the river and assessed by your pathologists, their death would always be put down to drowning or a simple heart attack.'

'But surely I have seen such displays of electricity before?' I protested. 'I understood them to be a kind of party trick. I thought they could do no serious harm.'

'Yes, and your conviction is entirely erroneous, even though you share it with most of the population,' said Bell. 'It is true that until recently they could not. Do you know, Doyle, when the first man in Europe was killed by electric current as that poor silver-haired man was tonight?'

I shook my head.

'Not more than four years ago, in Lyon, when a stage carpenter died at the hands of a Siemens dynamo like this one, though a great deal larger in size, for huge strides have been made in just a short time in the design of these machines. The first death in England was a year later in Birmingham in 1880 where a bandsman died, only this time it was a dynamo and a battery which he short-circuited. Of course it was only a matter of time before someone used such devices for murder and our friend Mr Hanbury may well take the dubious credit of being the first. I very much fear that where death is so efficient and reliable, there will be many more.'

It was a sobering thought. 'So it explains the strangeness of Jenny Galton's corpse when I saw it?'

'Certainly,' said Bell. 'By that time I had suspicions, but it was her autopsy that convinced me. I had been careful to read up on what little evidence we have and always the blood was extraordinarily liquid, especially in the heart, while rictus is very marked. It was not, I will admit, very pleasant to recall these effects when Hanbury was forcing me to touch it, using the cloth to keep clear himself. But even then, as I said, I did harbour certain hopes. For I had deduced that its originating power must be by hand and much time had elapsed, while despite my best efforts our poor friend with silver hair had taken considerable current. Also I could observe that the filament was not so bright, so the battery must have run lower. I did feel, therefore, that I had a chance, even if I should have preferred not to take it. And as you saw, Doyle, when I touched the thing I received only a small shock – my hair stood on end, I felt a little pain. But it was only the kind of harmless party trick you mentioned just now and which most people associate with electricity. Unfortunately, as we have seen, they will soon know better.'

Shortly after this, Inspector Miller's men returned to report that they had searched the whole place and found it was entirely empty of people other than the stupefied opium smokers. 'Well,' said the Inspector, 'we will have to begin clearing it out and I hate to think of half what we will find, but at least I will arrange for this contraption to go back where it came from at once. And we must make sure Macandrew does not let it out of his sight again.'

I cannot say I was sorry to walk up those steps for the last time and climb into the police cab Miller had arranged for us. Bell and he had some further words together and then we were on our way. 'We will visit Macandrew ourselves,' said Bell, looking at his watch. 'But before we do we have earned some refreshment.

It is not late and I have seen a satisfactory coffee house at Norfolk Street on the other side of the river. Let us take half an hour there.'

I knew the Doctor far too well to find this suggestion anything but highly unusual. He would surely want to compare notes with Macandrew and it was not his way to interrupt a case in its closing stages. I was also aware that he had been curiously silent on the matter which most concerned me, so I was not surprised when we sat down and he produced a few letters from his pocket.

'I was able to go through what was there quite carefully,' he said. 'The police will find much of it interesting. Without our guidance they would not have made anything of these. But you will.'

And he handed them to me.

The letters, dated several months earlier, were very much like the ones I had received, though he had made no attempt to disguise his hand, and rather than being posted it looked from the envelopes as if they had been brought to Hanbury by a mutual acquaintance, presumably a seaman. I picked up the first, addressed to Charles Hanbury, and this is what I read:

Your name is one often mentioned by seamen here as a fellow who will take on the out-of-the-way task if the price is right. I wish you to find the right Paphians for some amusement so I can play a trick upon a very dear friend. I have some girls in mind but you must find them out, write me of their particulars, and I will instruct you what to tell them to say and do when my friend comes calling. I would also like you to find an establishment with a child so we can play that joke upon him. You will be paid well, all the better since you may have to perform some tidying up for I don't want the girls to give trouble. If you agree, more particulars will follow.

My eye raced to the signature.

An American gentleman

And the address was a forwarding agent in Chicago.

Bell looked at me long and hard. 'So we may conclude he is not here?'

My hand was trembling and I was glad that he had left this until we were alone.

'But is it not possible,' I said, glancing at the dates, 'that this, too, is some blind? He would surely want to observe and enjoy my discomfort himself, never associating with Hanbury but staying in the shadows. These are very old letters, after all, and I have felt such a sense of him throughout this.'

'No doubt you have,' said Bell grimly. 'I have too. Who knows what pleasure he would have in the process we have just witnessed. It is so much what he looks for. The future of death. There is something more barbarous about that box of Hanbury's than the ugliest blade, for at least you have to drive that home.'

'Yet you say it is just coincidence that our enemy found this man?' I said bitterly, for in talking of such things I knew we were both thinking again of the beach and its message.

'I say no such thing,' said Bell. 'The legend of Hanbury's serpent head must have spread. No doubt he relished the power it gave him. And . . . Cream—' He hesitated a little before he spoke the name. It was a name I suppose we both tried not to speak for it seemed as if the mere act of pronouncing it gave its owner power and also summoned up so much old pain, 'would have heard these stories and sensed that a man like Hanbury, who undoubtedly had a reputation as a killer on many waterfronts, was someone he could use. I accept some doubts remain, Doyle, they always will. But my advice is that he has been playing at a distance.

'And,' he continued, 'I must apologise where I doubted you. I was wrong. My only defence is that I know the way he would like you to go, so perhaps I erred on the side of concern. I ask your forgiveness for that.'

I was, I will admit, somewhat consoled by these words, for the Doctor rarely apologised. As to the other matter, I had to acknowledge relief, for a part of me would have dreaded Cream appearing here in case he threatened the family for which I held such affection. 'Thank you,' I said. 'So we have some chance of rejoining the attack?'

The Doctor took a sip of tea. 'Perhaps he has provided us with a way.'

The Pool of Will

Bell would not speak very much further of his plan. But I know he was pleased by the fact that he had obtained a forwarding agent in Chicago from the letters to Hanbury.

'I intend also,' he said, 'to write to Inspector Miller and try to introduce him to the subject of what lies behind these letters. He knows what Hanbury was and I think he will be sympathetic. He is a potential ally in this matter, as no policeman in Edinburgh has ever been.'

Naturally I had expected Macandrew to be a little chastened by all these events when we called on him shortly after this conversation. It was, after all, his dynamo that had sent people to their deaths, and his appetite for 'materials' that had furnished Hanbury with a ready income.

But he opened the door with as wide a smile as I had yet seen and proved to be more animated than ever. 'My dear Dr Bell, and Dr Doyle,' he said, according me the title for almost the first time.

'Come in, I was told you were on your way. This is a remarkable case you have uncovered.'

He ushered us into the warm and well-appointed hall, and thence to the elegant drawing room, waving away a maid who had evidently appeared rather tardily as we sat down.

'I had no idea Hanbury was capable of such underhand things. He always made himself extremely useful to me, as you know. And I was happy for him to store the equipment when I did not need it.'

'You have your dynamo back, I take it,' said the Doctor politely, observing Macandrew extremely closely.

'Why yes,' said Macandrew. 'I will make sure from now on that it is either here or at the Polytechnic. I gather he had rigged up some trick with the thing.' And he took us over to it, only now when the box was opened it looked positively dull, just some wires and metal and the green light filament. And I marvelled a little at Hanbury's skill, for it had taken a kind of brilliance to transform this thing, though perhaps the Chinese helped him. The head of the serpent was, it is true, the crowning touch, but all the detail of the apparatus had been effectively disguised too and the use of coloured paper to cover it was ingenious.

'It was a very clever trick,' said Bell, who had noted Macandrew's blithe dismissal. 'He was an evil man but it took imagination.'

His words were obviously carefully chosen for, even though Macandrew smiled, I could see a slight irritation. 'I am a scientist,' he said. 'And I have no time for conjuring tricks. Now, can I offer you both some refreshment for I believe you have had a gruelling evening?'

'No,' said the Doctor. 'We have had something to sustain us and I came really to discuss your use of what Hanbury provided. Perhaps you could show us.'

'Of course,' said Macandrew, getting up. 'I would be delighted. You of all people would understand that aspect of my work. And I wished you to come and see my laboratory in any case.'

He showed us down the stairs and soon we were in his work place with its tank and dissecting tables and the Doctor was looking around with interest. 'So tell me,' he said after a while. 'How is it that Hanbury brought odd specimens of the river to you?'

'Oh,' said Macandrew, 'there are many men who help me with the equipment. I asked them to find me a rough hand who knew the river, had a boat and would not mind picking out the more grisly kinds of materials I needed. They soon directed me to Hanbury and he seemed ideal.'

'I see,' said Bell, 'and what did he bring you at first?'

'Why, animals that had drowned in the first instance. Cats, a dog or two. But I told him I would pay well for bodies provided they were legitimately obtained. And so on occasions he would bring them too, always with the paperwork. Naturally I insisted on that.'

'And, in the course of these duties, did he ever have access to these premises for I know you are away a great deal?'

Macandrew looked uninterested. 'Yes, my lecturing takes me everywhere, and on a few occasions I can recall he had the keys for he was delivering.'

'And then he provided you with corpses, did he not?' said Bell quietly.

'Yes,' said Macandrew, going to a filing drawer. 'But as I have said I always paid well, and insisted he had the necessary permissions. Here they are.'

He handed Bell a sheaf of papers.

'Yes I see,' said Bell, studying them. 'He went to a little trouble. And yet these are presumably forgeries.'

'I could have no idea of that,' said Macandrew, still standing beside him. 'And I appeal to you as a man of science, Dr Bell. I have a great interest in certain causes of death. Drowning, and also heart attacks. This is of course a sideline, not my main field I fully admit, but I am a polymath and such experiments may do us much good in the end. As the police recognised from these papers, I had no reason to question the sound provenance of what was brought here. Even now I feel sure some of them are genuine.'

'I doubt that,' said Bell, handing them back. 'And now are you aware of what in fact had happened to them?'

'In general, of course,' said Macandrew, replacing the files. 'I have no idea of the details.'

'Then,' said Bell with a stillness I always knew masked anger, 'let me tell you the *details*. They were derelicts, mainly, people who would not be missed, people who had some misfortune in their lives or were merely hopelessly poor and lured by a pipe of opium. They were stunned or killed by your electrical device, stripped of some clothing and any meagre

valuables they might have had and sent down a trap
door into the freezing river. Such were the deaths
feeding what you call your "sideline".'

Macandrew did not answer at once; he was quite
aware of the Doctor's point. 'Well, it is a debate,' he
said at last. 'I had no part in what you describe,
though it is true I benefited. But after all, you
yourself say these people will be missed by nobody.
And unless you, Dr Bell, go out into the East End and
save such people by distributing your money to them,
there is no point in lecturing anyone else. I fully
accept it is not possible or desirable to obtain
scientific material in the way you describe, but even
so I am happy to find another Hanbury. I will merely
check his paperwork more thoroughly, for nothing
can or should stand in the way of science.' He looked
rather pleased with this speech and I was a little
surprised that the Doctor seemed to concede ground
too.

'Ah yes,' said Bell, his tone lightening, 'the way of
science. Well, there is something to be said for that.
And you make your point well, so let us leave it there.
Now it had slipped my mind, but I meant to tell you
that I have myself a small scientific experiment, that
has been exercising my curiosity, and I wish to
discuss it with you particularly, while I inspect your
chambers below. Can we go down?'

'I would be delighted,' said Macandrew, getting up
with a great smile. 'Let us now officially say the
present discussion is at an end. And the scientific
one, infinitely more interesting in my view, and I
suspect yours too, begins.'

He led us through the door down the stone

staircase into the basement below. It was strange on this evening to be once again in a riverside establishment heading down to the water. When I had been here before I had felt impressed and important at being part of the advance of science. Now, as I thought back to that horrible room of clothes in the den and to Hanbury's evil box, I found the connection between the two riverside establishments unnerving, especially since they were inextricably linked by a grisly trade in cadavers. As we descended I looked again at the dim light of Macandrew's special carbon filaments, and found that they had become far less comforting than the gas I was used to.

We walked down along the dank tunnel and Bell stopped at the flood chamber. 'You use this for experiments on equipment, I understand,' he said. And I recalled then how interested he had been when I described it to him.

'Yes,' said Macandrew, leading the way in as Bell followed. There was not much room and, rather to my irritation, Bell stood blocking the doorway without even glancing back at me, forcing me to linger in the tunnel. 'What has been on my mind, to be truthful,' said Bell, 'is Hanbury's trap. Because on occasions he wanted his victims to be drowned as you wished, he would no doubt have to calculate how long they would survive and where in the river he was likely to find their corpses the next day. In some ways, indeed, his work was quite close to your study of how far the lungs survive in water. A tricky business. No doubt sometimes he missed them, which would have vexed him.'

'It is not something I have concerned myself with,

Dr Bell. He was useful but I had no idea how far he had sunk. And I thought we were to discuss matters scientific.'

'I promise that is where I am leading,' said the Doctor. 'And you say sometimes he had access to your laboratory and that, on these occasions, he was delivering cadavers.'

'Yes, as I recall.'

'Which were waiting for you on your return, were they not? You see, I will tell you what I think and you must say whether you agree. I think that, when he had the chance, he found a scientific way to make things far easier for himself. I do not think you knew that, but if you had stopped for a moment and applied your own scientific principles, you would have concluded as much.'

'Then I would be grateful if you would explain, for I still do not see the scientific application.'

'You see,' said Bell, 'using the box was one thing, but I think he had found a far easier way of drowning them, even than his trap. He only needed to bring his victims here, the very place where their bodies were required, show them the wonders of your laboratory, including this chamber, and then, while they stared at it, he would quite simply step outside . . .'

As he spoke the Doctor walked out.

'And close the door,' he added, and in an instant he too had closed it, tightening the wheeled waterproof seal. I could not believe my eyes and Macandrew was staggered. He came over to the door at once and pulled at it, staring at Bell though the porthole window.

'It is merely a demonstration,' the Doctor said, raising his voice so the astonished Macandrew could hear him. 'A chance for you to experience the effects of science.'

And with that he began to open the second wheel, which released the water into the chamber. I supposed he was joking and would in a second or so stop and open the door, but he kept on. Macandrew was looking away now and I could hear the noise of water. The ducts were opening and it was starting to flow into the room.

'Doctor, what are you doing?' I said in shock. But he did not even turn – he was opening the wheel further and further. Looking in I could see the water was already swirling around Macandrew's ankles, and a great roar was starting as the duct fully opened. Inside the chamber his expression, which had been angry, was turning to fear.

Now, as I remonstrated with the Doctor, Macandrew came and beat on the window, but Bell kept his hand hard on the wheel and did not even look. Soon Macandrew staggered back through the water to inspect the ducts, obviously seeing whether they could be blocked, but it was quite impossible. He had designed it himself so that the velocity of the water was enormous.

Once again I implored the Doctor, 'You must stop now at once. This is sheer folly.' I was trying to sound reasonable because I wanted to hide the truth, which was, strange though it is to relate, that I felt more fear now than I had even in the den. For I could quite well see that the Doctor was not himself. I had never before seen him so coldly angry. I shouted to him

433

again as he stood over the wheel but he merely consulted his watch.

Inside the chamber Macandrew had given up on the door and the porthole. He was staring about him, the water already at his knees and coming faster all the time. I looked around desperately, wondering if there was any other safety device beyond what Bell controlled, but I could see none. And when I turned back it seemed to me that the water was nearly at Macandrew's waist.

I began to scream at Bell as never before in my life. 'You will stop this. I do not care if the man turned his eye away from what was being done in his name. It is no excuse for drowning him.'

The Doctor turned and I saw the anger still in his eyes. 'If he has any scientific principles left in him at all, he will know quite well that he probably has another four minutes.'

Macandrew was beating on the door now, his face terrified. I turned back to Bell who was holding fast, but I no longer had any confidence in his calculation. When I looked back Macandrew was staggering around quite likely to collapse any second and drown himself even before the level reached the top.

I could bear it no longer. I hurled myself at Bell and physically dragged him away from the wheel. At first he resisted me and I wondered if I would be able to manage to get him away in time, for he still had his old wiry strength, but then he left it.

In the chamber I could see to my horror that Macandrew had fallen. I turned the wheel as fast as I could. Of course it was far harder this way than the other and there was massive pressure, but slowly I managed to make a seal.

And then I pulled the handle that opened the drain.

Looking through I could see Macandrew had his head up and that the water had stopped. But he was not looking at us. He was slumped against the far wall, his eyes fixed on the inlet.

At least the drainage was designed to be fast, so I could see the level dropping. And, while I made sure of the controls, it was Bell who opened the door. Over his shoulder I saw Macandrew pressed back against the wall, still white with fear.

'I think,' said Bell, 'I have demonstrated to you the alternative method Hanbury almost certainly used to provide you with what you wanted.'

'You are mad,' said Macandrew quietly. Though he still had a frightful appearance, he was recovering a little of his dignity.

'It is a question,' said the Doctor, 'of who is mad and who is sane. Some might think that performing scientific experiments on people who had been deliberately drowned was mad. I fully accept you had no legal guilt, but even so these things would never have happened without your contribution. And what sort of world, what sort of century lies before us if your science is to be conducted with that kind of wilful blindness?'

Little more was said as we went back upstairs and Macandrew dismissed us curtly from the house. But I admit I felt only relief. I had been half dreading that he would threaten the Doctor with some kind of lawsuit, for in many respects justice would have been

on his side, and I pointed this out as soon as we were
in the street.

The Doctor smiled at me. He looked utterly
exhausted but satisfied, exhilarated even. 'I am sorry
to have put *you* through that, Doyle, but not, I fear,
for any other reason. If Macandrew had shown the
slightest sympathy for the victims I would never have
done it, but he is the kind who thinks everything of
his science and himself and nothing whatsoever of its
effect. Even Hanbury, as I said, had more imagination
than that man. But I knew quite well that the famous
scientist would never let this affair be made public, so
we were quite safe.'

We strolled on slowly, not yet cold despite the
weather for we had got warm enough in Macandrew's
house, and also, I suppose, we wished to delay the
moment of parting. 'I also like to think,' he continued, 'though it is probably an illusion, that he
might have learned a lesson tonight.'

As we walked down that freezing yet well-lit
London street, he counselled me to try and forget
about this evening's horrors and get back to the sanity
and warmth of the Morland household. 'For my part,'
he said, 'I will be perfectly glad to return to
Edinburgh.' He was taking the train north the next
day and there was no way of knowing when we would
meet again.

Before he left me he said I should not allow myself
to be haunted. But there was something else.

'I do not want you to mistake me. On our terms,
Doyle, yes, but we will never give up the fight. To the
death, if necessary.'

And so we parted, and as I watched him disappear

in the direction of his hotel in a cab, a part of me felt almost reassured. Of course I knew that by far the greater business stood unfinished, but at least we had dealt with one immediate threat. I had quite forgotten his aphorism that the final and most dangerous stage of a Greek labyrinth is a single straight line.

THE UNCLE

I turned away after his cab disappeared round the corner of the street and buttoned up my overcoat to the top for the walk back to the Morlands's. Consulting my watch as I set off, I was amazed to find it was not even ten o'clock. But we had started for the opium den in early evening and it was hardly surprising that our sojourn there had felt like an eternity.

Looking around me, I saw that the frost had descended on London in earnest and the pavements were white and pretty. A small sprinkling of snow had evidently come down while we were in the scientist's house, making the streets seem much more cheerful, and I was suddenly pleased to think of Sally and Martin at their fireside, awaiting me. Of course, telling them of my adventures at the den would only raise unhappy memories for the family, so I resolved that I would hear about *their* day. At this moment I could think of nothing better than listening to Sally recounting her outings with the children, telling me what they had drawn or said or done, or even to

Martin chronicling his endless travails with the printer.

So I walked up to that little door with a light step, full of anticipation, and was not disappointed. For I had hardly opened it when Sally appeared looking radiant and excited in the candlelight which seemed, as I looked around, to be unusually abundant. Sally, who loved candles, had often talked to me about Christmas in the house when masses of extra ones were lit and flowers were everywhere. And now, as I stared round in astonishment, the household seemed to have decided to celebrate it early, for on every surface there were candles, sending out a soft dancing light and shining most of all in her face, which was utterly mischievous.

'We saw you coming,' she said, beaming in a way that reminded me of her little girl Lucy's exultant grin.

'Has Christmas arrived early?' I asked, for even I had not anticipated such a pleasant welcome, though it could hardly have come at a better time.

'No, but we have decided to add to it. And thanks to you it will be such a happy Christmas for we have no debts. But come. Here you are.'

And she picked up a glass from the table with a little smile.

I walked a few paces into that brilliant hallway and thought it had never seemed such a safe haven. 'What is it?' I held up the glass which contained a greenish liquid.

'Oh, it is a wonderful cordial. Prepared for you. You look so tired and anyway it is part of the surprise.'

'Very well,' said I, downing the drink in one. It

tasted deliciously refreshing, with a hint of apple and lime, though a little bitter.

'You see,' she said, 'someone is here. Someone who wants to meet you so badly. I have spoken to you of Uncle Tim and what his visits are like. It is such a shame Martin has to stay late working on the calendar, but he will be here soon. And the children have had Tim all to themselves and loved every moment of it.'

Of course I recalled her talk of Tim from before. Tim, who arrived from abroad, armed with presents for the children. And we moved on as if in a dream to the drawing room which was a little darker but here the firelight flickered merrily. I was happy but I thought also that it was a pity how tired I was, too tired to do justice to such a joyful occasion.

By the fire I saw a rocking chair that was usually in the window. Lucy and little Will were clustered around a smartly clad figure with longish hair who had his back towards me. The children turned around, all smiles and mischief like their mother, laughing uncontrollably at some secret joke, the firelight flickering on Lucy Morland's fair hair. And before them was the evidence of presents. Oranges and nuts and dates and other fruit, and Will was sucking at an orange.

Sally whispered in my ear, 'You see, I know now that it was Tim who learned of Dr Small's visit to Egypt when he was last here a year ago and mentioned you then. We had no idea you were known to Tim.'

I did not quite follow that as I sat down on the armchair, for my legs felt very tired. Yet, as he turned, I looked.

And there he was, smiling, so handsome, as he stroked Lucy's hair.

Though my senses were all but gone, I glimpsed the whole of it.

'It is so good to see you again, Doyle,' said Cream.

A Historical Note

People often want to know how much of my writing about Arthur Conan Doyle is based on actual events and whether I have made any fresh discoveries. The fact that the question still looms so large is in its own way a remarkable thing. Doyle ranks among the most famous of all Victorian writers, easily the most durable in terms of film and television, yet even today this man's life, particularly his early life, is shrouded in quite as much mystery as one of his own stories.

My own interest in the subject dates from a childhood in a Scottish seaside town only an hour away from where he grew up. This gave me an early acquaintance with the atmosphere of Edinburgh, not least its wind, and with Doyle's work. I still have a battered copy of the complete Holmes stories I bought when I was seven, a book I used to discuss avidly with a school friend, appropriately enough the son of a Professor of Anatomy.

Much to our surprise we were told by one of our teachers that the Holmes detective stories were not serious creations at all, but the playthings of a man who grew tried of their superficiality and killed off his detective. This summary never seemed quite right to me, although I had no idea then that T.S. Eliot harboured the same doubts and was himself so puzzled by Holmes's ambiguous connection to Doyle, that he called it the 'greatest' of the Sherlock Holmes mysteries. Today, re-reading Doyle's stories with some knowledge of the contradictions in their creator (and a little experience of what it is to write fiction), the whole notion of Holmes as a bit of casual fun, undertaken for commercial reasons, seems to me absurd. Just as Bram Stoker blamed Count Dracula on a meal of crab and Mary Shelley put Frankenstein down to a kind of literary party game, Doyle's reflections on his own gothic creation, written years after the event, reveal all the telltale hallmarks of a nineteenth-century author carefully, if unconsciously, sanitising a painful literary birth.

What lay behind this birth? Countless biographies have rehearsed what is known about Doyle, but to a very large extent this was dictated by the man himself. Not a single researcher has ever had unhampered access to his personal letters and papers. Indeed, following bitter legal battles, the bulk of these papers have not been seen by anyone for half a century and nobody can even say for sure where they are, or if they have been destroyed. As a result most recent chroniclers have had to do heroic detective work to arrive at new facts. That Arthur Conan Doyle himself suppressed many things is no longer in doubt and even the most cursory study of his life reveals a yawning gap between his public and private self. He could not keep the latter out of his writing, but he could keep it out of everything else with the result that, until quite recently, only the most public facts were available to us while Doyle himself stared out of his photos like a man in disguise. The school friend with whom I shared a liking for Holmes is now a distinguished consultant psychiatrist with a particular interest in the psychology of public people. In his view there is a greater tension between the public and the private in Conan Doyle than in any other historical figure he has ever studied, with the exception of the former American President Richard Nixon.

It is this paradox between the writing and the man which lies at the heart of Doyle for me. Here is the central mystery and every aspect of my own stories is an attempt to elucidate it, sometimes through documented fact and Doyle's own writing, sometimes by assumption based on evidence, sometimes by invention and metaphor. I was never interested in pure pastiche but I am very preoccupied by material Doyle would have known about, and considered in private, but could never publicly discuss, and also by events which challenge the whole basis of his most precious beliefs (the ending of *The Patient's Eyes* is intimately related to his belief in chivalry). He must, there is no way around it, have had to face such challenges, but how he did, and what effect they had on him, we can only conjecture.

I can lay claim to few major detective triumphs but I do still recall my amazement when, during my research, I stumbled on the fact that one of the nineteenth century's most notorious serial killers, an American and a doctor, studied medicine in Edinburgh in 1878, exactly the year that Doyle – a medical student at the same institution – met Joseph Bell. It seemed to me extraordinary that here, right in his creator's back yard, was exactly the kind of villain Holmes never encountered. Why?

And what of Doyle's teacher and inspiration, Joseph Bell? Here was the acknowledged basis of Holmes but, before we can reach any understanding of the meeting between the two men, it is necessary to explore the strange and appalling circumstances of Doyle's life when it happened, circumstances which he did everything in his power to conceal.

His attempts were so successful that thanks largely to a number of intrepid biographers the full story is only now starting to emerge, and it is quite as gothic as any fiction he ever wrote. By the late 1870s, his father Charles appears to have been enduring an agonised twilight existence in the Doyle family home as he made a spectacular decline into drunken insanity. Doyle, living at home throughout his student days, would have experienced this at close quarters. It was years before his father was committed to a mental institution, and even then he made at least one violent escape attempt. All of this was bad enough for the young Doyle in those crucial years and the horror of it is reflected in his work, not least in eerie Holmes stories like 'The Crooked Man' and 'The Yellow Face'. But there was far worse.

During this critical period Doyle's mother's affections had strayed. With his older sisters often away, he may well have been the sole grown-up witness to the spectacle of his father being cuckolded in his own home, and by a man who was only five years older than Doyle himself.

Bryan Waller, a young doctor, arrived first in the Doyle family home as a lodger, while Doyle was still away at school, but the emotional attachment to Doyle's mother was quickly formed and soon Waller took over all charge of the household with Charles Doyle still in it. The arrangement was therefore bizarre and, in almost every contemporary account,

Waller emerges as a cruel, arrogant and snobbish (if cultured) man with a notorious temper. A physical relationship between him and Mary Doyle, who was fifteen years older, cannot be proved. It may have been merely a close personal bond. Waller is also thought at one time to have considered an engagement to Doyle's sister, Annette. In a way it scarcely matters for, given the Victorian penchant for secrecy about such things, Doyle probably had no more idea of the truth than we do. The fact of this usurping father's presence while his own father failed would have been quite unbearable enough.

There are, however, some suggestive facts. The last child born to Doyle's mother, when her husband was already far into his illness and Waller ruled the roost, was christened Bryan Julia Doyle (Julia being the name of Bryan Waller's mother). Eventually Waller moved Mary Doyle to his estate in Masongill in the Pennines where she lived until she was eighty, and where rumours have survived to this day not merely about the relationship, but about the true parentage of Bryan Julia Doyle.

So what on earth can life have been like for Doyle living in this household, which bears a startling resemblance to *Hamlet* with Doyle as prince, throughout his most formative teenage years, years when he met Bell and the seeds of Sherlock Holmes were sown? As yet, we have no letters to consult. But Doyle's own silence on the subject is suggestive. According to many biographers, Waller must have been a crucial influence and probably determined Doyle's career choice. But in the whole of Conan Doyle's writing there is not a single solitary mention of him. Doyle's autobiography is written as if Waller never existed. Even so, this spectacularly evasive book, published well after Doyle's mother's death, does contain one chilling if elliptical reference to the whole affair, and it was surely placed by Doyle in the full knowledge that Waller himself, unlike his mother, was still alive to read it. 'My mother,' Doyle wrote of his student days, 'had adopted the device of sharing a large house, which may have eased her in some ways, but was disastrous in others . . .'

'Disastrous'? The adjective speaks volumes, but the author makes no further attempt to explain it, moving on instead to describe 'the most notable' encounter of his university life, and the man who represented everything that the vain and bullying Waller did not – Joseph Bell. 'For some reason I have never understood,' Doyle writes with obvious feeling, 'he singled me out. . .'

It is hard to imagine a more important moment for the young Doyle than the arrival of Joseph Bell at this desperate time. At home were two highly disturbing fathers, the one pathetic and insane, the other a threatening usurper. And then, like a miracle, enters the handsome charismatic teacher who 'singles' him out. Thin, wiry, dark, handsome, with the long fingers of a pianist and the aquiline features of an actor, Joseph Bell was one of the foremost medical academics of his generation, a consulting surgeon and also, incidentally, Queen Victoria's personal doctor when in Scotland. Even in the guarded prose of his autobiography Doyle was emphatic in describing the man as the most important person he met in all his crucial years in Edinburgh. Indeed in one of the few letters available (thanks to the Bell family) Doyle famously wrote to his former teacher: 'It is to you that I owe Sherlock Holmes.'

It is no surprise that the drama and emotional release of such a meeting in such extraordinary circumstances was the spark that ignited Holmes. And, for me, it was not merely an irresistible spur for a thriller, but for an imaginative reconstruction of Doyle's whole world. I decided to make the entry to this world not Edinburgh but the other most tortured and mysterious period of Doyle's life, namely the years leading up to the turn of the century. The writer had killed off his detective and was tending his invalid wife even though he had already fallen in love with another woman. Believing, as I do, that many of Doyle's best stories are grounded in his own conflicts and his pain, and that the outer man belies the inner, I found it productive and exciting to look back from this later period on a series of difficult and occasionally traumatic cases undertaken with Joseph Bell.

The idea of Bell and Doyle as a somewhat reluctant team is not quite as fantastical as it seems. For there is no question that Joseph Bell did have a secret. Shortly before Doyle met him in 1878 he had been called in by the Crown to sort out a murder case in Edinburgh which was going badly wrong. The murderer was a Frenchman called Eugene Chantrelle, the victim was Chantrelle's wife, but there had been many blunders in the case and Joseph Bell managed to steer the doctors and police back on the right track, before personally tracing the likely cause of death to a doctored gas pipe. At least three contemporary accounts by pathologists and colleagues attest to the Doctor's crucial role, yet Bell preferred to work in confidence and insisted his name was kept out of the trial.

He was especially careful not to attend the execution but on this occasion he had underestimated his man. For Chantrelle knew Bell's role at first hand and may well have seen a way of getting revenge. On the gallows itself, as many witnesses attest, Chantrelle made a point of airily asking the forensic pathologist Littlejohn to pass on his compliments to the absent Dr Bell for bringing him to justice.

This sudden unexpected publicity for Bell could explain why he sought anonymity in all the cases that followed. We know there were other cases, from many colleagues, but the details are far harder to establish. It was not until 1892 that the resourceful reporter Harry How made the connection between Holmes and Bell, shortly before Doyle decided to bring his own fictional detective's career to an end at Reichenbach.

What Doyle made of Bell's forensic and detective work remains a complete mystery. The Chantrelle case happened in the year the two men first met so he could hardly have avoided hearing about it. But Doyle never alluded to it in public, presumably because, like so much else in these Victorian lives, he knew it was confidential.

The obvious question then is what else was confidential? After Doyle's university training we can discover almost nothing of the relationship between the two men, but the few letters we have suggest there was one. Of course, there can be no certainty that Doyle's papers, if they ever appear, will solve all such questions. Doyle may well have guarded his inner world even from those closest to him but the frequent signs of cover up and destroyed evidence only arouse greater curiosity. When Bryan Waller died in Masongill in 1932, members of his staff were urgently instructed to go to the attic and hurl from the window on to the lawn all Waller's personal papers including notebooks and diaries. These were then taken to the back of the house and burned on a bonfire. But one servant glanced at a diary and according to her statement it contained a jealous lament, by the woman Waller married late in life, about her husband's continuing relationship with Mrs Doyle.

Later, Adrian Conan Doyle, son of Arthur and for many years guardian of the Doyle estate, restricted access and threatened legal action when any interpretation or fact did not suit him. Letters were made available at his whim, and withdrawn again, when the conclusions of this or that biographer did not appeal. After Adrian died, the long and complex legal case began, making it hard to establish even the whereabouts of many of the papers. One cache in Switzerland appears in the end to have yielded very little. But even as we await a resolution to the more practical aspects of the mystery I think we can already reach two conclusions. The first is that Doyle's casual and distanced account of the origins of Sherlock Holmes is not the whole truth. Given all the personal circumstances the author was trying to hide, the ambivalence he showed towards his great creation seems entirely understandable.

The second is that at last we are starting to get closer to a proper understanding of Doyle himself. And, while his greatness is not in question, indeed his reputation grows, everything points to a far more extraordinary, troubled and mysterious man than was ever dreamed of by his public.

If you enjoyed *The Night Calls* why not try further David Pirie titles in the *Murder Rooms* series . . .

David Pirie's new novel in the compelling
Murder Rooms series, *The Dark Water*,
is published in hardback by Century

THE DARK WATER

Imprisoned in a dank cottage deep in the English country-side Arthur Conan Doyle lies half-unconscious and at the mercy of his nemesis – Thomas Neill Cream. Gathering all his dwindling strength he smashes a window and crawls to safety. With a sharp piece of broken glass he awaits his torturer's return, but the man has eluded him once more, leaving behind the rotting body of a local miser and thwarted in his attempt to obtain money for his 'deadly' cause.

Securing the help of the remarkable pioneering criminal investigator Dr Joseph Bell, the two men return to the scene of the crime but find few clues. London reveals little more except the possibility that their archenemy has gone to the Suffolk coast under the name of Dr Mere. Full of legend the local community fear the 'Dunwich witch' has returned with her evil curse. A man has died in suspicious circumstances and it seems many are unwilling to talk about it. More hideous crimes are yet to come as Dr Bell and Doyle move closer and closer to confronting Cream: Bell to capture a notorious villain, Doyle to avenge himself for a crime which robbed him of his future happiness.

Dr Bell and Arthur Doyle are reunited once again in their quest to hunt down a criminal mastermind in a sinister tale of intrigue and violence, which reaches a terrifying and dramatic climax . . .

Read on for an extract . . .

THE WAKENING

The room was in darkness. I felt that even without opening my eyes. Sometimes there were sounds, though none that meant anything. I had no sense of physical space. When a proper memory threatened to drift into my consciousness, I resisted it at once, knowing how unwelcome it might prove. For the moment, I wanted only the dark.

So I slept again, I have no idea how long. Until at last, reluctantly, I opened my eyes. The room was black as I had anticipated and now I was forced to wonder where I was. As some sense of identity started to return, I guessed I had been taken ill with a fever, for the bedclothes smelt rank. But I could not be in the familiar bedroom of my house in Southsea: for one thing this place was too dark. And then I recalled the lodgings in London and my short-term position as a locum at a riverside practice.

Yet I was sure I could not be lying in the tiny bed-room I had rented from the Morland family. It was too quiet here and the bed was strange. After a time,

I forced myself away from its lumpy pillow but was quite unprepared for what followed. My head throbbed with a violent pain. This was bad enough but, what was worse, I suddenly recalled my last few minutes of consciousness.

Their climax was a face, the face of the only man I have ever met who deserves worse than the description 'evil'. I first knew Thomas Neill Cream in Edinburgh, indeed we had been friends until I discovered that he was a murderer. And then he murdered the woman I loved.

I swore to avenge her while my teacher at Edinburgh, Dr Joseph Bell – who had recruited me as his clerk and allowed me to help in his criminal investigations – declared a fight against the future of such crimes without motive. But in 1878, Cream disappeared into the American continent, sending only tormenting notes and, on one occasion, a lethal instrument that was designed to kill me.

Despite this, neither Bell nor I had forgotten our quest and chance had brought us together recently during a London case, when I became convinced Cream had returned to England. The Doctor disagreed. He was sure the strings were being pulled from far away and finally persuaded me he was right before he said his farewells.

I walked back to the my lodgings at the Morland house, a safe haven where Sally Morland, whom I loved as a friend and greatly admired, greeted me with the news that an American uncle, whom she sometimes mentioned, had made a surprise visit.

I thought nothing of this at the time but now, as I recalled it, I felt the hair stand on the back of my neck. Once again I saw Sally's flushed excitement, her eyes laughing in the light that flooded the hall from the candles that celebrated the uncle's visit. She had, I remembered, given me a cordial, a green drink he had prepared, which she said was part of the surprise and which tasted refreshing and bitter.

Then I had entered the living room and her children were there, laughing, with their oranges and nuts, and a figure in the rocking chair had turned around, smiling to see me. It was Cream.

Just before unconsciousness, I grasped some of it. How months earlier he must have set in train the events that led up to this moment; how he had befriended the Morlands (for the 'uncle' was only a family friend) and discreetly provided my name to a nearby practice.

All of this I saw with a kind of passive awe before losing my senses. Now, lying here in the darkness, I felt terror. Cream was an expert poisoner, indeed it was his preferred instrument of murder. If he had intended me to die, he could certainly have done it with his green cordial. Which could only mean his plans were more extensive. Was he somewhere beside me now in this black space?

The prospect was so awful I tried to gather my strength, forcing my head higher, opening my eyes as wide as I could. Still I could see nothing, only vague insubstantial shapes. There was a low noise from somewhere outside, perhaps a wind.

'Are you there?' The words came out as a whisper. My throat was parched and I began to sense body pains, no doubt masked by the poison. It occurred to me he could have done anything, even severed a limb.

I tried to move my legs. They seemed to function, but then a man feels his legs long after they are amputated, so I touched them quickly. Thank God they were whole but my legs and arms were feeble. I noticed too that I was drenched in perspiration. 'Are you there?' I tried to shout. There was nothing. Absolute silence.

I knew I must try to move though I felt so weak, even the simplest movement was horrible. I forced myself up further. And for the first time I realised that I was still wearing clothes, a shirt and under-garment, and the blankets on me were heavy.

Shutting my mind to the stench of this bed, I forced myself into a sitting position. It was still dark but there was a slight movement in the shadows before me and I expected him to step forward. Again something moved, this time accompanied by a low sound. I decided it must be some kind of reflection, and when it came again I was sure. The sound was wind, the shadows were of branches. That meant somewhere behind me was a window. Perhaps I could reach it.

I summoned all my strength and pushed my left leg out from under the blankets. It found support below me but I knew it would give way if I put any weight on it. I paused, not sure how to proceed, and suddenly had to endure a violent bout of shivering. This made me swing the other leg down. But, even with both feet on the ground, it was obvious there was no way I could stand and I sank quickly to a kneeling position, clutching the bedclothes.

My head was facing the bed, so if I crawled to my right I should come to the window that cast the reflection. I turned my body, registering the floor was stone and cold to the touch. If Cream were here, how he would be enjoying this humiliation. In London I had felt such an overwhelming presence of the man, now I could not sense him.

I began to crawl but it was painfully slow. As a distraction, I made myself think more about that last evening. My main dread was that Sally Morland and her children had been given the poison. I was sure my glass of cordial had been poured before I got there. Obviously he wanted everything to be normal, so no harm could have come to the Morlands up to that point. This gave me hope but I had also to face the plain truth, which was that Cream would think nothing of slaughtering them all.

Here was the worst possibility for me, far worse than the fact he might be watching me now. There had been nothing improper in my friendship with Sally Morland, whose world was built around her two young children and her husband. But she was so full of transparent joy and mischievousness, and reminded me so much of my first love, that when I began to suspect Cream had returned to the capital, I made a private pledge. Namely that if Sally Morland or her family came to harm because of me, then I must be better off embracing solitude, anonymity or even death. How could I do otherwise if all I brought was misery to those I cared for?

My movement forward was still agonisingly slow. As yet I had come to no furniture but sensed a shape ahead. Meanwhile, I took some small consolation from the knowledge that even Cream could not have the slightest suspicion of my private thoughts about

Sally Morland. Therefore, why should he bother with her? It was true he often killed for little reason but the wholesale slaughter of a respectable London family is not a common event. It would cause a full-scale alarm; and both of us would be key suspects. Would even Cream risk a manhunt on this scale when he merely needed to tell the Morlands I was in need of treatment and carry me anywhere he wished?

Of course I knew the answer. Yes he would happily take such a risk if he thought it would hurt me. It came down to that alone. And it was just at this point in my reflections that my hands felt cold stone blocking my way. I had reached a wall.

From above my head came the sound of wind. I succeeded in walking my hands up the wall till I was kneeling and finally, using this support, I pulled myself to my feet. At first I swayed and nearly fell but I had the wall to steady me and I leant against it, breathing heavily. There was cold air here, which cleared my head. I reached out and touched a curtain and then the ledge of a window. The material was rough and quite thick but I pushed it back. Outside there was just enough moonlight to show me I was at ground level and a dank overgrown wilderness lay beyond the window. A slight wind shook the branches of a small sycamore tree, the source of the moving shadow.

My last conscious memory had been of night-time, but I was sure this could not possibly be the same night. It was not just my pain and hunger. The air here was only mildly cold, yet the night at the Morlands' had been frosty, indeed there was snow on the streets. How long had I been unconscious and where was I?

As I stared, it did not even seem to me that I could be sure this was London. There was no gaslight, indeed not a flicker of artificial light anywhere. Of course I might be looking out on some large garden or park, but it hardly seemed cultivated and there were no lights of any kind from other buildings.

I tried to open the window but it was nailed shut so I turned back to the room. The opposite wall looked to be bare and without openings of any kind. In fact, as I discovered later, there was a small high window on that side but nothing else. Beside the bed, I could make out an armchair and, beyond that, a table. I staggered forward and rested myself on the back of the chair, which was ancient and badly in need of upholstering. This was no smart establishment, it was a hovel and how many hovels in the heart of London could boast a large garden out of sight of any houses?

To my right, I saw an old screen of some kind. Past that I thought I could make out the outline of a door. Knowing I had to reach it, I took a pace and nearly fell but managed to keep upright. I staggered three more paces until I was there and the handle supported me. But the thing was solid oak with two huge locks and, of course, no keys. I tried a feeble tug, but I might as well have been tugging at brickwork. In my present condition there was no hope here.

From somewhere beyond the door came an evil smell and I staggered back to the armchair where it was less pronounced. As I sat, knowing my strength was nearly exhausted, a new sensation assailed me. For suddenly I smelt and then spied food on the table beside the chair. Here was a bowl of milk, a half loaf of bread, even a slice of bacon. It was not very fresh but I was ravenous and did not care. I lifted the milk with trembling hands and drank it down. Then I clawed at the bread, which was hard but otherwise good, before gnawing the bacon. I swallowed as much as I could, wondering if, now that I had some relief from my hunger, I could smash the window.

But I knew in my heart I was far too weak. Even lifting that bowl of milk had been an effort. Already, despite the food, I could feel consciousness ebbing away, and I stumbled back to my bed. A little more rest I told myself, allowing a chance for the nourishment to do its work, and surely I could get up enough strength to break that window and get out before he returned.

But now, once again, the darkness descended upon me. It was many hours before I regained consciousness and heard what I took to be the noise of rain. Outside it seemed night but not, I was sure, the same night. My head was heavy and I felt a curious lassitude. What did it matter in the end if he came back here to torture and kill me? Ultimately, whatever happened, I would die and sink into this. What reason on earth was there then to fight the sensation of numbness in my limbs?

It was only when I thought of my enemy that I began to distrust this feeling. Slowly I became aware there was a flickering in the room behind me. With some difficulty I turned my throbbing head around and found that someone had lit a candle, now almost extinguished.

A fear ran through me, which at least dispelled some of that hideous complacency. Yet I could see

nobody. Using all my strength, I raised myself up.
There was the armchair I had inspected previously,
the table with the bread and milk, now replenished.
And the screen. But nothing else. Was he hiding?
There was no reason why he should bother and the
candle had burnt a good way down.

Of course I wanted to slump back into the darkness, but the shock of knowing he had been here
sharpened my senses. I had to eat and drink. So again
I got my feet to the ground and now, with the benefit
of light, I dragged myself to the table and slumped
into the chair. Suddenly from somewhere came a
sound, a soft rumbling clattering sound. I tensed,
waiting for footsteps, and the turn of a key in the
lock, but the noise receded. I decided it had been a
cart on the road outside.

I turned back to the table, getting the milk to my
lips and drank some of it down. It had been heavily
sugared and I was glad of it. Then I put out a hand
and pawed the bread into my mouth.

But suddenly I stopped. The bread was rough-
grained and wholesome, but I had begun to recognise
a taste. It was a chalky bitter undertaste I knew only
too well. With fury, I spat what was left of my mouthful on to the table and lashed out with my hand in an
attempt to knock the milk jug to the ground. But –
fortunately as it happened – the effort only made me
lose my balance and I missed the jug altogether,
falling hard to the floor.

How could I have been such a fool? Only my own
ravenous hunger and the weakness of my mind could
possibly have blinded me to what was obvious. Here
I was, meekly accepting day after day the sustenance

of an accomplished poisoner. The bread was certainly saturated in laudanum and the sugared milk would have contained even more. Little wonder every time I got up, I seemed to be slipping further into the darkness. As long as I survived on this fare, I was his prisoner and he could visit me whenever he wished and do whatever he wished. The diet would only make me weaker and weaker until I was a passive craving thing, entirely in his hands. No doubt he was looking forward to that, and would arrive soon enough to enjoy it.

In a feverish burst of activity, I determined now I must get out at all costs, even if I collapsed in the rain. I forced myself to my feet.

What I needed was an implement of some kind but there was nothing that I could see. The door was hopeless. The window must be the best opportunity and I turned back in that direction. But to my dawning horror I could already feel the effects of my meal. The black waters were rising in my brain and my feet felt like blocks of wood. There was no chance of fighting this. As it stole over me, I began to wonder if even my own memories were at fault. Perhaps this nightmare of Cream's return was some phantom conjured up by the laudanum. Had I merely, as Bell once feared, succumbed to addiction?

But then my eye fell on the milk and the bread. What addict ever went to the trouble of lacing his food with the stuff or of hiding the precious bottles? No, this was his work and at all costs I must hold on to my reason.

The only point in my favour had to be the realisation of what he was doing to me. With the last of my strength I disposed of the bread under the bed and spilt some of the milk there too. Let him suppose I had consumed most of my meal, while in truth I had taken much less. This was my final desperate thought as I collapsed.

When I woke up, he was by my bed. And he was singing.

Available in Arrow, David Pirie's first novel in the original and compelling *Murder Rooms* series . . .

THE PATIENT'S EYES

An eminent doctor . . .
A brilliant young medical student . . .
And a compelling series of mysteries which reveal the untold story behind the world's most celebrated detective.

In his first medical practice, young Arthur Conan Doyle meets sweet Heather Grace. He is puzzled not only by a strange eye complaint she suffers, but also by her visions of a phantom cyclist who vanishes as soon as he is followed.

However, Doyle soon finds himself embroiled in far more sinister events – including the murder of a rich Spanish businessman – and is forced to call on his mentor and later model for Sherlock Holmes, Dr Joseph Bell. But the perverse Dr Bell seems to consider the murder of Señor Garcia unimportant compared with the matter of the patient's eyes and the solitary cyclist . . .

'A pacey, enjoyable yarn, with a surprising twist, that ranks with the best of the Doyle canon'
Times Literary Supplement

'Pirie is delving deeper into the "real" origins . . . truly frightening'
Time Out

'A satisfying Borgesian mix of library riddle, fact and conjecture'
Guardian